#1 *New York Times* bestselling author **Stephanie Laurens** began writing romances as an escape from the dry world of professional science, a hobby that quickly became a career. Her novels set in Regency England have captivated readers around the globe, making her one of the romance world's most beloved and popular authors. Stephanie has published more than sixty works of historical romance, all of which remain in print and are readily available.

Stephanie lives with her husband and two cats in the hills outside Melbourne, Australia. When she isn't writing, she's reading, and if she isn't reading, she'll be tending her garden. For information on all published novels and upcoming releases, and to sign up for her newsletter, visit Stephanie's website: www.stephanielaurens.com.

Sophia James lives in Chelsea Bay, on Auckland, New Zealand's North Shore, with her husband, who is an artist. She has a degree in English and history from Auckland University and believes her love of writing was formed by reading Georgette Heyer during holidays at her grandmother's house. Sophia enjoys getting feedback at sophiajames.co.

STEPHANIE LAURENS

FOUR IN HAND

Ⓗ**HARLEQUIN**®BESTSELLING AUTHOR COLLECTION

ISBN-13: 978-0-373-01043-1

Four in Hand

Copyright © 2016 by Harlequin Books S.A.

The publisher acknowledges the copyright holders
of the individual works as follows:

Four in Hand
Copyright © 1993 by Stephanie Laurens

The Dissolute Duke
Copyright © 2013 by Sophia James

Recycling programs
for this product may
not exist in your area.

Printed in U.S.A.

CONTENTS

FOUR IN HAND

Stephanie Laurens

CHAPTER ONE

THE RATTLE OF the curtain rings sounded like thunder. The head of the huge four-poster bed remained wreathed in shadow yet Max was aware that for some mysterious reason Masterton was trying to wake him. Surely it couldn't be noon already?

Lying prone amid his warm sheets, his stubbled cheek cushioned in softest down, Max contemplated faking slumber. But Masterton knew he was awake. And knew that he knew, so to speak. Sometimes, the damned man seemed to know his thoughts before he did. And he certainly wouldn't go away before Max capitulated and acknowledged him.

Raising his head, Max opened one very blue eye. His terrifyingly correct valet was standing, entirely immobile, plumb in his line of vision. Masterton's face was impassive. Max frowned.

In response to this sign of approaching wrath, Masterton made haste to state his business. Not that it was *his* business, exactly. Only the combined vote of the rest of the senior staff of Delmere House had induced him to disturb His Grace's rest at the unheard-of hour of nine o'clock. He had every reason to know just how dangerous such an undertaking could be. He had been in the service of Max Rotherbridge, Viscount Delmere, for nine years. It was highly unlikely his master's recent elevation to the estate of His Grace the Duke of Twyford had in any way altered his temper. In fact, from what Masterton had seen, his master had had more to try his temper in dealing with his unexpected inheritance than in all the rest of his thirty-four years.

"Hillshaw wished me to inform you that there's a young lady to see you, Your Grace."

It was still a surprise to Max to hear his new title on his servants' lips. He had to curb an automatic reaction to look about him for whomever they were addressing. A lady. His frown deepened. "No." He dropped his head back into the soft pillows and closed his eyes.

"*No,* Your Grace?"

The bewilderment in his valet's voice was unmistakable. Max's head ached. He had been up until dawn. The evening had started badly, when he had felt constrained to attend a ball given by his maternal aunt, Lady Maxwell. He rarely attended such functions. They were too tame for his liking; the languishing sighs his appearance provoked among all the sweet young things were enough to throw even the most hardened reprobate entirely off his stride. And while he had every claim to that title, seducing débutantes was no longer his style. Not at thirty-four.

He had left the ball as soon as he could and repaired to the discreet villa wherein resided his latest mistress. But the beautiful Carmelita had been in a petulant mood. Why were such women invariably so grasping? And why did they imagine he was so besotted that he'd stand for it? They had had an almighty row, which had ended with him giving the luscious ladybird her congé in no uncertain terms.

From there, he had gone to White's, then Boodles. At that discreet establishment, he had found a group of his cronies and together they had managed to while the night away. And most of the morning, too. He had neither won nor lost. But his head reminded him that he had certainly drunk a lot.

He groaned and raised himself on his elbows, the better to fix Masterton with a gaze which, despite his condition, was remarkably lucid. Speaking in the voice of one instructing a dimwit, he explained. "If there's a woman to see me, she can't be a lady. No lady would call here."

Max thought he was stating the obvious but his henchman stared woodenly at the bedpost. The frown, which had temporarily left his master's handsome face, returned.

Silence.

Max sighed and dropped his head on to his hands. "Have you seen her, Masterton?"

"I did manage to get a glimpse of the young lady when Hillshaw showed her into the library, Your Grace."

Max screwed his eyes tightly shut. Masterton's insistence on using the term "young lady" spoke volumes. All of Max's servants were experienced in telling the difference between ladies and the sort of female who might be expected to call at a bachelor's residence. And if both Masterton and Hillshaw insisted the woman downstairs was a young lady, then a young lady she must be. But it was inconceivable that any young lady would pay a nine o'clock call on the most notorious rake in London.

Taking his master's silence as a sign of commitment to the day, Masterton crossed the large chamber to the wardrobe. "Hillshaw mentioned that the young lady, a Miss Twinning, Your Grace, was under the impression she had an appointment with you."

Max had the sudden conviction that this was a nightmare. He rarely made appointments with anyone and certainly not with young ladies for nine o'clock in the morning. And particularly not with unmarried young ladies. "Miss Twinning?" The name rang no bells. Not even a rattle.

"Yes, Your Grace." Masterton returned to the bed, various garments draped on his arm, a deep blue coat lovingly displayed for approval. "The Bath superfine would, I think, be most appropriate?"

Yielding to the inevitable with a groan, Max sat up.

ONE FLOOR BELOW, Caroline Twinning sat calmly reading His Grace of Twyford's morning paper in an armchair by his library hearth. If she felt any qualms over the propriety of her present position, she hid them well. Her charmingly candid countenance was free of all nervousness and, as she scanned a frankly libellous account of a garden party enlivened by the scandalous propensities of the ageing Duke of Cumberland, an engaging smile curved her generous lips. In truth, she was looking forward to her meeting with the Duke. She and her sisters had spent a most enjoyable eighteen months, the wine of freedom a heady tonic after their previously monastic existence. But it was time and more for them to embark on the serious business of securing their futures. To do that, they needs must enter the *ton,* that glittering arena thus far denied them. And, for them, the Duke of Twyford undeniably held the key to that particular door.

Hearing the tread of a masculine stride approach the library door, Caroline raised her head, then smiled confidently. Thank heavens the Duke was so easy to manage.

By the time he reached the ground floor, Max had exhausted every possible excuse for the existence of the mysterious Miss Twinning. He had taken little time to dress, having no need to employ extravagant embellishments to distract attention from his long and powerful frame. His broad shoulders and muscular thighs perfectly suited the prevailing fashion. His superbly cut coats looked as though they had been moulded on to him and his buckskin breeches showed not a crease. The understated waistcoat, perfectly tied cravat and shining top-boots which completed the picture were the envy of many an aspiring exquisite. His hair, black as night, was neatly cropped to frame a dark face on which the years had left nothing more than a trace of worldly cynicism. Disdaining the ornamentation common to the times, His Grace of Twyford wore no ring other than a gold signet on his left hand and displayed no fobs or seals. In spite of this, no one setting eyes on him could imagine he was other than he was—one of the most fashionable and wealthy men in the *ton*.

He entered his library, a slight frown in the depths of his midnight-blue eyes. His attention was drawn by a flash of movement as the young lady who had been calmly reading his copy of the morning *Gazette* in his favourite armchair by the hearth folded the paper and laid it aside, before rising to face him. Max halted, blue eyes suddenly intent, all trace of displeasure vanishing as he surveyed his unexpected visitor. His nightmare had transmogrified into a dream. The vision before him was unquestionably a houri. For a number of moments he remained frozen in rapturous contemplation. Then, his rational mind reasserted itself. Not a houri. Houris did not read the *Gazette*. At least, not in his library at nine o'clock in the morning. From the unruly copper curls clustering around her face to the tips of her tiny slippers, showing tantalisingly from under the simply cut and outrageously fashionable gown, there was nothing with which he could find fault. She was built on generous lines, a tall Junoesque figure, deep-bosomed and wide-hipped, but all in the most perfect proportions. Her apricot silk gown did justice to her ample charms, clinging suggestively to a figure of Grecian delight. When his eyes returned to her face, he had time to take in the straight nose and full lips and the dimple that peeked irrepressibly from one cheek before his gaze was drawn to the finely arched brows and long lashes which framed her large eyes. It was only when he looked into the cool grey-green orbs that he saw the twinkle of amusement lurking there. Unused to provoking such a response, he frowned.

"Who, exactly, are you?" His voice, he was pleased to find, was even and his diction clear.

The smile which had been hovering at the corners of those inviting lips finally came into being, disclosing a row of small pearly teeth. But instead of answering his question, the vision replied, "I was waiting for the Duke of Twyford."

Her voice was low and musical. Mentally engaged in considering how to most rapidly dispense with the formalities, Max answered automatically. "I am the Duke."

"You?" For one long moment, utter bewilderment was writ large across her delightful countenance.

For the life of her, Caroline could not hide her surprise. How could this man, of all men, be the Duke? Aside from the fact he was far too young to have been a crony of her father's, the gentleman before her was unquestionably a rake. And a rake of the first order, to boot. Whether the dark-browed, harsh-featured face with its aquiline nose and firm mouth and chin or the lazy assurance with which he had entered the room had contributed to her reading of his character, she could not have said. But the calmly arrogant way his intensely blue eyes had roved from the top of her curls all the way down to her feet, and then just as calmly returned by the same route, as if to make sure he had missed nothing, left her in little doubt of what sort of man she now faced. Secure in the knowledge of being under her guardian's roof, she had allowed the amusement she felt on seeing such decided appreciation glow in the deep blue eyes to show. Now, with those same blue eyes still on her, piercingly perceptive, she felt as if the rug had been pulled from beneath her feet.

Max could hardly miss her stunned look. "For my sins," he added in confirmation.

With a growing sense of unease, he waved his visitor to a seat opposite the huge mahogany desk while he moved to take the chair behind it. As he did so, he mentally shook his head to try to clear it of the thoroughly unhelpful thoughts that kept crowding in. Damn Carmelita!

Caroline, rapidly trying to gauge where this latest disconcerting news left her, came forward to sink into the chair indicated.

Outwardly calm, Max watched the unconsciously graceful glide of her walk, the seductive swing of her hips as she sat down. He would have to find a replacement for Carmelita. His gaze rested speculatively on the beauty before him. Hillshaw had been right. She was unquestionably a lady. Still, that had never stopped him before. And, now he came to look more closely, she was not, he thought, that young. Even better. No rings, which was odd. Another twinge of pain from behind his eyes lent a harshness to his voice. "Who the devil are you?"

The dimple peeped out again. In no way discomposed, she answered, "My name is Caroline Twinning.

And, if you really are the Duke of Twyford, then I'm very much afraid I'm your ward."

Her announcement was received in perfect silence. A long pause ensued, during which Max sat unmoving, his sharp blue gaze fixed unwaveringly on his visitor. She bore this scrutiny for some minutes, before letting her brows rise in polite and still amused enquiry.

Max closed his eyes and groaned. "Oh, God."

It had only taken a moment to work it out. The only woman he could not seduce was his own ward. And he had already decided he very definitely wanted to seduce Caroline Twinning. With an effort, he dragged his mind back to the matter at hand. He opened his eyes. Hopefully, she would put his reaction down to natural disbelief. Encountering the grey-green eyes, now even more amused, he was not so sure. "Explain, if you please. Simple language only. I'm not up to unravelling mysteries at the moment."

Caroline could not help grinning. She had noticed twinges of what she guessed to be pain passing spasmodically through the blue eyes. "If your head hurts that much, why don't you try an ice-pack? I assure you I won't mind."

Max threw her a look of loathing. His head felt as if it was splitting, but how dared she be so lost to all propriety as to notice, let alone mention it? Still, she was perfectly right. An ice-pack was exactly what he needed. With a darkling look, he reached for the bell pull.

Hillshaw came in answer to his summons and re-

ceived the order for an ice-pack without noticeable perturbation. "Now, Your Grace?"

"Of course now! What use will it be later?" Max
winced at the sound of his own voice.

"As Your Grace wishes." The sepulchral tones left
Max in no doubt of his butler's deep disapproval.

As the door closed behind Hillshaw, Max lay back
in the chair, his fingers at his temples, and fixed Caroline with an unwavering stare. "You may commence."

She smiled, entirely at her ease once more. "My father was Sir Thomas Twinning. He was an old friend of
the Duke of Twyford—the previous Duke, I imagine."

Max nodded. "My uncle. I inherited the title from
him. He was killed unexpectedly three months ago, together with his two sons. I never expected to inherit the
estate, so am unfamiliar with whatever arrangements
your parent may have made with the last Duke."

Caroline nodded and waited until Hillshaw, deliv-
ering the requested ice-pack on a silver salver to his
master, withdrew. "I see. When my father died eighteen
months ago, my sisters and I were informed that he had
left us to the guardianship of the Duke of Twyford."

"Eighteen months ago? What have you been doing
since then?"

"We stayed on the estate for a time. It passed to a distant cousin and he was prepared to let us remain. But it
seemed senseless to stay buried there forever. The Duke
wanted us to join his household immediately, but we
were in mourning. I persuaded him to let us go to my
late stepmother's family in New York. They'd always

wanted us to visit and it seemed the perfect opportunity. I wrote to him when we were in New York, telling him we would call on him when we returned to England and giving him the date of our expected arrival. He replied and suggested I call on him today. And so, here I am."

Max saw it all now. Caroline Twinning was yet another part of his damnably awkward inheritance. Having led a life of unfettered hedonism from his earliest days, a rakehell ever since he came on the town, Max had soon understood that his lifestyle required capital to support it. So he had ensured his estates were all run efficiently and well. The Delmere estates he had inherited from his father were a model of modern estate management. But his uncle Henry had never had much real interest in his far larger holdings. After the tragic boating accident which had unexpectedly foisted on to him the responsibilities of the dukedom of Twyford, Max had found a complete overhaul of all his uncle's numerous estates was essential if they were not to sap the strength from his more prosperous Delmere holdings. The last three months had been spent in constant upheaval, with the old Twyford retainers trying to come to grips with the new Duke and his very different style. For Max, they had been three months of unending work. Only this week, he had finally thought that the end of the worst was in sight. He had packed his long-suffering secretary, Joshua Cummings, off home for a much needed rest. And now, quite clearly, the next chapter in the saga of his Twyford inheritance was about to start.

"You mentioned sisters. How many?"

"My half-sisters, really. There are four of us, altogether."

The lightness of the answer made Max instantly suspicious. "How old?"

There was a noticeable hesitation before Caroline answered, "Twenty, nineteen and eighteen."

The effect on Max was electric. "Good Lord! They didn't accompany you here, did they?"

Bewildered, Caroline replied, "No. I left them at the hotel."

"Thank God for that," said Max. Encountering Caroline's enquiring gaze, he smiled. "If anyone had seen them entering here, it would have been around town in a flash that I was setting up a harem."

The smile made Caroline blink. At his words, her grey eyes widened slightly. She could hardly pretend not to understand. Noticing the peculiar light in the blue eyes as they rested on her, it seemed a very good thing she was the Duke's ward. From her admittedly small understanding of the morals of his type, she suspected her position would keep her safe as little else might.

Unbeknown to her, Max was thinking precisely the same thing. And resolving to divest himself of his latest inherited responsibility with all possible speed. Aside from having no wish whatever to figure as the guardian of four young ladies of marriageable age, he needed to clear the obstacles from his path to Caroline Twinning. It occurred to him that her explanation of her life history had been curiously glib and decidedly short on detail. "Start at the beginning. Who was your mother and when did she die?"

Caroline had come unprepared to recite her history, imagining the Duke to be cognizant of the facts. Still, in the circumstances, she could hardly refuse. "My mother was Caroline Farningham, of the Staffordshire Farninghams."

Max nodded. An ancient family, well-known and well-connected.

Caroline's gaze had wandered to the rows of books lining the shelves behind the Duke. "She died shortly after I was born. I never knew her. After some years, my father married again, this time to the daughter of a local family who were about to leave for the colonies. Eleanor was very good to me and she looked after all of us comfortably, until she died six years ago. Of course, my father was disappointed that he never had a son and he rarely paid any attention to the four of us, so it was all left up to Eleanor."

The more he heard of him, the more Max was convinced that Sir Thomas Twinning had had a screw loose. He had clearly been a most unnatural parent. Still, the others were only Miss Twinning's half-sisters. Presumably they were not all as ravishing as she. It occurred to him that he should ask for clarification on this point but, before he could properly phrase the question, another and equally intriguing matter came to mind.

"Why was it none of you was presented before? If your father was sufficiently concerned to organize a guardian for you, surely the easiest solution would have been to have handed you into the care of husbands?"

Caroline saw no reason not to satisfy what was, after all, an entirely understandable curiosity. "We were never presented because my father disapproved of such…oh, frippery pastimes! To be perfectly honest, I sometimes thought he disapproved of women in general."

Max blinked.

Caroline continued, "As for marriage, he had organized that after a fashion. I was supposed to have married Edgar Mulhall, our neighbour." Involuntarily, her face assumed an expression of distaste.

Max was amused. "Wouldn't he do?"

Caroline's gaze returned to the saturnine face. "You haven't met him or you wouldn't need to ask. He's…" She wrinkled her nose as she sought for an adequate description. "Righteous," she finally pronounced.

At that, Max laughed. "Clearly out of the question."

Caroline ignored the provocation in the blue eyes. "Papa had similar plans for my sisters, only, as he never noticed they were of marriageable age and I never chose to bring it to his attention, nothing came of them either."

Perceiving Miss Twinning's evident satisfaction, Max made a mental note to beware of her manipulative tendencies. "Very well. So much for the past. Now to the future. What was your arrangement with my uncle?"

The grey-green gaze was entirely innocent as it rested on his face. Max did not know whether to believe it or not.

"Well, it was really his idea, but it seemed a perfectly sensible one to me. He suggested we should be presented to the *ton*. I suspect he intended to find us suitable husbands and so bring his guardianship to an end." She paused, thinking. "I'm not aware of the terms of my father's will, but I assume such arrangements terminate should we marry?"

"Very likely," agreed Max. The throbbing in his head had eased considerably. His uncle's plan had much to recommend it, but, personally, he would much prefer not to have any wards at all. And he would be damned if he would have Miss Twinning as his ward—that would cramp his style far too much. There were a few things even reprobates such as he held sacred and guardianship was one.

He knew she was watching him but made no further comment, his eyes fixed frowningly on his blotter as he considered his next move. At last, looking up at her, he said, "I've heard nothing of this until now. I'll have to get my solicitors to sort it out. Which firm handles your affairs?"

"Whitney and White. In Chancery Lane."

"Well, at least that simplifies matters. They handle the Twyford estates as well as my others." He laid the ice-pack down and looked at Caroline, a slight frown in his blue eyes. "Where are you staying?"

"Grillon's. We arrived yesterday."

Another thought occurred to Max. "On what have you been living for the last eighteen months?"

"Oh, we all had money left us by our mothers. We

arranged to draw on that and leave our patrimony untouched."

Max nodded slowly. "But who had you in charge? You can't have travelled halfway around the world alone."

For the first time during this strange interview, Max saw Miss Twinning blush, ever so slightly. "Our maid and coachman, who acted as our courier, stayed with us."

The airiness of the reply did not deceive Max. "Allow me to comment, Miss Twinning, as your potential guardian, that such an arrangement will not do. Regardless of what may have been acceptable overseas, such a situation will not pass muster in London." He paused, considering the proprieties for what was surely the first time in his life. "At least you're at Grillon's for the moment. That's safe enough."

After another pause, during which his gaze did not leave Caroline's face, he said, "I'll see Whitney this morning and settle the matter. I'll call on you at two to let you know how things have fallen out." A vision of himself meeting a beautiful young lady and attempting to converse with her within the portals of fashionable Grillon's, under the fascinated gaze of all the other patrons, flashed before his eyes. "On second thoughts, I'll take you for a drive in the Park. That way," he continued in reply to the question in her grey-green eyes, "we might actually get a chance to talk."

He tugged the bell pull and Hillshaw appeared.

"Have the carriage brought around. Miss Twinning is returning to Grillon's."

"Yes, Your Grace."

"Oh, no! I couldn't put you to so much trouble," said Caroline.

"My dear child," drawled Max, "my wards would certainly not go about London in hacks. See to it, Hillshaw."

"Yes, Your Grace." Hillshaw withdrew, for once in perfect agreement with his master.

Caroline found the blue eyes, which had quizzed her throughout this exchange, still regarding her, a gently mocking light in their depths. But she was a lady of no little courage and smiled back serenely, unknowingly sealing her fate.

Never, thought Max, had he met a woman so attractive. One way or another, he would break the ties of guardianship. A short silence fell, punctuated by the steady ticking of the long case clock in the corner. Max took the opportunity afforded by Miss Twinning's apparent fascination with the rows of leather-bound tomes at his back to study her face once more. A fresh face, full of lively humour and a brand of calm self-possession which, in his experience, was rarely found in young women. Undoubtedly a woman of character.

His sharp ears caught the sound of carriage wheels in the street. He rose and Caroline perforce rose, too. "Come, Miss Twinning. Your carriage awaits."

Max led her to the front door but forbore to go any further, bowing over her hand gracefully before allow-

ing Hillshaw to escort her to the waiting carriage. The
less chance there was for anyone to see him with her
the better. At least until he had solved this guardianship tangle.

As SOON AS the carriage door was shut by the majestic
Hillshaw, the horses moved forward at a trot. Caroline
lay back against the squabs, her gaze fixed unseeingly
on the near-side window as the carriage traversed fashionable London. Bemused, she tried to gauge the effect
of the unexpected turn their futures had taken. Imagine
having a guardian like that!

Although surprised at being redirected from Twyford House to Delmere House, she had still expected
to meet the vague and amenable gentleman who had so
readily acquiesced, albeit by correspondence, to all her
previous suggestions. Her mental picture of His Grace
of Twyford had been of a man in late middle age, be-
wigged as many of her father's generation were, distinctly past his prime and with no real interest in dealing
with four lively young women. She spared a small smile
as she jettisoned her preconceived image. Instead of a
comfortable, fatherly figure, she would now have to deal
with a man who, if first impressions were anything to
go by, was intelligent, quick-witted and far too perceptive for her liking. To imagine the new Duke would not
know to a nicety how to manage four young women was
patently absurd. If she had been forced to express an
opinion, Caroline would have said that, with the present Duke of Twyford, managing women was a special-

ity. Furthermore, given his undoubted experience, she strongly suspected he would be highly resistant to feminine cajoling in any form. A frown clouded her grey-green eyes. She was not entirely sure she approved of the twist their fates had taken. Thinking back over the recent interview, she smiled. He had not seemed too pleased with the idea himself.

For a moment, she considered the possibility of coming to some agreement with the Duke, essentially breaking the guardianship clause of her father's will. But only for a moment. It was true she had never been presented to the *ton* but she had cut her social eyeteeth long ago. While the idea of unlimited freedom to do as they pleased might sound tempting, there was the undeniable fact that she and her half-sisters were heiresses of sorts. Her father, having an extremely repressive notion of the degree of knowledge which could be allowed mere females, had never been particularly forthcoming regarding their eventual state. Yet there had never been any shortage of funds in all the years Caroline could remember. She rather thought they would at least be comfortably dowered. Such being the case, the traps and pitfalls of society, without the protection of a guardian, such as the Duke of Twyford, were not experiences to which she would willingly expose her sisters.

As the memory of a certain glint in His Grace of Twyford's eye and the distinctly determined set of his jaw drifted past her mind's eye, the unwelcome possibility that he might repudiate them, for whatever reasons, hove into view. Undoubtedly, if there was any way to overset their guardianship, His Grace would find it. Unaccountably, she was filled with an inexplicable sense of disappointment.

Still, she told herself, straightening in a purposeful way, it was unlikely there was anything he could do about it. And she rather thought they would be perfectly safe with the new Duke of Twyford, as long as they *were* his wards. She allowed her mind to dwell on the question of whether she really wanted to be safe from the Duke of Twyford for several minutes before giving herself a mental shake. Great heavens! She had only just met the man and here she was, mooning over him like a green girl! She tried to frown but the action dissolved into a sheepish grin at her own susceptibility. Settling more comfortably in the corner of the luxurious carriage, she fell to rehearsing her description of what had occurred in anticipation of her sisters' eager questions.

WITHIN MINUTES OF Caroline Twinning's departure from Delmere House, Max had issued a succession of orders, one of which caused Mr. Hubert Whitney, son of Mr. Josiah Whitney, the patriarch of the firm Whitney and White, Solicitors, of Chancery Lane, to present himself at Delmere House just before eleven. Mr. Whitney was a dry, desiccated man of uncertain age, very correctly attired in dusty black. He was his father's son in every way and, now that his sire was no longer able to leave his bed, he attended to all his father's wealthier clients. As Hillshaw showed him into the well-appointed library, he breathed a sigh of relief, not for the first time, that it was Max Rotherbridge who had inherited the difficult Twyford estates. Unknown to Max, Mr. Whitney held him in particular esteem, frequently wishing that others among his clients could be equally straightforward and decisive. It really made life so much easier.

Coming face-to-face with his favourite client, Mr. Whitney was immediately informed that His Grace, the Duke of Twyford, was in no way amused to find he was apparently the guardian of four marriageable young ladies. Mr. Whitney was momentarily at a loss. Luckily, he had brought with him all the current Twyford papers and the Twinning documents were among these. Finding that his employer did not intend to upbraid him for not having informed him of a circumstance which, he was only too well aware, he should have brought forward long ago, he applied himself to assessing the terms of the late Sir Thomas Twinning's will. Having refreshed his memory on its details, he then turned to the late Duke's will.

Max stood by the fire, idly watching. He liked Whitney. He did not fluster and he knew his business.

Finally, Mr. Whitney pulled the gold pince-nez from his face and glanced at his client. "Sir Thomas Twinning predeceased your uncle, and, under the terms of your uncle's will, it's quite clear you inherit all his responsibilities."

Max's black brows had lowered. "So I'm stuck with this guardianship?"

Mr. Whitney pursed his lips. "I wouldn't go so far as to say that. The guardianship could be broken, I fancy, as it's quite clear Sir Thomas did not intend you, personally, to be his daughters' guardian." He gazed at the fire and solemnly shook his head. "No one, I'm sure, could doubt that."

Max smiled wryly.

"However," Mr. Whitney continued, "should you succeed in dissolving the guardianship clause, then the young ladies will be left with no protector. Did I understand you correctly in thinking they are presently in London and plan to remain for the Season?"

It did not need a great deal of intelligence to see where Mr. Whitney's discourse was heading. Exasperated at having his usually comfortably latent conscience pricked into life, Max stalked to the window and stood looking out at the courtyard beyond, hands clasped behind his straight back. "Good God, man! You can hardly think I'm a suitable guardian for four sweet young things!"

Mr. Whitney, thinking the Duke could manage very well if he chose to do so, persevered. "There remains the question of who, in your stead, would act for them."

The certain knowledge of what would occur if he abandoned four inexperienced, gently reared girls to the London scene, to the mercies of well-bred wolves who roamed its streets, crystallised in Max's unwilling mind. This was closely followed by the uncomfortable thought that he was considered the leader of one such pack, generally held to be the most dangerous. He could hardly refuse to be Caroline Twinning's guardian, only to set her up as his mistress. No. There was a limit to what even he could face down. Resolutely thrusting aside the memory, still vivid, of a pair of grey-green eyes, he turned to Mr. Whitney and growled, "All right, dammit! What do I need to know?"

Mr. Whitney smiled benignly and started to fill him in on the Twinning family history, much as Caroline had told it. Max interrupted him. "Yes, I know all that! Just tell me in round figures—how much is each of them worth?"

Mr. Whitney named a figure and Max's brows rose. For a moment, the Duke was entirely bereft of speech. He moved towards his desk and seated himself again.

"Each?"

Mr. Whitney merely inclined his head in assent. When the Duke remained lost in thought, he continued, "Sir Thomas was a very shrewd businessman, Your Grace."

"So it would appear. So each of these girls is an heiress in her own right?"

This time, Mr. Whitney nodded decisively.

Max was frowning.

"Of course," Mr. Whitney went on, consulting the documents on his knee, "you would only be responsible for the three younger girls."

Instantly he had his client's attention, the blue eyes oddly piercing. "Oh? Why is that?"

"Under the terms of their father's will, the Misses Twinning were given into the care of the Duke of Twyford until they attained the age of twenty-five or married. According to my records, I believe Miss Twinning to be nearing her twenty-sixth birthday. So she could, should she wish, assume responsibility for herself."

Max's relief was palpable. But hard on its heels came another consideration. Caroline Twinning had recognised his interest in her—hardly surprising as he had taken no pains to hide it. If she knew he was not her guardian, she would keep him at arm's length. Well, try to, at least. But Caroline Twinning was not a green girl. The aura of quiet self-assurance which clung to her suggested she would not be an easy conquest. Obviously, it would be preferable if she continued to believe she was protected from him by his guardianship. That way, he would have no difficulty in approaching her, his reputation notwithstanding. In fact, the more he thought of it, the more merits he could see in the situation. Perhaps, in this case, he could have his cake and eat it too? He eyed Mr. Whitney. "Miss Twinning knows nothing of the terms of her father's will. At present, she believes herself to be my ward, along with her half-sisters. Is there any pressing need to inform her of her change in status?"

Mr. Whitney blinked owlishly, a considering look suffusing his face as he attempted to unravel the Duke's motives for wanting Miss Twinning to remain as his ward. Particularly after wanting to dissolve the guardianship altogether. Max Rotherbridge did not normally vacillate.

Max, perfectly sensible of Mr. Whitney's thoughts, put forward the most acceptable excuses he could think of. "For a start, whether she's twenty-four or twenty-six, she's just as much in need of protection as her sisters. Then, too, there's the question of propriety. If it was generally known she was not my ward, it would be exceedingly difficult for her to be seen in my company. And as I'll still be guardian to her sisters, and as they'll be residing in one of my establishments, the situation could become a trifle delicate, don't you think?"

It was not necessary for him to elaborate. Mr. Whitney saw the difficulty clearly enough. It was his turn to frown. "What you say is quite true." Hubert Whitney had no opinion whatever in the ability of the young ladies to manage their affairs. "At present, there is nothing I can think of that requires Miss Twinning's agreement. I expect it can do no harm to leave her in ignorance of her status until she weds."

The mention of marriage brought a sudden check to Max's racing mind but he resolutely put the disturbing notion aside for later examination. He had too much to do today.

Mr. Whitney was continuing, "How do you plan to handle the matter, if I may make so bold as to ask?"

Max had already given the thorny problem of how four young ladies could be presented to the *ton* under his protection, without raising a storm, some thought. "I propose to open up Twyford House immediately. They can stay there. I intend to ask my aunt, Lady Benborough, to stand as the girls' sponsor. I'm sure she'll be only too thrilled. It'll keep her amused for the Season."

Mr. Whitney was acquainted with Lady Benborough. He rather thought it would. A smile curved his thin lips.

The Duke stood, bringing the interview to a close.

Mr. Whitney rose. "That seems most suitable. If there's anything further in which we can assist Your Grace, we'll be only too delighted."

Max nodded in response to this formal statement. As Mr. Whitney bowed, prepared to depart, Max, a past master of social intrigue, saw one last hole in the wall and moved to block it. "If there's any matter you wish to discuss with Miss Twinning, I suggest you do it through me, as if I was, in truth, her guardian. As you handle both our estates, there can really be no impropriety in keeping up appearances. For Miss Twinning's sake."

Mr. Whitney bowed again. "I foresee no problems, Your Grace."

CHAPTER TWO

AFTER MR. WHITNEY LEFT, Max issued a set of rapid and comprehensive orders to his majordomo Wilson. In response, his servants flew to various corners of London, some to Twyford House, others to certain agencies specializing in the hire of household staff to the élite of the *ton*. One footman was despatched with a note from the Duke to an address in Half Moon Street, requesting the favour of a private interview with his paternal aunt, Lady Benborough.

As Max had intended, his politely worded missive intrigued his aunt. Wondering what had prompted such a strange request from her reprehensible nephew, she immediately granted it and settled down to await his coming with an air of pleasurable anticipation.

Max arrived at the small house shortly after noon. He found his aunt attired in a very becoming gown of purple sarsenet with a new and unquestionably modish wig perched atop her commanding visage. Max, bowing elegantly before her, eyed the wig askance.

Augusta Benborough sighed. "Well, I suppose I'll have to send it back, if that's the way you feel about it!"

Max grinned and bent to kiss the proffered cheek. "Definitely not one of your better efforts, Aunt."

She snorted. "Unfortunately, I can hardly claim you know nothing about it. It's the very latest fashion, I'll have you know." Max raised one laconic brow. "Yes, well," continued his aunt, "I dare say you're right. Not quite my style."

As she waited while he disposed his long limbs in a chair opposite the corner of the chaise where she sat, propped up by a pile of colourful cushions, she passed a critical glance over her nephew's elegant figure. How he contrived to look so precise when she knew he cared very little how he appeared was more than she could tell. She had heard it said that his man was a genius. Personally, she was of the opinion it was Max's magnificent physique and dark good looks that carried the day.

"I hope you're going to satisfy my curiosity without a great deal of roundaboutation."

"My dear aunt, when have I ever been other than direct?"

She looked at him shrewdly. "Want a favour, do you? Can't imagine what it is but you'd better be quick about asking. Miriam will be back by one and I gather you'd rather not have her listening." Miriam Alford was a faded spinster cousin of Lady Benborough's who lived with her, filling the post of companion to the fashionable old lady. "I sent her to Hatchard's when I got your note," she added in explanation.

Max smiled. Of all his numerous relatives, his Aunt Benborough, his father's youngest sister, was his favourite. While the rest of them, his mother included, constantly tried to reform him by ringing peals over him, appealing to his sense of what was acceptable, something he steadfastly denied any knowledge of, Augusta Benborough rarely made any comment on his lifestyle or the numerous scandals this provoked. When he had first come on the town, it had rapidly been made plain to his startled family that in Max they beheld a reincarnation of the second Viscount Delmere. If even half the tales were true, Max's great-grandfather had been a thoroughly unprincipled character, entirely devoid of morals. Lady Benborough, recently widowed, had asked Max to tea and had taken the opportunity to inform him in no uncertain terms of her opinion of his behaviour. She had then proceeded to outline all his faults, in detail. However, as she had concluded by saying that she fully expected her tirade to have no effect whatsoever on his subsequent conduct, nor could she imagine how anyone in their right mind could think it would, Max had borne the ordeal with an equanimity which would have stunned his friends. She had eventually dismissed him with the words, "Having at least had the politeness to hear me out, you may now depart and continue to go to hell in your own fashion and with my good will."

Now a widow of many years' standing, she was still a force to be reckoned with. She remained fully absorbed in the affairs of the *ton* and continued to be seen at all the crushes and every gala event. Max knew she was as shrewd as she could hold together and, above all, had an excellent sense of humour. All in all, she was just what he needed.

"I've come to inform you that, along with all the other encumbrances I inherited from Uncle Henry, I seem to have acquired four wards."

"You?" Lady Benborough's rendering of the word was rather more forceful than Miss Twinning's had been.

Max nodded. "Me. Four young ladies, one, the only one I've so far set eyes on, as lovely a creature as any other likely to be presented this Season."

"Good God! Who was so besotted as to leave four young girls in your care?" If anything, her ladyship was outraged at the very idea. Then, the full impact of the situation struck her. Her eyes widened. "Oh, good lord!" She collapsed against her cushions, laughing uncontrollably.

Knowing this was an attitude he was going to meet increasingly in the next few weeks, Max sighed. In an even tone suggestive of long suffering, he pointed out the obvious. "They weren't left to me but to my esteemed and now departed uncle's care. Mind you, I can't see that he'd have been much use to 'em either."

Wiping the tears from her eyes, Lady Benborough considered this view. "Can't see it myself," she admitted. "Henry always was a slow-top. Who are they?"

"The Misses Twinning. From Hertfordshire." Max proceeded to give her a brief résumé of the life history of the Twinnings, ending with the information that it transpired all four girls were heiresses.

Augusta Benborough was taken aback. "And you say they're beautiful to boot?"

"The one I've seen, Caroline, the eldest, most definitely is."

"Well, if anyone should know it's you!" replied her ladyship testily. Max acknowledged the comment with the slightest inclination of his head.

Lady Benborough's mind was racing. "So, what do you want with me?"

"What I would *like,* dearest Aunt," said Max, with his sweetest smile, "is for you to act as chaperon to the girls and present them to the *ton.*" Max paused. His aunt said nothing, sitting quite still with her sharp blue eyes, very like his own, fixed firmly on his face. He continued. "I'm opening up Twyford House. It'll be ready for them tomorrow. I'll stand the nonsense—all of it." Still she said nothing. "Will you do it?"

Augusta Benborough thought she would like nothing better than to be part of the hurly-burly of the marriage game again. But four? All at once? Still, there was Max's backing, and that would count for a good deal. Despite his giving the distinct impression of total uninterest in anything other than his own pleasure, she knew from experience that, should he feel inclined, Max could and would perform feats impossible for those with lesser clout in the fashionable world. Years after the event, she had learned that, when her youngest son had embroiled himself in a scrape so hideous that even now she shuddered to think of it, it had been Max who had rescued him. And apparently for no better reason than it had been bothering her. She still owed him for that.

But there were problems. Her own jointure was not particularly large and, while she had never asked Max for relief, turning herself out in the style he would expect of his wards' chaperon was presently beyond her slender means. Hesitantly, she said, "My own wardrobe…"

"Naturally you'll charge all costs you incur in this business to me," drawled Max, his voice bored as he examined through his quizzing glass a china cat presently residing on his aunt's mantelpiece. He knew perfectly well his aunt managed on a very slim purse but was too wise to offer direct assistance which would, he knew, be resented, not only by the lady herself but also by her pompous elder son.

"Can I take Miriam with me to Twyford House?"

With a shrug, Max assented. "Aside from anything else, she might come in handy with four charges."

"When can I meet them?"

"They're staying at Grillon's. I'm taking Miss Twinning for a drive this afternoon to tell her what I've decided. I'll arrange for them to move to Twyford House tomorrow afternoon. I'll send Wilson to help you and Mrs. Alford in transferring to Mount Street. It would be best, I suppose, if you could make the move in the morning. You'll want to familiarize yourself with the staff and so on." Bethinking himself that it would be wise to have one of his own well-trained staff on hand, he added, "I suppose I can let you have Wilson for a week or two, until you settle in. I suggest you and I meet the Misses Twinning when they arrive—shall we say at three?"

Lady Benborough was entranced by the way her nephew seemed to dismiss complications like opening and staffing a mansion overnight. Still, with the efficient and reliable Wilson on the job, presumably it would be done. Feeling a sudden and unexpected surge of excitement at the prospect of embarking on the Season with a definite purpose in life, she drew a deep breath. "Very well. I'll do it!"

"Good!" Max stood. "I'll send Wilson to call on you this afternoon."

His aunt, already engrossed in the matter of finding husbands for the Twinning chits, looked up. "Have you seen the other three girls?"

Max shook his head. Imagining the likely scene should they be on hand this afternoon when he called for Miss Twinning, he closed his eyes in horror. He could just hear the *on-dits.* "And I hope to God I don't see them in Grillon's foyer either!"

Augusta Benborough laughed.

WHEN HE CALLED at Grillon's promptly at two, Max was relieved to find Miss Twinning alone in the foyer, seated on a chaise opposite the door, her bonnet beside her. He was not to know that Caroline had had to exert every last particle of persuasion to achieve this end. And she had been quite unable to prevent her three sisters from keeping watch from the windows of their bedchambers.

As she had expected, she had had to describe His Grace of Twyford in detail for her sisters. Looking up at the figure striding across the foyer towards her, she did not think she had done too badly. What had been hardest to convey was the indefinable air that hung about him—compelling, exciting, it immediately brought to mind a whole range of emotions well-bred young ladies were not supposed to comprehend, let alone feel. As he took her hand for an instant in his own, and smiled down at her in an oddly lazy way, she decided she had altogether underestimated the attractiveness of that sleepy smile. It was really quite devastating.

Within a minute, Caroline found herself on the box seat of a fashionable curricle drawn by a pair of beautiful but restive bays. She resisted the temptation to glance up at the first-floor windows where she knew the other three would be stationed. Max mounted to the driving seat and the diminutive tiger, who had been holding the horses' heads, swung up behind. Then they were off, tacking through the traffic towards Hyde Park.

Caroline resigned herself to silence until the safer precincts of the Park were reached. However, it seemed the Duke was quite capable of conversing intelligently while negotiating the chaos of the London streets.

"I trust Grillon's has met with your approval thus far?"

"Oh, yes. They've been most helpful," returned Caroline. "Were you able to clarify the matter of our guardianship?"

Max was unable to suppress a smile at her directness. He nodded, his attention temporarily claimed by the off-side horse which had decided to take exception to a monkey dancing on the pavement, accompanied by an accordion player.

"Mr. Whitney has assured me that, as I am the Duke of Twyford, I must therefore be your guardian." He had allowed his reluctance to find expression in his tone. As the words left his lips, he realised that the unconventional woman beside him might well ask why he found the role of protector to herself and her sisters so distasteful. He immediately went on the attack. "And, in that capacity, I should like to know how you have endeavoured to come by Parisian fashions?"

His sharp eyes missed little and his considerable knowledge of feminine attire told him Miss Twinning's elegant pelisse owed much to the French. But France was at war with England and Paris no longer the playground of the rich.

Initially stunned that he should know enough to come so close to the truth, Caroline quickly realised the source of his knowledge. A spark of amusement danced in her eyes. She smiled and answered readily, "I assure you we did not run away to Brussels instead of New York."

"Oh, I wasn't afraid of that!" retorted Max, perfectly willing to indulge in plain speaking. "If you'd been in Brussels, I'd have heard of it."

"Oh?" Caroline turned a fascinated gaze on him.

Max smiled down at her.

Praying she was not blushing, Caroline strove to get

the conversation back on a more conventional course. "Actually, you're quite right about the clothes, they are Parisian. But not from the Continent. There were two *couturières* from Paris on the boat going to New York. They asked if they could dress us, needing the business to become known in America. It was really most fortunate. We took the opportunity to get quite a lot made up before we returned—we'd been in greys for so long that none of us had anything suitable to wear."

"How did you find American society?"

Caroline reminded herself to watch her tongue. She did not delude herself that just because the Duke was engaged in handling a team of high-couraged cattle through the busy streets of London he was likely to miss any slip she made. She was rapidly learning to respect the intelligence of this fashionable rake. "Quite frankly, we found much to entertain us. Of course, our relatives were pleased to see us and organised a great many outings and entertainments." No need to tell him they had had a riotous time.

"Did the tone of the society meet with your approval?"

He had already told her he would have known if they had been in Europe. Did he have connections in New York? How much could he know of their junketing? Caroline gave herself a mental shake. How absurd! He had not known of their existence until this morning. "Well, to be sure, it wasn't the same as here. Many more cits and half-pay officers about. And, of course, nothing like the *ton*."

Unknowingly, her answer brought some measure of relief to Max. Far from imagining his new-found wards had been indulging in high living abroad, he had been wondering whether they had any social experience at all. Miss Twinning's reply told him that she, at least, knew enough to distinguish the less acceptable among society's hordes.

They had reached the gates of the Park and turned into the carriage drive. Soon, the curricle was bowling along at a steady pace under the trees, still devoid of any but the earliest leaves. A light breeze lifted the ends of the ribbons on Caroline's hat and playfully danced along the horses' dark manes.

Max watched as Caroline gazed about her with interest. "I'm afraid you'll not see many notables at this hour. Mostly nursemaids and their charges. Later, between three and five, it'll be crowded. The Season's not yet begun in earnest, but by now most people will have returned to town. And the Park is the place to be seen. All the old biddies come here to exchange the latest *on-dits* and all the young ladies promenade along the walks with their beaux."

"I see." Caroline smiled to herself, a secret smile as she imagined how she and her sisters would fit into this scene.

Max saw the smile and was puzzled. Caroline Twinning was decidedly more intelligent than the women with whom he normally consorted. He could not guess her thoughts and was secretly surprised at wanting to know them. Then, he remembered one piece of vital information he had yet to discover. "Apropos of my uncle's plan to marry you all off, satisfy my curiosity, Miss Twinning. What do your sisters look like?"

This was the question she had been dreading. Caroline hesitated, searching for precisely the right words with which to get over the difficult ground. "Well, they've always been commonly held to be well to pass."

Max noted the hesitation. He interpreted her careful phrasing to mean that the other three girls were no more than average. He nodded, having suspected as much, and allowed the subject to drop.

They rounded the lake and he slowed his team to a gentle trot. "As your guardian, I've made certain arrangements for your immediate future." He noticed the grey eyes had flown to his face. "Firstly, I've opened Twyford House. Secondly, I've arranged for my aunt, Lady Benborough, to act as your chaperon for the Season. She's very well-connected and will know exactly how everything should be managed. You may place complete confidence in her advice. You will remove from Grillon's tomorrow. I'll send my man, Wilson, to assist you in the move to Twyford House. He'll call for you at two tomorrow. I presume that gives you enough time to pack?"

Caroline assumed the question to be rhetorical. She was stunned. He had not known they existed at nine this morning. How could he have organised all that since ten?

Thinking he may as well clear all the looming fences while he was about it, Max added, "As for funds, I presume your earlier arrangements still apply. However, should you need any further advances, as I now hold the purse-strings of your patrimonies, you may apply directly to me."

His last statement succeeded in convincing Caroline that it would not be wise to underestimate this Duke. Despite having only since this morning to think about it, he had missed very little. And, as he held the purse-strings, he could call the tune. As she had foreseen, life as the wards of a man as masterful and domineering as the present Duke of Twyford was rapidly proving to be was definitely not going to be as unfettered as they had imagined would be the case with his vague and easily led uncle. There were, however, certain advantages in the changed circumstances and she, for one, could not find it in her to repine.

More people were appearing in the Park, strolling about the lawns sloping down to the river and gathering in small groups by the carriageway, laughing and chatting.

A man of slight stature, mincing along beside the carriage drive, looked up in startled recognition as they passed. He was attired in a bottle-green coat with the most amazing amount of frogging Caroline had ever seen. In place of a cravat, he seemed to be wearing a very large floppy bow around his neck. "Who on earth was that quiz?" she asked.

"That quiz, my dear ward, is none other than Walter Millington, one of the fops. In spite of his absurd clothes, he's unexceptionable enough but he has a sharp tongue so it's wise for young ladies to stay on his right side. Don't laugh at him."

Two old ladies in an ancient landau were staring at them with an intensity which in lesser persons would be considered rude.

Max did not wait to be asked. "And those are the Misses Berry. They're as old as bedamned and know absolutely everyone. Kind souls. One's entirely vague and the other's sharp as needles."

Caroline smiled. His potted histories were entertaining.

A few minutes later, the gates came into view and Max headed his team in that direction. Caroline saw a horseman pulled up by the carriage drive a little way ahead. His face clearly registered recognition of the Duke's curricle and the figure driving it. Then his eyes passed to her and stopped. At five and twenty, Caroline had long grown used to the effect she had on men, particularly certain sorts of men. As they drew nearer, she saw that the gentleman was impeccably attired and had the same rakish air as the Duke. The rider held up a hand in greeting and she expected to feel the curricle slow. Instead, it flashed on, the Duke merely raising a hand in an answering salute.

Amused, Caroline asked, "And who, pray tell, was that?"

Max was thinking that keeping his friends in ignorance of Miss Twinning was going to prove impossible. Clearly, he would be well-advised to spend some time planning the details of this curious seduction, or he might find himself with rather more competition than he would wish. "That was Lord Ramsleigh."

"A friend of yours?"

"Precisely."

Caroline laughed at the repressive tone. The husky sound ran tingling along Max's nerves. It flashed into his mind that Caroline Twinning seemed to understand a great deal more than one might expect from a woman with such a decidedly restricted past. He was prevented from studying her face by the demands of successfully negotiating their exit from the Park.

They were just swinging out into the traffic when an elegant barouche pulled up momentarily beside them, heading into the Park. The thin, middle-aged woman, with a severe, almost horsy countenance, who had been languidly lying against the silken cushions, took one look at the curricle and sat bolt upright. In her face, astonishment mingled freely with rampant curiosity. "Twyford!"

Max glanced down as both carriages started to move again. "My lady." He nodded and then they were swallowed up in the traffic.

Glancing back, Caroline saw the elegant lady remonstrating with her coachman. She giggled. "Who was she?"

"That, my ward, was Sally, Lady Jersey. A name to remember. She is the most inveterate gossip in London. Hence her nickname of Silence. Despite that, she's kind-hearted enough. She's one of the seven patronesses of

Almack's. You'll have to get vouchers to attend but I doubt that will be a problem."

They continued in companionable silence, threading their way through the busy streets. Max was occupied with imagining the consternation Lady Jersey's sighting of them was going to cause. And there was Ramsleigh, too. A wicked smile hovered on his lips. He rather thought he was going to spend a decidedly amusing evening. It would be some days before news of his guardianship got around. Until then, he would enjoy the speculation. He was certain he would not enjoy the mirth of his friends when they discovered the truth.

"OOOH, CARO! Isn't he magnificent?" Arabella's round eyes, brilliant and bright, greeted Caroline as she entered their parlour.

"Did he agree to be our guardian?" asked the phlegmatic Sarah.

And, "Is he nice?" from the youngest, Lizzie.

All the important questions, thought Caroline with an affectionate smile, as she threw her bonnet aside and subsided into an armchair with a whisper of her stylish skirts. Her three half-sisters gathered around eagerly. She eyed them fondly. It would be hard to find three more attractive young ladies, even though she did say so herself. Twenty-year-old Sarah, with her dark brown hair and dramatically pale face, settling herself on one arm of her chair. Arabella on her other side, chestnut curls rioting around her heart-shaped and decidedly mischievous countenance, and Lizzie, the youngest and quietest of them all, curling up at her feet, her grey-brown eyes shining with the intentness of youth, the light dusting of freckles on the bridge of her nose persisting despite the ruthless application of Denmark lotion, crushed strawberries and every other remedy ever invented.

"Commonly held to be well to pass." Caroline's own words echoed in her ears. Her smile grew. "Well, my loves, it seems we are, incontrovertibly and without doubt, the Duke of Twyford's wards."

"When does he want to meet us?" asked Sarah, ever practical.

"Tomorrow afternoon. He's opening up Twyford House and we're to move in then. He resides at Delmere House, where I went this morning, so the properties will thus be preserved. His aunt, Lady Benborough, is to act as our chaperon—she's apparently well-connected and willing to sponsor us. She'll be there tomorrow."

A stunned silence greeted her news. Then Arabella voiced the awe of all three. "Since ten this morning?"

Caroline's eyes danced. She nodded.

Arabella drew a deep breath. "Is he…masterful?"

"Very!" replied Caroline. "But you'll be caught out, my love, if you think to sharpen your claws on our guardian. He's a deal too shrewd, and experienced besides." Studying the pensive faces around her, she added. "Any flirtation between any of us and Max Rotherbridge would be doomed to failure. As his wards, we're out of court, and he won't stand any nonsense, I warn you."

"Hmm." Sarah stood and wandered to the windows before turning to face her. "So it's as you suspected? He won't be easy to manage?"

Caroline smiled at the thought and shook her head decisively. "I'm afraid, my dears, that any notions we may have had of setting the town alight while in the care of a complaisant guardian have died along with the last Duke." One slim forefinger tapped her full lower lip thoughtfully. "However," she continued, "provided we adhere to society's rules and cause him no trouble, I doubt our new guardian will throw any rub in our way. We did come to London to find husbands, after all. And that," she said forcefully, gazing at the three faces fixed on hers, "is, unless I miss my guess, precisely what His Grace intends us to do."

"So he's agreed to present us so we can find husbands?" asked Lizzie.

Again Caroline nodded. "I think it bothers him, to have four wards." She smiled in reminiscence, then added, "And from what I've seen of the *ton* thus far, I suspect the present Duke as our protector may well be a distinct improvement over the previous incumbent. I doubt we'll have to fight off the fortune-hunters."

Some minutes ticked by in silence as they considered their new guardian. Then Caroline stood and shook out her skirts. She took a few steps into the room before turning to address her sisters.

"Tomorrow we'll be collected at two and conveyed to Twyford House, which is in Mount Street." She paused to let the implication of her phrasing sink in. "As you love me, you'll dress demurely and behave with all due reticence. No playing off your tricks on the Duke." She looked pointedly at Arabella, who grinned roguishly back. "Exactly so! I think, in the circumstances, we should make life as easy as possible for our new guardian. I feel sure he could have broken the guardianship if he had wished and can only be thankful he chose instead to honour his uncle's obligations. But we shouldn't try him too far." She ended her motherly admonitions with a stern air, deceiving her sisters not at all.

As the other three heads came together, Caroline turned to gaze unseeingly out of the window. A bewitching smile curved her generous lips and a twinkle lit her grey-green eyes. Softly, she murmured to herself, "For I've a definite suspicion he's going to find us very trying indeed!"

THUP, THUP, THUP. The tip of Lady Benborough's thin cane beat a slow tattoo, muffled by the pile of the Aubusson carpet. She was pleasantly impatient, waiting with definite anticipation to see her new charges. Her sharp blue gaze had already taken in the state of the room, the perfectly organised furniture, everything tidy and in readiness. If she had not known it for fact, she would never have believed that, yesterday morn, Twyford House had been shut up, the knocker off the door, every piece of furniture shrouded in Holland covers. Wilson was priceless. There was even a bowl of early crocus on the side-table between the long windows. These stood open, giving access to the neat courtyard, flanked by flowerbeds bursting into colourful life. A marble fountain stood at its centre, a Grecian maiden pouring water never-endingly from an urn.

Her contemplation of the scene was interrupted by a peremptory knock on the street door. A moment later, she heard the deep tones of men's voices and relaxed. Max. She would never get used to thinking of him as Twyford—she had barely become accustomed to him being Viscount Delmere. Max was essentially Max—he needed no title to distinguish him.

The object of her vagaries strode into the room. As always, his garments were faultless, his boots beyond compare. He bowed with effortless grace over her hand, his blue eyes, deeper in shade than her own but alive with the same intelligence, quizzing her. "A vast improvement, Aunt."

It took a moment to realise he was referring to her latest wig, a newer version of the same style she had favoured for the past ten years. She was not sure whether she was pleased or insulted. She compromised and snorted. "Trying to turn me up pretty, heh?"

"I would never insult your intelligence so, ma'am," he drawled, eyes wickedly laughing.

Lady Benborough suppressed an involuntary smile in response. The trouble with Max was that he was such a thorough-going rake that the techniques had flowed into all spheres of his life. He would undoubtedly flirt outrageously with his old nurse! Augusta Benborough snorted again. "Wilson's left to get the girls. He should be back any minute. Provided they're ready, that is."

She watched as her nephew ran a cursory eye over the room before selecting a Hepplewhite chair and elegantly disposing his long length in it.

"I trust everything meets with your approval?"

She waved her hand to indicate the room. "Wilson's been marvellous. I don't know how he does it."

"Neither do I," admitted Wilson's employer. "And the rest of the house?"

"The same," she assured him, then continued, "I've been considering the matter of husbands for the chits. With that sort of money, I doubt we'll have trouble even if they have spots and squint."

Max merely inclined his head. "You may leave the fortune-hunters to me."

Augusta nodded. It was one of the things she particularly appreciated about Max—one never needed to spell things out. The fact that the Twinning girls were his wards would certainly see them safe from the attentions of the less desirable elements. The new Duke of Twyford was a noted Corinthian and a crack shot.

"Provided they're immediately presentable, I thought I might give a small party next week, to start the ball rolling. But if their wardrobes need attention, or they can't dance, we'll have to postpone it."

Remembering Caroline Twinning's stylish dress and her words on the matter, Max reassured her. "And I'd bet a monkey they can dance, too." For some reason, he felt quite sure Caroline Twinning waltzed. It was the only dance he ever indulged in; he was firmly convinced that she waltzed.

Augusta was quite prepared to take Max's word on such matters. If nothing else, his notorious career through the bedrooms and bordellos of England had left him with an unerring eye for all things feminine. "Next week, then," she said. "Just a few of the more useful people and a smattering of the younger crowd."

She looked up to find Max's eye on her.

"I sincerely hope you don't expect to see *me* at this event?"

"Good Lord, no! I want all attention on your wards, not on their guardian!"

Max smiled his lazy smile.

"If the girls are at all attractive, I see no problems at all in getting them settled. Who knows? One of them might snare Wolverton's boy."

"That milksop?" Max's mind rebelled at the vision of the engaging Miss Twinning on the arm of the future Earl of Wolverton. Then he shrugged. After all, he had yet to meet the three younger girls. "Who knows?"

"Do you want me to keep a firm hand on the reins, give them a push if necessary or let them wander where they will?"

Max pondered the question, searching for the right words to frame his reply. "Keep your eye on the three younger girls. They're likely to need some guidance. I haven't sighted them yet, so they may need more than that. But, despite her advanced years, I doubt Miss Twinning will need any help at all."

His aunt interpreted this reply to mean that Miss Twinning's beauty, together with her sizeable fortune, would be sufficient to overcome the stigma of her years. The assessment was reassuring, coming as it did from her reprehensible nephew, whose knowledge was extensive in such matters. As her gaze rested on the powerful figure, negligently at ease in his chair, she reflected that it really was unfair he had inherited only the best from both his parents. The combination of virility, good looks and power of both mind and body was overwhelming; throw the titles in for good measure and it was no wonder Max Rotherbridge had been the target of so many matchmaking mamas throughout his adult life. But he had shown no sign whatever of succumbing to the demure attractions of any débutante. His preference was, always had been, for women of far more voluptuous charms. The litany of his past mistresses attested to his devotion to his ideal. They had all, every last one, been well-endowed. Hardly surprising, she mused. Max was tall, powerful and vigorous. She could not readily imagine any of the delicate debs satisfying his appetites. Her wandering mind dwelt on the subject of his latest *affaire,* aside, of course, from his current *chère amie,* an opera singer, so she had been told. Emma, Lady Mortland, was a widow of barely a year's standing but she had returned to town determined, it seemed, to make up for time lost through her marriage to an ageing peer. If the *on-dits* were true, she had fallen rather heavily in Max's lap. Looking at the strikingly handsome face of her nephew, Augusta grinned. Undoubtedly, Lady Mortland had set her cap at a Duchess's tiara. Deluded woman! Max, for all his air of unconcern, was born to his position. There was no chance he would offer marriage to Emma or any of her ilk. He would certainly avail himself of their proffered charms. Then when he tired of them, he would dismiss them, generously rewarding those who had the sense to play the game with suitable grace, callously ignoring those who did not.

The sounds of arrival gradually filtered into the drawing-room. Max raised his head. A spurt of feminine chatter drifted clearly to their ears. Almost immediately, silence was restored. Then, the door opened and Millwade, the new butler, entered to announce, "Miss Twinning."

Caroline walked through the door and advanced into the room, her sunny confidence cloaking her like bright sunshine. Max, who had risen, blinked and then strolled forward to take her hand. He bowed over it, smiling with conscious charm into her large eyes.

Caroline returned the smile, thoroughly conversant with its promise. While he was their guardian, she could afford to play his games. His strong fingers retained their clasp on her hand as he drew her forward to meet his aunt.

Augusta Benborough's mouth had fallen open at first sight of her eldest charge. But by the time Caroline faced her, she had recovered her composure. No wonder Max had said she would need no help. Great heavens! The girl was…well, no sense in beating about the bush—she was devilishly attractive. Sensually so. Responding automatically to the introduction, Augusta recognised the amused comprehension in the large and friendly grey eyes. Imperceptibly, she relaxed.

"Your sisters?" asked Max.

"I left them in the hall. I thought perhaps…" Caroline's words died on her lips as Max moved to the bell pull. Before she could gather her wits, Millwade was in the room, receiving his instructions. Bowing to the inevitable, Caroline closed her lips on her unspoken excuses. As she turned to Lady Benborough, her ladyship's brows rose in mute question. Caroline smiled and, with a swish of her delicate skirts, sat beside Lady Benborough. "Just watch," she whispered, her eyes dancing.

Augusta Benborough regarded her thoughtfully, then turned her attention to the door. As she did so, it opened again. First Sarah, then Arabella, then Lizzie Twinning entered the room.

A curious hiatus ensued as both Max Rotherbridge and his aunt, with more than fifty years of town bronze between them, stared in patent disbelief at their charges. The three girls stood unselfconsciously, poised and confident, and then swept curtsies, first to Max, then to her ladyship.

Caroline beckoned and they moved forward to be presented, to a speechless Max, who had not moved from his position beside his chair, and then to a flabbergasted Lady Benborough.

As they moved past him to make their curtsy to his aunt, Max recovered the use of his faculties. He closed his eyes. But when he opened them again, they were still there. He was not hallucinating. There they were: three of the loveliest lovelies he had ever set eyes on—four if you counted Miss Twinning. They were scene-stealers, every one—the sort of young women whose appearance suspended conversations, whose passage engendered rampant curiosity, aside from other, less nameable emotions, and whose departure left onlookers wondering what on earth they had been talking about before. All from the same stable, all under one roof. Nominally his. Incredible. And then the enormity, the mind-numbing, all-encompassing reality of his inheritance struck him. One glance into Miss Twinning's grey eyes, brimming with mirth, told him she understood more than enough. His voice, lacking its customary strength and in a very odd register, came to his ears. "Impossible!"

His aunt Augusta collapsed laughing.

CHAPTER THREE

"No!" MAX SHOOK his head stubbornly, a frown of quite dramatic proportions darkening his handsome face.

Lady Benborough sighed mightily and frowned back. On recovering her wits, she had sternly repressed her mirth and sent the three younger Twinnings into the courtyard. But after ten minutes of carefully reasoned argument, Max remained adamant. However, she was quite determined her scapegrace nephew would not succeed in dodging his responsibilities. Aside from anything else, the situation seemed set to afford her hours of entertainment and, at her age, such opportunities could not be lightly passed by. Her lips compressed into a thin line and a martial light appeared in her blue eyes.

Max, recognising the signs, got in first. "It's impossible! Just *think* of the talk!"

Augusta's eyes widened to their fullest extent. "Why should you care?" she asked. "Your career to date would hardly lead one to suppose you fought shy of scandal." She fixed Max with a penetrating stare. "Besides, while there'll no doubt be talk, none of it will harm anyone. Quite the opposite. It'll get these girls into the limelight!"

The black frown on Max's face did not lighten.

Caroline wisely refrained from interfering between the two principal protagonists, but sat beside Augusta, looking as innocent as she could. Max's gaze swept over her and stopped on her face. His eyes narrowed. Caroline calmly returned his scrutiny.

There was little doubt in Max's mind that Caroline Twinning had deliberately concealed from him the truth about her sisters until he had gone too far in establishing himself as their guardian to pull back. He felt sure some retribution was owing to one who had so manipulated him but, staring into her large grey-green eyes, was unable to decide which of the numerous and varied punishments his fertile imagination supplied would be the most suitable. Instead, he said, in the tones of one goaded beyond endurance, "'Commonly held to be well to pass', indeed!"

Caroline smiled.

Augusta intervened. "Whatever you're thinking of, Max, it won't do! You're the girls' guardian—you told me so yourself. You cannot simply wash your hands of them. I can see it'll be a trifle awkward for you," her eyes glazed as she thought of Lady Mortland, "but if you don't concern yourself with them, who will?"

Despite his violent response to his first sight of all four Twinning sisters, perfectly understandable in the circumstances, Max had not seriously considered giving up his guardianship of them. His behaviour over the past ten minutes had been more in the nature of an emotional rearguard action in an attempt, which his rational brain acknowledged as futile, to resist the tide of change he could see rising up to swamp his hitherto well-ordered existence. He fired his last shot. "Do you seriously imagine that someone with my reputation will be considered a suitable guardian for four...?" He paused, his eyes on Caroline, any number of highly apt descriptions revolving in his head. "Excessively attractive virgins?" he concluded savagely.

Caroline's eyes widened and her dimple appeared.

"On the contrary!" Augusta answered. "Who better than you to act as their guardian? Odds are you know every ploy ever invented and a few more besides. And if you can't keep the wolves at bay, then no one can. I really don't know why you're creating all this fuss."

Max did not know either. After a moment of silence, he turned abruptly and crossed to the windows giving on to the courtyard. He had known from the outset that this was one battle he was destined to lose. Yet some part of his mind kept suggesting in panic-stricken accents that there must be some other way. He watched as the three younger girls—his wards, heaven forbid!—examined the fountain, prodding and poking in an effort to find the lever to turn it on. They were a breathtaking sight, the varied hues of their shining hair vying with the flowers, their husky laughter and the unconsciously seductive way their supple figures swayed this way and that causing him to groan inwardly. Up to the point when he had first sighted them, the three younger Twinnings had figured in his plans as largely irrelevant entities, easily swept into the background and of no possible consequence to his plans for their elder sister. One glimpse had been enough to scuttle that scenario. He was trapped—a guardian in very truth. And with what the Twinning girls had to offer he would have no choice but to play the role to the hilt. Every man in London with eyes would be after them!

Lady Benborough eyed Max's unyielding back with a frown. Then she turned to the woman beside her. She had already formed a high opinion of Miss Twinning. What was even more to the point, being considerably more than seven, Augusta had also perceived that her reprehensible nephew was far from indifferent to the luscious beauty. Meeting the grey-green eyes, her ladyship raised her brows. Caroline nodded and rose.

Max turned as Caroline laid her hand on his arm. She was watching her sisters, not him. Her voice, when she spoke, was tactfully low. "If it would truly bother you to stand as our guardian, I'm sure we could make some other arrangement." As she finished speaking, she raised her eyes to his.

Accustomed to every feminine wile known to woman, Max nevertheless could see nothing in the lucent grey eyes to tell him whether the offer was a bluff or not. But it only took a moment to realise that if he won this particular argument, if he succeeded in withdrawing as guardian to the Twinning sisters, Caroline Twinning would be largely removed from his orbit. Which would certainly make his seduction of her more difficult, if not impossible. Faced with those large grey-green eyes, Max did what none of the habitués of Gentleman Jackson's boxing salon had yet seen him do. He threw in the towel.

HAVING RESIGNED HIMSELF to the inevitable, Max departed, leaving the ladies to become better acquainted. As the street door closed behind him, Lady Benborough turned a speculative glance on Caroline. Her lips twitched. "Very well done, my dear. Clearly you need no lessons in how to manage a man."

Caroline's smile widened. "I've had some experience, I'll admit."

"Well, you'll need it all if you're going to tackle my nephew." Augusta grinned in anticipation. From where she sat, her world looked rosy indeed. Not only did she have four rich beauties to fire off, and unlimited funds to do it with, but, glory of glories, for the first time since he had emerged from short coats her reprehensible nephew was behaving in a less than predictable fashion. She allowed herself a full minute to revel in the wildest of imaginings, before settling down to extract all the pertinent details of their backgrounds and personalities from the Twinning sisters. The younger girls returned when the tea-tray arrived. By the time it was removed, Lady Benborough had satisfied herself on all points of interest and the conversation moved on to their introduction to the *ton*.

"I wonder whether news of your existence has leaked out yet," mused her ladyship. "Someone may have seen you at Grillon's."

"Lady Jersey saw me yesterday with Max in his curricle," said Caroline.

"Did she?" Augusta sat up straighter. "In that case, there's no benefit in dragging our heels. If Silence already has the story, the sooner you make your appearance, the better. We'll go for a drive in the Park tomorrow." She ran a knowledgeable eye over the sisters' dresses. "I must say, your dresses are very attractive. Are they all like that?"

Reassured on their wardrobes, she nodded. "So there's nothing to stop us wading into the fray immediately. Good!" She let her eyes wander over the four faces in front of her, all beautiful yet each with its own allure. Her gaze rested on Lizzie. "You—Lizzie, isn't it? You're eighteen?"

Lizzie nodded. "Yes, ma'am."

"If that's so, then there's no reason for us to be missish," returned her ladyship. "I assume you all wish to find husbands?"

They all nodded decisively.

"Good! At least we're all in agreement over the objective. Now for the strategy. Although your sudden appearance all together is going to cause a riot. I rather think that's going to be the best way to begin. At the very least, we'll be noticed."

"Oh, we're *always* noticed!" returned Arabella, hazel eyes twinkling.

Augusta laughed. "I dare say." From any other young lady, the comment would have earned a reproof. However, it was impossible to deny the Twinning sisters were rather more than just beautiful, and as they were all more than green girls it was pointless to pretend they did not fully comprehend the effect they had on the opposite sex. To her ladyship's mind, it was a relief not to have to hedge around the subject.

"Aside from anything else," she continued thoughtfully, "your public appearance as the Duke of Twyford's wards will make it impossible for Max to renege on his decision." Quite why she was so very firmly set on Max fulfilling his obligations she could not have said. But his guardianship would keep him in contact with Miss Twinning. And that, she had a shrewd suspicion, would be a very good thing.

THEIR DRIVE IN the Park the next afternoon was engineered by the experienced Lady Benborough to be tantalisingly brief. As predicted, the sight of four ravishing females in the Twyford barouche caused an immediate impact. As the carriage sedately bowled along the avenues, heads rapidly came together in the carriages they passed. Conversations between knots of elegant gentlemen and the more dashing of ladies who had descended from their carriages to stroll about the well-tended lawns halted in midsentence as all eyes turned to follow the Twyford barouche.

Augusta, happily aware of the stir they were causing, sat on the maroon leather seat and struggled to keep the grin from her face. Her charges were attired in a spectrum of delicate colours, for all the world like a posy of gorgeous blooms. The subtle peach of Caroline's round gown gave way to the soft turquoise tints of Sarah's. Arabella had favoured a gown of the most delicate rose muslin while Lizzie sat, like a quiet bluebell, nodding happily amid her sisters. In the soft spring sunshine, they looked like refugees from the fairy kingdom, too exquisite to be flesh and blood. Augusta lost her struggle and grinned widely at her fanciful thoughts. Then her eyes alighted on a landau drawn up to the side of the carriageway. She raised her parasol and tapped her coachman on the shoulder. "Pull up over there."

Thus it happened that Emily, Lady Cowper and Maria, Lady Sefton, enjoying a comfortable cose in the afternoon sunshine, were the first to meet the Twinning sisters. As the Twyford carriage drew up, the eyes of both experienced matrons grew round.

Augusta noted their response with satisfaction. She seized the opportunity to perform the introductions, ending with, "Twyford's wards, you know."

That information, so casually dropped, clearly stunned both ladies. *"Twyford's?"* echoed Lady Sefton. Her mild eyes, up to now transfixed by the spectacle that was the Twinning sisters, shifted in bewilderment to Lady Benborough's face. "How on *earth*…?"

In a few well-chosen sentences, Augusta told her. Once their ladyships had recovered from their amusement, both at once promised vouchers for the girls to attend Almack's.

"My dear, if your girls attend, we'll have to lay on more refreshments. The gentlemen will be there in droves," said Lady Cowper, smiling in genuine amusement.

"Who knows? We might even prevail on Twyford himself to attend," mused Lady Sefton.

While Augusta thought that might be stretching things a bit far, she was thankful for the immediate backing her two old friends had given her crusade to find four fashionable husbands for the Twinnings. The carriages remained together for some time as the two patronesses of Almack's learned more of His Grace of Twyford's wards. Augusta was relieved to find that all four girls could converse with ease. The two younger sisters prettily deferred to the elder two, allowing the more experienced Caroline, ably seconded by Sarah, to dominate the responses.

When they finally parted, Augusta gave the order to return to Mount Street. "Don't want to rush it," she explained to four enquiring glances. "Much better to let them come to us."

TWO DAYS LATER, the *ton* was still reeling from the discovery of the Duke of Twyford's wards. Amusement, from the wry to the ribald, had been the general reaction. Max had gritted his teeth and borne it, but the persistent demands of his friends to be introduced to his wards sorely tried his temper. He continued to refuse all such requests. He could not stop their eventual acquaintance but at least he did not need directly to foster it. Thus, it was in a far from benign mood that he prepared to depart Delmere House on that fine April morning, in the company of two of his particular cronies, Lord Darcy Hamilton and George, Viscount Pilborough.

As they left the parlour at the rear of the house and entered the front hallway, their conversation was interrupted by a knock on the street door. They paused in the rear of the hall as Hillshaw moved majestically past to answer it.

"I'm not at home, Hillshaw," said Max.

Hillshaw regally inclined his head. "Very good, Your Grace."

But Max had forgotten that Hillshaw had yet to experience the Misses Twinning *en masse*. Resistance was impossible and they came swarming over the threshold, in a frothing of lace and cambrics, bright smiles, laughing eyes and dancing curls.

The girls immediately spotted the three men, standing rooted by the stairs. Arabella reached Max first. "Dear guardian," she sighed languishingly, eyes dancing, "are you well?" She placed her small hand on his arm.

Sarah, immediately behind, came to his other side. "We hope you are because we want to ask your permission for something." She smiled matter-of-factly up at him.

Lizzie simply stood directly in front of him, her huge eyes trained on his face, a smile she clearly knew to be winning suffusing her countenance. "Please?"

Max raised his eyes to Hillshaw, still standing dumb by the door. The sight of his redoubtable henchman rolled up by a parcel of young misses caused his lips to twitch. He firmly denied the impulse to laugh. The Misses Twinning were outrageous already and needed no further encouragement. Then his eyes met Caroline's.

She had hung back, watching her sisters go through their paces, but as his eyes touched her, she moved forward, her hand outstretched. Max, quite forgetting the presence of all the others, took it in his.

"Don't pay any attention to them, Your Grace; I'm afraid they're sad romps."

"Not *romps,* Caro," protested Arabella, eyes fluttering over the other two men, standing mesmerized just behind Max.

"It's just that we heard it was possible to go riding in the Park but Lady Benborough said we had to have your permission," explained Sarah.

"So, here we are and can we?" asked Lizzie, big eyes beseeching.

"No," said Max, without further ado. As his aunt had observed, he knew every ploy. And the opportunities afforded by rides in the Park, where chaperons could be present but sufficiently remote, were endless. The first rule in a seduction was to find the opportunity to speak alone to the lady in question. And a ride in the Park provided the perfect setting.

Caroline's fine brows rose at his refusal. Max noticed that the other three girls turned to check their elder sister's response before returning to the attack.

"Oh, you can't mean that! How shabby!"

"Why on earth not?"

"We all ride well. I haven't been out since we were home."

Both Arabella and Sarah turned to the two gentlemen still standing behind Max, silent auditors to the extraordinary scene. Arabella fixed Viscount Pilborough with pleading eyes. "Surely there's nothing unreasonable in such a request?" Under the Viscount's besotted gaze, her lashes fluttered almost imperceptibly, before her lids decorously dropped, veiling those dancing eyes, the long lashes brushing her cheeks, delicately stained with a most becoming blush.

The Viscount swallowed. "Why on earth not, Max? Not an unreasonable request at all. Your wards would look very lovely on horseback."

Max, who was only too ready to agree on how lovely his wards would look in riding habits, bit back an oath. Ignoring Miss Twinning's laughing eyes, he glowered at the hapless Viscount.

Sarah meanwhile had turned to meet the blatantly admiring gaze of Lord Darcy. Not as accomplished a flirt as Arabella, she could nevertheless hold her own, and she returned his warm gaze with a serene smile. "Is there any real reason why we shouldn't ride?"

Her low voice, cool and strangely musical, made Darcy Hamilton wish there were far fewer people in Max's hall. In fact, his fantasies would be more complete if they were not in Max's hall at all. He moved towards Sarah and expertly captured her hand. Raising it to his lips, he smiled in a way that had thoroughly seduced more damsels than he cared to recall. He could well understand why Max did not wish his wards to ride. But, having met this Twinning sister, there was no way in the world he was going to further his friend's ambition.

His lazy drawl reached Max's ears. "I'm very much afraid, Max, dear boy, that you're going to have to concede. The opposition is quite overwhelming."

Max glared at him. Seeing the determination in his lordship's grey eyes and understanding his reasons only too well, he knew he was outnumbered on all fronts. His eyes returned to Caroline's face to find her regarding him quizzically. "Oh, very well!"

Her smile warmed him and at the prompting lift of her brows he introduced his friends, first to her, and then to her sisters in turn. The chattering voices washed over him, his friends' deeper tones running like a counterpoint in the cacophony. Caroline moved to his side.

"You're not seriously annoyed by us riding, are you?"

He glanced down at her. The stern set of his lips reluctantly relaxed. "I would very much rather you did not. However," he continued, his eyes roving to the group of her three sisters and his two friends, busy with noisy plans for their first ride that afternoon, "I can see that's impossible."

Caroline smiled. "We won't come to any harm, I assure you."

"Allow me to observe, Miss Twinning, that gallivanting about the London *ton* is fraught with rather more difficulty than you would have encountered in American society, nor yet within the circle to which you were accustomed in Hertfordshire."

A rich chuckle greeted his warning. "Fear not, dear guardian," she said, raising laughing eyes to his. Max noticed the dimple, peeking irrepressibly from beside her soft mouth. "We'll manage."

NATURALLY, MAX FELT obliged to join the riding party that afternoon. Between both his and Darcy Hamilton's extensive stables, they had managed to assemble suitable mounts for the four girls. Caroline had assured him that, like all country misses, they could ride very well. By the time they gained the Park, he had satisfied himself on that score. At least he need not worry over them losing control of the frisky horses and being thrown. But, as they were all as stunning as he had feared they would be, elegantly gowned in perfectly cut riding habits, his worries had not noticeably decreased.

As they ambled further into the Park, by dint of the simple expedient of reining in his dappled grey, he dropped to the rear of the group, the better to keep the three younger girls in view. Caroline, riding by his side, stayed with him. She threw him a laughing glance but made no comment.

As he had expected, they had not gone more than two hundred yards before their numbers were swelled by the appearance of Lord Tulloch and young Mr. Mitchell. But neither of these gentlemen seemed able to interrupt the rapport which, to Max's experienced eye, was developing with alarming rapidity between Sarah Twinning and Darcy Hamilton. Despite his fears, he grudgingly admitted the Twinning sisters knew a trick or two. Arabella flirted outrageously but did so with all gentlemen, none being able to claim any special consideration. Lizzie attracted the quieter men and was happy to converse on the matters currently holding the interest of the *ton*. Her natural shyness and understated youth, combined with her undeniable beauty, was a heady tonic for these more sober gentlemen. As they ventured deeper into the Park, Max was relieved to find Sarah giving Darcy no opportunity to lead her apart. Gradually, his watchfulness relaxed. He turned to Caroline.

"Have you enjoyed your first taste of life in London?"

"Yes, thank you," she replied, grey eyes smiling. "Your aunt has been wonderful. I can't thank you enough for all you've done."

Max's brow clouded. As it happened, the last thing he wanted was her gratitude. Here he was, thinking along lines not grossly dissimilar from Darcy's present preoccupation, and the woman chose to thank him. He glanced down at her as she rode beside him, her face free of any worry, thoroughly enjoying the moment. Her presence was oddly calming.

"What plans do you have for the rest of the week?" he asked.

Caroline was slightly surprised by his interest but replied readily. "We've been driving in the Park every afternoon except today. I expect we'll continue to appear, although I rather think, from now on, it will be on horseback." She shot him a measuring glance to see how he would take that. His face was slightly grim but he nodded in acceptance. "Last evening, we went to a small party given by Lady Malling. Your aunt said there are a few more such gatherings in the next week which we should attend, to give ourselves confidence in society."

Max nodded again. From the corner of his eye, he saw Sarah avoid yet another of Darcy's invitations to separate from the group. He saw the quick frown which showed fleetingly in his friend's eyes. Serve him right if the woman drove him mad. But, he knew, Darcy was made of sterner stuff. The business of keeping his wards out of the arms of his friends was going to be deucedly tricky. Returning to contemplation of Miss Twinning's delightful countenance, he asked, "Has Aunt Augusta got you vouchers for Almack's yet?"

"Yes. We met Lady Sefton and Lady Cowper on our first drive in the Park."

Appreciating his aunt's strategy, Max grinned. "Trust Aunt Augusta."

Caroline returned his smile. "She's been very good to us."

Thinking that the unexpected company of four lively young women must have been a shock to his aunt's system, Max made a mental note to do anything in his power to please his aunt Benborough.

They had taken a circuitous route through the Park and only now approached the fashionable precincts. The small group almost immediately swelled to what, to Max, were alarming proportions, with every available gentleman clamouring for an introduction to his beautiful wards. But, to his surprise, at a nod from Caroline, the girls obediently brought their mounts closer and refused every attempt to draw them further from his protective presence. To his astonishment, they all behaved with the utmost decorum, lightened, of course, by their natural liveliness but nevertheless repressively cool to any who imagined them easy targets. Despite his qualms, he was impressed. They continued in this way until they reached the gates of the Park, by which time the group had dwindled to its original size and he could relax again.

He turned to Caroline, still by his side. "Can you guarantee they'll always behave so circumspectly, or was that performance purely for my benefit?" As her laughing eyes met his, he tried to decide whether they were greeny-grey or greyish-green. An intriguing question.

"Oh, we're experienced enough to know which way to jump, I assure you," she returned. After a pause, she continued, her voice lowered so only he could hear. "In the circumstances, we would not willingly do anything to bring disrepute on ourselves. We are very much aware of what we owe to you and Lady Benborough."

Max knew he should be pleased at this avowal of good intentions. Instead, he was aware of a curious irritation. He would certainly do everything in his power to reinforce her expressed sentiment with respect to the three younger girls, but to have Caroline Twinning espousing such ideals was not in keeping with his plans.

Somehow, he was going to have to convince her that adherence to all the social strictures was not the repayment he, at least, would desire. The unwelcome thought that, whatever the case, she might now consider herself beholden to him, and would, therefore, grant him his wishes out of gratitude, very nearly made him swear aloud. His horse jibbed at the suddenly tightened rein and he pushed the disturbing thought aside while he dealt with the grey. Once the horse had settled again, he continued by Caroline's side as they headed back to Mount Street, a distracted frown at the back of his dark blue eyes.

Augusta Benborough flicked open her fan and plied it vigorously. Under cover of her voluminous skirts, she slipped her feet free of her evening slippers. She had forgotten how stifling the small parties, held in the run-up to the Season proper, could be. Every bit as bad as the crushes later in the Season. But there, at least, she would have plenty of her own friends to gossip with. The mothers and chaperons of the current batch of débutantes were a generation removed from her own and at these small parties they were generally the only older members present. Miriam Alford had elected to remain at Twyford House this evening, which left Augusta with little to do but watch her charges. And even that, she mused to herself, was not exactly riveting entertainment.

True, Max was naturally absent, which meant her primary interest in the entire business was in abeyance.

Still, it was comforting to find Caroline treating all the gentlemen who came her way with the same unfailing courtesy and no hint of partiality. Arabella, too, seemed to be following that line, although, in her case, the courtesy was entirely cloaked in a lightly flirtatious manner. In any other young girl, Lady Benborough would have strongly argued for a more demure style. But she had watched Arabella carefully. The girl had quick wits and a ready tongue. She never stepped beyond what was acceptable, though she took delight in sailing close to the wind. Now, convinced that no harm would come of Arabella's artful play, Augusta nodded benignly as that young lady strolled by, accompanied by the inevitable gaggle of besotted gentlemen.

One of their number was declaiming,

> "'My dearest flower,
> More beautiful by the hour,
> To you I give my heart.'"

Arabella laughed delightedly and quickly said, "My dear sir, I beg you spare my blushes! Truly, your verses do me more credit than I deserve. But surely, to do them justice, should you not set them down on parchment?" Anything was preferable to having them said aloud.

The budding poet, young Mr. Rawlson, beamed. "*Nothing* would give me greater pleasure, Miss Arabella. I'll away and transcribe them immediately. And dedicate them to your inspiration!" With a flourishing bow, he departed precipitately, leaving behind a silence pregnant with suppressed laughter.

This was broken by a snigger from Lord Shannon. "Silly puppy!"

As Mr. Rawlson was a year or two older than Lord Shannon, who himself appeared very young despite his attempts to ape the Corinthians, this comment itself caused some good-natured laughter.

"Perhaps, Lord Shannon, you would be so good as to fetch me some refreshment?" Arabella smiled sweetly on the hapless youngster. With a mutter which all interpreted to mean he was delighted to be of service to one so fair, the young man escaped.

With a smile, Arabella turned to welcome Viscount Pilborough to her side.

Augusta's eyelids drooped. The temperature in the room seemed to rise another degree. The murmuring voices washed over her. Her head nodded. With a start, she shook herself awake. Determined to keep her mind active for the half-hour remaining, she sought out her charges. Lizzie was chattering animatedly with a group of débutantes much her own age. The youngest Twinning was surprisingly innocent, strangely unaware of her attractiveness to the opposite sex, still little more than a schoolgirl at heart. Lady Benborough smiled. Lizzie would learn soon enough; let her enjoy her girlish gossiping while she might.

A quick survey of the room brought Caroline to light, strolling easily on the arm of the most eligible Mr. Willoughby.

"It's so good of you to escort your sister to these parties, sir. I'm sure Miss Charlotte must be very grateful." Caroline found conversation with the reticent Mr. Willoughby a particular strain.

A faint smile played at the corners of Mr. Willoughby's thin lips. "Indeed, I believe she is. But really, there is very little to it. As my mother is so delicate as to find these affairs quite beyond her, it would be churlish of me indeed to deny Charlotte the chance of becoming more easy in company before she is presented."

With grave doubts over how much longer she could endure such ponderous conversation without running amok, Caroline seized the opportunity presented by passing a small group of young ladies, which included the grateful Charlotte, to stop. The introductions were quickly performed.

As she stood conversing with a Miss Denbright, an occupation which required no more than half her brain, Caroline allowed her eyes to drift over the company. Other than Viscount Pilborough, who was dangling after Arabella in an entirely innocuous fashion, and Darcy Hamilton, who was pursuing Sarah in a far more dangerous way, there was no gentleman in whom she felt the least interest. Even less than her sisters did she need the opportunity of the early parties to gain confidence. Nearly eighteen months of social consorting in the ballrooms and banquet halls in New York had given them all a solid base on which to face the London *ton*. And even more than her sisters, Caroline longed to get on with it. Time, she felt, was slipping inexo-

rably by. Still, there were only four more days to go.
And then, surely their guardian would reappear? She
had already discovered that no other gentleman's eyes
could make her feel quite the same breathless excitement as the Duke of Twyford's did. He had not called on
them since that first ride in the Park, a fact which had
left her with a wholly resented feeling of disappointment. Despite the common sense on which she prided
herself, she had formed an irritating habit of compar-
ing all the men she met with His domineering Grace
and inevitably found them wanting. Such foolishness
would have to stop. With a small suppressed sigh, she
turned a charming smile on Mr. Willoughby, wishing
for the sixteenth time that his faded blue eyes were of
a much darker hue.

Satisfied that Caroline, like Lizzie and Arabella,
needed no help from her, Lady Benborough moved her
gaze on, scanning the room for Sarah's dark head. When
her first survey drew no result, she sat up straighter,
a slight frown in her eyes. Darcy Hamilton was here,
somewhere, drat him. He had attended every party they
had been to this week, a fact which of itself had already
drawn comment. His attentions to Sarah were becoming
increasingly marked. Augusta knew all the Hamiltons.
She had known Darcy's father and doubted not the truth
of the "like father, like son" adage. But surely Sarah
was too sensible to… She wasted no time in completing that thought but started a careful, methodical and
entirely well-disguised visual search. From her present
position, on a slightly raised dais to one side, she com-

manded a view of the whole room. Her gaze passed over the alcove set in the wall almost directly opposite her but then returned, caught by a flicker of movement within the shadowed recess.

There they were, Sarah and, without doubt, Darcy Hamilton. Augusta could just make out the blur of colour that was Sarah's green dress. How typical of Darcy. They were still in the room, still within sight, but, in the dim light of the alcove, almost private. As her eyes adjusted to the poor light, Augusta saw to her relief that, despite her fears and Darcy's reputation, they were merely talking, seated beside one another on a small settee. Still, to her experienced eye, there was a degree of familiarity in their pose, which, given that it must be unconscious, was all too revealing. With a sigh, she determined to have a word, if not several words, with Sarah, regarding the fascinations of men like Darcy Hamilton. She would have to do it, for Darcy's proclivities were too well-known to doubt.

She watched as Darcy leaned closer to Sarah.

"My dear," drawled Darcy Hamilton, "do you have any idea of the temptation you pose? Or the effect beauty such as yours has on mere men?"

His tone was lazy and warm, with a quality of velvety smoothness which fell like a warm cloak over Sarah's already hypersensitized nerves. He had flung one arm over the back of the settee and long fingers were even now twining in the soft curls at her nape. She knew she should move but could not. The sensations rippling down her spine were both novel and exhilarating. She was conscious of a ludicrous desire to snuggle into that warmth, to invite more soft words. But the desire which burned in his lordship's grey eyes was already frighteningly intense. She determinedly ignored the small reckless voice which urged her to encourage him and instead replied, "Why, no. Of course not."

Darcy just managed to repress a snort of disgust. Damn the woman! Her voice had held not the thread of a quaver. Calm and steady as a rock when his own pulses were well and truly racing. He simply did not believe it. He glanced down into her wide brown eyes, guileless as ever, knowing that his exasperation was showing. For a fleeting instant, he saw a glimmer of amusement and, yes, of triumph in the brown depths. But when he looked again, the pale face was once again devoid of emotion. His grey eyes narrowed.

Sarah saw his intent look and immediately dropped her eyes.

Her action confirmed Darcy's suspicions. By God, the chit was playing with him! The fact that Sarah could only be dimly aware of the reality of the danger she was flirting with was buried somewhere in the recesses of his mind. But, like all the Hamiltons, for him, desire could easily sweep aside all reason. In that instant, he determined he would have her, no matter what the cost. Not here, not now—neither place nor time was right. But some time, somewhere, Sarah Twinning would be his.

Augusta's attention was drawn by the sight of a mother gathering her two daughters and preparing to depart. As if all had been waiting for this signal, it suddenly seemed as if half the room was on their way. With relief, she turned to see Darcy lead Sarah from the alcove and head in her direction. As Caroline approached, closely followed by Lizzie and Arabella, Augusta Benborough wriggled her aching toes back into her slippers and rose. It was over. And in four days' time the Season would begin. As she smiled benignly upon the small army of gentlemen who had escorted her charges to her side, she reminded herself that, with the exception of Darcy Hamilton, there was none present tonight who would make a chaperon uneasy. Once in wider society, she would have no time to be bored. The Twinning sisters would certainly see to that.

CHAPTER FOUR

EMMA, LADY MORTLAND, thought Max savagely, had
no right to the title. He would grant she was attractive, in a blowsy sort of way, but her conduct left much
to be desired. She had hailed him almost as soon as
he had entered the Park. He rarely drove there except
when expediency demanded. Consequently, her ladyship had been surprised to see his curricle, drawn by
his famous match bays, advancing along the avenue.
He had been forced to pull up or run the silly woman
down. The considerable difficulty in conversing at any
length with someone perched six feet and more above
you, particularly when that someone displayed the most
blatant uninterest, had not discouraged Lady Mortland.
She had done her best to prolong the exchange in the
dim hope, Max knew, of gaining an invitation to ride
beside him. She had finally admitted defeat and archly
let him go, but not before issuing a thickly veiled invitation which he had had no compunction in declining. As
she had been unwise enough to speak in the hearing of
two gentlemen of her acquaintance, her resulting embarrassment was entirely her own fault. He knew she
entertained hopes, totally unfounded, of becoming his

Duchess. Why she should imagine he would consider taking a woman with the morals of an alley cat to wife was beyond him.

As he drove beneath the trees, he scanned the carriages that passed, hoping to find his wards. He had not seen them since that first ride in the Park, a feat of self-discipline before which any other he had ever accomplished in his life paled into insignificance. Darcy Hamilton had put the idea into his head. His friend had returned with him to Delmere House after that first jaunt, vociferous in his complaints of the waywardness of Sarah Twinning. The fact that she was Max's ward had not subdued him in the least. Max had not been surprised; Darcy could be ruthlessly singleminded when hunting. It had been Darcy who had suggested that a short absence might make the lady more amenable and had departed with the firm resolve to give the Twinning girls the go-by for at least a week.

That had been six days ago. The Season was about to get under way and it was time to reacquaint himself with his wards. Having ascertained that their horses had not left his stable, he had had the bays put to and followed them to the Park. He finally spied the Twyford barouche drawn up to the side of the avenue. He pulled up alongside.

"Aunt Augusta," he said as he nodded to her. She beamed at him, clearly delighted he had taken the trouble to find them. His gaze swept over the other occupants of the carriage in an appraising and approving manner, then came to rest on Miss Twinning. She smiled sunnily back at him. Suddenly alert, Max's mind returned from where it had wandered and again counted heads. There was a total of five in the carriage but Miriam Alford was there, smiling vaguely at him. Which meant one of his wards was missing. He quelled the urge to immediately question his aunt, telling himself there would doubtless be some perfectly reasonable explanation. Perhaps one was merely unwell. His mind reverted to its main preoccupation.

Responding automatically to his aunt's social chatter, he took the first opportunity to remark, "But I can't keep my horses standing, ma'am. Perhaps Miss Twinning would like to come for a drive?"

He was immediately assured that Miss Twinning would and she descended from the carriage. He reached down to help her up beside him and they were off.

Caroline gloried in the brush of the breeze on her face as the curricle bowled along. Even reined in to the pace accepted in the Park, it was still infinitely more refreshing than the funereal plod favoured by Lady Benborough. That was undoubtedly the reason her spirits had suddenly soared. Even the sunshine seemed distinctly brighter.

"Not riding today?" asked Max.

"No. Lady Benborough felt we should not entirely desert the matrons."

Max smiled. "True enough. It don't do to put people's backs up unnecessarily."

Caroline turned to stare at him. "Your philosophy?"

Augusta had told her enough of their guardian's past to realise this was unlikely.

Max frowned. Miss Caroline Twinning was a great deal too knowing. Unprepared to answer her query, he changed the subject. "Where's Sarah?"

"Lord Darcy took her up some time ago. Maybe we'll see them as we go around?"

Max suppressed the curse which rose to his lips. How many friends was he going to have left by the end of this Season? Another thought occurred. "Has she been seeing much of him?"

A deep chuckle answered this and his uneasiness grew. "If you mean has he taken to haunting us, no. On the other hand, he seems to have the entrée to all the salons we've attended this week."

He should, he supposed, have anticipated his friend's duplicity. Darcy was, after all, every bit as experienced as he. Still, it rankled. He would have a few harsh words to say to his lordship when next they met. "Has he been...particularly attentive towards her?"

"No," she replied in a careful tone, "not in any un-acceptable way."

He looked his question and she continued, "It's just that she's the only lady he pays any attention to at all. If he's not with Sarah, he either leaves or retires to the card tables or simply watches her from a distance."

The description was so unlike the Darcy Hamilton he knew that it was on the tip of his tongue to verify they were talking about the same man. A sneaking suspicion that Darcy might, just might, be seriously smitten awoke in his mind. One black brow rose.

They paused briefly to exchange greetings with Lady Jersey, then headed back towards the barouche. Coming to a decision, Max asked, "What's your next major engagement?"

"Well, we go to the first of Almack's balls tomorrow, then it's the Billingtons' ball the next night."

The start of the Season proper. But there was no way he was going to cross the threshold of Almack's. He had not been near the place for years. Tender young virgins were definitely not on his menu these days. He did not equate that description with Miss Twinning. Nor, if it came to that, to her sisters. Uncertain what to do for the best, he made no response to the information, merely inclining his head to show he had heard.

Caroline was silent as the curricle retraced its journey. Max's questions had made her uneasy. Lord Darcy was a particular friend of his—surely Sarah was in no real danger with him? She stifled a small sigh. Clearly, their guardian's attention was wholly concentrated on their social performance. Which, of course, was precisely what a guardian should be concerned with. Why, then, did she feel such a keen sense of disappointment?

They reached the barouche to find Sarah already returned. One glance at her stormy countenance was sufficient to answer Max's questions. It seemed Darcy's plans had not prospered. Yet.

As he handed Caroline to the ground and acknowledged her smiling thanks, it occurred to him she had not expressed any opinion or interest in his week-long absence. So much for that tactic. As he watched her climb into the barouche, shapely ankles temporarily exposed, he realised he had made no headway during their interlude. Her sister's affair with his friend had dominated his thoughts. Giving his horses the office, he grimaced to himself. Seducing a young woman while acting as guardian to her three younger sisters was clearly going to be harder going than he had imagined.

CLIMBING THE STEPS to Twyford House the next evening, Max was still in two minds over whether he was doing the right thing. He was far too wise to be overly attentive to Caroline, yet, if he did not make a push to engage her interest, she would shortly be the object of the attentions of a far larger circle of gentlemen, few of whom would hesitate to attend Almack's purely because they disliked being mooned over by very young women. He hoped, in his capacity as their guardian, to confine his attentions to the Twinning sisters and so escape the usual jostle of matchmaking mamas. They should have learned by now that he was not likely to succumb to their daughters' vapid charms. Still, he was not looking forward to the evening.

If truth were told, he had been hearing about his wards on all sides for the past week. They had caught the fancy of the *ton,* starved as it was of novelty. And their brand of beauty always had attraction. But what he had not heard was worrying him more. There had been more than one incident when, entering a room, he had been aware of at least one conversation abruptly halted, then smoothly resumed. Another reason to identify himself more closely with his wards. He reminded himself that three of them were truly his responsibility and, in the circumstances, the polite world would hold him responsible for Miss Twinning as well. His duty was clear.

Admitted to Twyford House, Max paused to exchange a few words with Millwade. Satisfied that all was running smoothly, he turned and stopped, all thought deserting him. Transfixed, he watched the Twinning sisters descend the grand staircase. Seen together, gorgeously garbed for the ball, they were quite the most heart-stopping sight he had beheld in many a year. His eyes rested with acclaim on each in turn, but stopped when they reached Caroline. The rest of the company seemed to dissolve in a haze as his eyes roamed appreciatively over the clean lines of her eau-de-Nil silk gown. It clung suggestively to her ripe figure, the neckline scooped low over her generous breasts. His hands burned with the desire to caress those tantalising curves. Then his eyes locked with hers as she crossed the room to his side, her hand extended to him. Automatically, he took it in his. Then she was speaking, smiling up at him in her usual confiding way.

"Thank you for coming. I do hope you'll not be too bored by such tame entertainment." Lady Benborough, on receiving Max's curt note informing them of his intention to accompany them to Almack's, had crowed with delight. When she had calmed, she had explained his aversion to the place. So it was with an unexpected feeling of guilt that Caroline had come forward to welcome him. But, gazing into his intensely blue eyes, she could find no trace of annoyance or irritation. Instead, she recognised the same emotion she had detected the very first time they had met. To add to her confusion, he raised her hand to his lips, his eyes warm and entirely too knowing.

"Do you know, I very much doubt that I'll be bored at all?" her guardian murmured wickedly.

Caroline blushed vividly. Luckily, this was missed by all but Max in the relatively poor light of the hall and the bustle as they donned their cloaks. Both Lady Benborough and Miriam Alford were to go, cutting the odds between chaperons and charges. Before Max's intervention, the coach would have had to do two trips to King Street. Now, Caroline found that Augusta and Mrs. Alford, together with Sarah and Arabella, were to go in the Twyford coach while she and Lizzie were to travel with Max. Suddenly suspicious of her guardian's intentions, she was forced to accept the arrangement with suitable grace. As Max handed her into the carriage and saw her settled comfortably, she told herself she was a fool to read into his behaviour anything other than an attempt to trip her up. He was only amusing himself.

As if to confirm her supposition, the journey was unremarkable and soon they were entering the hallowed precincts of the Assembly Rooms. The sparsely furnished halls were already well filled with the usual

mix of débutantes and unmarried young ladies, carefully chaperoned by their mamas in the hope of finding
a suitable connection among the unattached gentlemen strolling through the throng. It was a social club
to which it was necessary to belong. And it was clear
from their reception that, at least as far as the gentlemen were concerned, the Twinning sisters definitely
belonged. To Max's horror, they were almost mobbed.

He stood back and watched the sisters artfully manage their admirers. Arabella had the largest court with
all the most rackety and dangerous blades. A more
discerning crowd of eminently eligible gentlemen had
formed around Sarah while the youthful Lizzie had
gathered all the more earnest of the younger men to her.
But the group around Caroline drew his deepest consideration. There were more than a few highly dangerous roués in the throng gathered about her but all were
experienced and none was likely to attempt anything
scandalous without encouragement. As he watched, it
became clear that all four girls had an innate ability to
choose the more acceptable among their potential partners. They also had the happy knack of dismissing the
less favoured with real charm, a not inconsiderable feat.
The more he watched, the more intrigued Max became.
He was about to seek clarification from his aunt, standing beside him, when that lady very kindly answered
his unspoken query.

"You needn't worry, y'know. Those girls have got
heads firmly on their shoulders. Ever since they started

going about, I've been bombarded with questions on who's eligible and who's not. Even Arabella, minx that she is, takes good care to know who she's flirting with."

Max looked his puzzlement.

"Well," explained her ladyship, surprised by his obtuseness, "they're all set on finding husbands, of course!" She glanced up at him, eyes suddenly sharp, and added, "I should think you'd be thrilled—it means they'll be off your hands all the sooner."

"Yes. Of course," Max answered absently.

He stayed by his wards until they were claimed for the first dance. His sharp eyes had seen a number of less than desirable gentlemen approach the sisters, only to veer away as they saw him. If nothing else, his presence had achieved that much.

Searching through the crowd, he finally spotted Darcy Hamilton disappearing into one of the salons where refreshments were laid out.

"Going to give them the go-by for at least a week, huh?" he growled as he came up behind Lord Darcy.

Darcy choked on the lemonade he had just drunk.

Max gazed in horror at the glass in his friend's hand. "No! Bless me, Darcy! You turned temperate?"

Darcy grimaced. "Have to drink something and seemed like the best of a bad lot." His wave indicated the unexciting range of beverages available. "Thirsty work, getting a dance with one of your wards."

"Incidentally—" intoned Max in the manner of one about to pass judgement.

But Darcy held up his hand. "No. Don't start. I don't need any lectures from you on the subject. And you don't need to bother, anyway. Sarah Twinning has her mind firmly set on marriage and there's not a damned thing I can do about it."

Despite himself, Max could not resist a grin. "No luck?"

"None!" replied Darcy, goaded. "I'm almost at the stage of considering offering for her but I can't be sure she wouldn't reject me, and *that* I couldn't take."

Max, picking up a glass of lemonade himself, became thoughtful.

Suddenly, Darcy roused himself. "Do you know what she told me yesterday? Said I spent too much time on horses and not enough on matters of importance. *Can* you believe it?"

He gestured wildly and Max nearly hooted with laughter. Lord Darcy's stables were known the length and breadth of England as among the biggest and best producers of quality horseflesh.

"I very much doubt that she appreciates your interest in the field," Max said placatingly.

"Humph," was all his friend vouchsafed.

After a pause, Darcy laid aside his glass. "Going to find Maria Sefton and talk her into giving Sarah permission to waltz with me. One thing she won't be able to refuse." With a nod to Max, he returned to the main hall.

For some minutes, Max remained as he was, his abstracted gaze fixed on the far wall. Then, abruptly, he replaced his glass and followed his friend.

"YOU WANT ME to give *your ward* permission to waltz with you?" Lady Jersey repeated Max's request, clearly unable to decide whether it was as innocuous as he represented or whether it had an ulterior motive concealed within and if so, what.

"It's really not such an odd request," returned Max, unperturbed. "She's somewhat older than the rest and, as I'm here, it seems appropriate."

"Hmm." Sally Jersey simply did not believe there was not more to it. She had been hard-pressed to swallow her astonishment when she had seen His Grace of Twyford enter the room. And she was even more amazed that he had not left as soon as he had seen his wards settled. But he was, after all, Twyford. And Delmere and Rotherbridge, what was more. So, if he wanted to dance with his ward… She shrugged. "Very well. Bring her to me. If you can separate her from her court, that is."

Max smiled in a way that reminded Lady Jersey of the causes of his reputation. "I think I'll manage," he drawled, bowing over her hand.

CAROLINE WAS SURPRISED that Max had remained at the Assembly Rooms for so long. She lost sight of him for a while, and worked hard at forcing herself to pay attention to her suitors, for it was only to be expected their guardian would seek less tame entertainment elsewhere. But then his tall figure reappeared at the side of the room. He seemed to be scanning the multitude, then, over a sea of heads, his eyes met hers. Caroline fervently hoped the peculiar shock which went through her was not reflected in her countenance. After a moment, unobtrusively, he made his way to her side.

Under cover of the light flirtation she was engaged in with an ageing baronet, Caroline was conscious of the sudden acceleration of her heartbeat and the constriction that seemed to be affecting her breathing. Horrendously aware of her guardian's blue eyes, she felt her nervousness grow as he approached despite her efforts to remain calm.

But, when he gained her side and bowed over her hand in an almost bored way, uttering the most commonplace civilities and engaging her partner in a discussion of some sporting event, the anticlimax quickly righted her mind for her.

Quite how it was accomplished she could not have said, but Max succeeded in excusing them to her court, on the grounds that he had something to discuss with his ward. Finding herself on his arm, strolling apparently randomly down the room, she turned to him and asked, "What was it you wished to say to me?"

He glanced down at her and she caught her breath. That devilish look was back in his eyes as they rested on her, warming her through and through. What on earth was he playing at?

"Good heavens, my ward. And I thought you up to all the rigs. Don't you know a ruse when you hear it?"

The tones of his voice washed languorously over Caroline, leaving a sense of relaxation in their wake. She made a grab for her fast-disappearing faculties. Interpreting his remark to mean that his previously bored attitude had also been false, Caroline was left wondering what the present reality meant. She made a desperate bid to get their interaction back on an acceptable footing. "Where are we going?"

Max smiled. "We're on our way to see Lady Jersey."

"Why?"

"Patience, sweet Caroline," came the reply, all the more outrageous for its tone. "All will be revealed forthwith."

They reached Lady Jersey's side where she stood just inside the main room.

"There you are, Twyford!"

The Duke of Twyford smoothly presented his ward. Her ladyship's prominent eyes rested on the curtsying Caroline, then, as the younger woman rose, widened with a suddenly arrested expression. She opened her mouth to ask the question burning the tip of her tongue but caught His Grace's eye and, reluctantly swallowing her curiosity, said, "My dear Miss Twinning. Your guardian has requested you to be given permission to waltz and I have no hesitation in granting it. And, as he is here, I present the Duke as a suitable partner."

With considerable effort, Caroline managed to school her features to impassivity. Luckily, the musicians struck up at that moment, so that she barely had time to murmur her thanks to Lady Jersey before Max swept her on to the floor, leaving her ladyship, intrigued, staring after them.

Caroline struggled to master the unnerving sensation of being in her guardian's arms. He was holding her closer than strictly necessary, but, as they twirled down the room, she realised that to everyone else they presented a perfect picture of the Duke of Twyford doing the pretty by his eldest ward. Only she was close enough to see the disturbing glint in his blue eyes and hear the warmth in his tone as he said, "My dear ward, what a very accomplished dancer you are. Tell me, what other talents do you have that I've yet to sample?"

For the life of her, Caroline could not tear her eyes from his. She heard his words and understood their meaning but her brain refused to react. No shock, no scandalized response came to her lips. Instead, her mind was completely absorbed with registering the unbelievable fact that, despite their relationship of guardian and ward, Max Rotherbridge had every intention of seducing her. His desire was clear in the heat of his blue, blue gaze, in the way his hand at her back seemed to burn through the fine silk of her gown, in the gentle caress of his long fingers across her knuckles as he twirled her about the room under the long noses of the biggest gossips in London.

Mesmerized, she had sufficient presence of mind to keep a gentle smile fixed firmly on her face but her thoughts were whirling even faster than her feet. With a superhuman effort, she forced her lids to drop, screening her eyes from his. "Oh, we Twinnings have many accomplishments, dear guardian." To her relief, her voice was clear and untroubled. "But I'm desolated to have to admit that they're all hopelessly mundane."

A rich chuckle greeted this. "Permit me to tell you, my ward, that, for the skills I have in mind, your qualifications are more than adequate." Caroline's eyes flew to his. She could hardly believe her ears. But Max continued before she could speak, his blue eyes holding hers, his voice a seductive murmur. "And while you naturally lack experience, I assure you that can easily, and most enjoyably, be remedied."

It was too much. Caroline gave up the struggle to divine his motives and made a determined bid to reinstitute sanity. She smiled into the dark face above hers and said, quite clearly, "This isn't happening."

For a moment, Max was taken aback. Then, his sense of humour surfaced. "No?"

"Of course not," Caroline calmly replied. "You're my guardian and I'm your ward. Therefore, it is simply not possible for you to have said what you just did."

Studying her serene countenance, Max recognised the strategy and reluctantly admired her courage for adopting it. As things stood, it was not an easy defence for him to overcome. Reading in the grey-green eyes a determination not to be further discomposed, Max, too wise to push further, gracefully yielded.

"So what do you think of Almack's?" he asked.

Relieved, Caroline took the proffered olive branch and their banter continued on an impersonal level.

At the end of the dance, Max suavely surrendered her to her admirers, but not without a glance which, if she had allowed herself to think about it, would have made Caroline blush. She did not see him again until it

was time for them to quit the Assembly Rooms. In order
to survive the evening, she had sternly refused to let
her mind dwell on his behaviour. Consequently, it had
not occurred to her to arrange to exchange her place in
her guardian's carriage for one in the Twyford coach.
When Lizzie came to tug at her sleeve with the information that the others had already left, she perceived
her error. But the extent of her guardian's foresight did
not become apparent until they were halfway home.

She and Max shared the forward facing seat with
Lizzie curled up in a corner opposite them. On departing
King Street, they preserved a comfortable silence—due
to tiredness in Lizzie's case, from being too absorbed
with her thoughts in her case and, as she suddenly realised, from sheer experience in the case of her guardian.

They were still some distance from Mount Street
when, without warning, Max took her hand in his. Surprised, she turned to look up at him, conscious of his
fingers moving gently over hers. Despite the darkness
of the carriage, his eyes caught hers. Deliberately, he
raised her hand and kissed her fingertips. A delicious
tingle raced along Caroline's nerves, followed by a second of increased vigour as he turned her hand over
and placed a lingering kiss on her wrist. But they were
nothing compared to the galvanising shock that hit her
when, without giving any intimation of his intent, he
bent his head and his lips found hers.

From Max's point of view, he was behaving with
admirable restraint. He knew Lizzie was sound asleep

and that his manipulative and normally composed eldest ward was well out of her depth. Yet he reined in his desires and kept the kiss light, his lips moving gently over hers, gradually increasing the pressure until she parted her lips. He savoured the warm sweetness of her mouth, then, inwardly smiling at the response she had been unable to hide, he withdrew and watched as her eyes slowly refocused.

Caroline, eyes round, looked at him in consternation. Then her shocked gaze flew to Lizzie, still curled in her corner.

"Don't worry. She's sound asleep." His voice was deep and husky in the dark carriage.

Caroline, stunned, felt oddly reassured by the sound. Then she felt the carriage slow.

"And you're safe home," came the gently mocking voice.

In a daze, Caroline helped him wake Lizzie and then Max very correctly escorted them indoors, a smile of wicked contentment on his face.

ARABELLA STIFLED A wistful sigh and smiled brightly at the earnest young man who was guiding her around the floor in yet another interminable waltz. It had taken only a few days of the Season proper for her to sort through her prospective suitors. And come to the unhappy conclusion that none matched her requirements. The lads were too young, the men too old. There seemed to be no one in between. Presumably many were away with Wellington's forces, but surely there were those who could not leave the important business of keeping England running? And surely not all of them were old? She could not describe her ideal man, yet was sure she would instantly know when she met him. She was convinced she would feel it, like a thunderbolt from the blue. Yet no male of her acquaintance increased her heartbeat one iota.

Keeping up a steady and inconsequential conversation with her partner, something she could do half asleep, Arabella sighted her eldest sister, elegantly waltzing with their guardian. Now there was a coil. There was little doubt in Arabella's mind of the cause of Caroline's bright eyes and slightly flushed countenance. She looked radiant. But could a guardian marry his ward? Or, more to the point, was their guardian intent on marriage or had he some other arrangement in mind? Still, she had complete faith in Caroline. There had been many who had worshipped at her feet with something other than matrimony in view, yet her eldest sister had always had their measure. True, none had affected her as Max Rotherbridge clearly did. But Caroline knew the ropes, few better.

"I'll escort you back to Lady Benborough."

The light voice of her partner drew her thoughts back to the present. With a quick smile, Arabella declined. "I think I've torn my flounce. I'll just go and pin it up. Perhaps you could inform Lady Benborough that I'll return immediately?" She smiled dazzlingly upon the young man. Bemused, he bowed and moved away into the crowd. Her flounce was perfectly intact but she needed some fresh air and in no circumstances could she have borne another half-hour of that particular young gentleman's serious discourse.

She started towards the door, then glanced back to see Augusta receive her message without apparent perturbation. Arabella turned back to the door and immediately collided with a chest of quite amazing proportions.

"Oh!"

For a moment, she thought the impact had winded her. Then, looking up into the face of the mountain she had met, she realised it wasn't that at all. It was the thunderbolt she had been waiting for.

Unfortunately, the gentleman seemed unaware of this momentous happening. "My apologies, m'dear. Didn't see you there."

The lazy drawl washed over Arabella. He was tall, very tall, and seemed almost as broad, with curling blond hair and laughing hazel eyes. He had quite the most devastating smile she had ever seen. Her knees felt far too weak to support her if she moved, so she stood still and stared, mouthing she knew not what platitudes.

The gentleman seemed to find her reaction amusing. But, with a polite nod and another melting smile, he was gone.

Stunned, Arabella found herself standing in the doorway staring at his retreating back. Sanity returned with a thump. Biting back a far from ladylike curse, she swept out in search of the withdrawing-room. The use of a borrowed fan and the consumption of a glass of cool water helped to restore her outward calm. Inside, her resentment grew.

No gentleman simply excused himself and walked away from her. That was her role. Men usually tried to stay by her side as long as possible. Yet this man had seemed disinclined to linger. Arabella was not vain but wondered what was more fascinating than herself that he needs must move on so abruptly. Surely he had felt that strange jolt just as she had? Maybe he wasn't a ladies' man? But no. The memory of the decided appreciation which had glowed so warmly in his hazel eyes put paid to that idea. And, now she came to think of it, the comprehensive glance which had roamed suggestively over most of her had been decidedly impertinent.

Arabella returned to the ballroom determined to bring her large gentleman to heel, if for no better reason than to assure herself she had been mistaken in him. But frustration awaited her. He was not there. For the rest of the evening, she searched the throng but caught no glimpse of her quarry. Then, just before the last dance, another waltz, he appeared in the doorway from the card-room.

Surrounded by her usual court, Arabella was at her effervescent best. Her smile was dazzling as she openly debated, laughingly teasing, over who to bestow her hand on for this last dance. Out of the corner of her eye, she watched the unknown gentleman approach. And walk past her to solicit the hand of a plain girl in an outrageously overdecorated pink gown.

Arabella bit her lip in vexation but managed to conceal it as severe concentration on her decision. As the musicians struck up, she accepted handsome Lord Tulloch as her partner and studiously paid him the most flattering attention for the rest of the evening.

CHAPTER FIVE

MAX WAS WORRIED. Seriously worried. Since that first night at Almack's, the situation between Sarah Twinning and Darcy Hamilton had rapidly deteriorated to a state which, from experience, he knew was fraught with danger. As he watched Sarah across Lady Overton's ballroom, chatting with determined avidity to an eminently respectable and thoroughly boring young gentleman, his brows drew together in a considering frown. If, at the beginning of his guardianship, anyone had asked him where his sympathies would lie, with the Misses Twinning or the gentlemen of London, he would unhesitatingly have allied himself with his wards, on the grounds that four exquisite but relatively inexperienced country misses would need all the help they could get to defend their virtue successfully against the highly knowledgeable rakes extant within the *ton*. Now, a month later, having gained first-hand experience of the tenacious perversity of the Twinning sisters, he was not so sure.

His behaviour with Caroline on the night of their first visit to Almack's had been a mistake. How much of a mistake had been slowly made clear to him over the succeeding weeks. He was aware of the effect he had on her, had been aware of it from the first time he had seen her in his library at Delmere House. But in order to make any use of that weapon, he had to have her to himself. A fact, unfortunately, that she had worked out for herself. Consequently, whenever he approached her, he found her surrounded either by admirers who had been given too much encouragement for him to dismiss easily or one or more of her far too perceptive sisters. Lizzie, it was true, was not attuned to the situation between her eldest sister and their guardian. But he had unwisely made use of her innocence, to no avail as it transpired, and was now unhappily certain he would get no further opportunity by that route. Neither Arabella nor Sarah was the least bit perturbed by his increasingly blatant attempts to be rid of them. He was sure that, if he was ever goaded into ordering them to leave their sister alone with him, they would laugh and refuse. And tease him unmercifully about it, what was more. He had already had to withstand one episode of Arabella's artful play, sufficiently subtle, thank God, so that the others in the group had not understood her meaning.

His gaze wandered to where the third Twinning sister held court, seated on a chaise surrounded by ardent swains, her huge eyes wickedly dancing with mischief. As he watched, she tossed a comment to one of the circle and turned, her head playfully tilted, to throw a glance of open invitation into the handsome face of a blond giant standing before her. Max stiffened. Hell and the devil! He would have to put a stop to that game, and quickly. He had no difficulty in recognising the large frame of Hugo, Lord Denbigh. Although a few years younger than himself, in character and accomplishments there was little to choose between them. Under his horrified gaze, Hugo took advantage of a momentary distraction which had succeeded in removing attention temporarily from Arabella to lean forward and whisper something, Max could guess what, into her ear. The look she gave him in response made Max set his jaw grimly. Then, Hugo extended one large hand and Arabella, adroitly excusing herself to her other admirers, allowed him to lead her on to the floor. A waltz was just starting up.

Knowing there was only so much Hugo could do on a crowded ballroom floor, Max made a resolution to call on his aunt and wards on the morrow, firmly determined to acquaint them with his views on encouraging rakes. Even as the idea occurred, he groaned. How on earth could he tell Arabella to cease her flirtation with Hugo on the grounds he was a rake when he was himself trying his damnedest to seduce her sister and his best friend was similarly occupied with Sarah? He had known from the outset that this crazy situation would not work.

Reminded of what had originally prompted him to stand just inside the door between Lady Overton's ballroom and the salon set aside for cards and quietly study the company, Max returned his eyes to Sarah Twinning. Despite her assured manner, she was on edge, her hands betraying her nervousness as they played with the lace on her gown. Occasionally, her eyes would lift fleetingly to the door behind him. While to his experienced eye she was not looking her best, Darcy, ensconced in the card-room, was looking even worse. He had been drinking steadily throughout the evening and, although far from drunk, was fast attaining a dangerous state. Suffering from Twinning-induced frustration himself, Max could readily sympathise. He sincerely hoped his pursuit of the eldest Miss Twinning would not bring him so low. His friendship with Darcy Hamilton stretched back over fifteen years. In all that time he had never seen his friend so affected by the desire of a particular woman. Like himself, Darcy was an experienced lover who liked to keep his affairs easy and uncomplicated. If a woman proved difficult, he was much more likely to shrug and, with a smile, pass on to greener fields. But with Sarah Twinning, he seemed unable to admit defeat.

The thought that he himself had no intention of letting the elder Miss Twinning escape and was, even now, under the surface of his preoccupation with his other wards, plotting to get her into his arms, and, ultimately, into his bed, surfaced to shake his self-confidence. His black brows rose a little, in self-mockery. One could hardly blame the girls for keeping them at arm's length. The Twinning sisters had never encouraged them to believe they were of easy virtue, nor that they would accept anything less than marriage. Their interaction, thus far, had all been part of the game. By rights, it was they, the rakes of London, who should now acknowledge the evident truth that, despite their bountiful attractions, the Twinnings were virtuous females in search of husbands. And, having acknowledged that fact, to desist from their pursuit of the fair ladies. Without conscious thought on his part, his eyes strayed to where Caroline stood amid a group, mostly men, by the side of the dance floor. She laughed and responded to some comment, her copper curls gleaming like rosy gold in the bright light thrown down by the chandeliers. As if feeling his gaze, she turned and, across the intervening heads, their eyes met. Both were still. Then, she smoothly turned back to her companions and Max, straightening his shoulders, moved further into the crowd. The trouble was, he did not think that he, any more than Darcy, could stop.

Max slowly passed through the throng, stopping here and there to chat with acquaintances, his intended goal his aunt, sitting in a blaze of glorious purple on a chaise by the side of the room. But before he had reached her, a hand on his arm drew him around to face the sharp features of Emma Mortland.

"Your Grace! It's been such an age since we've… talked." Her ladyship's brown eyes quizzed him playfully.

Her arch tone irritated Max. It was on the tip of his tongue to recommend she took lessons in flirting from Arabella before she tried her tricks on him. Instead, he took her hand from his sleeve, bowed over it and pointedly returned to her, "As you're doubtless aware, Emma, I have other claims on my time."

His careless use of her first name was calculated to

annoy but Lady Mortland, having seen his absorption
with his wards, particularly his eldest ward, over the
past weeks, was fast coming to the conclusion that she
should do everything in her power to bring Twyford to
his knees or that tiara would slip through her fingers.
As she was a female of little intelligence, she sincerely
believed the attraction that had brought Max Rotherbridge to her bed would prove sufficient to induce him
to propose. Consequently, she coyly glanced up at him
through her long fair lashes and sighed sympathetically.
"Oh, my dear, *I know.* I do *feel* for you. This business
of being guardian to four country girls must be such a
bore to you. But surely, as a diversion, you could manage to spare us some few hours?"

Not for the first time, Max wondered where women
such as Emma Mortland kept their intelligence. In their
pockets? One truly had to wonder. As he looked down
at her, his expression unreadable, he realized that she
was a year or so younger than Caroline. Yet, from the
single occasion on which he had shared her bed, he
knew the frills and furbelows she favoured disguised
a less than attractive figure, lacking the curves that
characterized his eldest ward. And Emma Mortland's
energies, it seemed, were reserved for scheming. He
had not been impressed. As he knew that a number of
gentlemen, including Darcy Hamilton, had likewise
seen her sheets, he was at a loss to understand why she
continued to single him out. A caustic dismissal was
about to leave his lips when, amid a burst of hilarity

from a group just behind them, he heard the rich tones of his eldest ward's laugh.

On the instant, a plan, fully formed, came into his head and, without further consideration, he acted. He allowed a slow, lazy smile to spread across his face. "How well you read me, my sweet," he drawled to the relieved Lady Mortland. Encouraged, she put her hand tentatively on his arm. He took it in his hand, intending to raise it to his lips, but to his surprise he could not quite bring himself to do so. Instead, he smiled meaningfully into her eyes. With an ease born of countless hours of practice, he instituted a conversation of the risqué variety certain to appeal to Lady Mortland. Soon, he had her gaily laughing and flirting freely with her eyes and her fan. Deliberately, he turned to lead her on to the floor for the waltz just commencing, catching, as he did, a look of innocent surprise on Caroline's face.

Grinning devilishly, Max encouraged Emma to the limits of acceptable flirtation. Then, satisfied with the scene he had created, as they circled the room, he raised his head to see the effect the sight of Lady Mortland in his arms was having on Caroline. To his chagrin, he discovered his eldest ward was no longer standing where he had last seen her. After a frantic visual search, during which he ignored Emma entirely, he located Caroline, also dancing, with the highly suitable Mr. Willoughby. That same Mr. Willoughby who, he knew, was becoming very particular in his attentions. Smothering a curse, Max half-heartedly returned his attention to Lady Mortland.

He had intended to divest himself of the encumbrance of her ladyship as soon as the dance ended but, as the music ceased, he realized they were next to Caroline and her erstwhile partner. Again, Emma found herself the object of Max's undeniable, if strangely erratic charm. Under its influence, she blossomed and bloomed. Max, with one eye on Caroline's now unreadable countenance, leaned closer to Emma to whisper an invitation to view the beauties of the moonlit garden. As he had hoped, she crooned her delight and, with an air of anticipated pleasure, allowed him to escort her through the long windows leading on to the terrace.

"COUNT ME OUT." Darcy Hamilton threw his cards on to the table and pushed back his chair. None of the other players was surprised to see him leave. Normally an excellent player, tonight his lordship had clearly had his mind elsewhere. And the brandy he had drunk was hardly calculated to improve matters, although his gait, as he headed for the ballroom, was perfectly steady.

In the ballroom, Darcy paused to glance about. He saw the musicians tuning up and then sighted his prey.

Almost as if she sensed his approach, Sarah turned as he came up to her. The look of sudden wariness that came into her large eyes pricked his conscience and, consequently, his temper. "My dance, I think."

It was not, as he well knew, but before she could do more than open her mouth to deny him Darcy had swept her on to the floor.

They were both excellent dancers and, despite their

current difficulties, they moved naturally and easily together. Which was just as well, as their minds were each completely absorbed in trying to gauge the condition of the other. Luckily, they were both capable of putting on a display of calmness which succeeded in deflecting the interest of the curious.

Sarah, her heart, as usual, beating far too fast, glanced up under her lashes at the handsome face above her, now drawn and slightly haggard. Her heart sank. She had no idea what the outcome of this strange relationship of theirs would be, but it seemed to be causing both of them endless pain. Darcy Hamilton filled her thoughts, day in, day out. But he had steadfastly refused to speak of marriage, despite the clear encouragement she had given him to do so. He had side-stepped her invitations, offering, instead, to introduce her to a vista of illicit delights whose temptation was steadily increasing with time. But she could not, would not accept. She would give anything in the world to be his wife but had no ambition to be his mistress. Lady Benborough had, with all kindness, dropped her a hint that he was very likely a confirmed bachelor, too wedded to his equestrian interests to be bothered with a wife and family, satisfied instead with mistresses and the occasional *affaire*. Surreptitiously studying his rigid and unyielding face, she could find no reason to doubt Augusta's assessment. If that was so, then their association must end. And the sooner the better, for it was breaking her heart.

Seeing her unhappiness reflected in the brown pools of her eyes, Darcy inwardly cursed. There were times

he longed to hurt her, in retribution for the agony she
was putting him through, but any pain she felt seemed
to rebound, ten times amplified, back on him. He was,
as Lady Benborough had rightly surmised, well satisfied
with his bachelor life. At least, he had been, until he had
met Sarah Twinning. Since then, nothing seemed to be
right any more. Regardless of the response he knew he
awoke in her, she consistently denied any interest in the
delightful pleasures he was only too willing to introduce
her to. Or rather, held the prospect of said pleasures like
a gun at his head, demanding matrimony. He would be
damned if he would yield to such tactics. He had long
ago considered matrimony, the state of, in a calm and
reasoned way, and had come to the conclusion that it held
few benefits for him. The idea of being driven, forced,
pushed into taking such a step, essentially by the strength
of his own raging desires, horrified him, leaving him
annoyed beyond measure, principally with himself, but
also, unreasonably he knew, with the object of said desires. As the music slowed and halted, he looked down at
her lovely face and determined to give her one last chance
to capitulate. If she remained adamant, he would have to
leave London until the end of the Season. He was quite
sure he could not bear the agony any longer.

As Sarah drew away from him and turned towards
the room, Darcy drew her hand through his arm and
deftly steered her towards the long windows leading on
to the terrace. As she realized his intention, she hung
back. With a few quick words, he reassured her. "I just
want to talk to you. Come into the garden."

Thus far, Sarah had managed to avoid being totally private with him, too aware of her inexperience to chance such an interview. But now, looking into his pale grey eyes and seeing her own unhappiness mirrored there, she consented with a nod and they left the ballroom.

A stone terrace extended along the side of the house, the balustrade broken here and there by steps leading down to the gardens. Flambeaux placed in brackets along the walls threw flickering light down into the avenues and any number of couples could be seen, walking and talking quietly amid the greenery.

Unhurriedly, Darcy led her to the end of the terrace and then down the steps into a deserted walk. They both breathed in the heady freshness of the night air, calming their disordered senses and, without the need to exchange words, each drew some measure of comfort from the other's presence. At the end of the path, a secluded summer-house stood, white paintwork showing clearly against the black shadows of the shrubbery behind it.

As Darcy had hoped, the summer-house was deserted. The path leading to it was winding and heavily screened. Only those who knew of its existence would be likely to find it. He ushered Sarah through the narrow door and let it fall quietly shut behind them. The moonlight slanted through the windows, bathing the room in silvery tints. Sarah stopped in the middle of the circular floor and turned to face him. Darcy paused, trying to decide where to start, then crossed to stand before her, taking her hands in his. For some moments, they stood thus, the rake and the maid, gazing silently into each other's eyes. Then Darcy bent his head and his lips found hers.

Sarah, seduced by the setting, the moonlight and the man before her, allowed him to gather her, unresisting, into his arms. The magic of his lips on hers was a more potent persuasion than any she had previously encountered. Caught by a rising tide of passion, she was drawn, helpless and uncaring, beyond the bounds of thought. Her lips parted and gradually the kiss deepened until, with the moonlight washing in waves over them, he stole her soul.

It was an unintentionally intimate caress which abruptly shook the stars from her eyes and brought her back to earth with an unsteady bump. Holding her tightly within one arm, Darcy had let his other hand slide, gently caressing, over her hip, intending to draw her more firmly against him. But the feel of his hand, scorching through her thin evening dress, sent shock waves of such magnitude through Sarah's pliant body that she pulled back with a gasp. Then, as horrified realization fell like cold water over her heated flesh, she tore herself from his arms and ran.

For an instant, Darcy, stunned both by her response and by her subsequent reaction, stood frozen in the middle of the floor. A knot of jonquil ribbon from Sarah's dress had caught on the button of his cuff and impatiently he shook it free, then watched, fascinated, as it floated to the ground. The banging of the wooden door against its frame had stilled. Swiftly, he crossed the floor and, opening the door, stood in the aperture, listening to her footsteps dying in the spring night. Then, smothering a curse, he followed.

Sarah instinctively ran away from the main house, towards the shrubbery which lay behind the summer-house. She did not stop to think or reason, but just ran. Finally, deep within the tall clipped hedges and the looming bushes, her breath coming in gasps, she came to a clearing, a small garden at the centre of the shrubbery. She saw a marble bench set in an arbour. Thankfully, she sank on to it and buried her face in her hands.

Darcy, following, made for the shrubbery, her hurrying footsteps echoing hollowly on the gravel walks giving him the lead. But once she reached the grassed avenues between the high hedges, her feet made no sound. Penetrating the dark alleys, he was forced to go slowly, checking this way and that to make sure he did not pass her by. So quite fifteen minutes had passed before he reached the central garden and saw the dejected figure huddled on the bench.

In that time, sanity of sorts had returned to Sarah's mind. Her initial horror at her weakness had been replaced by the inevitable reaction. She was angry. Angry at herself, for being so weak that one kiss could overcome all her defences; angry at Darcy, for having engineered that little scene. She was busy whipping up the necessary fury to face the prospect of not seeing him ever again, when he materialized at her side. With a gasp, she came to her feet.

Relieved to find she was not crying, as he had thought, Darcy immediately caught her hand to prevent her flying from him again.

Stung by the shock his touch always gave her, intensified now, she was annoyed to discover, Sarah tried to pull her hand away. When he refused to let her go, she said, her voice infused with an iciness designed to freeze, "Kindly release me, Lord Darcy."

On hearing her voice, Darcy placed the emotion that was holding her so rigid. The knowledge that she was angry, nay, furious, did nothing to improve his own temper, stirred to life by her abrupt flight. Forcing his voice to a reasonableness he was far from feeling, he said, "If you'll give me your word you'll not run away from me, I'll release you."

Sarah opened her mouth to inform him she would not so demean herself as to run from him when the knowledge that she just had, and might have reason to do so again, hit her. She remained silent. Darcy, accurately reading her mind, held on to her hand.

After a moment's consideration, he spoke. "I had intended, my dear, to speak to you of our…curious relationship."

Sarah, breathing rapidly and anxious to end the interview, immediately countered, "I really don't think there's anything to discuss."

A difficult pause ensued, then, "So you would deny there's anything between us?"

The bleakness in his voice shook her, but she determinedly put up her chin, turning away from him as far as their locked hands would allow. "Whatever's between us is neither here nor there," she said, satisfied with the lightness she had managed to bring to her tone.

Her satisfaction was short-lived. Taking advantage of her movement, Darcy stepped quickly behind her, the hand still holding hers reaching across her, his arm wrapping around her waist and drawing her hard against him. His other hand came to rest on her shoulder, holding her still. He knew the shock it would give her, to feel his body against hers, and heard with grim satisfaction the hiss of her indrawn breath.

Sarah froze, too stunned to struggle, the sensation of his hard body against her back, his arm wound like steel about her waist, holding her fast, driving all rational thought from her brain. Then his breath wafted the curls around her ear. His words came in a deep and husky tone, sending tingling shivers up and down her spine.

"Well, sweetheart, there's very little between us now. So, perhaps we can turn our attention to our relationship?"

Sarah, all too well aware of how little there was between them, wondered in a moment of startling lucidity how he imagined that would improve her concentration. But Darcy's attention had already wandered. His lips were very gently trailing down her neck, creating all sorts of marvellous sensations which she tried very hard to ignore.

Then, he gave a deep chuckle. "As I've been saying these weeks past, my dear, you're wasted as a virgin.

Now, if you were to become my mistress, just think of all the delightful avenues we could explore."

"I don't want to become your mistress!" Sarah almost wailed, testing the arm at her waist and finding it immovable.

"No?" came Darcy's voice in her ear. She had the impression he considered her answer for a full minute before he continued, "Perhaps we should extend your education a trifle, my dear. So you fully appreciate what you're turning down. We wouldn't want you to make the wrong decision for lack of a few minutes' instruction, would we?"

Sarah had only a hazy idea of what he could mean but his lips had returned to her throat, giving rise to those strangely heady swirls of pleasure that washed through her, sapping her will. "Darcy, stop! You know you shouldn't be doing this!"

He stilled. "Do I?"

Into the silence, a nightingale warbled. Sarah held her breath.

But, when Darcy spoke again, the steel threading his voice, so often sensed yet only now recognised, warned her of the futility of missish pleas.

"Yes. You're right. I know I shouldn't." His lips moved against her throat, a subtle caress. "But what I want to do is make love to you. As you won't allow that, then this will have to do for now."

Sarah, incapable of further words, simply shook her head, powerless to halt the spreading fires he was so skilfully igniting.

Afterwards, Darcy could not understand how it had happened. He was as experienced with women as Max and had never previously lost control as he did that night. He had intended to do no more than reveal to the perverse woman her own desires and give her some inkling of the pleasures they could enjoy together. Instead, her responses were more than he had bargained for and his own desires stronger than he had been prepared to admit. Fairly early in the engagement, he had turned her once more into his arms, so he could capture her lips and take the lesson further. And further it had certainly gone, until the moon sank behind the high hedges and left them in darkness.

HOW THE HELL was he to get rid of her? Max, Lady Mortland on his arm, had twice traversed the terrace. He had no intention of descending to the shadowy avenues. He had no intention of paying any further attention to Lady Mortland at all. Lady Mortland, on the other hand, was waiting for his attentions to begin and was rather surprised at his lack of ardour in keeping to the terrace.

They were turning at the end of the terrace, when Max, glancing along, saw Caroline come out of the ballroom, alone, and walk quickly to the balustrade and peer over. She was clearly seeking someone. Emma Mortland, prattling on at his side, had not seen her. With the reflexes necessary for being one of the more successful rakes in the *ton,* Max whisked her ladyship back into the ballroom via the door they were about to pass.

Finding herself in the ballroom once more, with the

Duke of Twyford bowing over her hand in farewell, Lady Mortland put a hand to her spinning head. "Oh! But surely…"

"A guardian is never off duty for long, my dear," drawled Max, about to move off.

"Perhaps I'll see you in the Park, tomorrow?" asked Emma, convinced his departure had nothing to do with inclination.

Max smiled. "Anything's possible."

He took a circuitous route around the ballroom and exited through the same door he had seen his ward use. Gaining the terrace, he almost knocked her over as she returned to the ballroom, looking back over her shoulder towards the gardens.

"Oh!" Finding herself unexpectedly in her guardian's arms temporarily suspended Caroline's faculties.

From her face, Max knew she had not been looking for him. He drew her further into the shadows of the terrace, placing her hand on his arm and covering it comfortingly with his. "What is it?"

Caroline could not see any way of avoiding telling him. She fell into step beside him, unconsciously following his lead. "Sarah. Lizzie saw her leave the ballroom with Lord Darcy. More than twenty minutes ago. They haven't returned."

In the dim light, Max's face took on a grim look. He had suspected there would be trouble. He continued strolling towards the end of the terrace. "I know where they'll be. There's a summer-house deeper in the gardens. I think you had better come with me."

Caroline nodded and, unobtrusively, they made their way to the summer-house.

Max pushed open the door, then frowned at the empty room. He moved further in and Caroline followed. "Not here?"

Max shook his head, then bent to pick up a knot of ribbon from the floor.

Caroline came to see and took it from him. She crossed to the windows, turning the small cluster this way and that to gauge the colour.

"Is it hers?" asked Max as he strolled to her side.

"Yes. I can't see the colour well but I know the knot. It's a peculiar one. I made it myself."

"So they were here."

"But where are they now?"

"Almost certainly on their way back to the house," answered Max. "There's nowhere in this garden suitable for the purpose Darcy would have in mind. Presumably, your sister convinced him to return to more populated surroundings." He spoke lightly, but, in truth, was puzzled. He could not readily imagine Sarah turning Darcy from his purpose, not in his present mood, not in this setting. But he was sure there was nowhere else they could go.

"Well, then," said Caroline, dusting the ribbon, "we'd better go back, too."

"In a moment," said Max.

His tone gave Caroline an instant's warning. She put out a hand to fend him off. "No! This is *absurd*—you know it is."

Despite her hand, Max succeeded in drawing her into his arms, holding her lightly. "Absurd, is it? Well, you just keep on thinking how absurd it is, while I enjoy your very sweet lips." And he proceeded to do just that.

As his lips settled over hers, Caroline told herself she should struggle. But, for some mystical reason, her body remained still, her senses turned inward by his kiss. Under gentle persuasion, her lips parted and, with a thrill, she felt his gentle exploration teasing her senses, somehow drawing her deeper. Time seemed suspended and she felt her will weakening as she melted into his arms and they locked around her.

Max's mind was ticking in double time, evaluating the amenities of the summer-house and estimating how long they could remain absent from the ballroom. He decided neither answer was appropriate. Seduction was an art and should not be hurried. Besides, he doubted his eldest ward was quite ready to submit yet. Reluctantly, he raised his head and grinned wolfishly at her. "Still absurd?"

Caroline's wits were definitely not connected. She simply stared at him uncomprehendingly.

In face of this response, Max laughed and, drawing her arm through his, steered her to the door. "I think you're right. We'd better return."

SANITY RETURNED TO Sarah's mind like water in a bucket, slowing filling from a dripping tap, bit by bit, until it was full. For one long moment, she allowed her mind to remain blank, savouring the pleasure of being held so gently against him. Then, the world returned and demanded her response. She struggled to sit up and was promptly helped to her feet. She checked her gown and found it perfectly tidy, bar one knot of ribbon on her sleeve which seemed to have gone missing.

Darcy, who had returned to earth long before, had been engaged in some furious thinking. But, try as he might, he could not imagine how she would react. Like Max, it had been a long time since young virgins had been his prey. As she stood, he tried to catch a glimpse of her face in the dim light but she perversely kept it averted. In the end, he caught her hands and drew her to stand before him. "Sweetheart, are you all right?"

Strangely enough, it was the note of sincerity in his voice which snapped Sarah's control. Her head came up and, even in the darkness, her eyes flashed fire. "Of course I'm not all right! How *dare* you take advantage of me?"

She saw Darcy's face harden at her words and, in fury at his lack of comprehension, she slapped him.

For a minute, absolute silence reigned. Then a sob broke from Sarah as she turned away, her head bent to escape the look on Darcy's face.

Darcy, slamming a door on his emotions, so turbulent that even he had no idea what he felt, moved to rescue them both. In a voice totally devoid of all feeling, he said, "We had better get back to the house."

In truth, neither had any idea how long they had been absent. In silence, they walked side by side, careful not to touch each other, until, eventually, the terrace was reached. Sarah, crying but determined not to let the tears fall, blinked hard, then mounted the terrace steps by Darcy's side. At the top, he turned to her. "It would be better, I think, if you went in first."

Sarah, head bowed, nodded and went.

CAROLINE AND MAX regained the ballroom and both glanced around for their party. Almost immediately, Lizzie appeared by her sister's side on the arm of one of her youthful swains. She prettily thanked him and dismissed him before turning to her sister and their guardian. "Sarah came back just after you left to look for her. She and Lady Benborough and Mrs. Alford have gone home."

"Oh?" It was Max's voice which answered her. "Why?"

Lizzie cast a questioning look at Caroline and received a nod in reply. "Sarah was upset about something."

Max was already scanning the room when Lizzie's voice reached him. "Lord Darcy came in a little while after Sarah. He's left now, too."

With a sigh, Max realized there was nothing more to be done that night. They collected Arabella and departed Overton House, Caroline silently considering Sarah's problem and Max wondering if he was going to have to wait until his friend solved his dilemma before he would be free to settle his own affairs.

CHAPTER SIX

MAX TOOK A long sip of his brandy and savoured the smooth warmth as it slid down his throat. He stretched his legs to the fire. The book he had been trying to reach rested open, on his thighs, one strong hand holding it still. He moved his shoulders slightly, settling them into the comfort of well padded leather and let his head fall back against the chair.

It was the first night since the beginning of the Season that he had had a quiet evening at home. And he needed it. Who would have thought his four wards would make such a drastic change in a hitherto well-ordered existence? Then he remembered. He had. But he had not really believed his own dire predictions. And the only reason he was at home tonight was because Sarah, still affected by her brush with Darcy the night before, had elected to remain at home and Caroline had stayed with her. He deemed his aunt Augusta and Miriam Alford capable of chaperoning the two younger girls between them. After the previous night, it was unlikely they would allow any liberties.

Even now, no one had had an accounting of what had actually taken place between Darcy and Sarah. But,

knowing Darcy, his imagination had supplied a quantity
of detail. He had left Delmere House at noon that day
with the full intention of running his lordship to earth
and demanding an explanation. He had finally found
him at Manton's Shooting Gallery, culping wafer after
wafer with grim precision. One look at his friend's face
had been enough to cool his temper. He had patiently
waited until Darcy, having dispatched all the wafers
currently in place, had thrown the pistol down with an
oath and turned to him.

"Don't ask!"

So he had preserved a discreet silence on the subject
and together they had rolled about town, eventually ending in Cribb's back parlour, drinking Blue Ruin. Only
then had Darcy reverted to the topic occupying both
their minds. "I'm leaving town."

"Oh?"

His lordship had run a hand through his perfectly
cut golden locks, disarranging them completely, in a
gesture Max had never, in all their years together, seen
him use. "Going to Leicestershire. I need a holiday."

Max had nodded enigmatically. Lord Darcy's principal estates lay in Leicestershire and always, due to the
large number of horses he raised, demanded attention.
But in general, his lordship managed to run his business affairs quite comfortably from town.

"No, by God! I've got a better idea. I'll go to Ireland.
It's further away."

As Max knew, Lord Darcy's brother resided on the

family estates in Ireland. Still, he had said nothing, patiently waiting for what he had known would come.

Darcy had rolled his glass between his hands, studying the swirling liquid with apparent interest. "About Sarah."

"Mmm?" Max had kept his own eyes firmly fixed on his glass.

"I didn't."

"Oh?"

"No. But I'm not entirely sure she knows what happened." Darcy had drained his glass, using the opportunity to watch Max work this out.

Finally, comprehension had dawned. A glimmer of a smile had tugged at the corners of His Grace of Twyford's mouth. "Oh."

"Precisely. I thought I'd leave it in your capable hands."

"Thank you!" Max had replied. Then he had groaned and dropped his head into his hands. "How the hell do you imagine I'm going to find out what she believes and then explain it to her if she's wrong?" His mind had boggled at the awful idea.

"I thought you might work through Miss Twinning," Darcy had returned, grinning for the first time that day.

Relieved to see his friend smile, even at his expense, Max had grinned back. "I've not been pushing the pace quite as hard as you. Miss Twinning and I have some way to go before we reach the point where such intimate discussion would be permissible."

"Oh, well," Darcy had sighed. "I only hope you have better luck than I."

"Throwing in the towel?"

Darcy had shrugged. "I wish I knew." A silence had ensued which Darcy eventually broke. "I've got to get away."

"How long will you be gone?"

Another shrug. "Who knows? As long as it takes, I suppose."

He had left Darcy packing at Hamilton House and returned to the comfort of his own home to spend a quiet evening in contemplation of his wards. Their problems should really not cause surprise. At first sight, he had known what sort of men the Twinning girls would attract. And there was no denying they responded to such men. Even Arabella seemed hell-bent on tangling with rakes. Thankfully, Lizzie seemed too quiet and gentle to take the same road—three rakes in any family should certainly be enough.

Family? The thought sobered him. He sat, eyes on the flames leaping in the grate, and pondered the odd notion.

His reverie was interrupted by sounds of an arrival. He glanced at the clock and frowned. Too late for callers. What now? He reached the hall in time to see Hillshaw and a footman fussing about the door.

"Yes, it's all right, Hillshaw, I'm not an invalid, you know!"

The voice brought Max forward. "Martin!"

The tousled brown head of Captain Martin Rotherbridge turned to greet his older brother. A winning grin spread across features essentially a more boyish version of Max's own. "Hello, Max. I'm back, as you see. Curst Frenchies put a hole in my shoulder."

Max's gaze fell to the bulk of bandaging distorting the set of his brother's coat. He clasped the hand held out to him warmly, his eyes raking the other's face. "Come into the library. Hillshaw?"

"Yes, Your Grace. I'll see to some food."

When they were comfortably ensconced by the fire, Martin with a tray of cold meat by his side and a large balloon of his brother's best brandy in his hand, Max asked his questions.

"No, you're right," Martin answered to one of these. "It wasn't just the wound, though that was bad enough. They tell me that with rest it'll come good in time." Max waited patiently. His brother fortified himself before continuing. "No. I sold out simply because, now the action's over, it's deuced boring over there. We sit about and play cards half the day. And the other half, we just sit and reminisce about all the females we've ever had." He grinned at his brother in a way Caroline, for one, would have recognised. "Seemed to me I was running out of anecdotes. So I decided to come home and lay in a fresh stock."

Max returned his brother's smile. Other than the shoulder wound, Martin was looking well. The difficult wound and slow convalescence had not succeeded in erasing the healthy glow from outdoor living which burnished his skin and, although there were lines present which had not been there before, these merely seemed to emphasize the fact that Martin Rotherbridge had seen more than twenty-five summers and was an old hand in many spheres. Max was delighted to hear he had returned to civilian life. Aside from his genuine concern for a much loved sibling, Martin was now the heir to the Dukedom of Twyford. While inheriting the Delmere holdings, with which he was well-acquainted, would have proved no difficulty to Martin, the Twyford estates were a different matter. Max eyed the long, lean frame stretched out in the chair before him and wondered where to begin. Before he had decided, Martin asked, "So how do you like being 'Your Grace'?"

In a few pithy sentences, Max told him. He then embarked on the saga of horrors examination of his uncle's estate had revealed, followed by a brief description of their present circumstances. Seeing the shadow of tiredness pass across Martin's face, he curtailed his report, saying instead, "Time for bed, stripling. You're tired."

Martin started, then grinned sleepily at Max's use of his childhood tag. "What? Oh, yes. I'm afraid I'm not up to full strength yet. And we've been travelling since first light."

Max's hand at his elbow assisted him to rise from the depth of the armchair. On his feet, Martin stretched and yawned. Seen side by side, the similarity between the brothers was marked. Max was still a few inches taller and his nine years' seniority showed in the heavier musculature of his chest and shoulders. Other than that, the differences were few—Martin's hair was a shade lighter than Max's dark mane and his features retained a softness Max's lacked, but the intensely blue eyes of the Rotherbridges shone in both dark faces.

Martin turned to smile at his brother. "It's good to be home."

"GOOD MORNING. HILLSHAW, isn't it? I'm Lizzie Twinning. I've come to return a book to His Grace."

Although he had only set eyes on her once before, Hillshaw remembered his master's youngest ward perfectly. As she stepped daintily over the threshold of Delmere House, a picture in a confection of lilac muslin, he gathered his wits to murmur, "His Grace is not presently at home, miss. Perhaps his secretary, Mr. Cummings, could assist you." Hillshaw rolled one majestic eye toward a hovering footman who immediately, if reluctantly, disappeared in the direction of the back office frequented by the Duke's secretary.

Lizzie, allowing Hillshaw to remove her half-cape, looked doubtful. But all she said was, "Wait here for me, Hennessy. I shan't be long." Her maid, who had dutifully followed her in, sat primly on the edge of a chair by the wall and, under the unnerving stare of Hillshaw, lowered her round-eyed gaze to her hands.

Immediately, Mr. Joshua Cummings came hurrying forward from the dimness at the rear of the hall. "Miss Lizzie? I'm afraid His Grace has already left the house, but perhaps I may be of assistance?" Mr. Cummings was not what one might expect of a nobleman's secretary. He was of middle age and small and round and pale, and, as Lizzie later informed her sisters, looked as if he spent his days locked away perusing dusty papers. In a sense, he did. He was a single man and, until taking his present post, had lived with his mother on the Rotherbridge estate in Surrey. His family had long been associated with the Rotherbridges and he was sincerely devoted to that family's interests. Catching sight of the book in Lizzie's small hand, he smiled. "Ah, I see you have brought back Lord Byron's verses. Perhaps you'd like to read his next book? Or maybe one of Mrs. Linfield's works would be more to your taste?"

Lizzie smiled back. On taking up residence at Twyford House, the sisters had been disappointed to find that, although extensive, the library there did not hold any of the more recent fictional works so much discussed among the *ton*. Hearing of their complaint, Max had revealed that his own library did not suffer from this deficiency and had promised to lend them any books they desired. But, rather than permit the sisters free rein in a library that also contained a number of works less suitable for their eyes, he had delegated the task of looking out the books they wanted to his secretary. Consequently, Mr. Cummings felt quite competent to deal with the matter at hand.

"If you'd care to wait in the drawing room, miss?" Hillshaw moved past her to open the door. With another dazzling smile, Lizzie handed the volume she carried to Mr. Cummings, informing him in a low voice that one of Mrs. Linfield's novels would be quite acceptable, then turned to follow Hillshaw. As she did so, her

gaze travelled past the stately butler to rest on the figure emerging from the shadow of the library door. She
remained where she was, her grey-brown eyes growing
rounder and rounder, as Martin Rotherbridge strolled
elegantly forward.

After the best night's sleep he had had in months,
Martin had felt ready to resume normal activities but,
on descending to the breakfast parlour, had discovered
his brother had already left the house to call in at Tat-
tersall's. Suppressing the desire to pull on his coat and
follow, Martin had resigned himself to awaiting Max's
return, deeming it wise to inform his brother in person that he was setting out to pick up the reins of his
civilian existence before he actually did so. Knowing
his friends, and their likely reaction to his reappear-
ance among them, he was reasonably certain he would
not be returning to Delmere House until the following morning. And he knew Max would worry unless
he saw for himself that his younger brother was up to
it. So, with a grin for his older brother's affection, he
had settled in the library to read the morning's news
sheets. But, after months of semi-invalidism, his returning health naturally gave rise to returning spirits. Waiting patiently was not easy. He had been irritably pacing
the library when his sharp ears had caught the sound
of a distinctly feminine voice in the hall. Intrigued, he
had gone to investigate.

Setting eyes on the vision gracing his brother's hall,
Martin's immediate thought was that Max had taken to
allowing his ladybirds to call at his house. But the atti-

tudes of Hillshaw and Cummings put paid to that idea. The sight of a maid sitting by the door confirmed his startled perception that the vision was indeed a young lady. His boredom vanishing like a cloud on a spring day, he advanced.

Martin allowed his eyes to travel, gently, so as not to startle her, over the delicious figure before him. Very nice. His smile grew. The silence around him penetrated his mind, entirely otherwise occupied. "Hillshaw, I think you'd better introduce us."

Hillshaw almost allowed a frown to mar his impassive countenance. But he knew better than to try to avoid the unavoidable. Exchanging a glance of fellow feeling with Mr. Cummings, he obliged in sternly disapproving tones. "Captain Martin Rotherbridge, Miss Lizzie Twinning. The young lady is His Grace's youngest ward, sir."

With a start, Martin's gaze, which had been locked with Lizzie's, flew to Hillshaw's face. "Ward?" He had not been listening too well last night when Max had been telling him of the estates, but he was sure his brother had not mentioned any wards.

With a thin smile, Hillshaw inclined his head in assent.

Lizzie, released from that mesmerising gaze, spoke up, her soft tones a dramatic contrast to the masculine voices. "Yes. My sisters and I are the Duke's wards, you know." She held out her hand. "How do you do? I didn't know the Duke had a brother. I've only dropped by to exchange some books His Grace lent us. Mr. Cummings was going to take care of it."

Martin took the small gloved hand held out to him and automatically bowed over it. Straightening, he moved to her side, placing her hand on his arm and holding it there. "In that case, Hillshaw's quite right. You should wait in the drawing-room." The relief on Hillshaw's and Mr. Cummings's faces evaporated at his next words. "And I'll keep you company."

As Martin ushered Lizzie into the drawing-room and pointedly shut the door in Hillshaw's face, the Duke's butler and secretary looked at each other helplessly. Then Mr. Cummings scurried away to find the required books, leaving Hillshaw to look with misgiving at the closed door of the drawing-room.

Inside, blissfully unaware of the concern she was engendering in her guardian's servants, Lizzie smiled trustingly up at the source of that concern.

"Have you been my brother's ward for long?" Martin asked.

"Oh, no!" said Lizzie. Then, "That is, I suppose, yes." She looked delightfully befuddled and Martin could not suppress a smile. He guided her to the chaise and, once she had settled, took the chair opposite her so that he could keep her bewitching face in full view.

"It depends, I suppose," said Lizzie, frowning in her effort to gather her wits, which had unaccountably scattered, "on what you'd call long. Our father died eighteen months ago, but then the other Duke—your uncle, was he not?—was our guardian. But when we came back from America, your brother had assumed the title. So then he was our guardian."

Out of this jumbled explanation, Martin gleaned enough to guess the truth. "Did you enjoy America? Were you there long?"

Little by little his questions succeeded in their aim and in short order, Lizzie had relaxed completely and was conversing in a normal fashion with her guardian's brother.

Listening to her description of her home, Martin shifted, trying to settle his shoulder more comfortably. Lizzie's sharp eyes caught the awkward movement and descried the wad of bandaging cunningly concealed beneath his coat.

"You're injured!" She leaned forward in concern. "Does it pain you dreadfully?"

"No, no. The enemy just got lucky, that's all. Soon be right as rain, I give you my word."

"You were in the army?" Lizzie's eyes had grown round. "Oh, please tell me all about it. It must have been so exciting!"

To Martin's considerable astonishment, he found himself recounting for Lizzie's benefit the horrors of the campaign and the occasional funny incident which had enlivened their days. She did not recoil but listened avidly. He had always thought he was a dab hand at interrogation but her persistent questioning left him reeling. She even succeeded in dragging from him the reason he had yet to leave the house. Her ready sympathy, which he had fully expected to send him running, enveloped him instead in a warm glow, a sort of prideful care which went rapidly to his head.

Then Mr. Cummings arrived with the desired books. Lizzie took them and laid them on a side-table beside her, patently ignoring the Duke's secretary who was clearly waiting to escort her to the front door. With an ill-concealed grin, Martin dismissed him. "It's all right, Cummings. Miss Twinning has taken pity on me and decided to keep me entertained until my brother returns."

Lizzie, entirely at home, turned a blissful smile on Mr. Cummings, leaving that gentleman with no option but to retire.

AN HOUR LATER, Max crossed the threshold to be met by Hillshaw, displaying, quite remarkably, an emotion very near agitation. This was instantly explained. "Miss Lizzie's here. In the drawing-room with Mr. Martin."

Max froze. Then nodded to his butler. "Very good, Hillshaw." His sharp eyes had already taken in the bored face of the maid sitting in the shadows. Presumably, Lizzie had been here for some time. His face was set in grim lines as his hand closed on the handle of the drawing-room door.

The sight which met his eyes was not at all what he had expected. As he shut the door behind him, Martin's eyes lifted to his, amused understanding in the blue depths. He was seated in an armchair and Lizzie occupied the nearest corner of the chaise. She was presently hunched forward, pondering what lay before her on a small table drawn up between them. As Max rounded the chaise, he saw to his stupefaction that they were playing checkers.

Lizzie looked up and saw him. "Oh! You're back. I was just entertaining your brother until you returned." Max blinked but Lizzie showed no consciousness of the implication of her words and he discarded the notion of enlightening her.

Then Lizzie's eyes fell on the clock on the mantelshelf. "Oh, dear! I didn't realize it was so late. I must go. Where are those books Mr. Cummings brought?"

Martin fetched them for her and, under the highly sceptical gaze of his brother, very correctly took leave of her. Max, seeing the expression in his brother's eyes as they rested on his youngest ward, almost groaned aloud. This was really too much.

Max saw Lizzie out, then returned to the library. But before he could launch into his inquisition, Martin got in first. "You didn't tell me you had inherited four wards."

"Well, I have," said Max, flinging himself into an armchair opposite the one his brother had resumed.

"Are they all like that?" asked Martin in awe.

Max needed no explanation of what "that" meant. He answered with a groan, "Worse!"

Eyes round, Martin did not make the mistake of imagining the other Twinning sisters were antidotes. His gaze rested on his brother for a moment, then his face creased into a wide smile. "Good lord!"

Max brought his blue gaze back from the ceiling and fixed it firmly on his brother. "Precisely. That being so,

I suggest you revise the plans you've been making for Lizzie Twinning."

Martin's grin, if anything, became even broader. "Why so? It's you who's their guardian, not I. Besides, you don't seriously expect me to believe that, if our situations were reversed, you'd pay any attention to such restrictions?" When Max frowned, Martin continued. "Anyway, good heavens, you must have seen it for yourself. She's like a ripe plum, ready for the picking." He stopped at Max's raised hand.

"Permit me to fill you in," drawled his older brother. "For a start, I've nine years on you and there's nothing about the business you know that I don't. However, quite aside from that, I can assure you the Twinning sisters, ripe though they may be, are highly unlikely to fall into anyone's palms without a prior proposal of marriage."

A slight frown settled over Martin's eyes. Not for a moment did he doubt the accuracy of Max's assessment. But he had been strongly attracted to Lizzie Twinning and was disinclined to give up the idea of converting her to his way of thinking. He looked up and blue eyes met blue. "Really?"

Max gestured airily. "Consider the case of Lord Darcy Hamilton." Martin looked his question. Max obliged. "Being much taken with Sarah, the second of the four, Darcy's been engaged in storming her citadel for the past five weeks and more. No holds barred, I might add. And the outcome you ask? As of yesterday, he's retired to his estates, to lick his wounds and, unless I miss my guess, to consider whether he can stomach the idea of marriage."

"Good lord!" Although only peripherally acquainted with Darcy Hamilton, Martin knew he was one of Max's particular friends and that his reputation in matters involving the fairer sex was second only to Max's own.

"Exactly," nodded Max. "Brought low by a chit of a girl. So, brother dear, if it's your wish to tangle with any Twinnings, I suggest you first decide how much you're willing to stake on the throw."

As he pondered his brother's words, Martin noticed that Max's gaze had become abstracted. He only just caught the last words his brother said, musing, almost to himself. "For, brother mine, it's my belief the Twinnings eat rakes for breakfast."

THE COACH SWAYED as it turned a corner and Arabella clutched the strap swinging by her head. As equilibrium returned, she settled her skirts once more and glanced at the other two occupants of the carriage. The glow from a street lamp momentarily lit the interior of the coach, then faded as the four horses hurried on. Arabella grinned into the darkness.

Caroline had insisted that she and not Lizzie share their guardian's coach. One had to wonder why. Too often these days, her eldest sister had the look of the cat caught just after it had tasted the cream. Tonight, that look of guilty pleasure, or, more specifically, the anticipation of guilty pleasure, was marked.

She had gone up to Caroline's room to hurry her sis-

ter along. Caroline had been sitting, staring at her reflection in the mirror, idly twisting one copper curl to
sit more attractively about her left ear.

"Caro? Are you ready? Max is here."

"Oh!" Caroline had stood abruptly, then paused to
cast one last critical glance over her pale sea-green
dress, severely styled as most suited her ample charms,
the neckline daringly *décolleté*. She had frowned, her
fingers straying to the ivory swell of her breasts. "What
do you think, Bella? Is it too revealing? Perhaps a piece
of lace might make it a little less…?"

"Attractive?" Arabella had brazenly supplied. "To
be perfectly frank, I doubt our guardian would approve
a fichu."

The delicate blush that had appeared on Caroline's
cheeks had been most informative. But, "Too true," was
all her sister had replied.

Arabella looked across the carriage once more and
caught the gleam of warm approval that shone in their
guardian's eyes as they rested on Caroline. It was highly
unlikely that the conservative Mr. Willoughby was the
cause of her sister's blushes. That being so, what game
was the Duke of Twyford playing? And, even more to
the point, was Caro thinking of joining in?

Heaven knew, they had had a close enough call with
Sarah and Lord Darcy. Nothing had been said of Sarah's strange affliction, yet they were all close enough
for even the innocent Lizzie to have some inkling of the
root cause. And while Max had been the soul of discretion in speaking privately to Caroline and Sarah in the

hall before they had left, it was as plain as a pikestaff the information he had imparted had not included news of a proposal. Sarah's pale face had paled further. But the Twinnings were made of stern stuff and Sarah had shaken her head at Caro's look of concern.

The deep murmur of their guardian's voice came to her ears, followed by her sister's soft tones. Arabella's big eyes danced. She could not make out their words but those tones were oh, so revealing. But if Sarah was in deep waters and Caro was hovering on the brink, she, to her chagrin, had not even got her toes wet yet.

Arabella frowned at the moon, showing fleetingly between the branches of a tall tree. Hugo, Lord Denbigh. The most exasperating man she had ever met. She would give anything to be able to say she didn't care a button for him. Unfortunately, he was the only man who could make her tingle just by looking at her.

Unaware that she was falling far short of Caroline's expectations, Arabella continued to gaze out of the window, absorbed in contemplation of the means available for bringing one large gentleman to heel.

THE HEAVY TWYFORD coach lumbered along in the wake of the sleek Delmere carriage. Lady Benborough put up a hand to right her wig, swaying perilously as they rounded a particularly sharp corner. For the first time since embarking on her nephew's crusade to find the Twinning girls suitable husbands, she felt a twinge of nervousness. She was playing with fire and she knew it. Still, she could not regret it. The sight of Max and

Caroline together in the hall at Twyford House had sent
a definite thrill through her old bones. As for Sarah, she
doubted not that Darcy Hamilton was too far gone to
desist, resist and retire. True, he might not know it yet,
but time would certainly bring home to him the pen-
alty he would have to pay to walk away from the snare.
Her shrewd blue eyes studied the pale face opposite her.
Even in the dim light, the strain of the past few days
was evident. Thankfully, no one outside their party had
been aware of that contretemps. So, regardless of what
Sarah herself believed, Augusta had no qualms. Sarah
was home safe; she could turn her attention elsewhere.

Arabella, the minx, had picked a particularly difficult nut to crack. Still, she could hardly fault the girl's
taste. Hugo Denbigh was a positive Adonis, well-born,
well-heeled and easy enough in his ways. Unfortunately,
he was so easy to please that he seemed to find just as
much pleasure in the presence of drab little girls as he
derived from Arabella's rather more scintillating company. Gammon, of course, but how to alert Arabella to
that fact? Or would it be more to the point to keep quiet
and allow Hugo a small degree of success? As her mind
drifted down that particular path, Augusta suddenly
caught herself up and had the grace to look sheepish.
What appalling thoughts for a chaperon!

Her gaze fell on Lizzie, sweet but far from demure
in a gown of delicate silver gauze touched with colour
in the form of embroidered lilacs. A soft, introspective smile hovered over her classically moulded lips.

Almost a smile of anticipation. Augusta frowned. Had she missed something?

Mentally reviewing Lizzie's conquests, Lady Benborough was at a loss to account for the suppressed excitement evident, now she came to look more closely, in the way the younger girl's fingers beat an impatient if silent tattoo on the beads of her reticule. Clearly, whoever he was would be at the ball. She would have to watch her youngest charge like a hawk. Lizzie was too young, in all conscience, to be allowed the licence her more worldly sisters took for granted.

Relaxing back against the velvet squabs, Augusta smiled. Doubtless she was worrying over nothing. Lizzie might have the Twinning looks but surely she was too serious an innocent to attract the attentions of a rake? Three rakes she might land, the Twinnings being the perfect bait, but a fourth was bound to be wishful thinking.

CHAPTER SEVEN

MARTIN PUZZLED OVER Max's last words on the Twinnings but it was not until he met the sisters that evening, at Lady Montacute's drum, that he divined what had prompted his brother to utter them. He had spent the afternoon dropping in on certain old friends, only to be, almost immediately, bombarded with requests for introductions to the Twinnings. He had come away with the definite impression that the best place to be that evening would be wherever the Misses Twinning were destined. His batman and valet, Jiggins, had turned up the staggering information that Max himself usually escorted his wards to their evening engagements. Martin had found this hard to credit, but when, keeping an unobtrusive eye on the stream of arrivals from a vantage-point beside a potted palm in Lady Montacute's ballroom, he had seen Max arrive surrounded by Twinning sisters, he had been forced to accept the crazy notion as truth. When the observation that the fabulous creature on his brother's arm was, in fact, his eldest ward finally penetrated his brain all became clear.

Moving rapidly to secure a dance with Lizzie, who smiled up at him with flattering welcome, Martin was close enough to see the expression in his brother's eyes as he bent to whisper something in Miss Twinning's ear, prior to relinquishing her to the attention of the circle forming about her. His brows flew and he pursed his lips in surprise. As his brother's words of that morning returned to him, he grinned. How much was Max prepared to stake?

For the rest of the evening, Martin watched and plotted and planned. He used his wound as an excuse not to dance, which enabled him to spend his entire time studying Lizzie Twinning. It was an agreeable pastime. Her silvery dress floated about her as she danced and the candlelight glowed on her sheening brown curls. With her natural grace, she reminded him of a fairy sprite, except that he rather thought such mythical creatures lacked the fulsome charms with which the Twinning sisters were so well-endowed. Due to his experienced foresight, Lizzie accommodatingly returned to his side after every dance, convinced by his chatter of the morning that he was in dire need of cheering up. Lady Benborough, to whom he had dutifully made his bow, had snorted in disbelief at his die-away airs but had apparently been unable to dissuade Lizzie's soft heart from bringing him continual succour. By subtle degrees, he sounded her out on each of her hopeful suitors and was surprised at his own relief in finding she had no special leaning towards any.

He started his campaign in earnest when the musicians struck up for the dance for which he *had* engaged her. By careful manoeuvring, they were seated in a sheltered alcove, free for the moment of her swains. Schooling his features to grave disappointment, he said, "Dear Lizzie. I'm so sorry to disappoint you, but…" He let his voice fade away weakly.

Lizzie's sweet face showed her concern. "Oh! Do you not feel the thing? Perhaps I can get Mrs. Alford's smelling salts for you?"

Martin quelled the instinctive response to react to her suggestion in too forceful a manner. Instead, he waved aside her words with one limp hand. "No! No! Don't worry about me. I'll come about shortly." He smiled forlornly at her, allowing his blue gaze to rest, with calculated effect, on her grey-brown eyes. "But maybe you'd like to get one of your other beaux to dance with you? I'm sure Mr. Mallard would be only too thrilled." He made a move as if to summon this gentleman, the most assiduous of her suitors.

"Heavens, no!" exclaimed Lizzie, catching his hand in hers to prevent the action. "I'll do no such thing. If you're feeling poorly then of course I'll stay with you." She continued to hold his hand and, for his part, Martin made no effort to remove it from her warm clasp.

Martin closed his eyes momentarily, as if fighting off a sudden faintness. Opening them again, he said, "Actually, I do believe it's all the heat and noise in here that's doing it. Perhaps if I went out on to the terrace for a while, it might clear my head."

"The very thing!" said Lizzie, jumping up.

Martin, rising more slowly, smiled down at her in a

brotherly fashion. "Actually, I'd better go alone. Someone might get the wrong idea if we both left."

"Nonsense!" said Lizzie, slightly annoyed by his implication that such a conclusion could, of course, have no basis in fact. "Why should anyone worry? We'll only be a few minutes and anyway, I'm your brother's ward, after all."

Martin made some small show of dissuading her, which, as he intended, only increased her resolution to accompany him. Finally, he allowed himself to be bullied on to the terrace, Lizzie's small hand on his arm, guiding him.

As supper time was not far distant, there were only two other couples on the shallow terrace, and within minutes both had returned to the ballroom. Martin, food very far from his mind, strolled down the terrace, apparently content to go where Lizzie led. But his sharp soldier's eyes had very quickly adjusted to the moonlight. After a cursory inspection of the surroundings, he allowed himself to pause dramatically as they neared the end of the terrace. "I really think…" He waited a moment, as if gathering strength, then continued, "I really think I should sit down."

Lizzie looked around in consternation. There were no benches on the terrace, not even a balustrade.

"There's a seat under that willow, I think," said Martin, gesturing across the lawn.

A quick glance from Lizzie confirmed this observation. "Here, lean on me," she said. Martin obligingly draped one arm lightly about her shoulders. As he felt her small hands gripping him about his waist, a pang of guilt shook him. She really was so trusting. A pity to destroy it.

They reached the willow and brushed through the long strands which conveniently fell back to form a curtain around the white wooden seat. Inside the chamber so formed, the moonbeams danced, sprinkling sufficient light to lift the gloom and allow them to see. Martin sank on to the seat with a convincing show of weakness. Lizzie subsided in a susurration of silks beside him, retaining her clasp on his hand and half turning the better to look into his face.

The moon was behind the willow and one bright beam shone through over Martin's shoulder to fall gently on Lizzie's face. Martin's face was in shadow, so Lizzie, smiling confidingly up at him, could only see that he was smiling in return. She could not see the expression which lit his blue eyes as they devoured her delicate face, then dropped boldly to caress the round swell of her breasts where they rose and fell invitingly below the demurely scooped neckline of her gown. Carefully, Martin turned his hand so that now he was holding her hand, not she his. Then he was still.

After some moments, Lizzie put her head on one side and softly asked, "Are you all right?"

It was on the tip of Martin's tongue to answer truthfully. No, he was not all right. He had brought her out here to commence her seduction and now some magical power was holding him back. What was the matter with him? He cleared his throat and answered huskily, "Give me a minute."

A light breeze wafted the willow leaves and the light shifted. Lizzie saw the distracted frown which had settled over his eyes. Drawing her hand from his, she reached up and gently ran her fingers over his brow, as if to smooth the frown away. Then, to Martin's intense surprise, she leaned forward and, very gently, touched her lips to his.

As she drew away, Lizzie saw to her dismay that, if Martin had been frowning before, he was positively scowling now. "Why did you do that?" he asked, his tone sharp.

Even in the dim light he could see her confusion. "Oh, dear! I'm s...so sorry. Please excuse me! I shouldn't have done that."

"Damn right, you shouldn't have," Martin growled. His hand, which had fallen to the bench, was clenched hard with the effort to remain still and not pull the damn woman into his arms and devour her. He realized she had not answered his question. "But why did you?"

Lizzie hung her head in contrition. "It's just that you looked...well, so troubled. I just wanted to help." Her voice was a small whisper in the night.

Martin sighed in frustration. That sort of help he could do without.

"I suppose you'll think me very forward, but..." This time, her voice died away altogether.

What Martin did think was that she was adorable and he hurt with the effort to keep his hands off her. Now he came to think of it, while he had not had a headache when they came out to the garden, he certainly had one now. Repressing the desire to groan aloud, he straightened. "We'd better get back to the ballroom. We'll just forget the incident." As he drew her to her feet and placed her hand on his arm, an unwelcome thought struck him. "You don't go around kissing other men who look troubled, do you?"

The surprise in her face was quite genuine. "No! Of course not!"

"Well," said Martin, wondering why the information so thrilled him, "just subdue any of these sudden impulses of yours. Except around me, of course. I dare say it's perfectly all right with me, in the circumstances. You are my brother's ward, after all."

Lizzie, still stunned by her forward behaviour, and the sudden impulse that had driven her to it, smiled trustingly up at him.

CAROLINE SMILED HER practised smile and wished, for at least the hundredth time, that Max Rotherbridge were not their guardian. At least, she amended, not *her* guardian. He was proving a tower of strength in all other respects and she could only be grateful, both for his continuing support and protection, as well as his experienced counsel over the affair of Sarah and Lord Darcy. But there was no doubt in her mind that her own confusion would be immeasurably eased by dissolution of the guardianship clause which tied her so irrevocably to His Grace of Twyford.

While she circled the floor in the respectful arms of Mr. Willoughby who, she knew, was daily moving closer to a declaration despite her attempts to dampen his confidence, she was conscious of a wish that it was her guardian's far less gentle clasp she was in. Mr. Willoughby, she had discovered, was worthy. Which was almost as bad as righteous. She sighed and covered the lapse with a brilliant smile into his mild eyes, slightly below her own. It was not that she despised short men, just that they lacked the ability to make her feel delicate and vulnerable, womanly, as Max Rotherbridge certainly could. In fact, the feeling of utter helplessness that seemed to overcome her every time she found herself in his powerful arms was an increasing concern.

As she and her partner turned with the music, she sighted Sarah, dancing with one of her numerous court, trying, not entirely successfully, to look as if she was enjoying it. Her heart went out to her sister. They had stayed at home the previous night and, in unusual privacy, thrashed out the happenings of the night before. While Sarah skated somewhat thinly over certain aspects, it had been clear that she, at least, knew her heart. But Max had taken the opportunity of a few minutes' wait in the hall at Twyford House to let both herself and Sarah know, in the most subtle way, that Lord Darcy had left town for his estates. She swallowed another sigh and smiled absently at Mr. Willoughby.

As the eldest, she had, in recent years, adopted the role of surrogate mother to her sisters. One unfortunate aspect of that situation was that she had no one to turn to herself. If the gentleman involved had been anyone other than her guardian, she would have sought advice from Lady Benborough. In the circumstances, that avenue, too, was closed to her. But, after that interlude in the Overtons's summer-house, she was abysmally aware that she needed advice. All he had to do was to take her into his arms and her well-ordered defences fell flat. And his kiss! The effect of that seemed totally to disorder her mind, let alone her senses. She had not yet fathomed what, exactly, he was about, yet it seemed inconceivable that he would seduce his own ward. Which fact, she ruefully admitted, but only to herself when at her most candid, was at the seat of her desire to no longer be his ward.

It was not that she had any wish to join the *demi-monde*. But face facts she must. She was nearly twenty-six and she knew what she wanted. She wanted Max Rotherbridge. She knew he was a rake and, if she had not instantly divined his standing as soon as she had laid eyes on him, Lady Benborough's forthright remarks on the subject left no room for doubt. But every tiny particle of her screamed that he was the one. Which was why she was calmly dancing with each of her most ardent suitors, careful not to give any one of them the slightest encouragement, while waiting for her guardian to claim her for the dance before supper. On their arrival in the overheated ballroom, he had, in a sensual murmur that had wafted the curls over her ear and sent shivery tingles all the way down her spine, asked her to

hold that waltz for him. She looked into Mr. Willoughby's pale eyes. And sighed.

"SIR MALCOLM, I do declare you're flirting with me!"
Desperation lent Arabella's bell-like voice a definite
edge. Using her delicate feather fan to great purpose,
she flashed her large eyes at the horrendously rich but
essentially dim-witted Scottish baronet, managing
meanwhile to keep Hugo, Lord Denbigh, in view. Her
true prey was standing only feet away, conversing ami-
ably with a plain matron with an even plainer daughter. What was the matter with him? She had tried every
trick she knew to bring the great oaf to her tiny feet,
yet he persistently drifted away. He would be politely
attentive but seemed incapable of settling long enough
even to be considered one of her court. She had kept
the supper waltz free, declaring it to be taken to all her
suitors, convinced he would ask her for that most favoured dance. But now, with supper time fast approaching, she suddenly found herself facing the prospect of
having no partner at all. Her eyes flashing, she turned
in welcome to Mr. Pritchard and Viscount Molesworth.

She readily captivated both gentlemen, skilfully
steering clear of any lapse of her own rigidly imposed
standards. She was an outrageous flirt, she knew, but
a discerning flirt, and she had long made it her policy
never to hurt anyone with her artless chatter. She enjoyed the occupation but it had never involved her heart.
Normally, her suitors happily fell at her feet without the
slightest assistance from her. But, now that she had at

last found someone she wished to attract, she had, to her horror, found she had less idea of how to draw a man to her side than plainer girls who had had to learn the art.

To her chagrin, she saw the musicians take their places on the rostrum. There was only one thing to do. She smiled sweetly at the three gentlemen around her. "My dear sirs," she murmured, her voice mysteriously low, "I'm afraid I must leave you. No! Truly. Don't argue." Another playful smile went around. "Until later, Sir Malcolm, Mr. Pritchard, my lord." With a nod and a mysterious smile she moved away, leaving the three gentlemen wondering who the lucky man was.

Slipping through the crowd, Arabella headed for the exit to the ballroom. Doubtless there would be an antechamber somewhere where she could hide. She was not hungry anyway. She timed her exit to coincide with the movement of a group of people across the door, making it unlikely that anyone would see her retreat. Once in the passage, she glanced about. The main stairs lay directly in front of her. She glanced to her left in time to see two ladies enter one of the rooms. The last thing she needed was the endless chatter of a withdrawing-room. She turned purposefully to her right. At the end of the dimly lit corridor, a door stood open, light from the flames of a hidden fire flickering on its panels. She hurried down the corridor and, looking in, saw a small study. It was empty. A carafe and glasses set in readiness on a small table suggested it was yet another room set aside for the use of guests who found the heat of the ballroom too trying. With a sigh of relief, Arabella entered. After some consideration, she left the door open.

She went to the table and poured herself a glass of water. As she was replacing the glass, she heard voices approaching. Her eyes scanned the room and lit on the deep window alcove; the curtain across it, if fully drawn, would make it a small room. On the thought, she was through, drawing the heavy curtain tightly shut.

In silence, her heart beating in her ears, she listened as the voices came nearer and entered the room, going towards the fire. She waited a moment, breathless, but no one came to the curtain. Relaxing, she turned. And almost fell over the large pair of feet belonging to the gentleman stretched at his ease in the armchair behind the curtain.

"Oh!" Her hand flew to her lips in her effort to smother the sound. "What are you doing here?" she whispered furiously.

Slowly, the man turned his head towards her. He smiled. "Waiting for you, my dear."

Arabella closed her eyes tightly, then opened them again but he was still there. As she watched, Lord Denbigh unfurled his long length and stood, magnificent and, suddenly, to Arabella at least, oddly intimidating, before her. In the light of the full moon spilling through the large windows, his tawny eyes roved appreciatively over her. He caught her small hand in his and raised it to his lips. "I didn't think you'd be long."

His lazy tones, pitched very low, washed languidly over Arabella. With a conscious effort, she tried to break free of their hypnotic hold. "How could you know I was coming here? *I* didn't."

"Well," he answered reasonably, "I couldn't think where else you would go, if you didn't have a partner for the supper waltz."

He *knew!* In the moonlight, Arabella's fiery blush faded into more delicate tints but the effect on her temper was the same. "You oaf!" she said in a fierce whisper, aiming a stinging slap at the grin on his large face. But the grin grew into a smile as he easily caught her hand and drew it down and then behind her, drawing her towards him. He captured her other hand as well and imprisoned that in the same large hand behind her back.

"Lord Denbigh! Let me go!" Arabella pleaded, keeping her voice low for fear the others beyond the curtain would hear. How hideously embarrassing to be found in such a situation. And now she had another problem. What was Hugo up to? As her anger drained, all sorts of other emotions came to the fore. She looked up, her eyes huge and shining in the moonlight, her lips slightly parted in surprise.

Hugo lifted his free hand and one long finger traced the curve of her full lower lip.

Even with only the moon to light his face, Arabella saw the glimmer of desire in his eyes. "Hugo, let me go. Please?"

He smiled lazily down at her. "In a moment, sweetheart. After I've rendered you incapable of scratching my eyes out."

His fingers had taken hold of her chin and he waited

to see the fury in her eyes before he chuckled and bent his head until his lips met hers.

Arabella had every intention of remaining aloof from his kisses. Damn him—he'd tricked her! She tried to whip up her anger, but all she could think of was how wonderfully warm his lips felt against hers. And what delicious sensations were running along her nerves. Everywhere. Her body, entirely of its own volition, melted into his arms.

She felt, rather than heard, his deep chuckle as his arms shifted and tightened about her. Finding her hands free and resting on his shoulders, she did not quite know what to do with them. Box his ears? In the end, she twined them about his neck, holding him close.

When Hugo finally lifted his head, it was to see the stars reflected in her eyes. He smiled lazily down at her. "Now you have to admit that's more fun than waltzing."

Arabella could think of nothing to say.

"No quips?" he prompted.

She blushed slightly. "We should be getting back." She tried to ease herself from his embrace but his arms moved not at all.

Still smiling in that sleepy way, he shook his head. "Not yet. That was just the waltz. We've supper to go yet." His lips lightly brushed hers. "And I'm ravenously hungry."

Despite the situation, Arabella nearly giggled at the boyish tone. But she became much more serious when his lips returned fully to hers, driving her into far deeper waters than she had ever sailed before.

But he was experienced enough to correctly gauge
her limits, to stop just short and retreat, until they were
sane again. Later, both more serious than was their
wont, they returned separately to the ballroom.

DESPITE HER STRATEGIES, Arabella was seen as she slipped
from the ballroom. Max, returning from the card-room
where he had been idly passing his time until he could,
with reasonable excuse, gravitate to the side of his eldest ward, saw the bright chestnut curls dip through the
doorway and for an instant had thought that Caroline
was deserting him. But his sharp ears had almost immediately caught the husky tone of her laughter from a
knot of gentlemen near by and he realised it must have
been Arabella, most like Caroline in colouring, whom
he had seen.

But he had more serious problems on his mind than
whether Arabella had torn her flounce. His pursuit of
the luscious Miss Twinning, or, rather, the difficulties
which now lay in his path to her, were a matter for concern. The odd fact that he actually bothered to dance
with his eldest ward had already been noted. As there
were more than a few ladies among the *ton* who could
give a fairly accurate description of his preferences in
women, the fact that Miss Twinning's endowments
brought her very close to his ideal had doubtless not
been missed. However, he cared very little for the opin-
ions of others and foresaw no real problem in placating
the *ton* after the deed was done. What was troubling him

was the unexpected behaviour of the two principals in the affair, Miss Twinning and himself.

With respect to his prey, he had miscalculated on two counts. Firstly, he had imagined it would take a concerted effort to seduce a twenty-five-year-old woman who had lived until recently a very retired life. Instead, from the first, she had responded so freely that he had almost lost his head. He was too experienced not to know that it would take very little of his persuasion to convince her to overthrow the tenets of her class and come to him. It irritated him beyond measure that the knowledge, far from spurring him on to take immediate advantage of her vulnerability, had made him pause and consider, in a most disturbing way, just what he was about. His other mistake had been in thinking that, with his intensive knowledge of the ways of the *ton,* he would have no difficulty in using his position as her guardian to create opportunities to be alone with Caroline. Despite—or was it because of?—her susceptibility towards him, she seemed able to avoid his planned tête-à-têtes with ease and, with the exception of a few occasions associated with some concern over one or other of her sisters, had singularly failed to give him the opportunities he sought. And seducing a woman whose mind was filled with worry over one of her sisters was a task he had discovered to be beyond him.

He had, of course, revised his original concept of what role Caroline was to play in his life. However, he was fast coming to the conclusion that he would have to in some way settle her sisters' affairs before either he or Caroline would have time to pursue their own destinies. But life, he was fast learning, was not all that simple. In the circumstances, the *ton* would expect Miss Twinning's betrothal to be announced before that of her sisters. And he was well aware he had no intention of giving his permission for any gentleman to pay his addresses to Miss Twinning. As he had made no move to clarify for her the impression of his intentions he had originally given her, he did not delude himself that she might not accept some man like Willoughby, simply to remove herself from the temptation of her guardian. Yet if he told her she was not his ward, she would undoubtedly be even more vigilant with respect to himself and, in all probability, even more successful in eluding him.

There was, of course, a simple solution. But he had a perverse dislike of behaving as society dictated. Consequently, he had formed no immediate intention of informing Caroline of his change of plans. There was a challenge, he felt, in attempting to handle their relationship his way. Darcy had pushed too hard and too fast and, consequently, had fallen at the last fence. He, on the other hand, had no intention of rushing things. Timing was everything in such a delicate matter as seduction.

The congestion of male forms about his eldest ward brought a slight frown to his face. But the musicians obligingly placed bow to string, allowing him to extricate her from their midst and sweep her on to the floor.

He glanced down into her grey-green eyes and saw his own pleasure in dancing with her reflected there.

His arm tightened slightly and her attention focused. "I do hope your sisters are behaving themselves?"

Caroline returned his weary question with a smile. "Assuming your friends are doing likewise, I doubt there'll be a problem."

Max raised his brows. So she knew at least a little of what had happened. After negotiating a difficult turn to avoid old Major Brumidge and his similarly ancient partner, he jettisoned the idea of trying to learn more of Sarah's thoughts in favour of spiking a more specific gun. "Incidently, apropos of your sisters' and your own fell intent, what do you wish me to say to the numerous beaux who seem poised to troop up the steps of Delmere House?"

He watched her consternation grow as she grappled with the sticky question. He saw no reason to tell her that, on his wards' behalf, he had already turned down a number of offers, none of which could be considered remotely suitable. He doubted they were even aware of the interest of the gentlemen involved.

Caroline, meanwhile, was considering her options. If she was unwise enough to tell him to permit any acceptable gentlemen to address them, they could shortly be bored to distraction with the task of convincing said gentlemen that their feelings were not reciprocated. On the other hand, giving Max Rotherbridge a free hand to choose their husbands seemed equally unwise. She temporized. "Perhaps it would be best if we were to let you know if we anticipated receiving an offer from any particular gentleman that we would wish to seriously consider."

Max would have applauded if his hands had not been so agreeably occupied. "A most sensible suggestion, my ward. Tell me, how long does it take to pin up a flounce?"

Caroline blinked at this startling question.

"The reason I ask," said Max as they glided to a halt, "is that Arabella deserted the room some minutes before the music started and, as far as I can see, has yet to return."

A frown appeared in Caroline's fine eyes but, in deference to the eyes of others, she kept her face free of care and her voice light. "Can you see if Lord Denbigh is in the room?"

Max did not need to look. "Not since I entered it." After a pause, he asked, "Is she seriously pursuing that line? If so, I fear she'll all too soon reach point non plus."

Caroline followed his lead as he offered her his arm and calmly strolled towards the supper-room. A slight smile curled her lips as, in the increasing crowd, she leaned closer to him to answer. "With Arabella, it's hard to tell. She seems so obvious, with her flirting. But that's really all superficial. In reality, she's rather reticent about such things."

Max smiled in reply. Her words merely confirmed his own reading of Arabella. But his knowledge of the relationship between Caroline and her sisters prompted him to add, "Nevertheless, you'd be well-advised to sound her out on that score. Hugo Denbigh, when all is said and done, is every bit as dangerous as…" He paused to capture her eyes with his own before, smiling in a devilish way, he continued, "I am."

Conscious of the eyes upon them, Caroline strove to maintain her composure. "How very…reassuring, to be sure," she managed.

The smile on Max's face broadened. They had reached the entrance of the supper-room and he paused in the doorway to scan the emptying ballroom. "If she hasn't returned in ten minutes, we'll have to go looking. But come, sweet ward, the lobster patties await."

With a flourish, Max led her to a small table where they were joined, much to his delight, by Mr. Willoughby and a plain young lady, a Miss Spence. Mr. Willoughby's transparent intention of engaging the delightful Miss Twinning in close converse, ignoring the undemanding Miss Spence and Miss Twinning's guardian, proved to be rather more complicated than Mr. Willoughby, for one, had imagined. Under the subtle hand of His Grace of Twyford, Mr. Willoughby found himself the centre of a general discussion on philosophy. Caroline listened in ill-concealed delight as Max blocked every move poor Mr. Willoughby made to polarise the conversation. It became apparent that her guardian understood only too well Mr. Willoughby's state and she found herself caught somewhere between embarrassment and relief. In the end, relief won the day.

Eventually, routed, Mr. Willoughby rose, ostensibly to return Miss Spence to her parent. Watching his

retreat with laughing eyes, Caroline returned her gaze
to her guardian, only to see him look pointedly at the
door from the ballroom. She glanced across and saw
Arabella enter, slightly flushed and with a too-bright
smile on her lips. She made straight for the table where
Sarah was sitting with a number of others and, with her
usual facility, merged with the group, laughing up at the
young man who leapt to his feet to offer her his chair.

Caroline turned to Max, a slight frown in her eyes,
to find his attention had returned to the door. She followed his gaze and saw Lord Denbigh enter.

To any casual observer, Hugo was merely coming
late to the supper-room, his languid gaze and sleepy
smile giving no hint of any more pressing emotion than
to discover whether there were any lobster patties left.
Max Rotherbridge, however, was a far from casual observer. As he saw the expression in his lordship's heavy-
lidded eyes as they flicked across the room to where
Arabella sat, teasing her company unmercifully, His
Grace of Twyford's black brows rose in genuine astonishment. Oh, God! Another one?

RESIGNED TO YET another evening spent with no progress in the matter of his eldest ward, Max calmly escorted her back to the ballroom and, releasing her to
the attentions of her admirers, not without a particularly
penetrating stare at two gentlemen of dubious standing
who had had the temerity to attempt to join her circle,
he prepared to quit the ballroom. He had hoped to have
persuaded Miss Twinning to view the moonlight from

the terrace. There was a useful bench he knew of, under a concealing willow, which would have come in handy. However, he had no illusions concerning his ability to make love to a woman who was on tenterhooks over the happiness of not one but two sisters. So he headed for the card-room.

On his way, he passed Arabella, holding court once again in something close to her usual style. His blue gaze searched her face. As if sensing his regard, she turned and saw him. For a moment, she looked lost. He smiled encouragingly. After a fractional pause, she flashed her brilliant smile back and, putting up her chin, turned back to her companions, laughing at some comment.

Max moved on. Clearly, Caroline did have another problem on her hands. He paused at the entrance to the card-room and, automatically, scanned the packed ballroom. Turning, he was about to cross the threshold when a disturbing thought struck him. He turned back to the ballroom.

"Make up your mind! Make up your mind! Oh, it's you, Twyford. What are you doing at such an occasion? Hardly your style these days, what?"

Excusing himself to Colonel Weatherspoon, Max moved out of the doorway and checked the room again. Where was Lizzie? He had not seen her at supper, but then again he had not looked. He had mentally dubbed her the baby of the family but his rational mind informed him that she was far from too young. He was about to cross the room to where his aunt Augusta sat, resplendent in bronze bombazine, when a movement by the windows drew his eyes.

Lizzie entered from the terrace, a shy and entirely guileless smile on her lips. Her small hand rested with easy assurance on his brother's arm. As he watched, she turned and smiled up at Martin, a look so full of trust that a newborn lamb could not have bettered it. And Martin, wolf that he was, returned the smile readily.

Abruptly, Max turned on his heel and strode into the card-room. He needed a drink.

CHAPTER EIGHT

ARABELLA SWATTED AT the bumble-bee blundering noisily by her head. She was lying on her stomach on the stone surround of the pond in the courtyard of Twyford House, idly trailing her fingers in the cool green water. Her delicate mull muslin, petal-pink in hue, clung revealingly to her curvaceous form while a straw hat protected her delicate complexion from the afternoon sun. Most other young ladies in a similar pose would have looked childish. Arabella, with her strangely wistful air, contrived to look mysteriously enchanting.

Her sisters were similarly at their ease. Sarah was propped by the base of the sundial, her *bergère* hat shading her face as she threaded daisies into a chain. The dark green cambric gown she wore emphasized her arrestingly pale face, dominated by huge brown eyes, darkened now by the hint of misery. Lizzie sat beside the rockery, poking at a piece of embroidery with a noticeable lack of enthusiasm. Her sprigged mauve muslin proclaimed her youth yet its effect was ameliorated by her far from youthful figure.

Caroline watched her sisters from her perch in a cushioned hammock strung between two cherry trees.

If her guardian could have seen her, he would undoubtedly have approved of the simple round gown of particularly fine amber muslin she had donned for the warm day. The fabric clung tantalizingly to her mature figure while the neckline revealed an expanse of soft ivory breasts.

The sisters had gradually drifted here, one by one, drawn by the warm spring afternoon and the heady scents rising from the rioting flowers which crammed the beds and overflowed on to the stone flags. The period between luncheon and the obligatory appearance in the Park was a quiet time they were coming increasingly to appreciate as the Season wore on. Whenever possible, they tended to spend it together, a last vestige, Caroline thought, of the days when they had only had each other for company.

Sarah sighed. She laid aside her hat and looped the completed daisy chain around her neck. Cramming her headgear back over her dark curls, she said, "Well, what are we going to do?"

Three pairs of eyes turned her way. When no answer was forthcoming, she continued, explaining her case with all reasonableness, "Well, we can't go on as we are, can we? None of us is getting anywhere."

Arabella turned on her side better to view her sisters. "But what can we do? In your case, Lord Darcy's not even in London."

"True," returned the practical Sarah. "But it's just occurred to me that he must have friends still in London. Ones who would write to him, I mean. Other than our guardian."

Caroline grinned. "Whatever you do, my love, kindly explain all to me before you set the *ton* ablaze. I don't think I could stomach our guardian demanding an explanation and not having one to give him."

Sarah chuckled. "Has he been difficult?"

But Caroline would only smile, a secret smile of which both Sarah and Arabella took due note.

"He hasn't said anything about me, has he?" came Lizzie's slightly breathless voice. Under her sisters' gaze, she blushed. "About me and Martin," she mumbled, suddenly becoming engrossed in her *petit point*.

Arabella laughed. "Artful puss. As things stand, you're the only one with all sails hoisted and a clear wind blowing. The rest of us are becalmed, for one reason or another."

Caroline's brow had furrowed. "Why do you ask? Has Max given you any reason to suppose he disapproves?"

"Well," temporized Lizzie, "he doesn't seem entirely...happy, about us seeing so much of each other."

Her attachment to Martin Rotherbridge had progressed in leaps and bounds. Despite Max's warning and his own innate sense of danger, Martin had not been able to resist the temptation posed by Lizzie Twinning. From that first undeniably innocent kiss he had, by subtle degrees, led her to the point where, finding herself in his arms in the gazebo in Lady Malling's garden, she had permitted him to kiss her again. Only this time, it had been Martin leading the way. Lizzie, all innocence, had been thoroughly enthralled by the experience and stunned by her own response to the delightful sensations it had engendered. Unbeknownst to her, Martin Rotherbridge had been stunned, too.

Belatedly, he had tried to dampen his own increasing desires, only to find, as his brother could have told him, that that was easier imagined than accomplished. Abstinence had only led to intemperance. In the end, he had capitulated and returned to spend every moment possible at Lizzie's side, if not her feet.

Lizzie was right in her assessment that Max disapproved of their association but wrong in her idea of the cause. Only too well-acquainted with his brother's character, their guardian entertained a grave concern that the frustrations involved in behaving with decorum in the face of Lizzie Twinning's bounteous temptations would prove overwhelming long before Martin was brought to admit he was in love with the chit. His worst fears had seemed well on the way to being realized when he had, entirely unintentionally, surprised them on their way back to the ballroom. His sharp blue eyes had not missed the glow in Lizzie's face. Consequently, the look he had directed at his brother, which Lizzie had intercepted, had not been particularly encouraging. She had missed Martin's carefree response.

Caroline, reasonably certain of Max's thoughts on the matter, realized these might not be entirely clear to Lizzie. But how to explain Max's doubts of his own brother to the still innocent Lizzie? Despite the fact that only a year separated her from Arabella, the disparity in their understandings, particularly with respect to the male of the species, was enormous. All three elder Twinnings had inherited both looks and dispositions from their father's family, which in part explained his aversion to women. Thomas Twinning had witnessed firsthand the dance his sisters had led all the men of their acquaintance before finally settling in happily wedded bliss. The strain on his father and himself had been considerable. Consequently, the discovery that his daughters were entirely from the same mould had prompted him to immure them in rural seclusion. Lizzie, however, had only inherited the Twinning looks, her gentle and often quite stubborn innocence deriving from the placid Eleanor. Viewing the troubled face of her youngest half-sister, Caroline decided the time had come to at least try to suggest to Lizzie's mind that there was often more to life than the strictly obvious. Aside from anything else, this time, she had both Sarah and Arabella beside her to help explain.

"I rather think, my love," commenced Caroline, "that it's not that Max would disapprove of the connection. His concern is more for your good name."

Lizzie's puzzled frown gave no indication of lightening. "But why should my being with his brother endanger my good name?"

Sarah gave an unladylike snort of laughter. "Oh, Lizzie, love! You're going to have to grow up, my dear. Our guardian's concerned because he knows what his brother's like and that, generally speaking, young ladies are not safe with him."

The effect of this forthright speech on Lizzie was galvanizing. Her eyes blazed in defence of her absent love. "Martin's not like that at all!"

"Oh, sweetheart, you're going to have to open your eyes!" Arabella bought into the discussion, sitting up the better to do so. "He's not only 'like that,' Martin Rotherbridge has made a career specializing in being 'like that.' He's a rake. The same as Hugo and Darcy Hamilton, too. And, of course, the greatest rake of them all is our dear guardian, who has his eye firmly set on Caro here. Rakes and Twinnings go together, I'm afraid. We attract them and they—" she put her head on one side, considering her words "—well, they attract us. It's no earthly good disputing the evidence."

Seeing the perturbation in Lizzie's face, Caroline sought to reassure her. "That doesn't mean that the end result is not just the same as if they were more conservative. It's just that, well, it very likely takes longer for such men to accept the…the desirability of marriage." Her eyes flicked to Sarah who, head bent and eyes intent on her fingers, was plaiting more daisies. "Time will, I suspect, eventually bring them around. The danger is in the waiting."

Lizzie was following her sister's discourse with difficulty. "But Martin's never…well, you know, tried to make love to me."

"Do you mean to say he's never kissed you?" asked Arabella in clear disbelief.

Lizzie blushed. "Yes. But I kissed him first."

"Lizzie!" The startled exclamation was drawn from all three sisters who promptly thereafter fell about laughing. Arabella was the last to recover. "Oh, my dear, you're more a Twinning than we'd thought!"

"Well, it was nice, I thought," said Lizzie, fast losing her reticence in the face of her sisters' teasing. "Anyway, what am I supposed to do? Avoid him? That wouldn't be much fun. And I don't think I could stop him kissing me, somehow. I rather like being kissed."

"It's not the kissing itself that's the problem," stated Sarah. "It's what comes next. And that's even more difficult to stop."

"Very true," confirmed Arabella, studying her slippered toes. "But if you want lessons in how to hold a rake at arm's length you shouldn't look to me. Nor to Sarah either. It's only Caro who's managed to hold her own so far." Arabella's eyes started to dance as they rested on her eldest sister's calm face. "But, I suspect, that's only because our dear guardian is playing a deep game."

Caroline blushed slightly, then reluctantly smiled. "Unfortunately, I'm forced to agree with you."

A silence fell as all four sisters pondered their rakes. Eventually, Caroline spoke. "Sarah, what are you planning?"

Sarah wriggled her shoulders against the sundial's pedestal. "Well, it occurred to me that perhaps I should make some effort to bring things to a head. But if I did the obvious, and started wildly flirting with a whole bevy of gentlemen, then most likely I'd only land myself in the suds. For a start, Darcy would very likely not believe it and I'd probably end with a very odd reputation. I'm not good at it, like Bella."

Arabella put her head on one side, the better to observe her sister. "I could give you lessons," she offered.

"No," said Caroline. "Sarah's right. It wouldn't wash." She turned to Lizzie to say, "Another problem, my love, is that rakes know all the tricks, so bamming them is very much harder."

"Too true," echoed Arabella. She turned again to Sarah. "But if not that, what, then?"

A wry smile touched Sarah's lips. "I rather thought the pose of the maiden forlorn might better suit me. Nothing too obvious, just a subtle withdrawing. I'd still go to all the parties and balls, but I'd just become quieter and ever so gradually, let my…what's the word, Caro? My despair? My broken heart? Well, whatever it is, show through."

Her sisters considered her plan and found nothing to criticise. Caroline summed up their verdict. "In truth, my dear, there's precious little else you could do."

Sarah's eyes turned to Arabella. "But what are you going to do about Lord Denbigh?"

Arabella's attention had returned to her toes. She wrinkled her pert nose. "I really don't know. I can't make him jealous; as Caro said, he knows all those tricks. And the forlorn act would not do for me."

Arabella had tried every means possible to tie down the elusive Hugo but that large gentleman seemed to view her attempts with sleepy humour, only bestirring himself to take advantage of any tactical error she made. At such times, as Arabella had found to her confusion and consternation, he could move with ruthless efficiency. She was now very careful not to leave any opening he could exploit to be private with her.

"Why not try...?" Caroline broke off, suddenly assailed by a twinge of guilt at encouraging her sisters in their scheming. But, under the enquiring gaze of Sarah and Arabella, not to mention Lizzie, drinking it all in, she mentally shrugged and continued. "As you cannot convince him of your real interest in any other gentleman, you'd be best not to try, I agree. But you could let him understand that, as he refused to offer marriage, and you, as a virtuous young lady, are prevented from accepting any other sort of offer, then, with the utmost reluctance and the deepest regret, you have been forced to turn aside and consider accepting the attentions of some other gentleman."

Arabella stared at her sister. Then, her eyes started to dance. "Oh, Caro!" she breathed. "What a perfectly marvellous plan!"

"Shouldn't be too hard for you to manage," said Sarah. "Who are the best of your court for the purpose? You don't want to raise any overly high expectations on their parts but you've loads of experience in playing that game."

Arabella was already deep in thought. "Sir Humphrey Bullard, I think. And Mr. Stone. They're both sober enough and in no danger of falling in love with me. They're quite coldly calculating in their approach to matrimony; I doubt they have hearts to lose. They both want an attractive wife, preferably with money, who would not expect too much attention from them. To their minds, I'm close to perfect but to scramble for my favours would be beneath them. They should be perfect for my charade."

Caroline nodded. "They sound just the thing."

"Good! I'll start tonight," said Arabella, decision burning in her huge eyes.

"But what about you, Caro?" asked Sarah with a grin. "We've discussed how the rest of us should go on, but you've yet to tell us how you plan to bring our dear guardian to his knees."

Caroline smiled, the same gently wistful smile that frequently played upon her lips these days. "If I knew that, my dears, I'd certainly tell you." The last weeks had seen a continuation of the unsatisfactory relationship between His Grace of Twyford and his eldest ward. Wary of his ability to take possession of her senses should she give him the opportunity, Caroline had consistently avoided his invitations to dally alone with him. Indeed, too often in recent times her mind had been engaged in keeping a watchful eye over her sisters, something their perceptive guardian seemed to understand. She could not fault him for his support and was truly grateful for the understated manner in which he frequently set aside his own inclinations to assist her in her concern for her siblings. In fact, it had occurred to her that, far from being a lazy guardian, His Grace of Twyford was very much *au fait* with the activities of each of his wards. Lately, it had seemed to her that her sisters' problems were deflecting a considerable amount of his energies from his pursuit of herself. So, with a twinkle in her eyes, she said, "If truth be told, the best plan I can think of to further my own ends is to assist you all in achieving your goals as soon as may be. Once free of you three, perhaps our dear guardian will be able to concentrate on me."

IT WAS LIZZIE who initiated the Twinning sisters' friendship with the two Crowbridge girls, also being presented that year. The Misses Crowbridge, Alice and Amanda, were very pretty young ladies in the manner which had been all the rage until the Twinnings came to town. They were pale and fair, as ethereal as the Twinnings were earthy, as fragile as the Twinnings were robust, and, unfortunately for them, as penniless as the Twinnings were rich. Consequently, the push to find well-heeled husbands for the Misses Crowbridge had not prospered.

Strolling down yet another ballroom, Lady Mott's as it happened, on the arm of Martin, of course, Lizzie had caught the sharp words uttered by a large woman of horsey mien to a young lady, presumably her daughter, sitting passively at her side. "Why can't you two be like that? Those girls simply walk off with any man they fancy. All it needs is a bit of push. But you and Alice…" The rest of the tirade had been swallowed up by the hubbub around them. But the words returned to

Lizzie later, when, retiring to the withdrawing-room to mend her hem which Martin very carelessly had stood upon, she found the room empty except for the same young lady, huddled in a pathetic bundle, trying to stifle her sobs.

As a kind heart went hand in hand with Lizzie's innocence, it was not long before she had befriended Amanda Crowbridge and learned of the difficulty facing both Amanda and Alice. Lacking the Twinning sisters' confidence and abilities, the two girls, thrown without any preparation into the heady world of the *ton*, found it impossible to converse with the elegant gentlemen, becoming tongue-tied and shy, quite unable to attach the desired suitors. To Lizzie, the solution was obvious.

Both Arabella and Sarah, despite having other fish to fry, were perfectly willing to act as tutors to the Crowbridge girls. Initially, they agreed to this more as a favour to Lizzie than from any more magnanimous motive, but as the week progressed they became quite absorbed with their protégées. For the Crowbridge girls, being taken under the collective wing of the three younger Twinnings brought a cataclysmic change to their social standing. Instead of being left to decorate the wall, they now spent their time firmly embedded amid groups of chattering young people. Drawn ruthlessly into conversations by the artful Arabella or Sarah at her most prosaic, they discovered that talking to the swells of the *ton* was not, after all, so very different from conversing with the far less daunting lads at home. Under the steady encouragement provided by the Twinnings, the Crowbridge sisters slowly unfurled their petals.

Caroline and His Grace of Twyford watched the growing friendship from a distance and were pleased to approve, though for very different reasons. Having ascertained that the Crowbridges were perfectly acceptable acquaintances, although their mother, for all her breeding, was, as Lady Benborough succinctly put it, rather too pushy, Caroline was merely pleased that her sisters had found some less than scandalous distraction from their romantic difficulties. Max, on the other hand, was quick to realize that with the three younger girls busily engaged in this latest exploit, which kept them safely in the ballrooms and salons, he stood a much better chance of successfully spending some time, in less populated surroundings, with his eldest ward.

In fact, as the days flew past, his success in his chosen endeavour became so marked that Caroline was forced openly to refuse any attempt to detach her from her circle. She had learned that their relationship had become the subject of rampant speculation and was now seriously concerned at the possible repercussions, for herself, for her sisters and for him. Max, reading her mind with consummate ease, paid her protestations not the slightest heed. Finding herself once more in His Grace's arms and, as usual, utterly helpless, Caroline was moved to remonstrate. "What on earth do you expect to accomplish by all this? I'm your *ward,* for heaven's sake!"

A deep chuckle answered her. Engaged in tracing her left brow, first with one long finger, then with his lips, Max had replied, "Consider your time spent with me as an educational experience, sweet Caro. As Aunt Augusta was so eager to point out," he continued, transferring his attention to her other brow, "who better than your guardian to demonstrate the manifold dangers to be met with among the *ton?*"

She was prevented from telling him what she thought of his reasoning, in fact, was prevented from thinking at all, when his lips moved to claim hers and she was swept away on a tide of sensation she was coming to appreciate all too well. Emerging, much later, pleasantly witless, she found herself the object of His Grace's heavy-lidded blue gaze. "Tell me, my dear, if you were not my ward, would you consent to be private with me?"

Mentally adrift, Caroline blinked in an effort to focus her mind. For the life of her she could not understand his question, although the answer seemed clear enough. "Of course not!" she lied, trying unsuccessfully to ease herself from his shockingly close embrace.

A slow smile spread across Max's face. As the steel bands around her tightened, Caroline was sure he was laughing at her.

Another deep chuckle, sending shivers up and down her spine, confirmed her suspicion. Max bent his head until his lips brushed hers. Then, he drew back slightly and blue eyes locked with grey. "In that case, sweet ward, you have some lessons yet to learn."

Bewildered, Caroline would have asked for enlightenment but, reading her intent in her eyes, Max avoided her question by the simple expedient of kissing her again. Irritated by his cat-and-mouse tactics, Caroline tried to withdraw from participation in this strange game whose rules were incomprehensible to her. But she quickly learned that His Grace of Twyford had no intention of letting her backslide. Driven, in the end, to surrender to the greater force, Caroline relaxed, melting into his arms, yielding body, mind and soul to his experienced conquest.

IT WAS AT Lady Richardson's ball that Sir Ralph Keighly first appeared as a cloud on the Twinnings's horizon. Or, more correctly, on the Misses Crowbridge's horizon, although by that stage, it was much the same thing. Sir Ralph, with a tidy estate in Gloucestershire, was in London to look for a wife. His taste, it appeared, ran to sweet young things of the type personified by the Crowbridge sisters, Amanda Crowbridge in particular. Unfortunately for him, Sir Ralph was possessed of an overwhelming self-conceit combined with an unprepossessing appearance. He was thus vetoed on sight as beneath consideration by the Misses Crowbridge and their mentors.

However, Sir Ralph was rather more wily than he appeared. Finding his attentions to Amanda Crowbridge compromised by the competing attractions of the large number of more personable young men who formed the combined Twinning-Crowbridge court, he retired from the lists and devoted his energies to cultivating Mr. and

Mrs. Crowbridge. In this, he achieved such notable success that he was invited to attend Lady Richardson's ball with the Crowbridges. Despite the tearful protestations of both Amanda and Alice at his inclusion in their party, when they crossed the threshold of Lady Richardson's ballroom, Amanda, looking distinctly seedy, had her hand on Sir Ralph's arm.

At her parents' stern instruction, she was forced to endure two waltzes with Sir Ralph. As Arabella acidly observed, if it had been at all permissible, doubtless Amanda would have been forced to remain at his side for the entire ball. As it was, she dared not join her friends for supper but, drooping with dejection, joined Sir Ralph and her parents.

To the three Twinnings, the success of Sir Ralph was like waving a red rag to a bull. Without exception, they took it as interference in their, up until then, successful development of their protégées. Even Lizzie was, metaphorically speaking, hopping mad. But the amenities offered by a ball were hardy conducive to a council of war, so, with admirable restraint, the three younger Twinnings devoted themselves assiduously to their own pursuits and left the problem of Sir Ralph until they had leisure to deal with it appropriately.

Sarah was now well down the road to being acknowledged as having suffered an unrequited love. She bore up nobly under the strain but it was somehow common knowledge that she held little hope of recovery. Her brave face, it was understood, was on account of her sisters, as she did not wish to ruin their Season by retiring into seclusion, despite this being her most ardent wish. Her large brown eyes, always fathomless, and her naturally pale and serious face were welcome aids in the projection of her new persona. She danced and chatted, yet the vitality that had burned with her earlier in the Season had been dampened. That, at least, was no more than the truth.

Arabella, all were agreed, was settling down to the sensible prospect of choosing a suitable connection. As Hugo Denbigh had contrived to be considerably more careful in his attentions to Arabella than Darcy Hamilton had been with Sarah, the gossips had never connected the two. Consequently, the fact that Lord Denbigh's name was clearly absent from Arabella's list did not in itself cause comment. But, as the Twinning sisters had been such a hit, the question of who precisely Arabella would choose was a popular topic for discussion. Speculation was rife and, as was often the case in such matters, a number of wagers had already been entered into the betting books held by the gentlemen's clubs. According to rumour, both Mr. Stone and Sir Humphrey Bullard featured as possible candidates. Yet not the most avid watcher could discern which of these gentlemen Miss Arabella favoured.

Amid all this drama, Lizzie Twinning continued as she always had, accepting the respectful attentions of the sober young men who sought her out while reserving her most brilliant smiles for Martin Rotherbridge. As she was so young and as Martin wisely refrained from any overtly amorous or possessive act in public, most observers assumed he was merely helping his brother with what must, all were agreed, constitute a definite handful. Martin, finding her increasingly difficult to lead astray, was forced to live with his growing frustrations and their steadily diminishing prospects for release.

The change in Amanda Crowbridge's fortunes brought a frown to Caroline's face. She would not have liked the connection for any of her sisters. Still, Amanda Crowbridge was not her concern. As her sisters appeared to have taken the event philosophically enough, she felt justified in giving it no further thought, reserving her energies, mental and otherwise, for her increasingly frequent interludes with her guardian.

Despite her efforts to minimize his opportunities, she found herself sharing his carriage on their return journey to Mount Street. Miriam Alford sat beside her and Max, suavely elegant and exuding a subtle aura of powerful sensuality, had taken the seat opposite her. Lady Benborough and her three sisters were following in the Twyford coach. As Caroline had suspected, their chaperon fell into a sound sleep before the carriage had cleared the Richardson House drive.

Gazing calmly at the moonlit fields, she calculated they had at least a forty-minute drive ahead of them. She waited patiently for the move she was sure would come and tried to marshal her resolve to deflect it. As the minutes ticked by, the damning knowledge slowly seeped into her consciousness that, if her guardian was to suddenly become afflicted with propriety and the journey was accomplished without incident, far from being relieved, she would feel let down, cheated of an eagerly anticipated treat. She frowned, recognizing her already racing pulse and the tense knot in her stomach that restricted her breathing for the symptoms they were. On the thought, she raised her eyes to the dark face before her.

He was watching the countryside slip by, the silvery light etching the planes of his face. As if feeling her gaze, he turned and his eyes met hers. For a moment, he read her thoughts and Caroline was visited by the dreadful certainty that he knew the truth she was struggling to hide. Then, a slow, infinitely wicked smile spread across his face. Caroline stopped breathing. He leaned forward. She expected him to take her hand and draw her to sit beside him. Instead, his strong hands slipped about her waist and, to her utter astonishment, he lifted her across and deposited her in a swirl of silks on his lap.

"Max!" she gasped.

"Sssh. You don't want to wake Mrs. Alford. She'd have palpitations."

Horrified, Caroline tried to get her feet to the ground, wriggling against the firm clasp about her waist. Almost immediately, Max's voice sounded in her ear, in a tone quite different from any she had previously heard. "Sweetheart, unless you cease wriggling your delightful *derriére* in such an enticing fashion, this lesson is likely to go rather further than I had intended."

Caroline froze. She held her breath, not daring to so

much as twitch. Then Max's voice, the raw tones of an instant before no longer in evidence, washed over her in warm approval. "Much better."

She turned to face him, carefully keeping her hips still. She placed her hands on his chest in an effort, futile, she knew, to fend him off. "Max, this is madness. You must stop doing this!"

"Why? Don't you like it?" His hands were moving gently on her back, his touch scorching through the thin silk of her gown.

Caroline ignored the sardonic lift of his black brows and the clear evidence in his eyes that he was laughing at her. She found it much harder to ignore the sensations his hands were drawing forth. Forcing her face into strongly disapproving lines, she answered his first question, deeming it prudent to conveniently forget the second. "I'm your *ward,* remember? You know I am. You told me so yourself."

"A fact you should strive to bear in mind, my dear."

Caroline wondered what he meant by that. But Max's mind, and hands, had shifted their focus of attention. As his hands closed over her breasts, Caroline nearly leapt to her feet. *"Max!"*

But, "Sssh," was all her guardian said as his lips settled on hers.

CHAPTER NINE

THE TWYFORD COACH was also the scene of considerable activity, though of a different sort. Augusta, in sympathy with Mrs. Alford, quickly settled into a comfortable doze which the whisperings of the other occupants of the carriage did nothing to disturb. Lizzie, Sarah and Arabella, incensed by Amanda's misfortune, spent some minutes giving vent to their feelings.

"It's not as if Sir Ralph's such a good catch, even," Sarah commented.

"Certainly not," agreed Lizzie with uncharacteristic sharpness. "It's really too bad! Why, Mr. Minchbury is almost at the point of offering for her and he has a much bigger estate, besides being much more attractive. And Amanda *likes* him, what's more."

"Ah," said Arabella, wagging her head sagely, "but he's not been making up to Mrs. Crowbridge, has he? That woman must be all about in her head, to think of giving little Amanda to Keighly."

"Well," said Sarah decisively, "what are we going to do about it?"

Silence reigned for more than a mile as the sisters considered the possibilities. Arabella eventually spoke into the darkness. "I doubt we'd get far discussing matters with the Crowbridges."

"Very true," nodded Sarah. "And working on Amanda's equally pointless. She's too timid."

"Which leaves Sir Ralph," concluded Lizzie. After a pause, she went on: "I know we're not precisely to his taste, but do you think you could do it, Bella?"

Arabella's eyes narrowed as she considered Sir Ralph. Thanks to Hugo, she now had a fairly extensive understanding of the basic attraction between men and women. Sir Ralph was, after all, still a man. She shrugged. "Well, it's worth a try. I really can't see what else we can do."

For the remainder of the journey, the sisters' heads were together, hatching a plan.

ARABELLA STARTED HER campaign to steal Sir Ralph from Amanda the next evening, much to the delight of Amanda. When she was informed in a whispered aside of the Twinnings' plan for her relief, Amanda's eyes had grown round. Swearing to abide most faithfully by any instructions they might give her, she had managed to survive her obligatory two waltzes with Sir Ralph in high spirits, which Sarah later informed her was not at all helpful. Chastised, she begged pardon and remained by Sarah's side as Arabella took to the floor with her intended.

As Sir Ralph had no real affection for Amanda, it took very little of Arabella's practised flattery to make him increasingly turn his eyes her way. But, to the

Twinnings' consternation, their plan almost immediately developed a hitch.

Their guardian was not at all pleased to see Sir Ralph squiring Arabella. A message from him, relayed by both Caroline and Lady Benborough, to the effect that Arabella should watch her step, pulled Arabella up short. A hasty conference, convened in the withdrawing-room, agreed there was no possibility of gaining His Grace's approval for their plan. Likewise, none of the three sisters had breathed a word of their scheme to Caroline, knowing that, despite her affection for them, there were limits to her forbearance.

"But we can't just give up!" declared Lizzie in trenchant tones.

Arabella was nibbling the end of one finger. "No. We won't give up. But we'll have to reorganize. You two," she said, looking at Sarah and Lizzie, quite ignoring Amanda and Alice who were also present, "are going to have to cover for me. That way, I won't be obviously spending so much time with Sir Ralph, but he'll still be thinking about me. You must tell Sir Ralph that our guardian disapproves but that, as I'm head over heels in love with him, I'm willing to go against the Duke's wishes and continue to see him." She frowned, pondering her scenario. "We'll have to be careful not to paint our dear guardian in too strict colours. The story is that we're sure he'll eventually come around, when he sees how attached I am to Sir Ralph. Max knows I'm a flighty, flirtatious creature and so doubts of the strength of my affections. That should be believable enough."

"All right," Sarah nodded. "We'll do the groundwork and you administer the *coup de grâce*."

And so the plan progressed.

For Arabella, the distraction of Sir Ralph came at an opportune time in her juggling of Sir Humphrey and Mr. Stone. It formed no part of her plans for either of these gentlemen to become too particular. And while her sober and earnest consideration of their suits had, she knew, stunned and puzzled Lord Denbigh, who watched with a still sceptical eye, her flirtation with Sir Ralph had brought a strange glint to his hazel orbs.

In truth, Hugo had been expecting Arabella to flirt outrageously with her court in an attempt to make him jealous and force a declaration. He had been fully prepared to sit idly by, watching her antics from the sidelines with his usual sleepily amused air, waiting for the right moment to further her seduction. But her apparent intention to settle for a loveless marriage had thrown him. It was not a reaction he had expected. Knowing what he did of Arabella, he could not stop himself from thinking what a waste it would be. True, as the wife of a much older man, she was likely to be even more receptive to his own suggestions of a discreet if illicit relationship. But the idea of her well-endowed charms being brutishly enjoyed by either of her ageing suitors set his teeth on edge. Her sudden pursuit of Sir Ralph Keighly, in what he was perceptive enough to know was not her normal style, seriously troubled him, suggesting as it did some deeper intent. He wondered whether she knew what she was about. The fact that she continued to encourage Keighly despite Twyford's clear disapproval further increased his unease.

Arabella, sensing his perturbation, continued to tread the difficult path she had charted, one eye on him, the other on her guardian, encouraging Sir Ralph with one hand while using the other to hold back Sir Humphrey and Mr. Stone. As she confessed to her sisters one morning, it was exhausting work.

Little by little, she gained ground with Sir Ralph, their association camouflaged by her sisters' ploys. On the way back to the knot of their friends, having satisfactorily twirled around Lady Summerhill's ballroom, Arabella and Sir Ralph were approached by a little lady, all in brown.

Sir Ralph stiffened.

The unknown lady blushed. "How do you do?" she said, taking in both Arabella and Sir Ralph in her glance. "I'm Harriet Jenkins," she explained helpfully to Arabella, then, turning to Sir Ralph, said, "Hello, Ralph," in quite the most wistful tone Arabella had ever heard.

Under Arabella's interested gaze, Sir Ralph became tongue-tied. He perforce bowed over the small hand held out to him and managed to say, "Mr. Jenkins's estates border mine."

Arabella's eyes switched to Harriet Jenkins. "My father," she supplied.

Sir Ralph suddenly discovered someone he had to exchange a few words with and precipitately left them. Arabella looked down into Miss Jenkins's large eyes, brown, of course, and wondered. "Have you lately come to town, Miss Jenkins?"

Harriet Jenkins drew her eyes from Sir Ralph's departing figure and dispassionately viewed the beauty before her. What she saw in the frank hazel eyes prompted her to reply, "Yes. I was…bored at home. So my father suggested I come to London for a few weeks. I'm staying with my aunt, Lady Cottesloe."

Arabella was only partly satisfied with this explanation. Candid to a fault, she put the question in her mind. "Pardon me, Miss Jenkins, but are you and Sir Ralph…?"

Miss Jenkins's wistfulness returned. "No. Oh, you're right in thinking I want him. But Ralph has other ideas. I've known him from the cradle, you see. And I suppose familiarity breeds contempt." Suddenly realizing to whom she was speaking, she blushed and continued, "Not that I could hope to hold a candle to the London beauties, of course."

Her suspicions confirmed, Arabella merely laughed and slipped an arm through Miss Jenkins's. "Oh, I shouldn't let that bother you, my dear." As she said the words, it occurred to her that, if anything, Sir Ralph was uncomfortable and awkward when faced with beautiful women, as evidenced by his behaviour with either herself or Amanda. It was perfectly possible that some of his apparent conceit would drop away when he felt less threatened; for instance, in the presence of Miss Jenkins.

Miss Jenkins had stiffened at Arabella's touch and

her words. Then, realizing the kindly intent behind them, she relaxed. "Well, there's no sense in deceiving myself. I suppose I shouldn't say so, but Ralph and I were in a fair way to being settled before he took this latest notion of looking about before he made up his mind irrevocably. I sometimes think it was simply fear of tying the knot that did it."

"Very likely," Arabella laughingly agreed as she steered Miss Jenkins in the direction of her sisters.

"My papa was furious and said I should give him up. But I convinced him to let me come to London, to see how things stood. Now, I suppose, I may as well go home."

"Oh, on no account should you go home yet awhile, Miss Jenkins!" said Arabella, a decided twinkle in her eye. "May I call you Harriet? Harriet, I'd like you to meet my sisters."

THE ADVENT OF Harriet Jenkins caused a certain amount of reworking of the Twinnings' plan for Sir Ralph. After due consideration, she was taken into their confidence and willingly joined the small circle of conspirators. In truth, her appearance relieved Arabella's mind of a nagging worry over how she was to let Sir Ralph down after Amanda accepted Mr. Minchbury, who, under the specific guidance of Lizzie, was close to popping the question. Now, all she had to do was to play the hardened flirt and turn Sir Ralph's bruised ego into Harriet's tender care. All in all, things were shaping up nicely.

However, to their dismay, the Twinnings found that

Mrs. Crowbridge was not yet vanquished. The news of her latest ploy was communicated to them two days later, at Beckenham, where they had gone to watch a balloon ascent. The intrepid aviators had yet to arrive at the field, so the three Twinnings had descended from their carriage and, together with the Misses Crowbridge and Miss Jenkins, were strolling elegantly about the field, enjoying the afternoon sunshine and a not inconsiderable amount of male attention. It transpired that Mrs. Crowbridge had invited Sir Ralph to pay a morning call and then, on the slightest of pretexts, had left him alone with Amanda for quite twenty minutes. Such brazen tactics left them speechless. Sir Ralph, to do him justice, had not taken undue advantage.

"He probably didn't have time to work out the odds against getting Arabella versus the benefits of Amanda," said Sarah with a grin. "Poor man! I can almost pity him, what with Mrs. Crowbridge after him as well."

All the girls grinned but their thoughts quickly returned to their primary preoccupation. "Yes, but," said Lizzie, voicing a fear already in both Sarah's and Arabella's minds, "if Mrs. Crowbridge keeps behaving like this, she might force Sir Ralph to offer for Amanda by tricking him into compromising her."

"I'm afraid that's only too possible," agreed Harriet. "Ralph's very gullible." She shook her head in such a deploring way that Arabella and Sarah were hard put to it to smother their giggles.

"Yes, but it won't do," said Amanda, suddenly. "I know my mother. She'll keep on and on until she succeeds. You've got to think of some way of…of removing Sir Ralph quickly."

"For his sake as well as your own," agreed Harriet. "The only question is, how?"

Silence descended while this conundrum revolved in their minds. Further conversation on the topic was necessarily suspended when they were joined by a number of gentlemen disinclined to let the opportunity of paying court to such a gaggle of very lovely young ladies pass by. As His Grace of Twyford's curricle was conspicuously placed among the carriages drawn up to the edge of the field, the behaviour of said gentlemen remained every bit as deferential as within the confines of Almack's, despite the sylvan setting.

Mr. Mallard was the first to reach Lizzie's side, closely followed by Mr. Swanston and Lord Brookfell. Three other fashionable exquisites joined the band around Lizzie, Amanda, Alice and Harriet, and within minutes an unexceptionable though thoroughly merry party had formed. Hearing one young gentleman allude to the delicate and complementary tints of the dresses of the four younger girls as "pretty as a posy," Sarah could not resist a grimace, purely for Arabella's benefit. Arabella bit hard on her lip to stifle her answering giggle. Both fell back a step or two from the younger crowd, only to fall victim to their own admirers.

Sir Humphrey Bullard, a large man of distinctly florid countenance, attempted to capture Arabella's undivided attention but was frustrated by the simultaneous arrival of Mr. Stone, sleekly saturnine, on her other side. Both offered their arms, leaving Arabella, with a sunshade to juggle, in a quandary. She laughed and shook her head at them both. "Indeed, gentlemen, you put me to the blush. What can a lady do under such circumstances?"

"Why, make your choice, m'dear," drawled Mr. Stone, a strangely determined glint in his eye.

Arabella's eyes widened at this hint that Mr. Stone, at least, was not entirely happy with being played on a string. She was rescued by Mr. Humphrey, irritatingly aware that he did not cut such a fine figure as Mr. Stone. "I see the balloonists have arrived. Perhaps you'd care to stroll to the enclosure and watch the inflation, Miss Arabella?"

"We'll need to get closer if we're to see anything at all," said Sarah, coming up on the arm of Lord Tulloch.

By the time they reached the area cordoned off in the centre of the large field, a crowd had gathered. The balloon was already filling slowly. As they watched, it lifted from the ground and slowly rose to hover above the cradle slung beneath, anchored to the ground by thick ropes.

"It looks like such a flimsy contraption," said Arabella, eyeing the gaily striped silk balloon. "I wonder that anyone could trust themselves to it."

"They don't always come off unscathed, I'm sorry to say," answered Mr. Stone, his schoolmasterish tones evincing strong disapproval of such reckless behaviour.

"Humph!" said Sir Humphrey Bullard.

Arabella's eyes met Sarah's in mute supplication. Sarah grinned.

It was not until the balloon had taken off, successfully, to Arabella's relief, and the crowd had started to disperse that the Twinnings once more had leisure to contemplate the problem of Sir Ralph Keighly. Predictably, it was Sarah and Arabella who conceived the plot. In a few whispered sentences, they developed its outline sufficiently to see that it would require great attention to detail to make it work. As they would have no further chance that day to talk with the others in private, they made plans to meet the next morning at Twyford House. Caroline had mentioned her intention of visiting her old nurse, who had left the Twinnings' employ after her mother had died and hence was unknown to the younger Twinnings. Thus, ensconced in the back parlour of Twyford House, they would be able to give free rein to their thoughts. Clearly, the removal of Sir Ralph was becoming a matter of urgency.

Returning to their carriage, drawn up beside the elegant equipage bearing the Delmere crest, the three youngest Twinnings smiled serenely at their guardian, who watched them from the box seat of his curricle, a far from complaisant look in his eyes.

Max was, in fact, convinced that something was in the wind but had no idea what. His highly developed social antennae had picked up the undercurrents of his wards' plotting and their innocent smiles merely confirmed his suspicions. He was well aware that Caroline, seated beside him in a fetching gown of figured muslin, was not privy to their schemes. As he headed his team from the field, he smiled. His eldest ward had had far too much on her mind recently to have had any time free for scheming.

Beside him, Caroline remained in blissful ignorance of her sisters' aims. She had spent a thoroughly enjoyable day in the company of her guardian and was in charity with the world. They had had an excellent view of the ascent itself from the height of the box seat of the curricle. And when she had evinced the desire to stroll among the crowds, Max had readily escorted her, staying attentively by her side, his acerbic comments forever entertaining and, for once, totally unexceptionable. She looked forward to the drive back to Mount Street with unimpaired calm, knowing that in the curricle, she ran no risk of being subjected to another of His Grace's "lessons." In fact, she was beginning to wonder how many more lessons there could possibly be before the graduation ceremony. The thought brought a sleepy smile to her face. She turned to study her guardian.

His attention was wholly on his horses, the bays, as sweet a pair as she had ever seen. Her eyes fell to his hands as they tooled the reins, strong and sure. Remembering the sensations those hands had drawn forth as they had knowledgeably explored her body, she caught her breath and rapidly looked away. Keeping her eyes fixed on the passing landscape, she forced her thoughts into safer fields.

The trouble with Max Rotherbridge was that he invaded her thoughts, too, and, as in other respects, was well-nigh impossible to deny. She was fast coming to the conclusion that she should simply forget all else and give herself up to the exquisite excitements she found in his arms. All the social and moral strictures ever intoned, all her inhibitions seemed to be consumed to ashes in the fire of her desire. She was beginning to feel it was purely a matter of time before she succumbed. The fact that the idea did not fill her with trepidation but rather with a pleasant sense of anticipation was in itself, she felt, telling.

As the wheels hit the cobbles and the noise that was London closed in around them, her thoughts flew ahead to Lady Benborough, who had stayed at home recruiting her energies for the ball that night. It was only this morning, when, with Max, she had bid her ladyship goodbye, that the oddity in Augusta's behaviour had struck her. While the old lady had been assiduous in steering the girls through the shoals of the acceptable gentlemen of the *ton,* she had said nothing about her eldest charge's association with her nephew. No matter how Caroline viewed it, invoke what reason she might, there was something definitely odd about that. As she herself had heard the rumours about His Grace of Twyford's very strange relationship with his eldest ward, it was inconceivable that Lady Benborough had not been edified with their tales. However, far from urging her to behave with greater discretion towards Max, impossible task though that might be, Augusta continued to

behave as if there was nothing at all surprising in Max
Rotherbridge escorting his wards to a balloon ascent.
Caroline wondered what it was that Augusta knew that
she did not.

THE TWINNING SISTERS attended the opera later that week.
It was the first time they had been inside the ornate
structure that was the Opera House; their progress to
the box organized for them by their guardian was perforce slow as they gazed about them with interest. Once
inside the box itself, in a perfect position in the first
tier, their attention was quickly claimed by their fellow
opera-goers. The pit below was a teeming sea of heads;
the stylish crops of the fashionable young men who took
perverse delight in rubbing shoulders with the masses
bobbed amid the unkempt locks of the hoi polloi. But
it was upon the occupants of the other boxes that the
Twinnings' principal interest focused. These quickly
filled as the time for the curtain to rise approached. All
four were absorbed in nodding and waving to friends
and acquaintances as the lights went out.

The first act consisted of a short piece by a little-
known Italian composer, as the prelude to the opera itself, which would fill the second and third acts, before
another short piece ended the performance. Caroline sat,
happily absorbed in the spectacle, beside and slightly in
front of her guardian. She was blissfully content. She
had merely made a comment to Max a week before that
she would like to visit the opera. Two days later, he had
arranged it all. Now she sat, superbly elegant in a sil-

ver satin slip overlaid with bronzed lace, and revelled in the music, conscious, despite her preoccupation, of the warmth of the Duke of Twyford's blue gaze on her bare shoulders.

Max watched her delight with satisfaction. He had long ago ceased to try to analyze his reactions to Caroline Twinning; he was besotted and knew it. Her happiness had somehow become his happiness; in his view, nothing else mattered. As he watched, she turned and smiled, a smile of genuine joy. It was, he felt, all the thanks he required for the effort organizing such a large box at short notice had entailed. He returned her smile, his own lazily sensual. For a moment, their eyes locked. Then, blushing, Caroline turned back to the stage.

Max had little real interest in the performance, his past experiences having had more to do with the singer than the song. He allowed his gaze to move past Caroline to dwell on her eldest half-sister. He had not yet fathomed exactly what Sarah's ambition was, yet felt sure it was not as simple as it appeared. The notion that any Twinning would meekly accept unwedded solitude as her lot was hard to swallow. As Sarah sat by Caroline's side, dramatic as ever in a gown of deepest green, the light from the stage lit her face. Her troubles had left no mark on the classical lines of brow and cheek but the peculiar light revealed more clearly than daylight the underlying determination in the set of the delicate mouth and chin. Max's lips curved in a wry grin. He doubted that Darcy had heard the last of Sarah Twinning, whatever the outcome of his self-imposed exile.

Behind Sarah sat Lord Tulloch and Mr. Swanston, invited by Max to act as squires for Sarah and Arabella respectively. Neither was particularly interested in the opera, yet both had accepted the invitations with alacrity. Now, they sat, yawning politely behind their hands, waiting for the moment when the curtain would fall and they could be seen by the other attending members of the *ton,* escorting their exquisite charges through the corridors.

Arabella, too, was fidgety, settling and resettling her pink silk skirts and dropping her fan. She appeared to be trying to scan the boxes on the tier above. Max smiled. He could have told her that Hugo Denbigh hated opera and had yet to be seen within the portals of Covent Garden.

Lady Benborough, dragon-like in puce velvet, sat determinedly following the aria. Distracted by Arabella's antics, she turned to speak in a sharp whisper, whereat Arabella grudgingly subsided, a dissatisfied frown marring her delightful visage.

At the opposite end of the box sat Martin, with Lizzie by the parapet beside him. She was enthralled by the performance, hanging on every note that escaped the throat of the soprano performing the lead. Martin, most improperly holding her hand, evinced not the slightest interest in the buxom singer but gazed solely at Lizzie, a peculiar smile hovering about his lips. Inwardly, Max sighed. He just hoped his brother knew what he was about.

The aria ended and the curtain came down. As the

applause died, the large flambeaux which lit the pit were brought forth and re-installed in their brackets. Noise erupted around them as everyone talked at once.

Max leaned forward to speak by Caroline's ear. "Come. Let's stroll."

She turned to him in surprise and he smiled. "That's what going to the opera is about, my dear. To see and be seen. Despite appearances, the most important performances take place in the corridors of Covent Garden, not on the stage."

"Of course," she returned, standing and shaking out her skirts. "How very provincial of me not to realize." Her eyes twinkled. "How kind of you, dear guardian, to attend so assiduously to our education."

Max took her hand and tucked it into his arm. As they paused to allow the others to precede them, he bent to whisper in her ear, "On the contrary, sweet Caro. While I'm determined to see your education completed, my interest is entirely selfish."

The wicked look which danced in his dark blue eyes made Caroline blush. But she was becoming used to the highly improper conversations she seemed to have with her guardian. "Oh?" she replied, attempting to look innocent and not entirely succeeding. "Won't I derive any benefit from my new-found knowledge?"

They were alone in the box, hidden from view of the other boxes by shadows. For a long moment, they were both still, blue eyes locked with grey-green, the rest of the world far distant. Caroline could not breathe; the intensity of that blue gaze and the depth of the passion which smouldered within it held her mesmerized. Then, his eyes still on hers, Max lifted her hand and dropped a kiss on her fingers. "My dear, once you find the key, beyond that particular door lies paradise. Soon, sweet Caro, very soon, you'll see."

Once in the corridor, Caroline's cheeks cooled. They were quickly surrounded by her usual court and Max, behaving more circumspectly than he ever had before, relinquished her to the throng. Idly, he strolled along the corridors, taking the opportunity to stretch his long legs. He paused here and there to exchange a word with friends but did not stop for long. His preoccupation was not with extending his acquaintance of the *ton*. His ramblings brought him to the corridor serving the opposite arm of the horseshoe of boxes. The bell summoning the audience to their seats for the next act rang shrilly. Max was turning to make his way back to his box when a voice hailed him through the crush.

"Your Grace!"

Max closed his eyes in exasperation, then opened them and turned to face Lady Mortland. He nodded curtly. "Emma."

She was on the arm of a young man whom she introduced and immediately dismissed, before turning to Max. "I think perhaps we should have a serious talk, Your Grace."

The hard note in her voice and the equally rock-like glitter in her eyes were not lost on the Duke of Twyford. Max had played the part of the fashionable rake for fifteen years and knew well the occupational hazards.

He lifted his eyes from an uncannily thorough contemplation of Lady Mortland and sighted a small alcove, temporarily deserted. "I think perhaps you're right, my dear. But I suggest we improve our surroundings."

His hand under her elbow steered Emma towards the alcove. The grip of his fingers through her silk sleeve and the steely quality in his voice were a surprise to her ladyship, but she was determined that Max Rotherbridge should pay, one way or another, for her lost dreams.

They reached the relative privacy of the alcove. "Well, Emma, what's this all about?"

Suddenly, Lady Mortland was rather less certain of her strategy. Faced with a pair of very cold blue eyes and an iron will she had never previously glimpsed, she vacillated. "Actually, Your Grace," she cooed, "I had rather hoped you would call on me and we could discuss the matter in…greater privacy."

"Cut line, Emma," drawled His Grace. "You knew perfectly well I have no wish whatever to be private with you."

The bald statement ignited Lady Mortland's temper. "Yes!" she hissed, fingers curling into claws. "Ever since you set eyes on that little harpy you call your ward, you've had no time for me!"

"I wouldn't, if I were you, make scandalous statements about a young lady to her guardian," said Max, unmoved by her spleen.

"Guardian, ha! Love, more like!"

One black brow rose haughtily.

"Do you deny it? No, of course not! Oh, there are whispers aplenty, let me tell you. But they're as nothing to the storm there'll be when I get through with you. I'll tell—Ow!"

Emma broke off and looked down at her wrist, imprisoned in Max's right hand. "L…let me go. Max, you're hurting me."

"Emma, you'll say nothing."

Lady Mortland looked up and was suddenly frightened. Max nodded, a gentle smile, which was quite terrifyingly cold, on his lips. "Listen carefully, Emma, for I'll say this once only. You'll not, verbally or otherwise, malign my ward—any of my wards—in any way whatever. Because, if you do, rest assured I'll hear about it. Should that happen, I'll ensure your stepson learns of the honours you do his father's memory by your retired lifestyle. Your income derives from the family estates, does it not?"

Emma had paled. "You…you wouldn't."

Max released her. "No. You're quite right. I wouldn't," he said. "Not unless you do first. Then, you may be certain that I would." He viewed the woman before him, with understanding if not compassion. "Leave be, Emma. What Caroline has was never yours and you know it. I suggest you look to other fields."

With a nod, Max left Lady Mortland and returned through the empty corridors to his box.

Caroline turned as he resumed his seat. She studied his face for a moment, then leaned back to whisper, "Is anything wrong?"

Max's gaze rested on her sweet face, concern for his peace of mind the only emotion visible. He smiled reassuringly and shook his head. "A minor matter of no moment." In the darkness he reached for her hand and raised it to his lips. With a smile, Caroline returned her attention to the stage. When she made no move to withdraw her hand, Max continued to hold it, mimicking Martin, placating his conscience with the observation that, in the dark, no one could see the Duke of Twyford holding hands with his eldest ward.

CHAPTER TEN

EXECUTION OF THE first phase of the Twinnings' master plot to rescue Amanda and Sir Ralph from the machinations of Mrs. Crowbridge fell to Sarah. An evening concert was selected as the venue most conducive to success. As Sir Ralph was tone deaf, enticing him from the real pleasure of listening to the dramatic voice of *Señorita Muscariña,* the Spanish soprano engaged for the evening, proved easier than Sarah had feared.

Sir Ralph was quite content to escort Miss Sarah for a stroll on the balcony, ostensibly to relieve the stuffiness in Miss Twinning's head. In the company of the rest of the *ton,* he knew Sarah was pining away and thus, he reasoned, he was safe in her company. That she was one of the more outstandingly opulent beauties he had ever set eyes on simply made life more complete. It was rare that he felt at ease with such women and his time in London had made him, more than once, wish he was back in the less demanding backwoods of Gloucestershire. Even now, despite his successful courtship of the beautiful, the effervescent, the gorgeous Arabella Twinning, there were times Harriet Jenkins's face reminded him of how much more comfortable their al-

most finalized relationship had been. In fact, although
he tried his best to ignore them, doubts kept appearing in his mind, of whether he would be able to live
up to Arabella's expectations once they were wed. He
was beginning to understand that girls like Arabella—
well, she was a woman, really—were used to receiving
the most specific advances from the more hardened of
the male population. Sir Ralph swallowed nervously,
woefully aware that he lacked the abilities to compete
with such gentlemen. He glanced at the pale face of the
beauty beside him. A frown marred her smooth brow.
He relaxed. Clearly, Miss Sarah's mind was not bent
on illicit dalliance.

In thinking this, Sir Ralph could not have been further from the truth. Sarah's frown was engendered by
her futile attempts to repress the surge of longing that
had swept through her—a relic of that fateful evening in
Lady Overton's shrubbery, she felt sure—when she had
seen Darcy Hamilton's tall figure negligently propped
by the door. She had felt the weight of his gaze upon
her and, turning to seek its source, had met his eyes
across the room. Fool that she was! She had had to
fight to keep herself in her seat and not run across the
room and throw herself into his arms. Then, an arch
look from Arabella, unaware of Lord Darcy's return,
had reminded her of her duty. She had put her hand
to her head and Lizzie had promptly asked if she was
feeling the thing. It had been easy enough to claim Sir
Ralph's escort and leave the music-room. But the thun-

derous look in Darcy's eyes as she did so had tied her stomach in knots.

Pushing her own concerns abruptly aside, she transferred her attention to the man beside her. "Sir Ralph, I hope you won't mind if I speak to you on a matter of some delicacy?"

Taken aback, Sir Ralph goggled.

Sarah ignored his startled expression. Harriet had warned her how he would react. It was her job to lead him by the nose. "I'm afraid things have reached a head with Arabella. I know it's not obvious; she's so reticent about such things. But I feel it's my duty to try to explain it to you. She's in such low spirits. Something must be done or she may even go into a decline."

It was on the tip of Sir Ralph's tongue to say that he had thought it was Sarah who was going into the decline. And the suggestion that Arabella, last seen with an enchanting sparkle in her big eyes, was in low spirits confused him utterly. But Sarah's next comment succeeded in riveting his mind. "You're the only one who can save her."

The practical tone in which Sarah brought out her statement lent it far greater weight than a more dramatic declaration. In the event, Sir Ralph's attention was all hers. "You see, although she would flay me alive for telling you, you should know that she was very seriously taken with a gentleman earlier in the Season, before you arrived. He played on her sensibilities and she was so vulnerable. Unfortunately, he was not interested in marriage. I'm sure I can rely on your discretion. Luckily, she learned of his true intentions before he had time to achieve them. But her heart was sorely bruised, of course. Now that she's found such solace in your company, we had hoped, my sisters and I, that you would not let her down."

Sir Ralph was heard to mumble that he had no intention of letting Miss Arabella down.

"Ah, but you see," said Sarah, warming to her task, "what she needs is to be taken out of herself. Some excitement that would divert her from the present round of balls and parties and let her forget her past hurts in her enjoyment of a new love."

Sir Ralph, quite carried away by her eloquence, muttered that yes, he could quite see the point in that.

"So you see, Sir Ralph, it's imperative that she be swept off her feet. She's very romantically inclined, you know."

Sir Ralph, obediently responding to his cue, declared he was only too ready to do whatever was necessary to ensure Arabella's happiness.

Sarah smiled warmly, "In that case, I can tell you exactly what you must do."

It took Sarah nearly half an hour to conclude her instructions to Sir Ralph. Initially, he had been more than a little reluctant even to discuss such an enterprise. But, by dwelling on the depth of Arabella's need, appealing quite brazenly to poor Sir Ralph's chivalrous instincts, she had finally wrung from him his sworn agreement to the entire plan.

In a mood of definite self-congratulation, she led the way back to the music-room and, stepping over the door sill, all but walked into Darcy Hamilton. His hand at her elbow steadied her, but, stung by his touch, she abruptly pulled away. Sir Ralph, who had not previously met Lord Darcy, stopped in bewilderment, his eyes going from Sarah's burning face to his lordship's pale one. Then, Darcy Hamilton became aware of his presence. "I'll return Miss Twinning to her seat."

Responding to the commanding tone, Sir Ralph bowed and departed.

Sarah drew a deep breath. "How *dare* you?" she uttered furiously as she made to follow Sir Ralph.

But Darcy's hand on her arm detained her. "What's that…country bumpkin to you?" The insulting drawl in his voice drew a blaze of fire from Sarah's eyes.

But before she could wither him where she stood, several heads turned their way. "Sssh!"

Without a word, Darcy turned her and propelled her back out of the door.

"Disgraceful!" said Lady Malling to Mrs. Benn, nodding by her side.

On the balcony, Sarah stood very still, quivering with rage and a number of other more interesting emotions, directly attributable to the fact that Darcy was standing immediately behind her.

"Perhaps you'd like to explain what you were doing with that gentleman on the balcony for half an hour and more?"

Sarah almost turned, then remembered how close

he was. She lifted her chin and kept her temper with an effort. "That's hardly any affair of yours, my lord."

Darcy frowned. "As a friend of your guardian—"

At that Sarah did turn, uncaring of the consequences, her eyes flashing, her voice taut. "As a friend of my guardian, you've been trying to seduce me ever since you first set eyes on me!"

"True," countered Darcy, his face like granite. "But not even Max has blamed me for that. Besides, it's what you Twinning girls expect, isn't it? Tell me, my dear, how many other lovesick puppies have you had at your feet since I left?"

It was on the tip of Sarah's tongue to retort that she had had no lack of suitors since his lordship had quit the scene. But, just in time, she saw the crevasse yawning at her feet. In desperation, she willed herself to calm, and coolly met his blue eyes, her own perfectly candid. "Actually, I find the entertainments of the *ton* have palled. Since you ask, I've formed the intention of entering a convent. There's a particularly suitable one, the Ursulines, not far from our old home."

For undoubtedly the first time in his adult life, Darcy Hamilton was completely nonplussed. A whole range of totally unutterable responses sprang to his lips. He swallowed them all and said, "You wouldn't be such a fool."

Sarah's brows rose coldly. For a moment she held his gaze, then turned haughtily to move past him.

"Sarah!" The word was wrung from him and then she was in his arms, her lips crushed under his, her head spinning as he gathered her more fully to him.

For Sarah, it was a repeat of their interlude in the shrubbery. As the kiss deepened, then deepened again, she allowed herself a few minutes' grace, to savour the paradise of being once more in his arms.

Then, she gathered her strength and tore herself from his hold. For an instant, they remained frozen, silently staring at each other, their breathing tumultuous, their eyes liquid fire. Abruptly, Sarah turned and walked quickly back into the music-room.

With a long-drawn-out sigh, Darcy Hamilton leaned upon the balustrade, gazing unseeingly at the well-manicured lawns.

HIS GRACE OF TWYFORD carefully scrutinized Sarah Twinning's face as she returned to the music-room and joined her younger sisters in time to applaud the singer's operatic feats. Caroline, seated beside him, had not noticed her sister's departure from the room, nor her short-lived return. As his gaze slid gently over Caroline's face and noted the real pleasure the music had brought her, he decided that he had no intention of informing her of her sister's strange behaviour. That there was something behind the younger Twinnings's interest in Sir Ralph Keighly he did not doubt. But whatever it was, he would much prefer that Caroline was not caught up in it. He was becoming accustomed to having her complete attention and found himself reluctant to share it with anyone.

He kept a watchful eye on the door to the balcony and, some minutes later, when the singer was once more in full flight, saw Darcy Hamilton enter and, unobtrusively, leave the room. His eyes turning once more to the bowed dark head of Sarah Twinning, Max sighed. Darcy Hamilton had been one of the coolest hands in the business. But in the case of Sarah Twinning his touch seemed to have deserted him entirely. His friend's disintegration was painful to watch. He had not yet had time to do more than nod a greeting to Darcy when he had seen him enter the room. Max wondered what conclusions he had derived from his sojourn in Ireland. Whatever they were, he wryly suspected that Darcy would be seeking him out soon enough.

Which, of course, was likely to put a time limit on his own affair. His gaze returned to Caroline and, as if in response, she turned to smile up at him, her eyes unconsciously warm, her lips curving invitingly. Regretfully dismissing the appealing notion of creating a riot by kissing her in the midst of the cream of the *ton,* Max merely returned the smile and watched as she once more directed her attention to the singer. No, he did not need to worry. She would be his long before her sisters' affairs became pressing.

THE MASKED BALL given by Lady Penbright was set to be one of the highlights of an already glittering Season. Her ladyship had spared no expense. Her ballroom was draped in white satin and the terraces and trellised walks with which Penbright House was lavishly endowed were lit by thousands of Greek lanterns. The music of a small orchestra drifted down from the minstrels' gallery, the notes falling like petals on the gloriously covered heads of the *ton*. By decree, all the guests wore long dominos, concealing their evening dress, hoods secured over the ladies' curls to remove even that hint of identity. Fixed masks concealing the upper face were the order, far harder to penetrate than the smaller and often more bizarre hand-held masks, still popular in certain circles for flirtation. By eleven, the Penbright ball had been accorded the ultimate accolade of being declared a sad crush and her ladyship retired from her position by the door to join in the revels with her guests.

Max, wary of the occasion and having yet to divine the younger Twinnings' secret aim, had taken special note of his wards' dresses when he arrived at Twyford House to escort them to the ball. Caroline he would have no difficulty in detecting; even if her domino in a subtle shade of aqua had not been virtually unique, the effect her presence had on him, he had long ago noticed, would be sufficient to enable him to unerringly find her in a crowded room blindfold. Sarah, looking slightly peaked but carrying herself with the grace he expected of a Twinning, had flicked a moss-green domino over her satin dress which was in a paler shade of the same colour. Arabella had been struggling to settle the hood of a delicate rose-pink domino over her bright curls while Lizzie's huge grey eyes had watched from the depths of her lavender hood. Satisfied he had fixed the particular tints in his mind, Max had ushered them forth.

On entering the Penbright ballroom, the three younger Twinnings melted into the crowd but Caroline remained beside Max, anchored by his hand under her elbow. To her confusion, she found that one of the major purposes of a masked ball seemed to be to allow those couples who wished to spend an entire evening together without creating a scandal to do so. Certainly, her guardian appeared to have no intention of quitting her side.

While the musicians were tuning up, she was approached in a purposeful manner by a grey domino, under which she had no difficulty in recognizing the slight frame of Mr. Willoughby. The poor man was not entirely sure of her identity and Caroline gave him no hint. He glared at the tall figure by her side, which resulted in a slow, infuriating grin spreading across that gentleman's face. Then, as Mr. Willoughby cleared his throat preparatory to asking the lady in the aqua domino for the pleasure of the first waltz, Max got in before him.

After her second waltz with her guardian, who was otherwise behaving impeccably, Caroline consented to a stroll about the rooms. The main ballroom was full and salons on either side took up the overflow. A series of interconnecting rooms made Caroline's head spin. Then, Max embarked on a long and involved anecdote which focused her attention on his masked face and his wickedly dancing eyes.

She should, of course, have been on her guard, but Caroline's defences against her dangerous guardian had long since fallen. Only when she had passed through the door he held open for her, and discovered it led into a bedroom, clearly set aside for the use of any guests overcome by the revels downstairs, did the penny drop. As she turned to him, she heard the click of the lock falling into its setting. And then Max stood before her, his eyes alight with an emotion she dared not define. That slow grin of his, which by itself turned her bones to jelly, showed in the shifting light from the open windows.

She put her hands on his shoulders, intending to hold him off, yet there was no strength behind the gesture and instead, as he drew her against him, her arms of their own accord slipped around his neck. She yielded in that first instant, as his lips touched hers, and Max knew it. But he saw no reason for undue haste. Savouring the feel of her, the taste of her, he spun out their time, giving her the opportunity to learn of each pleasure as it came, gently guiding her to the chaise by the windows, never letting her leave his arms or that state of helpless surrender she was in.

Caroline Twinning was heady stuff, but Max remembered he had a question for her. He drew back to gaze at her as she lay, reclining against the colourful cushions, her eyes unfocused as his long fingers caressed the satin smoothness of her breasts as they had once before in the carriage on the way back from the Richardsons' ball, with Miriam Alford snoring quietly in the corner. "Caro?"

Caroline struggled to make sense of his voice through the haze of sensation clouding her mind. "Mmm?"

"Sweet Caro," he murmured wickedly, watching her

efforts. "If you recall, I once asked you if, were I not your guardian, you would permit me to be alone with you. Do you still think, if that was the case, you'd resist?"

To Caroline, the question was so ridiculous that it broke through to her consciousness, submerged beneath layers of pleasurable sensation. A slight frown came to her eyes as she wondered why on earth he kept asking such a hypothetical question. But his hands had stilled so it clearly behoved her to answer it. "I've always resisted you," she declared. "It's just that I've never succeeded in impressing that fact upon you. Even if you weren't my guardian, I'd still try to resist you." Her eyes closed and she gave up the attempt at conversation as his hands resumed where they had left off. But all too soon they stilled again.

"What do you mean, *even* if I weren't your guardian?"

Caroline groaned. "Max!" But his face clearly showed that he wanted her answer, so she explained with what patience she could muster. "This, you and me, together, would be scandalous enough if you weren't my guardian, but you are, so it's ten times worse." She closed her eyes again. "You must know that."

Max did, but it had never occurred to him that she would have readily accepted his advances even had he not had her guardianship to tie her to him. His slow smile appeared. He should have known. Twinnings and rakes, after all. Caroline, her eyes still closed, all senses focused on the movement of his hands upon her breasts, did not see the smile, nor the glint in her guard-

ian's very blue eyes that went with it. But her eyes flew
wide open when Max bent his head and took one rosy
nipple into his mouth.

"Oh!" She tensed and Max lifted his head to grin
wolfishly at her. He cocked one eyebrow at her but she
was incapable of speech. Then, deliberately, his eyes
holding hers, he lowered his head to her other breast,
feeling her tense in his arms against the anticipated
shock. Gradually, she relaxed, accepting that sensation
too. Slowly, he pushed her further, knowing he would
meet no resistance. She responded freely, so much so
that he was constantly drawing back, trying to keep a
firm hold on his much tried control. Experienced as he
was, Caroline Twinning was something quite outside
his previous knowledge.

Soon, they had reached that subtle point beyond
which there would be no turning back. He knew it,
though he doubted she did. And, to his amazement, he
paused, then gently disengaged, drawing her around
to lean against his chest so that he could place kisses
in the warm hollow of her neck and fondle her breasts,
ensuring she would stay blissfully unaware while he
did some rapid thinking.

The pros were clear enough, but she would obviously
come to him whenever he wished, now or at any time
in the future. Such as tomorrow. The cons were rather
more substantial. Chief among these was that tonight
they would have to return to the ball afterwards, usually
a blessing if one merely wanted to bed a woman, not
spend the entire night with her. But, if given the choice,

he would prefer to spend at least twenty-four hours in bed with Caroline, a reasonable compensation for his forbearance to date. Then, too, there was the very real problem of her sisters. Despite the preoccupation of his hands, he knew that a part of his mind was taken up with the question of what they were doing while he and his love were otherwise engaged. He would infinitely prefer to be able to devote his entire attention to the luscious person in his arms. He sighed. His body did not like what his mind was telling it. Before he could change his decision, he pulled Caroline closer and bent to whisper in her ear. "Caro?"

She murmured his name and put her hand up to his face. Max smiled. "Sweetheart, much as I'd like to complete your education here and now, I have a dreadful premonition of what hideous scandals your sisters might be concocting with both of us absent from the ballroom."

He knew it was the right excuse to offer, for her mind immediately reasserted itself. "Oh, dear," she sighed, disappointment ringing clearly in her tone, deepening Max's smile. "I suspect you're right."

"I know I'm right," he said, straightening and sitting her upright. "Come, let's get you respectable again."

As soon as she felt sufficiently camouflaged from her guardian's eye by the gorgeously coloured throng, Lizzie Twinning made her way to the ballroom window further from the door. It was the meeting place Sarah had stipulated where Sir Ralph was to await further instructions. He was there, in a dark green domino and a black mask.

Lizzie gave him her hand. "Good!" The hand holding hers trembled. She peered into the black mask. "You're not going to let Arabella down, are you?"

To her relief, Sir Ralph swallowed and shook his head. "No. Of course not. I've got my carriage waiting, as Miss Sarah suggested. I wouldn't dream of deserting Miss Arabella."

Despite the weakness in his voice, Lizzie was satisfied. "It's all right," she assured him. "Arabella is wearing a rose-pink domino. It's her favourite colour so you should recognise it. We'll bring her to you, as we said we would. Don't worry," she said, giving his hand a squeeze, "it'll all work out for the best, you'll see." She patted his hand and, returning it to him, left him. As she moved down the ballroom, she scanned the crowd and picked out Caroline in her aqua domino waltzing with a black domino who could only be their guardian. She grinned to herself and the next instant, walked smack into a dark blue domino directly in her path.

"Oh!" She fell back and put up a hand to her mask, which had slipped.

"Lizzie," said the blue domino in perfectly recognizable accents, "what were you doing talking to Keighly?"

"Martin! What a start you gave me. My mask nearly fell. Wh…what do you mean?"

"I mean, Miss Innocence," said Martin sternly, taking her arm and compelling her to walk beside him on to the terrace, "that I saw you come into the ballroom and then, as soon as you were out of Max's sight, make a bee-line for Keighly. Now, out with it! What's going on?"

Lizzie was in shock. What was she to do? Not for a moment did she imagine that Martin would agree to turn a blind eye to their scheme. But she was not a very good liar. Still, she would have to try. Luckily, the mask hid most of her face and her shock had kept her immobile, gazing silently up at him in what could be taken for her usual innocent manner. "But I don't know what you mean, Martin. I know I talked to Sir Ralph, but that was because he was the only one I recognized."

The explanation was so reasonable that Martin felt his sudden suspicion was as ridiculous as it had seemed. He felt decidedly foolish. "Oh."

"But now you're here," said Lizzie, putting her hand on his arm. "So I can talk to you."

Martin's usual grin returned. "So you can." He raised his eyes to the secluded walks, still empty as the dancing had only just begun. "Why don't we explore while we chat?"

Lately, Lizzie had been in the habit of refusing such invitations but tonight she was thankful for any suggestion that would distract Martin from their enterprise. So she nodded and they stepped off the terrace on to the gravel. They followed a path into the shrubbery. It wended this way and that until the house was a glimmer of light and noise beyond the screening bushes. They found an ornamental stream and followed it to a lake. There was a small island in the middle with a tiny summer-house, reached by a rustic bridge. They crossed over and found the door of the summer-house open.

"Isn't this lovely?" said Lizzie, quite enchanted by the scene. Moonbeams danced in a tracery of light created by the carved wooden shutters. The soft swish of the water running past the reed-covered banks was the only sound to reach their ears.

"Mmm, yes, quite lovely," murmured Martin, enchanted by something quite different. Even Lizzie in her innocence heard the warning in his tone but she turned only in time to find herself in his arms. Martin tilted her face up and smiled gently down at her. "Lizzie, sweet Lizzie. Do you have any idea how beautiful you are?"

Lizzie's eyes grew round. Martin's arms closed around her, gentle yet quite firm. It seemed unbelievable that their tightness could be restricting her breathing, yet she found herself quite unable to draw breath. And the strange light in Martin's eyes was making her dizzy. She had meant to ask her sisters for guidance on how best to handle such situations but, due to her absorption with their schemes, it had slipped her mind. She suspected this was one of those points where using one's wits came into it. But, as her tongue seemed incapable of forming any words, she could only shake her head and hope that was acceptable.

"Ah," said Martin, his grin broadening. "Well, you're so very beautiful, sweetheart, that I'm afraid I can't resist. I'm going to kiss you again, Lizzie. And it's going to be thoroughly enjoyable for both of us." Without further words, he dipped his head and, very gently, kissed her. When she did not draw back, he continued the caress, prolonging the sensation until he felt her response. Gradually, with the moonlight washing over them, he deepened the kiss, then, as she continued to respond easily, gently drew her further into his arms. She came willingly and Martin was suddenly unsure of the ground rules. He had no wish to frighten her, innocent as she was, yet he longed to take their dalliance further, much further. He gently increased the pressure of his lips on hers until they parted for him. Slowly, continually reminding himself of her youth, he taught her how pleasurable a kiss could be. Her responses drove him to seek more.

Kisses were something Lizzie felt she could handle. Being held securely in Martin's arms was a delight. But when his hand closed gently over her breast she gasped and pulled away. The reality of her feelings hit her. She burst into tears.

"Lizzie?" Martin, cursing himself for a fool, for pushing her too hard, gathered her into his arms, ignoring her half-hearted resistance. "I'm sorry, Lizzie. It was too soon, I know. Lizzie? Sweetheart?"

Lizzie gulped and stifled her sobs. "It's true!" she said, her voice a tear-choked whisper. "They said you were a rake and you'd want to take me to bed and I didn't believe them but it's *true*." She ended this astonishing speech on a hiccup.

Martin, finding much of her accusation difficult to deny, fastened on the one aspect that was not clear. "They—who?"

"Sarah and Bella and Caro. They said you're *all* rakes. You and Max and Lord Darcy and Lord Denbigh. They said there's something about us that means we attract rakes."

Finding nothing in all this that he wished to dispute, Martin kept silent. He continued to hold Lizzie, his face half buried in her hair. "What did they suggest you should do about it?" he eventually asked, unsure if he would get an answer.

The answer he got was unsettling. "Wait."

Wait. Martin did not need to ask what for. He knew.

Very much later in the evening, when Martin had escorted Lizzie back to the ballroom, Max caught sight of them from the other side of the room. He had been forced to reassess his original opinion of the youngest Twinning's sobriety. Quite how such a youthful innocent had managed to get Martin into her toils he could not comprehend, but one look at his brother's face, even with his mask in place, was enough to tell him she had succeeded to admiration. Well, he had warned him.

ARABELLA'S ROLE IN the great plan was to flirt so outrageously that everyone in the entire room would be certain that it was indeed the vivacious Miss Twinning under the rose-pink domino. None of the conspirators had imagined this would prove at all difficult and, true to form, within half an hour Arabella had convinced the better part of the company of her identity. She left one group of revellers, laughing gaily, and was moving around the room, when she found she had walked into the arms of a large, black-domino-clad figure. The shock she received from the contact immediately informed her of the identity of the gentleman.

"Oh, sir! You quite overwhelm me!"

"In such a crowd as this, my dear? Surely you jest?"

"Would you contradict a lady, sir? Then you're no gentlemen, in truth."

"In truth, you're quite right, sweet lady. Gentlemen lead such boring lives."

The distinctly seductive tone brought Arabella up short. He could not know who she was, could he? As if in answer to her unspoken question, he asked, "And who might you be, my lovely?"

Arabella's chin went up and she playfully retorted, "Why, that's not for you to know, sir. My reputation might be at stake, simply for talking to so unconventional a gentleman as you."

To her unease, Hugo responded with a deep and attractive chuckle. Their light banter continued, Arabella making all the customary responses, her quick ear for repartee saving her from floundering when his returns made her cheeks burn. She flirted with Hugo to the top of her bent. And hated every minute of it. He did not know who she was, yet was prepared to push an unknown lady to make an assignation with him for later in the evening. She was tempted to do so and then confront him with her identity. But her heart failed her. Instead, when she could bear it no longer, she made a weak excuse and escaped.

THEY HAD TIMED their plan carefully, to avoid any possible mishap. The unmasking was scheduled for one o'clock. At precisely half-past twelve, Sarah and Sir Ralph left the ballroom and strolled in a convincingly relaxed manner down a secluded walk which led to a little gazebo. The gazebo was placed across the path and, beyond it, the path continued to a gate giving access to the carriage drive.

Within sight of the gazebo, Sarah halted. "Arabella's inside. I'll wait here and ensure no one interrupts."

Sir Ralph swallowed, nodded once and left her. He climbed the few steps and entered the gazebo. In the dimness, he beheld the rose-pink domino, her mask still in place, waiting nervously for him to approach. Reverently, he went forward and then went down on one knee.

Sarah, watching from the shadows outside, grinned in delight. The dim figures exchanged a few words, then Sir Ralph rose and kissed the lady. Sarah held her breath, but all went well. Hand in hand, the pink domino and her escort descended by the opposite door of the gazebo and headed for the gate. To make absolutely sure of their success, Sarah entered the gazebo and stood watching the couple disappear through the gate. She waited, silently, then the click of horses' hooves came distantly on the breeze. With a quick smile, she turned to leave. And froze.

Just inside the door to the gazebo stood a tall, black-domino-clad figure, his shoulders propped negligently against the frame in an attitude so characteristic Sarah would have known him anywhere. "Are you perchance waiting for an assignation, my dear?"

Sarah made a grab for her fast-disappearing wits. She drew herself up but, before she could speak, his voice came again. "Don't run away. A chase through the bushes would be undignified at best and I would catch you all the same."

Sarah's brows rose haughtily. She had removed her mask which had been irritating her and it hung by its strings from her fingers. She swung it back and forth nervously. "Run? Why should I run?" Her voice, she was pleased to find, was calm.

Darcy did not answer. Instead, he pushed away from the door and crossed the floor to stand in front of her. He reached up and undid his mask. Then his eyes caught hers. "Are you still set on fleeing to a convent?"

Sarah held his gaze steadily. "I am."

A wry smile, self-mocking, she thought, twisted his mobile mouth. "That won't do, you know. You're not cut out to be a bride of Christ."

"Better a bride of Christ than the mistress of any man." She watched the muscles in his jaw tighten.

"You think so?"

Despite the fact that she had known it would happen, had steeled herself to withstand it, her defences crumbled at his touch and she was swept headlong into abandonment, freed from restraint, knowing where the road led and no longer caring.

But when Darcy stooped and lifted her, to carry her to the wide cushioned seats at the side of the room, she shook her head violently. "Darcy, no!" Her voice caught on a sob. "Please, Darcy, let me go."

Her tears sobered him as nothing else could have. Slowly, he let her down until her feet touched the floor. She was openly crying, as if her heart would break. "Sarah?" Darcy put out a hand to smooth her brown hair.

Sarah had found her handkerchief and was mopping her streaming eyes, her face averted. "Please go, Darcy."

Darcy stiffened. For the first time in his adult life, he wanted to take a woman into his arms purely to comfort her. All inclinations to make love to her had vanished at the first hint of her distress. But, sensing behind her whispered words a confusion she had yet to resolve, he sighed and, with a curt bow, did as she asked.

Sarah listened to his footsteps die away. She remained in the gazebo until she had cried herself out. Then, thankful for the at least temporary protection of her mask, she returned to the ballroom to tell her sisters and their protégées of their success.

Hugo scanned the room again, searching through the sea of people for Arabella. But the pink domino was nowhere in sight. He was as thoroughly disgruntled as only someone of a generally placid nature could become. Arabella had flirted outrageously with an unknown man. Admittedly him, but she had not known that. Here he had been worrying himself into a state over her getting herself stuck in a loveless marriage for no reason and underneath she was just a heartless flirt. A jade. Where the hell was she?

A small hand on his arm made him jump. But, contrary to the conviction of his senses, it was not Arabella but a lady in a brown domino with a brown mask fixed firmly in place. "'Ello, kind sir. You seem strangely lonely."

Hugo blinked. The lady's accent was heavily middle European, her tone seductively low.

"I'm all alone," sighed the lady in brown. "And as you seemed also alone, I thought that maybe we could cheer one another up, no?"

In spite of himself, Hugo's glance flickered over the lady. Her voice suggested a wealth of experience yet her skin, what he could see of it, was as delicate as a young girl's. The heavy mask she wore covered most of her face, even shading her lips, though he could see these were full and ripe. The domino, as dominos did, concealed her figure. Exasperated, Hugo sent another searching glance about the room in vain. Then, he looked down and smiled into the lady's hazel eyes. "What a very interesting idea, my dear. Shall we find somewhere to further develop our mutual acquaintance?"

He slipped an arm around the lady's waist and found that it was indeed very neat. She seemed for one instant to stiffen under his arm but immediately relaxed. Damn Arabella! She had driven him mad. He would forget her existence and let this lovely lady restore his sanity. "What did you say your name was, my dear?"

The lady smiled up at him, a wickedly inviting smile. "Maria Pavlovska," she said as she allowed him to lead her out of the ballroom.

They found a deserted ante-room without difficulty and, without wasting time in further, clearly unnecessary talk, Hugo drew Maria Pavlovska into his arms. She allowed him to kiss her and, to his surprise, raised no demur when he deepened the kiss. His senses were racing and her responses drove him wild. He let his hand wander and she merely chuckled softly, the sound suggesting that he had yet to reach her limit. He found a convenient armchair and pulled her on to his lap and let her drive him demented. She was the most satisfyingly responsive woman he had ever found. Bewildered by his good fortune, he smiled understandingly when she whispered she would leave him for a moment.

He sighed in anticipation and stretched his long legs in front of him as the door clicked shut.

As the minutes ticked by and Maria Pavlovska did not return, sanity slowly settled back into Hugo's fevered brain. Where the hell was she? She'd deserted him. Just like Arabella. The thought hit him with the force of a sledgehammer. *Just like Arabella?* No, he was imagining things. True, Maria Pavlovska had aroused him in a way he had begun to think only Arabella could. *Hell!* She had even *tasted* like Arabella. But Arabella's domino was pink. Maria Pavlovska's domino was brown. And, now he came to think of it, it had been a few inches too short; he had been able to see her pink slippers and the pink hem of her dress. Arabella's favourite colour was pink but pink was, after all, a very popular colour. Damn, where was she? Where were they? With a long-suffering sigh, Hugo rose and, forswearing all women, left to seek the comparative safety of White's for the rest of the night.

CHAPTER ELEVEN

AFTER RETURNING TO the ballroom with Caroline, Max found his temper unconducive to remaining at the ball. In short, he had a headache. His wards seemed to be behaving themselves, despite his premonitions, so there was little reason to remain at Penbright House. But the night was young and his interlude with Caroline had made it unlikely that sleep would come easily, so he excused himself to his eldest ward and his aunt, and left to seek entertainment of a different sort.

He had never got around to replacing Carmelita. There hardly seemed much point now. He doubted he would have much use for such women in future. He grinned to himself, then winced. Just at that moment, he regretted not having a replacement available. He would try his clubs—perhaps a little hazard might distract him.

The carriage had almost reached Delmere House when, on the spur of the moment, he redirected his coachman to a discreet house on Bolsover Street. Sending the carriage back to Penbright House, he entered the newest gaming hell in London. Naturally, the door was opened to His Grace of Twyford with an alacrity that brought a sardonic grin to His Grace's face. But the play was entertaining enough and the beverages varied and of a quality he could not fault. The hell claimed to be at the forefront of fashion and consequently there were a number of women present, playing the green baize tables or, in some instances, merely accompanying their lovers. To his amusement, Max found a number of pairs of feminine eyes turned his way, but was too wise to evince an interest he did not, in truth, feel. Among the patrons he found more than a few refugees from the Penbright ball, among them Darcy Hamilton.

Darcy was leaning against the wall, watching the play at the hazard table. He glowered as Max approached. "I noticed both you and your eldest ward were absent from the festivities for an inordinately long time this evening. Examining etchings upstairs, I suppose?"

Max grinned. "We were upstairs, as it happens. But it wasn't etchings I was examining."

Darcy nearly choked on his laughter. "Damn you, Max," he said when he could speak. "So you've won through, have you?"

A shrug answered him. "Virtually. But I decided the ball was not the right venue." The comment stunned Darcy but before he could phrase his next question Max continued. "Her sisters seem to be hatching some plot, though I'm dashed if I can see what it is. But when I left all seemed peaceful enough." Max's blue eyes went to his friend's face. "What are you doing here?"

"Trying to avoid thinking," said Darcy succinctly.

Max grinned. "Oh. In that case, come and play a hand of piquet."

The two were old adversaries who only occasionally found the time to play against each other. Their skills were well-matched and before long their game had resolved into an exciting tussle which drew an increasing crowd of spectators. The owners of the hell, finding their patrons leaving the tables to view the contest, from their point an unprofitable exercise, held an urgent conference. They concluded that the cachet associated with having hosted a contest between two such well-known players was worth the expense. Consequently, the two combatants found their glasses continually refilled with the finest brandy and new decks of cards made readily available.

Both Max and Darcy enjoyed the battle, and as both were able to stand the nonsense, whatever the outcome, they were perfectly willing to continue the play for however long their interest lasted. In truth, both found the exercise a welcome outlet for their frustrations of the past weeks.

The brandy they both consumed made absolutely no impression on their play or their demeanour. Egged on by a throng of spectators, all considerably more drunk than the principals, the game was still underway at the small table in the first parlour when Lord McCubbin, an ageing but rich Scottish peer, entered with Emma Mortland on his arm.

Drawn to investigate the cause of the excitement, Emma's bright eyes fell on the elegant figure of the

Duke of Twyford. An unpleasant smile crossed her sharp features. She hung on Lord McCubbin's arm, pressing close to whisper to him.

"Eh? What? Oh, yes," said his lordship, somewhat incoherently. He turned to address the occupants of the table in the middle of the crowd. "Twyford! There you are! Think you've lost rather more than money tonight, what?"

Max, his hand poised to select his discard, let his eyes rise to Lord McCubbin's face. He frowned, an unwelcome premonition filling him as his lordship's words sank in. "What, exactly, do you mean by that, my lord?" The words were even and precise and distinctly deadly.

But Lord McCubbin seemed not to notice. "Why, dear boy, you've lost one of your wards. Saw her, clear as daylight. The flighty one in the damned pink domino. Getting into a carriage with that chap Keighly outside the Penbright place. Well, if you don't know, it's probably too late anyway, don't you know?"

Max's eyes had gone to Emma Mortland's face and seen the malicious triumph there. But he had no time to waste on her. He turned back to Lord McCubbin. "Which way did they go?"

The silence in the room had finally penetrated his lordship's foggy brain. "Er—didn't see. I went back to the ballroom."

MARTIN ROTHERBRIDGE PAUSED, his hand on the handle of his bedroom door. It was past seven in the morning. He had sat up all night since returning from the ball, with his brother's brandy decanter to keep him company, going over his relationship with Lizzie Twinning. And still he could find only one solution. He shook his head and opened the door. The sounds of a commotion in the hall drifted up the stairwell. He heard his brother's voice, uplifted in a series of orders to Hillshaw, and then to Wilson. The tone of voice was one he had rarely heard from Max. It brought him instantly alert. Sleep forgotten, he strode back to the stairs.

In the library, Max was pacing back and forth before the hearth, a savage look on his face. Darcy Hamilton stood silently by the window, his face showing the effects of the past weeks, overlaid by the stress of the moment. Max paused to glance at the clock on the mantelshelf. "Seven-thirty," he muttered. "If my people haven't traced Keighly's carriage by eight-thirty, I'll have to send around to Twyford House." He stopped as a thought struck him. Why hadn't they sent for him anyway? It could only mean that, somehow or other, Arabella had managed to conceal her disappearance. He resumed his pacing. The idea of his aunt in hysterics, not to mention Miriam Alford, was a sobering thought. His own scandalous career would be nothing when compared to the repercussions from this little episode. He would wring Arabella's neck when he caught her.

The door opened. Max looked up to see Martin enter. "What's up?" asked Martin.

"Arabella!" said his brother, venom in his voice. "The stupid chit's done a bunk with Keighly."

"Eloped?" said Martin, his disbelief patent.

Max stopped pacing. "Well, I presume he means to marry her. Considering how they all insist on the proposal first, I can't believe she'd change her spots quite so dramatically. But if I have anything to say about it, she won't be marrying Keighly. I've a good mind to shove her into a convent until she comes to her senses!"

Darcy started, then smiled wryly. "I'm told there's a particularly good one near their old home."

Max turned to stare at him as if he had gone mad.

"But think of the waste," said Martin, grinning.

"Precisely my thoughts," nodded Darcy, sinking into an armchair. "Max, unless you plan to ruin your carpet, for God's sake sit down."

With something very like a growl, Max threw himself into the other armchair. Martin drew up a straight-backed chair from the side of the room and sat astride it, his arms folded over its back. "So what now?" he asked. "I've never been party to an elopement before."

His brother's intense blue gaze, filled with silent warning, only made him grin more broadly. "Well, how the hell should I know?" Max eventually exploded.

Both brothers turned to Darcy. He shook his head, his voice unsteady as he replied. "Don't look at me. Not in my line. Come to think of it, none of us has had much experience in trying to get women to marry us."

"Too true," murmured Martin. A short silence fell, filled with uncomfortable thoughts. Martin broke it. "So, what's your next move?"

"Wilson's sent runners out to all the posting houses. I can't do a thing until I know which road they've taken."

At that moment, the door silently opened and shut again, revealing the efficient Wilson, a small and self-effacing man, Max's most trusted servitor. "I thought you'd wish to know, Your Grace. There's been no sightings of such a vehicle on any of the roads leading north, north-east or south. The man covering the Dover road has yet to report back, as has the man investigating the road to the south-west."

Max nodded. "Thank you, Wilson. Keep me informed as the reports come in."

Wilson bowed and left as silently as he had entered.

The frown on Max's face deepened. "Where would they go? Gretna Green? Dover? I know Keighly's got estates somewhere, but I never asked where." After a moment, he glanced at Martin. "Did Lizzie ever mention it?"

Martin shook his head. Then, he frowned. "Not but what I found her talking to Keighly as soon as ever they got to the ball this evening. I asked her what it was about but she denied there was anything in it." His face had become grim. "She must have known."

"I think Sarah knew too," said Darcy, his voice unemotional. "I saw her go out with Keighly, then found her alone in a gazebo not far from the carriage gate."

"Hell and the devil!" said Max. "They can't all simultaneously have got a screw loose. What I can't understand is what's so attractive about *Keighly*?"

A knock on the door answered this imponderable question. At Max's command, Hillshaw entered. "Lord Denbigh desires a word with you, Your Grace."

For a moment, Max's face was blank. Then, he sighed. "Show him in, Hillshaw. He's going to have to know sooner or later."

As it transpired, Hugo already knew. As he strode into the library, he was scowling furiously. He barely waited to shake Max's hand and exchange nods with the other two men before asking, "Have you discovered which road they've taken?"

Max blinked and waved him to the armchair he had vacated, moving to take the chair behind the desk. "How did you know?"

"It's all over town," said Hugo, easing his large frame into the chair. "I was at White's when I heard it. And if it's reached that far, by later this morning your ward is going to be featuring in the very latest *on-dit* all over London. I'm going to wring her neck!"

This last statement brought a tired smile to Max's face. But, "You'll have to wait in line for that privilege," was all he said.

The brandy decanter, replenished after Martin's inroads, had twice made the rounds before Wilson again slipped noiselessly into the room. He cleared his throat to attract Max's attention. "A coach carrying a gentleman and a young lady wearing a rose-pink domino put in at the Crown at Acton at two this morning, Your Grace."

The air of despondency which had settled over the room abruptly lifted. "Two," said Max, his eyes going to the clock. "And it's well after eight now. So they must be past Uxbridge. Unless they made a long stop?"

Wilson shook his head. "No, Your Grace. They only stopped long enough to change horses." If anything, the little man's impassive face became even more devoid of emotion. "It seems the young lady was most anxious to put as much distance as possible behind them."

"As well she might," said Max, his eyes glittering. "Have my curricle put to. And good work, Wilson."

"Thank you, Your Grace." Wilson bowed and left. Max tossed off the brandy in his glass and rose.

"I'll come with you," said Hugo, putting his own glass down. For a moment, his eyes met Max's, then Max nodded.

"Very well." His gaze turned to his brother and Darcy Hamilton. "Perhaps you two could break the news to the ladies at Twyford House?"

Martin nodded.

Darcy grimaced at Max over the rim of his glass. "I thought you'd say that." After a moment, he continued, "As I said before, I'm not much of a hand at elopements and I don't know Keighly at all. But it occurs to me, Max, dear boy, that it's perfectly possible he might not see reason all that easily. He might even do something rash. So, aside from Hugo here, don't you think you'd better take those along with you?"

Darcy pointed at a slim wooden case that rested on top of the dresser standing against the wall at the side of the room. Inside, as he knew, reposed a pair of Mr. Joseph Manton's duelling pistols, with which Max was considered a master.

Max hesitated, then shrugged. "I suppose you're

right." He lifted the case to his desk-top and, opening it, quickly checked the pistols. They looked quite lethal, the long black barrels gleaming, the silver mountings glinting wickedly. He had just picked up the second, when the knocker on the front door was plied with a ruthlessness which brought a definite wince to all four faces in the library. The night had been a long one. A moment later, they heard Hillshaw's sonorous tones, remonstrating with the caller. Then, an unmistakably feminine voice reached their ears. With an oath, Max strode to the door.

Caroline fixed Hillshaw with a look which brooked no argument. "I wish to see His Grace *immediately,* Hillshaw."

Accepting defeat, Hillshaw turned to usher her to the drawing-room, only to be halted by his master's voice.

"Caro! What are you doing here?"

From the library door, Max strolled forward to take the hand Caroline held out to him. Her eyes widened as she took in the pistol he still held in his other hand. "Thank God I'm in time!" she said, in such heartfelt accents that Max frowned.

"It's all right. We've found out which road they took. Denbigh and I were about to set out after them. Don't worry, we'll bring her back."

Far from reassuring her as he had intended, his matter-of-fact tone seemed to set her more on edge. Caroline clasped both her small hands on his arm. "No! You don't understand."

Max's frown deepened. He decided she was right. He

could not fathom why she wished him to let Arabella ruin herself. "Come into the library."

Caroline allowed him to usher her into the apartment where they had first met. As her eyes took in the other occupants, she coloured slightly. "Oh, I didn't realize," she said.

Max waved her hesitation aside. "It's all right. They already know." He settled her in the armchair Hugo had vacated. "Caro, do you know where Keighly's estates are?"

Caroline was struggling with his last revelation. They already knew? How? "Gloucestershire, I think," she replied automatically. Then, her mind registered the fact that Max had laid the wicked-looking pistol he had been carrying on his desk, with its mate, no less, and was putting the box which she thought ought to contain them back, empty, on the dresser. A cold fear clutched at her stomach. Her voice seemed thin and reedy. "Max, what are you going to do with those?"

Max, still standing behind the desk, glanced down at the pistols. But it was Hugo's deep voice which answered her. "Have to make sure Keighly sees reason, ma'am," he explained gently. "Need to impress on him the wisdom of keeping his mouth shut over this."

Her mind spinning, Caroline looked at him blankly. "But why? I mean, what can he say? Well, it's all so ridiculous."

"Ridiculous?" echoed Max, a grim set to his mouth.

"I'm afraid you don't quite understand, Miss Twinning," broke in Darcy. "The story's already all over town. But if Max can get her back and Keighly keeps his mouth shut, then it's just possible it'll all blow over, you see."

"But…but why should Max interfere?" Caroline put a hand to her head, as if to still her whirling thoughts.

This question was greeted by stunned silence. It was Martin who broke it. "But, dash it all! He's her *guardian!*"

For an instant, Caroline looked perfectly blank. "Is he?" she whispered weakly.

This was too much for Max. "You know perfectly well I am." It appeared to him that his Caro had all but lost her wits with shock. He reined in his temper, sorely tried by the events of the entire night, and said, "Hugo and I are about to leave to get Arabella back—"

"No!" The syllable was uttered with considerable force by Caroline as she leapt to her feet. It had the desired effect of stopping her guardian in his tracks. One black brow rose threateningly, but before he could voice his anger she was speaking again. "You *don't* understand! I didn't *think* you did, but you kept telling me you *knew.*"

Caroline's eyes grew round as she watched Max move around the desk and advance upon her. She waved one hand as if to keep him back and enunciated clearly, "Arabella did not go with Sir Ralph."

Max stopped. Then his eyes narrowed. "She was seen getting into a carriage with him in the Penbrights' drive."

Caroline shook her head as she tried to work this out.

Then she saw the light. "A rose-pink domino was seen getting into Sir Ralph's carriage?"

At her questioning look, Max thought back to Lord McCubbin's words. Slowly, he nodded his head. "And you're sure it wasn't Arabella?"

"When I left Twyford House, Arabella was at the breakfast table."

"So who…?"

"Sarah?" came the strangled voice of Darcy Hamilton.

Caroline looked puzzled. "No. She's at home, too."

"Lizzie?"

Martin's horrified exclamation startled Caroline. She regarded him in increasing bewilderment. "Of course not. She's at Twyford House."

By now, Max could see the glimmer of reason for what seemed like the first time in hours. "So who went with Sir Ralph?"

"Miss Harriet Jenkins," said Caroline.

"Who?" The sound of four male voices in puzzled unison was very nearly too much for Caroline. She sank back into her chair and waved them back to their seats. "Sit down and I'll explain."

With wary frowns, they did as she bid them.

After a pause to marshal her thoughts, Caroline began. "It's really all Mrs. Crowbridge's fault. She decided she wanted Sir Ralph for a son-in-law. Sir Ralph had come to town because he took fright at the thought of the marriage he had almost contracted with Miss Jenkins in Gloucestershire." She glanced up, but none of her audience seemed to have difficulty understanding events thus far. "Mrs. Crowbridge kept throwing Amanda in Sir Ralph's way. Amanda did not like Sir Ralph and so, to help out, and especially because Mr. Minchbury had almost come to the point with Amanda and she favoured his suit, Arabella started flirting with Sir Ralph, to draw him away from Amanda." She paused, but no questions came. "Well, you, Max, made that a bit difficult when you told Arabella to behave herself with respect to Sir Ralph. But they got around that by sharing the work, as it were. It was still Arabella drawing Sir Ralph off, but the other two helped to cover her absences. Then, Miss Jenkins came to town, following Sir Ralph. She joined in the...the plot. I gather Arabella was to hold Sir Ralph off until Mr. Minchbury proposed and then turn him over to Miss Jenkins."

Max groaned and Caroline watched as he put his head in his hand. "Sir Ralph has my heart-felt sympathy," he said. He gestured to her. "Go on."

"Well, then Mrs. Crowbridge tried to trap Sir Ralph by trying to put him in a compromising situation with Amanda. After that, they all decided something drastic needed to be done, to save both Sir Ralph and Amanda. At the afternoon concert, Sarah wheedled a declaration of sorts from Sir Ralph over Arabella and got him to promise to go along with their plan. He thought Arabella was about to go into a decline and had to be swept off her feet by an elopement."

"My sympathy for Sir Ralph has just died," said Max. "What a slow-top if he believed that twaddle!"

"So that's what she was doing on the balcony with him," said Darcy. "She was there for at least half an hour."

Caroline nodded. "She said she had had to work on him. But Harriet Jenkins has known Sir Ralph from the cradle and had told her how best to go about it."

When no further comment came, Caroline resumed her story. "At the Penbrights's ball last night, Lizzie had the job of making sure Sir Ralph had brought his carriage and would be waiting for Sarah when she came to take him to the rendezvous later."

"And that's why she went to talk to Keighly as soon as you got in the ballroom," said Martin, putting his piece of the puzzle into place.

"All Arabella had to do was flirt outrageously as usual, so that everyone, but particularly Sir Ralph, would be convinced it was her in the rose-pink domino. At twelve-twenty, Arabella swapped dominos with Harriet Jenkins and Harriet went down to a gazebo by the carriage gate."

"Oh, God!" groaned Hugo Denbigh. The horror in his voice brought all eyes to him. He had paled. "What was the colour? Of the second domino?"

Caroline stared at him. "Brown."

"Oh, no! I should have guessed. But her *accent*." Hugo dropped his head into his large hands.

For a moment, his companions looked on in total bewilderment. Then Caroline chuckled, her eyes dancing. "Oh. Did you meet Maria Pavlovska?"

"Yes, I did!" said Hugo, emerging from his depression. "Allow me to inform you, Miss Twinning, that your sister is a minx!"

"I know that," said Caroline. "Though I must say, it's rather trying of her." In answer to Max's look of patent enquiry, she explained. "Maria Pavlovska was a character Arabella acted in a play on board ship. A Polish countess of—er—" Caroline broke off, blushing.

"Dubious virtue," supplied Hugo, hard pressed.

"Well, she was really very good at it," said Caroline.

Looking at Hugo's flushed countenance, none of the others doubted it.

"Where was I?" asked Caroline, trying to appear unconscious. "Oh, yes. Well, all that was left to do was to get Sir Ralph to the gazebo. Sarah apparently did that."

Darcy nodded. "Yes. I saw her."

Max waited for more. His friend's silence brought a considering look to his eyes.

"So, you see, it's all perfectly all right. It's Harriet Jenkins who has gone with Sir Ralph. I gather he proposed before they left and Miss Jenkins's family approved the match, and as they are headed straight back to Gloucestershire, I don't think there's anything to worry about. Oh, and Mr. Minchbury proposed last night and the Crowbridges accepted him, so all's ended well after all and everyone's happy."

"Except for the four of us, who've all aged years in one evening," retorted Max acerbically.

She had the grace to blush. "I came as soon as I found out."

Hugo interrupted. "But they've forgotten one thing. It's all over town that Arabella eloped with Keighly."

"Oh, no. I don't think that can be right," said Caroline, shaking her head. "Anyone who was at the unmasking at the Penbrights' ball would know Arabella was there until the end." Seeing the questioning looks, she explained. "The unmasking was held at one o'clock. And someone suggested there should be a…a competition to see who was the best disguised. People weren't allowed to unmask until someone correctly guessed who they were. Well, no one guessed who Maria Pavlovska was, so Arabella was the toast of the ball."

Max sat back in his chair and grinned tiredly. "So anyone putting about the tale of my ward's elopement will only have the story rebound on them. I'm almost inclined to forgive your sisters their transgression for that one fact."

Caroline looked hopeful, but he did not elaborate. Max stood and the others followed suit. Hugo, still shaking his head in disbelief, took himself off, and Darcy left immediately after. Martin retired for a much needed rest and Caroline found herself alone with her guardian.

Max crossed to where she sat and drew her to her feet and into his arms. His lips found hers in a reassuring kiss. Then, he held her, her head on his shoulder, and laughed wearily. "Sweetheart, if I thought your sisters would be on my hands for much longer, I'd have Whitney around here this morning to instruct him to break that guardianship clause."

"I'm sorry," mumbled Caroline, her hands engrossed

in smoothing the folds of his cravat. "I did come as soon as I found out."

"I know you did," acknowledged Max. "And I'm very thankful you did, what's more! Can you imagine how Hugo and I would have looked if we *had* succeeded in overtaking Keighly's carriage and demanded he return the lady to us? God!" He shuddered. "It doesn't bear thinking about." He hugged her, then released her. "Now you should go home and rest. And I'm going to get some sleep."

"One moment," she said, staying within his slackened hold, her eyes still on his cravat. "Remember I said I'd tell you whether there were any gentlemen who we'd like to consider seriously, should they apply to you for permission to address us?"

Max nodded. "Yes. I remember." Surely she was not going to mention Willoughby? What had gone on last night, after he had left? He suddenly felt cold.

But she was speaking again. "Well, if Lord Darcy should happen to ask, then you know about that, don't you?"

Max nodded. "Yes. Darcy would make Sarah a fine husband. One who would keep her sufficiently occupied so she wouldn't have time for scheming." He grinned at Caroline's blush. "And you're right. I'm expecting him to ask at any time. So that's Sarah dealt with."

"And I'd rather thought Lord Denbigh for Arabella, though I didn't know then about Maria Pavlovska."

"Oh, I wouldn't deal Hugo short. Maria Pavlovska might be a bit hard to bear but I'm sure he'll come about.

And, as I'm sure Aunt Augusta has told you, he's perfectly acceptable as long as he can be brought to pop the question."

"And," said Caroline, keeping her eyes down, "I'm not perfectly sure, but…"

"You think Martin might ask for Lizzie," supplied Max, conscious of his own tiredness. It was sapping his will. All sorts of fantasies were surfacing in his brain and the devil of it was they were all perfectly achievable. But he had already made other plans, better plans. "I foresee no problems there. Martin's got more money than is good for him. I'm sure Lizzie will keep him on his toes, hauling her out of the scrapes her innocence will doubtless land her in. And I'd much rather it was him than me." He tried to look into Caroline's face but she kept her eyes—were they greyish-green or greenish-grey? He had never decided—firmly fixed on his cravat.

"I'm thrilled that you approve of my cravat, sweetheart, but is there anything more? I'm dead on my feet," he acknowledged with a rueful grin, praying that she did not have anything more to tell him.

Caroline's eyes flew to his, an expression he could not read in their depths. "Oh, of course you are! No. There's nothing more."

Max caught the odd wistfulness in her tone and correctly divined its cause. His grin widened. As he walked her to the door, he said, "Once I'm myself again, and have recovered from your sisters' exploits, I'll call on you—say at three this afternoon? I'll take you for a drive. There are some matters I wish to discuss with you." He guided her through the library door and into the hall. In answer to her questioning look, he added. "About your ball."

"Oh. I'd virtually forgotten about it," Caroline said as Max took her cloak from Hillshaw and placed it about her shoulders. They had organized to hold a ball in the Twinnings' honour at Twyford House the following week.

"We'll discuss it at three this afternoon," said Max as he kissed her hand and led her down the steps to her carriage.

CHAPTER TWELVE

SARAH WRINKLED HER nose at the piece of cold toast lying on her plate. Pushing it away, she leaned back in her chair and surveyed her elder sister. With her copper curls framing her expressive face, Caroline sat at the other end of the small table in the breakfast-room, a vision of palest cerulean blue. A clearly distracted vision. A slight frown had settled in the greeny eyes, banishing the lively twinkle normally lurking there. She sighed, apparently unconsciously, as she stared at her piece of toast, as cold and untouched as Sarah's, as if concealed in its surface were the answers to all unfathomable questions. Sarah was aware of a guilty twinge. Had Max cut up stiff and Caroline not told them?

They had all risen early, being robust creatures and never having got into the habit of lying abed, and had gathered in the breakfast parlour to examine their success of the night before. That it had been a complete and unqualified success could not have been divined from their faces; all of them had looked drawn and peaked. While Sarah knew the cause of her own unhappiness, and had subsequently learned of her younger sisters' reasons for despondency, she had been and still was at a loss to explain Caroline's similar mood. She had been in high feather at the ball. Then Max had left early, an unusual occurrence which had made Sarah wonder if they had had a falling-out. But her last sight of them together, when he had taken leave of Caroline in the ballroom, had not supported such a fancy. They had looked…well, intimate. Happily so. Thoroughly immersed in each other. Which, thought the knowledgeable Sarah, was not especially like either of them. She sent a sharp glance to the other end of the table.

Caroline's bloom had gradually faded and she had been as silent as the rest of them during the drive home. This morning, on the stairs, she had shared their quiet mood. And then, unfortunately, they had had to make things much worse. They had always agreed that Caroline would have to be told immediately after the event. That had always been their way, ever since they were small children. No matter the outcome, Caroline could be relied on to predict unerringly the potential ramifications and to protect her sisters from any unexpected repercussions. This morning, as they had recounted to her their plan and its execution, she had paled. When they had come to a faltering halt, she had, uncharacteristically, told them in a quiet voice to wait as they were while she communicated their deeds to their guardian forthwith. She had explained nothing. Rising from the table without so much as a sip of her coffee, she had immediately called for the carriage and departed for Delmere House.

She had returned an hour and a half later. They had

not left the room; Caroline's orders, spoken in that particular tone, were not to be dismissed lightly. In truth, each sunk in gloomy contemplation of her state, they had not noticed the passage of time. Caroline had reentered the room, calmly resumed her seat and accepted the cup of coffee Arabella had hastily poured for her. She had fortified herself from this before explaining to them, in quite unequivocal terms, just how close they had come to creating a hellish tangle. It had never occurred to them that someone might see Harriet departing and, drawing the obvious conclusion, inform Max of the fact, especially in such a public manner. They had been aghast at the realization of how close to the edge of scandal they had come and were only too ready to behave as contritely as Caroline wished. However, all she had said was, "I don't really think there's much we should do. Thankfully, Arabella, your gadding about as Maria Pavlovska ensured that everyone knows you did not elope from the ball. I suppose we could go riding." She had paused, then added, "But I really don't feel like it this morning."

They had not disputed this, merely shaken their heads to convey their agreement. After a moment of silence, Caroline had added, "I think Max would expect us to behave as if nothing had happened, other than there being some ridiculous tale about that Bella had eloped. You'll have to admit, I suppose, that you swapped dominos with Harriet Jenkins, but that could have been done in all innocence. And remember to show due interest in the surprising tale that Harriet left the

ball with Sir Ralph." An unwelcome thought reared its
head. "Will the Crowbridge girls have the sense to keep
their mouths shut?"

They had hastened to assure her on this point. "Why,
it was all for Amanda's sake, after all," Lizzie had
pointed out.

Caroline had not been entirely convinced but had
been distracted by Arabella. Surmising from Caroline's
use of her shortened name that the worst was over, she
had asked, "Is Max very annoyed with us?"

Caroline had considered the question while they had
all hung, unexpectedly nervous, on her answer. "I think
he's resigned, now that it's all over and no real harm
done, to turn a blind eye to your misdemeanours. However, if I were you, I would not be going out of my way
to bring myself to his notice just at present."

Their relief had been quite real. Despite his reputation, their acquaintance with the Duke of Twyford had
left his younger wards with the definite impression that
he would not condone any breach of conduct and was
perfectly capable of implementing sufficiently draco-
nian measures in response to any transgression. In years
past, they would have ignored the potential threat and
relied on Caroline to make all right in the event of any
trouble. But, given that the man in question was Max
Rotherbridge, none was sure how successful Caroline
would be in turning him up sweet. Reassured that their
guardian was not intending to descend, in ire, upon
them, Lizzie and Arabella, after hugging Caroline and
avowing their deepest thanks for her endeavours on

their behalf, had left the room. Sarah suspected they would both be found in some particular nook, puzzling out the uncomfortable feeling in their hearts.

Strangely enough, she no longer felt the need to emulate them. In the long watches of a sleepless night, she had finally faced the fact that she could not live without Darcy Hamilton. In the gazebo the previous evening, it had been on the tip of her tongue to beg him to take her from the ball, to some isolated spot where they could pursue their lovemaking in greater privacy. She had had to fight her own nearly overwhelming desire to keep from speaking the words. If she had uttered them, he would have arranged it all in an instant, she knew; his desire for her was every bit as strong as her desire for him. Only her involvement in their scheme and the consternation her sudden disappearance would have caused had tipped the scales. Her desire for marriage, for a home and family, was still as strong as ever. But, if he refused to consider such an arrangement, she was now prepared to listen to whatever alternative suggestions he had to offer. There was Max's opposition to be overcome, but presumably Darcy was aware of that. She felt sure he would seek her company soon enough and then she would make her acquiescence plain. That, at least, she thought with a small, introspective smile, would be very easy to do.

Caroline finally pushed the unhelpful piece of toast aside. She rose and shook her skirts in an unconsciously flustered gesture. In a flash of unaccustomed insight, Sarah wondered if her elder sister was in a similar state to the rest of them. After all, they were all Twinnings. Although their problems were superficially quite different, in reality, they were simply variations on the same theme. They were all in love with rakes, all of whom seemed highly resistant to matrimony. In her case, the rake had won. But surely Max wouldn't win, too? For a moment, Sarah's mind boggled at the thought of the two elder Twinnings falling by the wayside. Then, she gave herself a mental shake. No, of course not. He was their guardian, after all. Which, Sarah thought, presumably meant Caroline would even the score. Caroline was undoubtedly the most capable of them all. So why, then, did she look so troubled?

Caroline was indeed racked by the most uncomfortable thoughts. Leaving Sarah to her contemplation of the breakfast table, she drifted without purpose into the drawing-room and thence to the small courtyard beyond. Ambling about, her delicate fingers examining some of the bountiful blooms, she eventually came to the hammock, slung under the cherry trees, protected from the morning sun by their leafy foliage. Climbing into it, she rested her aching head against the cushions with relief and prepared to allow the conflicting emotions inside her to do battle.

Lately, it seemed to her that there were two Caroline Twinnings. One knew the ropes, was thoroughly acquainted with society's expectations and had no hesitation in laughing at the idea of a gentlewoman such as herself sharing a man's bed outside the bounds of marriage. She had been acquainted with this Caroline

Twinning for as long as she could remember. The other woman, for some mysterious reason, had only surfaced in recent times, since her exposure to the temptations of Max Rotherbridge. There was no denying the increasing control this second persona exerted over her. In truth, it had come to the point where she was seriously considering which Caroline Twinning she preferred.

She was no green girl and could hardly pretend she had not been perfectly aware of Max's intentions when she had heard the lock fall on that bedroom door. Nor could she comfort herself that the situation had been beyond her control—at least, not then. If she had made any real effort to bring the illicit encounter to a halt, as she most certainly should have done, Max would have instantly acquiesced. She could hardly claim he had forced her to remain. But it had been that other Caroline Twinning who had welcomed him into her arms and had proceeded to enjoy, all too wantonly, the delights to be found in his.

She had never succeeded in introducing marriage as an aspect of their relationship. She had always been aware that what Max intended was an illicit affair. What she had underestimated was her own interest in such a scandalous proceeding. But there was no denying the pleasure she had found in his arms, nor the disappointment she had felt when he had cut short their interlude. She knew she could rely on him to ensure that next time there would be no possible impediment to the completion of her education. And she would go to his arms with neither resistance nor regrets. Which, to the original Caroline Twinning, was a very lowering thought.

Swinging gently in the hammock, the itinerant breeze wafting her curls, she tried to drum up all the old arguments against allowing herself to become involved in such an improper relationship. She had been over them all before; they held no power to sway her. Instead, the unbidden memory of Max's mouth on her breast sent a thrill of warm desire through her veins. "Fool!" she said, without heat, to the cherry tree overhead.

MARTIN ROTHERBRIDGE KICKED a stone out of his path. He had been walking for nearly twenty minutes in an effort to rid himself of a lingering nervousness over the act he was about to perform. He would rather have raced a charge of Chasseurs than do what he must that day. But there was nothing else for it—the events of the morning had convinced him of that. That dreadful instant when he had thought, for one incredulous and heart-stopping moment, that Lizzie had gone away with Keighly was never to be repeated. And the only way of ensuring that was to marry the chit.

It had certainly not been his intention, and doubtless Max would laugh himself into hysterics, but there it was. Facts had to be faced. Despite his being at her side for much of the time, Lizzie had managed to embroil herself very thoroughly in a madcap plan which, even now, if it ever became known, would see her ostracized by those who mattered in the *ton*. She was a damned sight too innocent to see the outcome of her actions; either that, or too naïve in her belief in her abilities to come about. She needed a husband to keep a firm hand on her reins, to steer her clear of the perils her beauty and innocence would unquestionably lead her into. And, as he desperately wanted the foolish woman, and had every intention of fulfilling the role anyway, he might as well officially be it.

He squared his shoulders. No sense in putting off the evil moment any longer. He might as well speak to Max.

He turned his steps toward Delmere House. Rounding a corner, some blocks from his destination, he saw the impressive form of Lord Denbigh striding along on the opposite side of the street, headed in the same direction. On impulse, Martin crossed the street.

"Hugo!"

Lord Denbigh halted in his purposeful stride and turned to see who had hailed him. Although a few years separated them, he and Martin Rotherbridge had many interests in common and had been acquainted even before the advent of the Twinnings. His lordship's usual sleepy grin surfaced. "Hello, Martin. On your way home?"

Martin nodded and fell into step beside him. At sight of Hugo, his curiosity over Maria Pavlovska had returned. He experimented in his head with a number of suitable openings before settling for, "Dashed nuisances, the Twinning girls!"

"Very!" The curt tone in Hugo's deep voice was not very encouraging.

Nothing loath, Martin plunged on. "Waltz around, tying us all in knots. What exactly happened when Arabella masqueraded as that Polish countess?"

To his amazement, Hugo coloured. "Never you mind," he said, then, at the hopeful look in Martin's eyes, relented. "If you must know, she behaved in a manner which…well, in short, it was difficult to tell who was seducing whom."

Martin gave a burst of laughter, which he quickly controlled at Hugo's scowl. By way of returning the confidence, he said, "Well, I suppose I may as well tell you, as it's bound to be all over town all too soon. I'm on my way to beg Max's permission to pay my addresses to Lizzie Twinning."

Hugo's mild eyes went to Martin's face in surprise. He murmured all the usual condolences, adding, "Didn't really think you'd be wanting to get leg-shackled just yet."

Martin shrugged. "Nothing else for it. Aside from making all else blessedly easy, it's only as her husband I'd have the authority to make certain she didn't get herself involved in any more hare-brained schemes."

"There is that," agreed Hugo ruminatively. They continued for a space in silence before Martin realized they were nearing Delmere House.

"Where are you headed?" he enquired of the giant by his side.

For the second time, Hugo coloured. Looking distinctly annoyed by this fact, he stopped. Martin, puzzled, stopped by his side, but before he could frame any question, Hugo spoke. "I may as well confess, I suppose. I'm on my way to see Max, too."

Martin howled with laughter and this time made no effort to subdue it. When he could speak again, he clapped Hugo on the back. "Welcome to the family!" As they turned and fell into step once more, Martin's eyes lifted. "And lord, what a family it's going to be! Unless I miss my guess, that's Darcy Hamilton's curricle."

Hugo looked up and saw, ahead of them, Lord Darcy's curricle drawn up outside Delmere House. Hamilton himself, elegantly attired, descended and turned to give instructions to his groom, before strolling towards the steps leading up to the door. He was joined by Martin and Hugo.

Martin grinned. "Do you want to see Max, too?"

Darcy Hamilton's face remained inscrutable. "As it happens, I do," he answered equably. As his glance flickered over the unusually precise picture both Martin and Hugo presented, he added, "Am I to take it there's a queue?"

"Afraid so," confirmed Hugo, grinning in spite of himself. "Maybe we should draw lots?"

"Just a moment," said Martin, studying the carriage waiting by the pavement in front of Darcy's curricle. "That's Max's travelling chaise. Is he going somewhere?"

This question was addressed to Darcy Hamilton, who shook his head. "He's said nothing to me."

"Maybe the Twinnings have proved too much for him and he's going on a repairing lease?" suggested Hugo.

"Entirely understandable, but I don't somehow think that's it," mused Darcy. Uncertain, they stood on the pavement, and gazed at the carriage. Behind them the door of Delmere House opened. Masterton hurried down the steps and climbed into the chaise. As soon as the door had shut, the coachman flicked his whip and the carriage pulled away. Almost immediately, the vacated position was filled with Max's curricle, the bays stamping and tossing their heads.

Martin's brows had risen. "Masterton and baggage," he said. "Now why?"

"Whatever the reason," said Darcy succinctly, "I suspect we'd better catch your brother now or he'll merrily leave us to our frustrations for a week or more."

The looks of horror which passed over the two faces before him brought a gleam of amusement to his eyes.

"Lord, yes!" said Hugo.

Without further discussion, they turned *en masse* and started up the steps. At that moment, the door at the top opened and their prey emerged. They stopped.

Max, eyeing them as he paused to draw on his driving gloves, grinned. The breeze lifted the capes of his greatcoat as he descended the steps.

"Max, we need to talk to you."

"Where are you going?"

"You can't leave yet."

With a laugh, Max held up his hand to stem the tide. When silence had fallen, he said, "I'm so glad to see you all." His hand once more quelled the surge of explanation his drawling comment drew forth. "No! I find I have neither the time nor the inclination to discuss the matters. My answers to your questions are yes, yes and yes. All right?"

Darcy Hamilton laughed. "Fine by me."

Hugo nodded bemusedly.

"Are you going away?" asked Martin.

Max nodded. "I need a rest. Somewhere tranquil."

His exhausted tone brought a grin to his brother's face. "With or without company?"

Max's wide grin showed fleetingly. "Never you mind, brother dear. Just channel your energies into keeping Lizzie from engaging in any further crusades to help the needy and I'll be satisfied." His gaze took in the two curricles beside the pavement, the horses fretting impatiently. "In fact, I'll make life easy for you. For all of you. I suggest we repair to Twyford House. I'll engage to remove Miss Twinning. Aunt Augusta and Mrs. Alford rest all afternoon. And the house is a large one. If you can't manage to wrest agreement to your proposals from the Misses Twinning under such circumstances, I wash my hands of you."

They all agreed very readily. Together, they set off immediately, Max and his brother in his curricle, Lord Darcy and Hugo Denbigh following in Darcy's carriage.

THE SOUND OF male voices in the front hall drifted to Caroline's ears as she sat with her sisters in the back parlour. With a sigh, she picked up her bonnet and bade the three despondent figures scattered through the room goodbye. They all looked distracted. She felt much the same. Worn out by her difficult morning and from tossing and turning half the night, tormented by a longing she had tried valiantly to ignore, she had fallen asleep in the hammock under the cherry trees. Her sisters had found her but had left her to recover, only waking her for a late lunch before her scheduled drive with their guardian.

As she walked down the corridor to the front hall, she was aware of the leaping excitement the prospect of seeing Max Rotherbridge always brought her. At the mere thought of being alone with him, albeit on the box seat of a curricle in broad daylight in the middle of fashionable London, she could feel that other Caroline Twinning taking over.

Her sisters had taken her words of the morning to heart and had wisely refrained from joining her in greeting their guardian. Alone, she emerged into the hallway. In astonishment, she beheld, not one elegantly turned out gentleman, but four.

Max, his eyes immediately drawn as if by some magic to her, smiled and came forward to take her hand. His comprehensive glance swept her face, then dropped to her bonnet, dangling loosely by its ribbons from one hand. His smile broadened, bringing a delicate colour to her cheeks. "I'm glad you're ready, my dear. But where are your sisters?"

Caroline blinked. "They're in the back parlour," she answered, turning to greet Darcy Hamilton.

Max turned. "Millwade, escort these gentlemen to the back parlour."

Millwade, not in Hillshaw's class, looked slightly scandalized. But an order from his employer was not to be disobeyed. Caroline, engaged in exchanging courtesies with the gentlemen involved, was staggered. But before she could remonstrate, her cloak appeared about her shoulders and she was firmly propelled out the door. She was constrained to hold her fire until Max had dismissed the urchin holding the bays and climbed up beside her.

"You're supposed to be our guardian! Don't you think it's a little unconventional to leave three gentlemen with your wards unchaperoned?"

Giving his horses the office, Max chuckled. "I don't think any of them need chaperoning at present. They'd hardly welcome company when trying to propose."

"Oh! You mean they've asked?"

Max nodded, then glanced down. "I take it you're still happy with their suits?"

"Oh, yes! It's just that...well, the others didn't seem to hold out much hope." After a pause, she asked, "Weren't you surprised?"

He shook his head. "Darcy I've been expecting for weeks. After this morning, Hugo was a certainty. And Martin's been more sternly silent than I've ever seen him before. So, no, I can't say I was surprised." He turned to grin at her. "Still, I hope your sisters have suffered as much as their swains—it's only fair."

She was unable to repress her answering grin, the dimple by her mouth coming delightfully into being. A subtle comment of Max's had the effect of turning the conversation into general fields. They laughed and discussed, occasionally with mock seriousness, a number of tonnish topics, then settled to determined consideration of the Twyford House ball.

This event had been fixed for the following Tuesday, five days distant. More than four hundred guests were expected. Thankfully, the ballroom was huge and the house would easily cater for this number. Under Lady Benborough's guidance, the Twinning sisters had coped with all the arrangements, a fact known to Max. He had a bewildering array of questions for Caroline. Absorbed with answering these, she paid little attention to her surroundings.

"You don't think," she said, airing a point she and her sisters had spent much time pondering, "that, as it's not really a proper come-out, in that we've been about for the entire Season and none of us is truly a débutante, the whole thing might fall a little flat?"

Max grinned. "I think I can assure you that it will very definitely not be flat. In fact," he continued, as if pondering a new thought, "I should think it'll be one of the highlights of the Season."

Caroline looked her question but he declined to explain.

As usual when with her guardian, time flew and it was only when a chill in the breeze penetrated her thin cloak that Caroline glanced up and found the afternoon gone. The curricle was travelling smoothly down a well surfaced road, lined with low hedges set back a little from the carriageway. Beyond these, neat fields stretched sleepily under the waning sun, a few scattered sheep and cattle attesting to the fact that they were deep in the country. From the direction of the sun, they were travelling south, away from the capital. With a puzzled frown, she turned to the man beside her. "Shouldn't we be heading back?"

Max glanced down at her, his devilish grin in evidence. "We aren't going back."

Caroline's brain flatly refused to accept the implications of that statement. Instead, after a pause, she asked conversationally, "Where are we?"

"A little past Twickenham."

"Oh." If they were that far out of town, then it was difficult to see how they could return that evening even if he was only joking about not going back. But he had to be joking, surely?

The curricle slowed and Max checked his team for the turn into a beech-lined drive. As they whisked through the gateway, Caroline caught a glimpse of a coat of arms worked into the impressive iron gates. The Delmere arms, Max's own. She looked about her with interest, refusing to give credence to the suspicion growing in her mind. The drive led deep into the beechwood, then opened out to run along a ridge bordered by cleared land, close-clipped grass dropping away on one side to run down to a distant river. On the other side, the beechwood fell back as the curricle continued towards a rise. Cresting this, the road descended in a broad sweep to end in a gravel courtyard before an old stone house. It nestled into an unexpected curve of a small stream, presumably a tributary of the larger river which Caroline rather thought must be the Thames. The roof sported many gables. Almost as many chimneys, intricate pots capping them, soared high above the tiles. In the setting sun, the house glowed mellow and warm. Along one wall, a rambling white rose nodded its blooms and released its perfume to the freshening breeze. Caroline thought she had seen few more appealing houses.

They were expected, that much was clear. A groom came running at the sound of the wheels on the gravel. Max lifted her down and led her to the door. It opened at his touch. He escorted her in and closed the door behind them.

Caroline found herself in a small hall, neatly panelled in oak, a small round table standing in the middle of the tiled floor. Max's hand at her elbow steered her to a corridor giving off the back of the hall. It terminated in a beautifully carved oak door. As Max reached around her to open it, Caroline asked, "Where are the servants?"

"Oh, they're about. But they're too well trained to show themselves."

Her suspicions developing in leaps and bounds, Caroline entered a large room, furnished in a fashion she had never before encountered.

The floor was covered in thick, silky rugs, executed in the most glorious hues. Low tables were scattered amid piles of cushions in silks and satins of every conceivable shade. There was a bureau against one wall, but the room was dominated by a dais covered with silks and piled with cushions, more silks draping down from above to swirl about it in semi-concealing mystery. Large glass doors gave on to a paved courtyard. The doors stood slightly ajar, admitting the comforting gurgle of the stream as it passed by on the other side of the courtyard wall. As she crossed to peer out, she noticed the ornate brass lamps which hung from the ceiling. The courtyard was empty and, surprisingly, entirely enclosed. A wooden gate was set in one side-wall and another in the wall opposite the house presumably gave on to the stream. As she turned back into the room, Caroline thought it had a strangely relaxing effect on the senses—the silks, the glowing but not overbright colours, the soothing murmur of the stream. Then, her eyes lit on the silk-covered dais. And grew round. Seen from this angle, it was clearly a bed, heavily disguised beneath the jumble of cushions and silks, but a bed nevertheless. Her suspicions confirmed, her gaze flew to her guardian's face.

What she saw there tied her stomach in knots. "Max…" she began uncertainly, the conservative Miss Twinning hanging on grimly.

But then he was standing before her, his eyes glinting devilishly and that slow smile wreaking havoc with her good intentions. "Mmm?" he asked.

"What are we doing here?" she managed, her pulse racing, her breath coming more and more shallowly, her nerves stretching in anticipation.

"Finishing your education," the deep voice drawled.

Well, what had she expected? asked that other Miss Twinning, ousting her competitor and taking total possession as Max bent his head to kiss her. Her mouth opened welcomingly under his and he took what she offered, gradually drawing her into his embrace until she was crushed against his chest. Caroline did not mind; breathing seemed unimportant just at that moment.

When Max finally raised his head, his eyes were bright under their hooded lids and, she noticed with smug satisfaction, his breathing was almost as ragged as hers. His eyes searched her face, then his slow smile appeared. "I notice you've ceased reminding me I'm your guardian."

Caroline, finding her arms twined around his neck, ran her fingers through his dark hair. "I've given up," she said in resignation. "You never paid the slightest attention, anyway."

Max chuckled and bent to kiss her again, then pulled back and turned her about. "Even if I were your guardian, I'd still have seduced you, sweetheart."

Caroline obligingly stood still while his long fingers unlaced her gown. She dropped her head forward to move her curls, which he had loosed, out of his way. Then, the oddity of his words struck her. Her head came up abruptly. "*Even?* Max…" She tried to turn around but his hand pushed her back.

"Stand still," he commanded. "I have no intention of making love to you with your clothes on."

Having no wish to argue that particular point, Caroline, seething with impatience, stood still until she felt the last ribbon freed. Then, she turned. "What do you mean, *even* if you were my guardian? You are my guardian. You told me so yourself." Her voice tapered away as one part of her mind tried to concentrate on her questions while the rest was more interested in the fact that Max had slipped her dress from her shoulders and it had slid, in a softly sensuous way, down to her feet. In seconds, her petticoats followed.

"Yes, I know I did," Max agreed helpfully, his fingers busy with the laces of the light stays which restrained her ample charms. "I lied. Most unwisely, as it turned out."

"Wh…what?" Caroline was having a terrible time trying to focus her mind. It kept wandering. She supposed she really ought to feel shy about Max undressing her. The thought that there were not so many pieces of her clothing left for him to remove, spurred her to ask, "What do you mean, you lied? And why unwisely?"

Max dispensed with her stays and turned his attention to the tiny buttons of her chemise. "You were never my ward. You ceased to be a ward of the Duke of Twyford when you turned twenty-five. But I arranged to let you believe I was still your guardian, thinking that if you knew I wasn't you would never let me near you." He grinned wolfishly at her as his hands slipped over her shoulders and her chemise joined the rest of her clothes at her feet. "I didn't then know that the Twinnings are…susceptible to rakes."

His smug grin drove Caroline to shake her head. "We're not…susceptible."

"Oh?" One dark brow rose.

Caroline closed her eyes and her head fell back as his hands closed over her breasts. She heard his deep chuckle and smiled to herself. Then, as his hands drifted, and his lips turned to hers, her mind went obligingly blank, allowing her senses free rein. As her bones turned to jelly and her knees buckled, Max's arm helpfully supported her. Then, her lips were free and she was swung up into his arms. A moment later, she was deposited in the midst of the cushions and silks on the dais.

Feeling excitement tingling along every nerve, Caroline stretched sensuously, smiling at the light that glowed in Max's eyes as they watched her while he dispensed with his clothes. But when he stretched out beside her, and her hands drifted across the hard muscles of his chest, she felt him hold back. In unconscious entreaty, she turned towards him, her body arching against his. His response was immediate and the next instant his lips had returned to hers, his arms gathering her to him. With a satisfied sigh, Caroline gave her full concentration to her last lesson.

CHAPTER THIRTEEN

"SARAH?" DARCY TRIED to squint down at the face under the dark hair covering his chest.

"Mmm," Sarah replied sleepily, snuggling comfortably against him.

Darcy grinned and gave up trying to rouse her. His eyes drifted to the ceiling as he gently stroked her back. Serve her right if she was exhausted.

Together with Martin and Hugo, he had followed the strongly disapproving Millwade to the back parlour. He had announced them, to the obvious consternation of the three occupants. Darcy's grin broadened as he recalled the scene. Arabella had looked positively stricken with guilt, Lizzie had not known what to think and Sarah had simply stood, her back to the windows, and watched him. At his sign, she had come to his side and they had left the crowded room together.

At his murmured request to see her privately, she had led the way to the morning-room. He had intended to speak to her then, but she had stood so silently in the middle of the room, her face quite unreadable, that before he had known it he was kissing her. Accomplished rake that he was, her response had been staggering. He had always known her for a sensual woman but previously her reactions had been dragged unwillingly from her. Now that they came freely, their potency was enhanced a thousand-fold. After five minutes, he had forcibly disengaged to return to the door and lock it. After that, neither of them had spared a thought for anything save the quenching of their raging desires.

Much later, when they had recovered somewhat, he had managed to find the time, in between other occupations, to ask her to marry him. She had clearly been stunned and it was only then that he realized she had not expected his proposal. He had been oddly touched. Her answer, given without the benefit of speech, had been nevertheless comprehensive and had left him in no doubt of her desire to fill the position he was offering. His wife. The idea made him laugh. Would he survive?

The rumble in his chest disturbed Sarah but she merely burrowed her head into his shoulder and returned to her bliss-filled dreams. Darcy moved slightly, settling her more comfortably.

Her eagerness rang all sorts of warning bells in his mind. Used to taking advantage of the boredom of sensual married women, he made a resolution to ensure that his Sarah never came within arm's reach of any rakes. It would doubtless be wise to establish her as his wife as soon as possible, now he had whetted her appetite for hitherto unknown pleasures. Getting her settled in Hamilton House and introducing her to his country residences, and perhaps giving her a child or two, would no doubt keep her occupied. At least, he amended, sufficiently occupied to have no desire left over for any other than himself.

The light was fading. He glanced at the window to find the afternoon far advanced. With a sigh, he shook Sarah's white shoulder gently.

"Mmm," she murmured protestingly, sleepily trying to shake off his hand.

Darcy chuckled. "I'm afraid, my love, that you'll have to awaken. The day is spent and doubtless someone will come looking for us. I rather think we should be dressed when they do."

With a long-drawn-out sigh, Sarah struggled to lift her head, propping her elbows on his chest to look into his face. Then, her gaze wandered to take in the scene about them. They were lying on the accommodatingly large sofa before the empty fireplace, their clothes strewn about the room. She dropped her head into her hands. "Oh, God. I suppose you're right."

"Undoubtedly," confirmed Darcy, smiling. "And allow me to add, sweetheart, that, as your future husband, I'll always be right."

"Oh?" Sarah enquired innocently. She sat up slightly, her hair in chaos around her face, straggling down her back to cover his hands where they lay, still gently stroking her satin skin.

Darcy viewed her serene face with misgiving. Thinking to distract her, he asked, "Incidentally, when should we marry? I'm sure Max won't care what we decide."

Sarah's attention was drawn from tracing her finger along the curve of his collarbone. She frowned in concentration. "I rather think," she eventually said, "that it had better be soon."

Having no wish to disagree with this eminently sensible conclusion, Darcy said, "A wise decision. Do you want a big wedding? Or shall we leave that to Max and Caroline?"

Sarah grinned. "A very good idea. I think our guardian should be forced to undergo that pleasure, don't you?"

As this sentiment exactly tallied with his own, Darcy merely grinned in reply. But Sarah's next question made him think a great deal harder.

"How soon is it possible to marry?"

It took a few minutes to check all the possible pros and cons. Then he said, uncertain of her response, "Well, theoretically speaking, it would be possible to get married tomorrow."

"Truly? Well, let's do that," replied his prospective bride, a decidedly wicked expression on her face.

Seeing it, Darcy grinned. And postponed their emergence from the morning-room for a further half-hour.

THE FIRST THOUGHT that sprang to Arabella's mind on seeing Hugo Denbigh enter the back parlour was how annoyed he must have been to learn of her deception. Caroline had told her of the circumstances; they would have improved his temper. Oblivious to all else save the object of her thoughts, she did not see Sarah leave the room, nor Martin take Lizzie through the long windows into the garden. Consequently, she was a little perturbed to suddenly find herself alone with Hugo Denbigh.

"Maria Pavlovska, I presume?" His tone was perfectly equable but Arabella did not place any reliance on that. He came to stand before her, dwarfing her by his height and the breadth of his magnificent chest.

Arabella was conscious of a devastating desire to throw herself on that broad expanse and beg forgiveness for her sins. Then she remembered how he had responded to Maria Pavlovska. Her chin went up enough to look his lordship in the eye. "I'm so glad you found my little…charade entertaining."

Despite having started the conversation, Hugo abruptly found himself at a loss for words. He had not intended to bring up the subject of Maria Pavlovska, at least not until Arabella had agreed to marry him. But seeing her standing there, obviously knowing he knew and how he found out, memory of the desire Arabella-Maria so readily provoked had stirred disquietingly and he had temporarily lost his head. But now was not the time to indulge in a verbal brawl with a woman who, he had learned to his cost, could match his quick tongue in repartee. So, he smiled lazily down at her, totally confusing her instead, and rapidly sought to bring the discussion to a field where he knew she possessed few defences. "Mouthy baggage," he drawled, taking her in his arms and preventing any riposte by the simple expedient of placing his mouth over hers.

Arabella was initially too stunned by this unexpected manoeuvre to protest. And by the time she realized what had happened, she did not want to protest. Instead, she twined her arms about Hugo's neck and kissed him back with all the fervour she possessed. Unbeknownst to her, this was a considerable amount, and Hugo suddenly found himself desperately searching for a control he had somehow misplaced.

Not being as hardened a rake as Max or Darcy, he struggled with himself until he won some small measure of rectitude; enough, at least, to draw back and sit in a large armchair, drawing Arabella onto his lap. She snuggled against his chest, drawing comfort from his warmth and solidity.

"Well, baggage, will you marry me?"

Arabella sat bolt upright, her hands braced against his chest, and stared at him. "Marry you? Me?"

Hugo chuckled, delighted to have reduced her to dithering idiocy.

But Arabella was frowning. "Why do you want to marry me?"

The frown transferred itself to Hugo's countenance. "I should have thought the answer to that was a mite obvious, m'dear."

Arabella brushed that answer aside. "I mean, besides the obvious."

Hugo sighed and, closing his eyes, let his head fall back against the chair. He had asked himself the same question and knew the answer perfectly well. But he had not shaped his arguments into any coherent form, not contemplating being called on to recite them. He opened his eyes and fixed his disobliging love with a grim look. "I'm marrying you because the idea of you flirting with every Tom, Dick and Harry drives me insane. I'll tear anyone you flirt with limb from limb. So, unless you wish to be responsible for murder, you'd better stop flirting." A giggle, quickly suppressed, greeted this threat. "Incidentally," Hugo continued, "you don't go around kissing men like that all the time, do you?"

Arabella had no idea of what he meant by "like that" but as she had never kissed any other man, except in a perfectly chaste manner, she could reply with perfect truthfulness, "No, of course not! That was only you."

"Thank God for that!" said a relieved Lord Denbigh. "Kindly confine all such activities to your betrothed in future. Me," he added, in case this was not yet plain.

Arabella lifted one fine brow but said nothing. She was conscious of his hands gently stroking her hips and wondered if it would be acceptable to simply blurt out "yes". Then, she felt Hugo's hand tighten about her waist.

"And one thing more," he said, his eyes kindling. "No more Maria Pavlovska. Ever."

Arabella grinned. "No?" she asked wistfully, her voice dropping into the huskily seductive Polish accent.

Hugo stopped and considered this plea. "Well," he temporized, inclined to be lenient, "Only with me. I dare say I could handle closer acquaintance with Madame Pavlovska."

Arabella giggled and Hugo took the opportunity to kiss her again. This time, he let the kiss develop as he had on other occasions, keeping one eye on the door,

YOUR PARTICIPATION IS REQUESTED!

Dear Reader,

Since you are a lover of our books – we would like to get to know you!

Inside you will find a short Reader's Survey. Sharing your answers with us will help our editorial staff understand who you are and what activities you enjoy.

To thank you for your participation, we would like to send you 2 books and 2 gifts – **ABSOLUTELY FREE!**

Enjoy your gifts with our appreciation,

Pam Powers

**SEE INSIDE
FOR READER'S
SURVEY**

For Your Reading Pleasure...

We'll send you 2 books and 2 gifts
ABSOLUTELY FREE
just for completing our Reader's Survey!

YOUR READER'S SURVEY
"THANK YOU" FREE GIFTS INCLUDE:
- ▶ 2 FREE books
- ▶ 2 lovely surprise gifts

PLEASE FILL IN THE CIRCLES COMPLETELY TO RESPOND

1) What type of fiction books do you enjoy reading? (Check all that apply)
- ○ Suspense/Thrillers ○ Action/Adventure ○ Modern-day Romances
- ○ Historical Romance ○ Humor ○ Paranormal Romance

2) What attracted you most to the last fiction book you purchased on impulse?
- ○ The Title ○ The Cover ○ The Author ○ The Story

3) What is usually the greatest influencer when you <u>plan</u> to buy a book?
- ○ Advertising ○ Referral ○ Book Review

4) How often do you access the internet?
- ○ Daily ○ Weekly ○ Monthly ○ Rarely or never.

5) How many NEW paperback fiction novels have you purchased in the past 3 months?
- ○ 0 - 2 ○ 3 - 6 ○ 7 or more

YES! I have completed the Reader's Survey. Please send me the 2 FREE books and 2 FREE gifts (gifts are worth about $10) for which I qualify. I understand that I am under no obligation to purchase any books, as explained on the back of this card.

246/349 HDL GKFX

FIRST NAME	LAST NAME

ADDRESS

APT.#	CITY

STATE/PROV.   ZIP/POSTAL CODE

READER SERVICE—Here's how it works:

the other on the windows and his mind solely on her responses. Eventually, he drew back and, retrieving his hands from where they had wandered, bringing a blush to his love's cheeks, he gripped her about her waist and gently shook her. "You haven't given me your answer yet."

"Yes, please," said Arabella, her eyes alight. "I couldn't bear not to be able to be Maria Pavlovska every now and again."

Laughing, Hugo drew her back into his arms. "When shall we wed?"

Tracing the strong line of his jaw with one small finger, Arabella thought for a minute, then replied, "Need we wait very long?"

The undisguised longing in her tone brought her a swift response. "Only as long as you wish."

Arabella chuckled. "Well, I doubt we could be married tomorrow."

"Why not?" asked Hugo, his eyes dancing.

His love looked puzzled. "Is it possible? I thought all those sorts of things took forever to arrange."

"Only if you want a big wedding. If you do, I warn you it'll take months. My family's big and distributed all about. Just getting in touch with half of them will be bad enough."

But the idea of waiting for months did not appeal to Arabella. "If it can be done, can we really be married tomorrow? It would be a lovely surprise—stealing a march on the others."

Hugo grinned. "For a baggage, you do have some good ideas sometimes."

"Really?" asked Maria Pavlovska.

FOR MARTIN ROTHERBRIDGE, the look on Lizzie's face as he walked into the back parlour was easy to read. Total confusion. On Lizzie, it was a particularly attractive attitude and one with which he was thoroughly conversant. With a grin, he went to her and took her hand, kissed it and tucked it into his arm. "Let's go into the garden. I want to talk to you."

As talking to Martin in gardens had become something of a habit, Lizzie went with him, curious to know what it was he wished to say and wondering why her heart was leaping about so uncomfortably.

Martin led her down the path that bordered the large main lawn until they reached an archway formed by a rambling rose. This gave access to the rose gardens. Here, they came to a stone bench bathed in softly dappled sunshine. At Martin's nod, Lizzie seated herself with a swish of her muslin skirts. After a moment's consideration, Martin sat beside her. Their view was filled with ancient rosebushes, the spaces beneath crammed with early summer flowers. Bees buzzed sleepily and the occasional dragonfly darted by, on its way from the shrubbery to the pond at the bottom of the main lawn. The sun shone warmly and all was peace and tranquillity.

All through the morning, Lizzie had been fighting the fear that in helping Amanda Crowbridge she had unwittingly earned Martin's disapproval. She had no idea why his approval mattered so much to her, but with the single-mindedness of youth, was only aware that it did. "Wh…what did you wish to tell me?"

Martin schooled his face into stern lines, much as he would when bawling out a young lieutenant for some silly but understandable folly. He took Lizzie's hand in his, his strong fingers moving comfortingly over her slight ones. "Lizzie, this scheme of yours, m'dear. It really was most unwise." Martin kept his eyes on her slim fingers. "I suppose Caroline told you how close-run the thing was. If she hadn't arrived in the nick of time, Max and Hugo would have been off and there would have been no way to catch them. And the devil to pay when they came up with Keighly."

A stifled sob brought his eyes to her, but she had averted her face. "Lizzie?" No lieutenant he had ever had to speak to had sobbed. Martin abruptly dropped his stance of stern mentor and gathered Lizzie into his arms. "Oh, sweetheart. Don't cry. I didn't mean to upset you. Well, yes, I did. Just a bit. You upset me the devil of a lot when I thought you had run off with Keighly."

Lizzie had muffled her face in his coat but she looked up at that. "You thought… But whyever did you think such a silly thing?"

Martin flushed slightly. "Well, yes. I know it was silly. But it was just the way it all came out. At one stage, we weren't sure who had gone in that blasted coach." He paused for a moment, then continued in more serious vein. "But, really, sweetheart, you mustn't start up these schemes to help people. Not when they involve sailing so close to the wind. You'll set all sorts of people's backs up, if ever they knew."

Rather better acquainted with Lizzie than his brother was, Martin had no doubt at all whose impulse had started the whole affair. It might have been Arabella who had carried out most of the actions and Sarah who had worked out the details, but it was his own sweet Lizzie who had set the ball rolling.

Lizzie was hanging her head in contrition, her fingers idly playing with his coat buttons. Martin tightened his arms about her until she looked up. "Lizzie, I want you to promise me that if you ever get any more of these helpful ideas you'll immediately come and tell me about them, before you do anything at all. Promise?"

Lizzie's downcast face cleared and a smile like the sun lit her eyes. "Oh, yes. That will be safer." Then, a thought struck her and her face clouded again. "But you might not be about. You'll…well, now your wound is healed, you'll be getting about more. Meeting lots of l-ladies and…things."

"Things?" said Martin, struggling to keep a straight face. "What things?"

"Well, you know. The sort of things you do. With l-ladies." At Martin's hoot of laughter, she set her lips firmly and doggedly went on. "Besides, you might marry and your wife wouldn't like it if I was hanging on your sleeve." There, she had said it. Her worst fear had been brought into the light.

But, instead of reassuring her that all would, somehow, be well, Martin was in stitches. She glared at him. When that had no effect, she thumped him hard on his chest.

Gasping for breath, Martin caught her small fists and then a slow grin, very like his brother's, broke across his face as he looked into her delightfully enraged countenance. He waited to see the confusion show in her fine eyes before drawing her hands up, pulling her hard against him and kissing her.

Lizzie had thought he had taught her all about kissing, but this was something quite different. She felt his arms lock like a vice about her waist, not that she had any intention of struggling. And the kiss went on and on. When she finally emerged, flushed, her eyes sparkling, all she could do was gasp and stare at him.

Martin uttered a laugh that was halfway to a groan. "Oh, Lizzie! Sweet Lizzie. For God's sake, say you'll marry me and put me out of my misery."

Her eyes grew round. "Marry you?" The words came out as a squeak.

Martin's grin grew broader. "Mmm. I thought it might be a good idea." His eyes dropped from her face to the lace edging that lay over her breasts. "Aside from ensuring I'll always be there for you to discuss your hare-brained schemes with," he continued conversationally, "I could also teach you about all the things I do with l-ladies."

Lizzie's eyes widened as far as they possibly could.

Martin grinned devilishly. "Would you like that, Lizzie?"

Mutely, Lizzie nodded. Then, quite suddenly, she found her voice. "Oh, yes!" She flung her arms about Martin's neck and kissed him ferociously. Emerging from her wild embrace, Martin threw back his head and laughed. Lizzie did not, however, confuse this with rejection. She waited patiently for him to recover.

But, "Lizzie, oh, Lizzie. What a delight you are!" was all Martin Rotherbridge said, before gathering her more firmly into his arms to explore her delights more thoroughly.

A considerable time later, when Martin had called a halt to their mutual exploration on the grounds that there were probably gardeners about, Lizzie sat comfortably in the circle of his arms, blissfully happy, and turned her thought to the future. "When shall we marry?" she asked.

Martin, adrift in another world, came back to earth and gave the matter due consideration. If he had been asked the same question two hours ago, he would have considered a few months sufficiently soon. Now, having spent those two hours with Lizzie in unfortunately restrictive surroundings, he rather thought a few days would be too long to wait. But presumably she would want a big wedding, with all the trimmings.

However, when questioned, Lizzie disclaimed all interest in wedding breakfasts and the like. Hesitantly, not sure how he would take the suggestion, she toyed with the pin in his cravat and said, "Actually, I wonder if it would be possible to be married quite soon. Tomorrow, even?"

Martin stared at her.

"I mean," Lizzie went on, "that there's bound to be quite a few weddings in the family—what with Arabella and Sarah."

"And Caroline," said Martin.

Lizzie looked her question.

"Max has taken Caroline off somewhere. I don't know where, but I'm quite sure why."

"Oh." Their recent occupation in mind, Lizzie could certainly see how he had come to that conclusion. It was on the tip of her tongue to ask for further clarification of the possibilities Caroline might encounter, but her tenacious disposition suggested she settle the question of her own wedding first. "Yes, well, there you are. With all the fuss and bother, I suspect we'll be at the end of the list."

Martin looked much struck by her argument.

"But," Lizzie continued, sitting up as she warmed to her theme, "if we get married tomorrow, without any of the others knowing, then it'll be done and we shan't have to wait." In triumph, she turned to Martin.

Finding her eyes fixed on him enquiringly, Martin grinned. "Sweetheart, you put together a very convincing argument. So let's agree to be married tomorrow. Now that's settled, it seems to me you're in far too composed a state. From what I've learned, it would be safest for everyone if you were kept in a perpetual state of confusion. So come here, my sweet, and let me confuse you a little."

Lizzie giggled and, quite happily, gave herself up to delighted confusion.

THE CLINK OF crockery woke Caroline. She stretched languorously amid the soft cushions, the sensuous drift of the silken covers over her still tingling skin bringing back clear memories of the past hours. She was alone in the bed. Peering through the concealing silk canopy, she spied Max, tastefully clad in a long silk robe, watching a small dapper servant laying out dishes on the low tables on the other side of the room. The light from the brass lamps suffused the scene with a soft glow. She wondered what the time was.

Lying back in the luxurious cushions, she pondered her state. Her final lesson had been in two parts. The first was concluded fairly soon after Max had joined her in the huge bed; the second, a much more lingering affair, had spun out the hours of the evening. In between, Max had, to her lasting shock, asked her to marry him. She had asked him to repeat his request three times, after which he had refused to do it again, saying she had no choice in the matter anyway as she was hopelessly compromised. He had then turned his attention to compromising her even further. As she had no wish to argue the point, she had meekly gone along with his evident desire to examine her responses to him in even greater depth than he had hitherto, a proceeding which had greatly contributed to their mutual content. She was, she feared, fast becoming addicted to Max's particular expertise; there were, she had discovered, certain benefits attached to going to bed with rakes.

She heard the door shut and Max's tread cross the floor. The silk curtains were drawn back and he stood by the bed. His eyes found her pale body, covered only by the diaphanous silks, and travelled slowly from her legs all the way up until, finally, they reached her face, and he saw she was awake and distinctly amused. He grinned and held out a hand. "Come and eat. I'm ravenous."

It was on the tip of Caroline's tongue to ask what his appetite craved, but the look in his eyes suggested that might not be wise if she wished for any dinner. She struggled to sit up and looked wildly around for her clothes. They had disappeared. She looked enquiringly at Max. He merely raised one black brow.

"I draw the line at sitting down to dinner with you clad only in silk gauze," Caroline stated.

With a laugh, Max reached behind him and lifted a pale blue silk wrap from a chair and handed it to her. She struggled into it and accepted his hand to help her from the depths of the cushioned dais.

The meal was well cooked and delicious. Max contrived to turn eating into a sensual experience of a different sort and Caroline eagerly followed his lead. At the end of the repast, she was lying, relaxed and content, against his chest, surrounded by the inevitable cushions and sipping a glass of very fine chilled wine.

Max, equally content, settled one arm around her comfortably, then turned to a subject they had yet to broach. "When shall we be married?"

Caroline raised her brows. "I hadn't really thought that far ahead."

"Well, I suggest you do, for there are certain cavils to be met."

"Oh?"

"Yes," said Max. "Given that I left my brother, Darcy Hamilton and Hugo Denbigh about to pay their addresses to my three wards, I suspect we had better return to London tomorrow afternoon. Then, if you want a big wedding, I should warn you that the Rotherbridge family is huge and, as I am its head, all will expect to be invited."

Caroline was shaking her head. "Oh, I don't think a big wedding would be at all wise. I mean, it looks as though the Twinning family will have a surfeit of weddings. But," she paused, "maybe your family will expect it?"

"I dare say they will, but they're quite used to me doing outrageous things. I should think they'll be happy enough that I'm marrying at all, let alone to someone as suitable as yourself, my love."

Suddenly, Caroline sat bolt upright. "Max! I just remembered. What's the time? They'll all be in a flurry because I haven't returned…."

But Max drew her back against his chest. "Hush. It's all taken care of. I left a note for Aunt Augusta. She knows you're with me and will not be returning until tomorrow."

"But…won't she be upset?"

"I should think she'll be dancing a jig." He grinned as she turned a puzzled face to him. "Haven't you worked out Aunt Augusta's grand plan yet?" Bemused, Caroline shook her head. "I suspect she had it in mind that I should marry you from the moment she first met you. That was why she was so insistent that I keep my wards. Initially, I rather think she hoped that by her throwing us forever together I would notice you." He chuckled. "Mind you, a man would have to be blind not to notice your charms at first sight, m'dear. By that first night at Almack's, I think she realized she didn't need to do anything further, just give me plenty of opportunity. She knows me rather well, you see, and knew that, despite my reputation, you were in no danger of being offered a *carte blanche* by me."

"I did wonder why she never warned me about you," admitted Caroline.

"But to return to the question of our marriage. If you wish to fight shy of a full society occasion, then it still remains to fix the date."

Caroline bent her mind to the task. Once they returned to London, she would doubtless be caught up in all the plans for her sisters' weddings, and, she supposed, her own would have to come first. But it would all take time. And meanwhile, she would be living in Twyford House, not Delmere House. The idea of returning to sleeping alone in her own bed did not appeal. The end of one slim finger tapping her lower lip, she asked, "How soon could we be married?"

"Tomorrow, if you wish." As she turned to stare at him again, Max continued. "Somewhere about here," he waved his arm to indicate the room, "lies a special licence. And our neighbour happens to be a retired bishop, a long-time friend of my late father's, who will be only too thrilled to officiate at my wedding. If you truly wish it, I'll ride over tomorrow morning and we can be married before luncheon, after which we had better get back to London. Does that programme meet with your approval?"

Caroline leaned forward and placed her glass on the table. Then she turned to Max, letting her hands slide under the edge of his robe. "Oh, yes," she purred. "Most definitely."

Max looked down at her, a glint in his eyes. "You, madam, are proving to be every bit as much a houri as I suspected."

Caroline smiled slowly. "And do you approve, my lord?"

"Most definitely," drawled Max as his lips found hers.

THE DUKE OF TWYFORD returned to London the next afternoon, accompanied by his Duchess. They went directly to Twyford House, to find the entire household at sixes and sevens. They found Lady Benborough in the back parlour, reclining on the chaise, her wig askew, an expression of smug satisfaction on her face. At sight of them, she abruptly sat up, struggling to control the wig. "There you are! And about time, too!" Her shrewd blue eyes scanned their faces, noting the inner glow that lit Caroline's features and the contented satisfaction in her nephew's dark face. "What have you been up to?"

Max grinned wickedly and bent to kiss her cheek. "Securing my Duchess, as you correctly imagined."

"You've tied the knot already?" she asked in disbelief.

Caroline nodded. "It seemed most appropriate. That way, our wedding won't get in the way of the others."

"Humph!" snorted Augusta, disgruntled at missing the sight of her reprehensible nephew getting leg-shackled. She glared at Max.

His smile broadened. "Strange, I had thought you would be pleased to see us wed. Particularly considering your odd behaviour. Why, even Caro had begun to wonder why you never warned her about me, despite the lengths to which I went to distract her mind from such concerns."

Augusta blushed. "Yes, well," she began, slightly flustered, then saw the twinkle in Max's eye. "You know very well I'm *aux anges* to see you married at last, but I would have given my best wig to have seen it!"

Caroline laughed. "I do assure you we are truly married. But where are the others?"

"And that's another thing!" said Augusta, turning to Max. "The next time you set about creating a bordello in a household I'm managing, at least have the goodness to warn me beforehand! I come down after my nap to find Arabella in Hugo Denbigh's lap. That was bad enough, but the door to the morning-room was locked. Sarah and Darcy Hamilton *eventually* emerged, but only much later." She glared at Max but was obviously having difficulty keeping her face straight. "Worst of all," she continued in a voice of long suffering, "Miriam went to look at the roses just before sunset. Martin had apparently chosen the rose garden to further his affair with Lizzie, don't ask me why. It was an hour before Miriam's palpitations had died down enough for her to go to bed. I've packed her off to her sister's to recuperate. Really, Max, you've had enough experience to have foreseen what would happen."

Both Max and Caroline were convulsed with laughter.

"Oh, dear," said Caroline when she could speak, "I wonder what would have happened if she had woken up on the way back from the Richardsons' ball?"

Augusta looked interested but, before she could request further information, the door opened and Sarah entered, followed by Darcy Hamilton. From their faces it was clear that all their troubles were behind them—Sarah looked radiant, Darcy simply looked besotted. The sisters greeted each other affectionately, then Sarah drew back and surveyed the heavy gold ring on Caroline's left hand. "Married already?"

"We thought to do you the favour of getting our marriage out of the way forthwith," drawled Max, releasing Darcy's hand. "So there's no impediment to your own nuptials."

Darcy and Sarah exchanged an odd look, then burst out laughing. "I'm afraid, dear boy," said Darcy, "that we've jumped the gun, too."

Sarah held out her left hand, on which glowed a slim gold band.

While the Duke and Duchess of Twyford and Lord and Lady Darcy exchanged congratulations all around, Lady Benborough looked on in disgust. "What I want to know," she said, when she could make herself heard once more, "is if I'm to be entirely done out of weddings, even after all my efforts to see you all in parson's mouse-trap?"

"Oh, there are still two Twinnings to go, so I wouldn't give up hope," returned her nephew, smiling down at her with transparent goodwill. "Apropos of which, has anyone seen the other two lately?"

No one had. When applied to, Millwade imparted the information that Lord Denbigh had called for Miss Arabella just before two. They had departed in Lord Denbigh's carriage. Mr. Martin had dropped by for Miss Lizzie at closer to three. They had left in a hack.

"A hack?" queried Max.

Millwade merely nodded. Dismissed, he withdrew.

Max was puzzled. "Where on earth could they have gone?"

As if in answer, voices were heard in the hall. But it was Arabella and Hugo who had returned. Arabella danced in, her curls bouncing, her big eyes alight with happiness. Hugo ambled in her wake, his grin suggesting that he suspected his good fortune was merely a dream and he would doubtless wake soon enough. Meanwhile, he was perfectly content with the way this particular dream was developing. Arabella flew to embrace Caroline and Sarah, then turned to the company at large and announced, "Guess what!"

A pregnant silence greeted her words, the Duke and his Duchess, the Lord and his Lady, all struck dumb by a sneaking suspicion. Almost unwillingly, Max voiced it. "You're married already?"

Arabella's face fell a little. "How did you guess?" she demanded.

"No!" moaned Augusta. "Max, see what happens when you leave town? I won't have it!"

But her words fell on deaf ears. Too blissfully happy themselves to deny their friends the same pleasures, the Duke and his Duchess were fully engaged in wishing the new Lady Denbigh and her Lord all manner of felicitations. And then, of course, there was their own news to hear, and that of the Hamiltons. The next ten minutes were filled with congratulations and good wishes.

Left much to herself, Lady Benborough sat in a corner of the chaise and watched the group with an indulgent eye. Truth to tell, she was not overly concerned with the absence of weddings. At her age, they constituted a definite trial. She smiled at the thought of the stories she would tell of the rapidity with which the three rakes before her had rushed their brides to the altar. Between them, they had nearly forty years of experience in evading parson's mouse-trap, yet, when the right lady had loomed on their horizon, they had found it expedient to wed her with all speed. She wondered whether that fact owed more to their frustrations or their experience.

Having been assured by Arabella that Martin had indeed proposed and been accepted, the Duke and Duchess allowed themselves to be distracted by the question of the immediate housing arrangements. Eventually, it was decided that, in the circumstances, it was perfectly appropriate that Sarah should move into Hamilton House immediately, and Arabella likewise to Denbigh House. Caroline, of course, would henceforth be found at Delmere House. Relieved to find their ex-guardian so accommodating, Sarah and Arabella were about to leave to attend to their necessary packing, when the door to the drawing-room opened.

Martin and Lizzie entered.

It was Max, his sharp eyes taking in the glow in Lizzie's face and the ridiculously proud look stamped across Martin's features, who correctly guessed their secret.

"Don't tell me!" he said, in a voice of long suffering. "You've got married, too?"

NEEDLESS TO SAY, the Twyford House ball four days later was hardly flat. In fact, with four blushing brides, sternly watched over by their four handsome husbands, it was, as Max had prophesied, one of the highlights of the Season.

* * * * *

Visit the Author Profile page
at Harlequin.com for more titles.

THE DISSOLUTE DUKE

Sophia James

I would like to dedicate this book
to my sister-in-law, Susie.
Thanks for being a fan.

CHAPTER ONE

England—1831

HER BROTHERS WOULD kill her for this.

Lady Lucinda Wellingham knew that they would. Of all the hare-brained schemes that she had ever been involved with, this was the most foolish of the lot. She would be ruined and it would be entirely her fault.

'Just a kiss,' the man whispered, pressing her against a wall in the corridor, the smell of strong liquor on his breath. His hands wandered across the line of her breasts, and in the ridiculously flimsy dress that she had allowed Posy Tompkins to talk her into wearing, Lucinda could feel where his next thoughts lay.

Richard Allenby, third Earl of Halsey, had been attractive at London society balls, but here at a country party in Bedfordshire he was intolerably cloying. Pushing him away, she stood up straight, pleased that her height allowed her a good few inches above his own.

'I think, sir, that you have somehow got the wrong idea about my wish to…'

The words were cut off as his lips covered hers, a wet, limp kiss that made her turn her head away quickly before wiping her mouth. Goodness, the man was almost panting and it did not suit him at all.

'You are here at the most infamous party of the Season and my room isn't far.' His fingers closed across her forearm as he hailed two others who looked to have had as much to drink as he had. Both leered at her in the very same way that Halsey was. A mistake. She should have fled moments ago when the chance had been hers and the bedrooms had not been so perilously close. In this den of iniquity it seemed anything went, the morals of the man whose house it was fallen beyond all redemption.

A spike of fear brought her elbow against the wall, loosening Halsey's fingers and allowing a hard-won freedom which she took the chance on and ran.

Twisted and narrow corridors lay before her. There were close to twenty bedchambers on this floor alone and, moving quickly, Lucinda discovered double doors at the very end. With the corners she had taken she was certain those following would not see which door she had chanced upon and without a backward glance she turned an ornate ivory handle and slipped into the room.

It was dark inside save for a candle burning next to the bed, where a man sat reading, thick-rimmed glasses balanced on the end of his nose.

When he looked up she placed one finger to her lips, asking for his silence before turning back to the door. Outside she could hear the noise of those who followed her, the uncertainty of where she was adding to their urgency. Surely they would not dare to try their luck with any number of closed doors? A good few minutes passed, the whispers becoming less audible, and then they were gone, retracing their steps in the quest for the escaped quarry and ruing the loss of a night's entertainment. Relief filled her.

'Can I speak now?' The voice was laconic and deep, an inflection of something on the edge that Lucinda could not understand.

'If you are very quiet, I think it might be safe.' She looked around uncertainly.

A ripe swear word was her only answer and as the sheets were pushed back Lucinda saw the naked form of a man unfold from within them and her mouth gaped open. Not just any man either, but the scandalous host of this weekend's licentiousness: Taylen Ellesmere, the Sixth Duke of Alderworth. The Dissolute Duke, they called him, a rakehell who obeyed no laws of morality with his wanton disregard of any manners and his degenerate ways.

He was wearing absolutely nothing as he ambled across to the door behind her and locked it. The sound seared into Lucinda's brain, but she found she could not even move a muscle.

He was beautiful. At least he was that, his dark hair falling to his shoulders and eyes the colour of wet leaves after a forest storm at Falder. She did not glance below the line of his neck, though every fibre of her being seemed to want her to. His smile said that he knew her thought, the creases around his eyes falling into humour.

'Lady Lucinda Wellingham?'

He knew her name. She nodded, trying to find her voice. What might happen next? She felt like a chicken in a fox's lair.

'Do your three brothers know that you are here?'

Her shake of the head was tempered by a lack of breath that indicated panic and she could barely take in air. Every single thing had gone wrong since dawn, so when her hands tried to open the stays of her bodice a little she was glad when they gave, allowing breath to come more easily. The deep false cleavage so desired by society women disappeared as the fasteners loosened, her breasts spilling back into their natural and fairly meagre form. The lurid red dress she wore fell away from the rise of her bosom in a particularly suggestive manner and she knew he observed it.

'Choosing my room to hide in might not have been the wisest of options.' He glanced tellingly towards the large bed.

Lucinda ignored the remark altogether. 'Richard Allenby, the Earl of Halsey, and his friends gave me little other choice, your Grace. I had the need of a safe place.'

At that he laughed, the sound of mirth echoing about the chamber.

'Drink loosens the choking ties of societal pressure. Good manners and foppish decency is something most men cannot tolerate for more than a few weeks upon end and this place allows them to blow off steam, if you will.'

'At the expense of women who are saying no?'

'Most ladies here encourage such behaviour and dress accordingly.'

His eyes ran across the low-cut *décolletage* of her attire before returning to her face.

'This is not London, my lady, and nor does it pretend to be. If Halsey has indeed insulted you, he would have done so because he thought you were…available. Free will is a concept I set great store by here at Alderworth.'

The challenge in his eyes was unrepentant. Indeed, were she to describe his features she would say a measured indolence sat across them, like a lizard playing with a fly whose wings had already been disposed of. Her fingers went back to the door handle, but, looking for the key, she saw it had been removed. A quick sleight of hand. She had not seen him do it.

'As free will is so important to you, I would now like to exercise my own and ask you to open the door.'

He simply leaned over to a pile of clothes roughly deposited on a chair and hauled out a fob watch.

'Unfortunately it is that strange time of the evening: too early for guests to be properly drunk and therefore harmless and too late to expect the conduct of gentlemen to be above reproach. Any movement through the house at this point is more dangerous than remaining here with me.'

'Remaining in here?' Could he possibly mean what she thought he did?

His eyes lightened. 'I have room.'

'You have known me for two minutes and half of

those have been conducted in silence.' She tried to insert as much authority as she could into her announcement.

'All the better to observe your…many charms.' His green eyes were hooded with a sensual and languorous invitation.

'You sound like the wolf from the Grimm brothers' fairy tales, your Grace, though I doubt any character from a nursery rhyme exhibits the flair for nudity that you seem to display.'

Moving back from him, she was pleased when he pulled on a long white shirt, the sleeves billowing into wide folds from the shoulder. A garment a pirate might have worn or a highwayman. It suited him entirely.

'Is that better, my lady?'

When she nodded he smiled and lifted two glasses from a cabinet behind him. 'Perhaps good wine might loosen your inhibitions.'

'It certainly will not.' Her voice sounded strict even to her own ears and her eyes went to the book deposited on the counterpane. 'Machiavelli's *Il Principe* is a surprising choice for a man who seems to have no care for the name of the generations of Ellesmeres who have come before him.'

'You think all miscreants should be illiterate?'

Amazingly she began to laugh, so ridiculous was this conversation. 'Well, they are not usually tucked up in bed at ten o'clock wearing nothing but a pair of strong spectacles and reading a book of political philosophy in Italian, your Grace.'

'Believe me, degeneracy has a certain exhausting

quality to it. The expectations for even greater acts of debauchery can be rather wearisome when age creeps up on one.'

'How old are you?'

'Twenty-five. But I have been at it for a while.'

He was only a year older than she was and her few public scrapes had always been torturous. Still he was a man, she reasoned, though the double standards of behaviour excusing his sex did not even come close to exonerating his numerous and shocking depravities.

'Did your mother not teach you the basics of human kindness to others, your Grace?'

'Oh, indeed she did. One husband and six lovers later I understood it exactly. I was her only child, you see, and a very fast learner.'

She had heard the sordid story of the Ellesmere family many times, but not from the angle of a disenchanted son. Patricia Ellesmere had died far from her kin. There were those who said a broken heart had caused her death, but six lovers sounded particularly messy.

'What happened to your father?' She knew she should not have asked, but interest overcame any sense of reticence.

'He did what any self-respecting Duke might have done on discovering that his wife had cuckolded him six times over.'

'He killed himself?'

He laughed. 'No. He gambled away his fortune and then lost his woes in strong brandy. My parents died within a day of the other, at different ends of the country, and in the company of their newest lovers. Liver failure and a self-inflicted shot through the head. At least it made the funeral sum less expensive. Two for the price of one cuts the costs considerably.' His lips curled around the words and his green eyes were sharp. 'I was eleven at the time.'

Such candour was astonishing. No one had ever spoken to her like this before, a lack of apology in every new and dreadful thing he uttered.

Her own problems paled into insignificance at the magnitude of his and she could only be thankful for her close and supportive family ties.

'You had other relatives…to help you?'

'Mary Shields, my grandmother, took me in.'

'Lady Shields?' My God, who in society did not know of her proclivity for gossip and meanness? She had been dead for three years now, but Lucinda still remembered her beady black eyes and her vitriolic proclamations. And this was the woman whom an orphan child had been dispatched to?

'I see by your expression that you knew her?' He upended his tumbler and poured himself another. A generous another.

He wore rings on every finger on his left hand, she noticed, garish rings save for the band on his middle finger which was embellished with an engraving. She could not quite make out the letters.

A woman, no doubt. He was rumoured to have had many a lover, old and young, large and thin, married and unmarried. *He does not make distinction when appe-*

tite pounces. She remembered hearing a rumour saying exactly that as it swirled around in society—a diverting scandal with the main player showing no sense of remorse.

The Duke of Alderworth. She knew that most of the ladies in society watched him, many a beating heart hoping that she might be the one to change him, but with his having reached twenty-five Lucinda doubted he would reform for anyone.

Foolish fancies were the prerogative of inexperienced girls. As the youngest sister of three rambunctious and larger-than-life brothers she found herself immune to the wiles of the opposite sex and seldom entertained any romantic notions about them.

Surprisingly, the lengthening silence between them was not awkward. That astonishing fact was made even more so by the thought that had he pushed himself upon her like Richard Allenby, the Earl of Halsey, she might have been quite pleased to see the result. But he did not advance on her in any way. Outside the screams of delight permeated this end of the corridor again, women's laughing shouts mingled with the deeper tone of their drunken pursuers. A hunting horn also blasted close, the loudness of it making her jump.

'A successful night, by the sounds. The hunters and the hunted in the pursuit of ecstasy. Soon enough there will be the silence of the damned.' He watched her carefully.

'I think you are baiting me, your Grace. I do not think you can be half as bad as they say you are.'

His expression changed completely.

'In that you would be very wrong, Lady Lucinda, for I am all that they say of me and more.' A new danger cloaked him, a hard implacability in his eyes that made him look older. 'The fact is that I could have you in my bed in a trice and you would be begging me not to stop doing any of the tantalising things to your body that I might want to.'

The pure punch of his words had her heart pounding fast, because in such a boast lay a good measure of truth. She was more aware of him as a man than she had ever been of any other. Horrified, Lucinda turned to the window and made much of looking out into the gardens, lit tonight by a number of burning torches positioned along various pathways. Two lovers lay entwined amidst the bushes, bare skin pale in the light. Around them other couples lingered, their intentions visible even from this distance. The intemperance of it all shocked her to the core.

'If you touch me, my brothers would kill you, most probably.' She attempted to keep fear from the threat and failed.

He laughed. 'They could try, I suppose, but...' The rest was left unsaid, but the menace in him was magnified. The indolence that she imagined before was now honed into cold hard steel, a man who existed in the underbelly of London's society even though he was high born. The contradictions in him confused her, the quicksilver change unnerving.

'I came to the party with Lady Posy Tompkins and

she assured me that it was a respectable affair. Obviously she and I share a completely different idea of the word "respectable" and I suppose I should have made more of asking exactly where we were going before I said yes, but she was most insistent about the fun we might have and the fact that her godmother was coming made it sound more than respectable...'

He stopped her by laying his finger across the movement of her mouth. 'Do you always talk so much, Lady Lucinda?'

Her whole body jerked in response to the touch. 'I do, your Grace, because when I am nervous I seem to be unable to stop although I don't quite remember another occasion when I have been as nervous as I am right at this moment, so if you were to let me walk from this room this instant I should go gladly and find—'

His mouth came to the place where his finger had lingered, and Lucinda's world dissolved into hot colourful fragments of itself, tipping any sense of reality on its head and replacing ordinariness with a dangerous molten pleasure.

CHAPTER TWO

TAY JUST WANTED her to stop talking, the edge of panic in her voice bringing forth a guilt that he hadn't felt for years. The slight curve of her breasts fitted into his chest and he liked the softness. Usually he had to bend down to women, but this one stood only a few inches below him, her thinness accentuating her willowy figure in an almost boyish way.

Her nails were short and the calluses between her second and third fingers told him she was left handed and that she participated in some sort of sport. Archery, perhaps. The thought of her standing, aiming at a target and her blonde hair lifting in the breeze was strangely arousing. He should, of course, escort her from Alderworth post-haste and make certain that she was delivered home safely into the bosom of her family.

But he knew that he would not, and when he took her mouth against his, another feeling surfaced which he refused to dwell on altogether.

He did not imagine she had been kissed much before because her full lips were held in a tight line and, as he opened her mouth with his tongue, her eyes widened.

Eyes of pale blue etched with a darker shade—eyes

a man could lose himself in completely and never recover from.

Softening his assault, he threaded his hands through
her hair, tilting her face. This time he did not hurry or
demand more as the heat of a slow burn built. God, she
smelt so good, like the flowers in an early springtime,
fresh and clean. He had become so used to the heady
over-ripe perfumes of his many experienced *amours*
that he had forgotten the difference.

Innocence. It smelt strangely like hope.

Sealing his mouth across hers, he brought his fingers
behind her nape. Closer. Warmer.

The power of connection winded him, the first ten-
tative exploration of her tongue poignant in a way that
made him melancholy. It had been a long time since he
had kissed a woman who watched him as if he might
unlock the secrets of the universe.

Lust ignited, an incendiary living torch of need burning bright, like the wick of gunpowder snaking down
through his being. Unstoppable.

'Are you a virgin?'

He knew she was by the way she was breathing,
barely enough air to fill her up, lost in the moment and
her lips parted. 'Yes.'

'Why the hell did you come to this party, then?' The
layer of civilisation that he had tried to keep in place
was gone with the feel of her, but there was no with-
drawal as he asked the question. Rather she pressed in
closer and shut her eyes, as though trying in the darkness to find an answer. He felt the feathery waft of her

breath in the sensitive folds of his neck and wondered if she was quite as innocent as he presumed. If this was a game she played, then it was one that he had long been practised in and she would need to be careful. His hands went around her back of their own accord, like a pathway memorised.

Salvation.

The word came unbidden and blossomed into something that he could not deny and his pulse began to quicken. It had been years since he had felt like this with any woman and surprise spurred him onwards.

He twisted her and his mouth fell lower, laving at the skin at her neck, his attention bringing whorls of redness to the pale. Her breath matched his own now, neither quiet nor measured, for the power of the body had taken over and his thumb caressed the budding hardness of one nipple through crimson silk.

She arched back, thighs locked tight, her breasts twin beacons of temptation.

He wanted her as he had never wanted another in all his life, the feel of her, the softness, her hair light-spun gold against his dark. With a small motion he had her bodice loosened and his palm around the bounty of one breast, cupping flesh, stroking the firmness. He needed her devoid of clothing, wanting pure knowledge without a covering. If she had not been the lady he knew she was, he would have simply ripped the garment off from neckline to hemline, and transported her naked to his bed to take his fill. His mouth ached for the intimacy of her curves.

'The taste of a lover is part of the attraction,' he stated simply as he raised his head, watching as understanding dawned. Uncertainty chased on the heels of wariness, but still she did not pull away as he thought she might. Only a slight frown marred her brow, measuring intent without any fear whatsoever. A guileless allowance.

Such an emotion was something he had rarely experienced. His reputation had protected him, he supposed, and kept others at a distance. But Lucinda Wellingham was different and more dangerous than all of the sirens who had stalked him across so many years. The connection between them was unexpected and startling as it drew him in, his body tightening in the echo of an old knowledge. His head dipped and he brought one soft peak into his mouth, the force of the action ripping stretched red silk and the seam shirring into uncountable and damaged threads. He liked the way she arched into him, her fingers combing through his hair, nails hard-edged with want, taking his offering and giving him back her own.

His hands now moved from the rise of her bottom around the front to feel for the hidden folds of womanhood, the silk only a thin barrier to taking. He pressed in to find her centre.

'No.' A single word, moaned more than stated, but enough.

'No?' He had to make certain that that was what she had meant, his breath coming thick with need. She shook her head this time, sky-blue eyes devoid of everything, a frown on her forehead and her chest rising and falling.

No, because she could not envisage what a yes might mean? No, because he was a man with enough of a reputation to destroy her?

Breaking away he moved back, the anger in him mounting with a pounding awareness of guilt. The road to ruin was a short one and he knew a lady of her ilk would have no possible defence against his persuasions. Suddenly his own chosen life path seemed seedy and vulgar.

'I will take you home.'

She did not repair the damage to her dress as she watched him so that one breast stood out naked from the loosened fabric, a pink-rosebud nipple beckoning against scarlet silk. With her glassy eyes and stillness she was like a sensual and pliant Madonna fallen from heaven to land at the feet of the devil. Indecision welled, but he had no shield against such goodness, no way to safeguard his yearning against her righteousness.

Stepping forwards, he readjusted her gown, retying the laces on the flimsy bodice so that some measure of decency was reinstated. He could do nothing to repair the ruined seam and his eyes were drawn to the show of flesh that curved outwards beneath it, calling for his attentions. Swearing, he took a blanket from his bed and laid it around her, the wool almost the same shade as her hair. Then he collected his clothes, pulling on his breeches and placing a jacket over the shirt. He did not stop for a cravat. His boots were shoved on stockingless feet at the door as he retrieved the key and unlocked it.

'Come, sweetheart,' he murmured and found her hand, liking the way her slender fingers curled around his own.

Trust.

Another barrier breached. He yearned for others.

OUTSIDE IT WAS quiet and, as the stables materialised before them, a lad came to his side.

'Ye'd be wanting the carriage at this time of the night, your Grace?' Disbelief was evident in the query. Normally conveyances were not sent for until well into the noon hours of the next day. Or the one after that.

'Indeed. Find Stephens and have it readied. I need to go to London.'

When the boy left them Lucinda Wellingham began to speak, her voice low and uncertain. 'My cloak is still in the house and my hat and reticule. Should I not get them?'

'No.' Tay wanted only to be gone. He had no idea who would talk about her appearance at one of the most infamous and least salubrious parties of the Season, but if he had her home at the Wellingham town house before the morning surely her brothers would be able to fashion a story which would dispel all rumour.

'My friend Posy Tompkins might wonder what has happened to me. I hope that she is safe.' She did not meet his eyes at all, a contrite Venus who had tripped into the underworld unbidden and now only wanted to be released from it.

'Safe?' He could not help laughing, though the sound was anything but humorous. 'No one at my parties is safe. It is generally their singular intention not to be.'

'Enjoying herself, then?' she countered without missing a beat, the damn dimples in her cheeks another timely reminder of her innate goodness.

'Oh, I can almost swear that she will be that. The thrall of a good orgasm is highly conducive to contentment.'

Silence reigned, but he had to let her know. Who he was. What he was. Her muteness heartened him.

'I am not safe, Lady Lucinda, and neither am I repentant. When you came to Alderworth dressed in the sort of gown that raises dark fantasies in the minds of any red-blooded man, surely you understood at least that?'

Tears glittered and Tay swore, causing more again to pool beneath the light of the lamp.

'Lord knows, you are far too sweet for a sinner like me and tomorrow you will realise exactly just how close to ruin you were and be thankful that I took you home, no matter the loss of a few possessions.'

ASHER, TARIS AND Cristo would not have called her sweet. Not in a million years. She was a failure and a liability to the Wellingham name and she always had been. That was the trouble. She was 'intrinsically flawed'. The gypsy who had read her palm in a stall

outside the Leadenhall Market had looked directly into
her eyes and told her so.

Intrinsically flawed.

And she was. Tonight was living proof of the ridiculous things she did, without thought for responsibility or consequence. With a little less luck she could
have been in the Duke of Alderworth's bed right now,
knees up around his bare and muscled thighs and knowing what a great many of the less principled women of
English society already did. It was only his good sense
that had stopped her, for she had been far beyond putting a halt to anything. With just a little persuasion she
would have followed him to his bed in the candlelight.
Shame coated her, the thick ignominy making her feel
ill. Such a narrow escape.

An older man came towards them, carrying a light,
and behind him again a whole plethora of busy servants. Lucinda did not meet their eyes as they observed
her, plastering a look on her face that might pass for
indifference. Goodness, how she hoped that there was
none amongst these servants of Alderworth who might
have a channel of communication into the empire of
the Wellinghams.

At her side Alderworth made her feel both excited
and nervous, his heat calling her to him in a way that
scorched sense. When his arm came against her own
she did not pull away, the feel of him exciting and forbidden before he moved back. She took in one deep
breath and then let it out slowly, trying to find logic
and reason and failing.

His gaze swept across her with all the intensity of a ranging and predatory tiger.

Within moments the conveyance was ready to leave, the lamps lit and the driver in place. Without touching her Taylen Ellesmere indicated that she climb up and when she sat on a plush leather seat, he chose the opposite side to rest on, his green eyes brittle.

'It will take us four hours to reach Mayfair. If you are still cold…?'

'No, I am fine.' She pulled the blanket further about her, liking the shelter.

'Good.' Short and harsh.

Glancing out of the window, she saw in the faded reflection her stricken and uncertain face.

What did the Duke of Alderworth make of her? Was he as irritated by her uncertainty as he was with her intemperance? She could sense he wanted her gone just as soon as he could get her there, a woman who had strayed unbidden into a place she had no reason to be in; a woman who did not play the games that he was so infamous for.

Why he should hoist himself into the carriage in the first place was a mystery. He looked like a man who would wish to be anywhere but opposite her in a small moving space.

It was the kiss, probably, and the fact that she did not know quite how to kiss a man back. Her denial of anything more between them would have also rankled, an innocent who had played with fire and had burnt them both because of it. Granted, two or three forward beaux had planted their lips on her mouth across the years, but the offerings had always been chaste and tepid and nothing like…

No, she would not think about that. Taylen Ellesmere was a fast-living and dissolute rake who would be far from attracted to the daughter of one of London's most respectable families. He had all the women he wanted, after all, loose women, beautiful women, and she had heard it said time after time that he did not wish to be shackled by the permanency of marriage.

She shook her head hard and listened to what he was saying now.

'I shall deny that you were at Alderworth tonight should I be questioned about it. Instruct your brothers to do the same.'

'They might not need to know anything if I am lucky…'

'It is my experience that scandal does not exist in the same breath as luck, Lucinda.'

A strange warmth infused her as he said her name. She had never really liked 'Lucinda' much, but when he pronounced it he made it sound…sensual. The timbre of some other promise lay on the edge of his words.

'Believe me, with good management any damage can be minimised.'

Damage. Reality flared. She was only a situation to be managed. The night crawled in about them, small shafts of moonlight illuminating the interior of the coach. Outside the rain had begun to fall heavily, a sudden shower in a windless night.

Taylen Ellesmere was exactly like her brothers, a man who liked control and power over everything about him. No surprises or unwanted quandaries. The thought made her frown.

'I do not envisage problems,' he said. 'If you play your part well, there should not be—'

A shout split the air, and then the carriage simply rolled to one side further and further, the wild scrunch of metal upon wood and a jerking lurch.

Leaping over beside her, the Duke braced her in his arms, protecting her from the splintering glass as it shattered inwards, a cushion against the rocking chaos and the rush of cold air. He held her so tightly she felt the punching hardness of metal on his body, drawing blood and making him grimace.

Then there was only darkness.

LUCINDA WAS IN her own room at Falder House in Mayfair, the curtains billowing in a quiet afternoon breeze, the sounds of the wind in the trees and further off in the park the voices of children calling.

Everything exactly normal save for her three sisters-in-law dressed in sombre shades and sitting in a row of chairs watching her.

'You are awake?'

Beatrice-Maude came forwards and lifted Lucinda's head carefully before offering a sip of cold lemonade that sat in a glass on the bedside table. 'The doctor said he thought you would return to us today and he was right.' She smiled as she carefully blotted any trace of moisture from Lucinda's lips. 'How do you feel?'

'How should I feel?'

Something was not right. Some quiet and creeping thing was being hidden from her, crouched in the shadows of truth.

'Why am I here? What happened?'

'You don't remember?' Emerald now joined Beatrice-Maude and her face was solemn. 'You don't remember an accident, Lucy?'

'Where?' Panic had begun to consume her and she tried to sit up, but nothing seemed to work, her arms, her legs, her back. All numb and useless. The feel of her heart pumping in her chest was the only thing that still functioned and she felt light headed at the fear of paralysis.

'I cannot move.'

'Doctor Cameron said that was a normal thing. He said many people regain the use of their bodies after the swelling has subsided.'

'Swelling?'

'You suffered a blow to the neck and a nasty bang on the head. It was lucky that the coach to Leicester was passing by the other way, because otherwise...'

'You could have been there all night and Doctor Cameron said you may not have lived.' Eleanor, her youngest brother's wife, had joined in now, but unlike the others her voice shook and her face was blotchy. She had been crying. A lot.

This realisation frightened Lucinda more than anything else had.

'How did it happen?'

'Your carriage overturned. There was a corner, it seems, and the vehicle was moving too fast. It plummeted down a hill a good many yards and came to rest at the bottom of the incline.'

Agitation made her shake as more and more words tumbled into the chasm of blankness her brain had become.

Beatrice took over, holding her hand tightly, and managing a forced smile. 'It is over now, sweetheart. You are home and you are safe and that is all that is important.'

'How did I get here?'

'Asher brought you back three days ago.'

Lucinda swallowed. Three days. Her mind tried its hardest to find any recollection of the passage of time and failed.

And now she was cast upon this bed as a figure of stone, her head and heart the only parts of her body that she could still feel. A tear leaked its way from her left eye and fell warm down her cheek into the line of her hair. Swallowing, her throat thick and raw, she had the taste of blood on her tongue.

Screaming. A flash of sound came back through the ether. *Screaming and screaming. Her voice and another calming her. Quiet and sad, warm hands holding her neck so that she did not move, the night air cold and wet and the rain joining blood.*

'Doctor Cameron said it was a miracle you did not move another inch as you would have been dead. He says it was fortunate that when they found you, your head had been stabilised between two heavy planks of wood to restrain any motion.'

'Lucky,' she countered, the sentiment falling into question.

They were not telling her the whole of it. She could see it in the shared looks and feel it in the hushed un-spoken reticence. She wondered why her brothers were not here in the room and knew the answer to the question as soon as she thought it.

They would not be able to hide things from her as easily as her sisters-in-law, although Cristo was still most efficient at keeping his own council.

'Was anyone else hurt?'

The hesitation told her there had been.

'There was a man in the carriage with you, Lucy.' Emerald now took her other hand, rubbing at it in a way that was supposed to be comforting, she supposed, though it felt vaguely annoying because her skin was so numb.

'I was alone with him?' Nothing made sense. What could she have been doing on the open road at night and in the company of a stranger? It was all too odd. 'Who was he?'

'The sixth Duke of Alderworth.' Beatrice took up the story now.

'Alderworth?' Lucinda knew the name despite not remembering anything at all about the accident.

My God. The Dissolute Duke was infamous across London and it seemed he kept to the company of whores and harpies almost exclusively. Why would she have been there alone with him and so far from home?

'Does Asher know he was there?' She looked up at Emerald.

'Unfortunately he does.'

'Do other people also know?

'Unfortunately they do.'

'How many know?'

'All of London would not be putting too fine a point on it, I think.'

'I see. It is a scandal then and I am ruined?'

'No.' Beatrice-Maude's voice was strong. 'Your brothers would never allow that to happen and neither will we.'

Lucinda swallowed, the whole conundrum more than she could deal with. Eleanor and Emerald watched her with a certain worry in their eyes and even Beatrice, who was seldom flustered, seemed out of sorts.

Intrinsically flawed. The words came from nowhere as she closed her eyes and slept.

CHAPTER THREE

TAY ELLESMERE SAT in the library of the Carisbrook family town house in Mayfair and looked at the three Wellingham brothers opposite him.

His head ached, his right leg was swollen above the knee and the top of his left arm was encased in a heavy white bandage, as were his ribs, strapped tightly so that breathing was not quite so agonising. Besides this he had myriad other cuts and grazes from the glass and wood splintering as the carriage had overturned.

But these injuries were the very least of his worries. A far more pressing matter lingered in the air between him and his hosts.

'You were dressed most inappropriately and Lucinda was barely dressed at all, for God's sake. The scandal is the talk of the town and has been for the past week.'

Asher Wellingham, Duke of Carisbrook, seldom minced words and Tay did not dissemble, either.

'Our lack of clothing was the result of being thrown over and over down a hill in a somersaulting carriage. One does not generally emerge from such a mishap faultlessly attired,' he drawled the reply, knowing that it would annoy them, but short of verifying their sister's presence at his party he could do little else but blame the accident.

'We thought Lucinda had gone with Lady Posy Tompkins to her aunt's country home for the weekend. I cannot for the life of me imagine how instead she ended up alone in the middle of the night with the most dissolute Duke in all of London town and dressed as a harpy.'

'Did you ask her?'

'She can remember nothing.' Taris Wellingham broke in now, his stillness as menacing as his older brother's fury.

'Nothing?'

'Nothing before the accident, nothing during the accident and nothing just after the accident.'

Hope flared. Perhaps it might give him an escape after all. If the lady was not baying for his blood, then her brothers might also give up the chase should he play his cards well.

'Your sister informed me that she was trying to reach the Wellingham town house after being separated somehow from her friend. She merely asked me to give her a lift home and I immediately assented.'

'Her reticule, hat and cloak were returned to us from your country seat. A coincidence, would you not say, to be left at the very place you swear she was not.'

Cristo Wellingham's voice sounded as flat as his brothers'.

'Richard Allenby, the Earl of Halsey, has also told

half of London that she was a guest at your weekend soirée. Others verify his story.'

'He lies. I was the host and your sister was not there.'

'The problem is, Duke, Lucinda is facing certain ruin and you do not seem to be taking your part in her downfall seriously.'

Taylen had had enough.

'Ruin is a strong word, Lord Taris.'

'As strong as retribution.'

Asher Wellingham's hand hit the table and Tay stood. Even with his arm in a bandage he could give the three of them a good run for their money. The art of gentlemanly fighting had been a lesson missing from his life, the tough school of displacement and abuse honing the rudiments of the craft instead. Hell, he had been beaten enough himself to understand exactly the best places to hit back.

'We will kill you for this, Alderworth, I swear that we will.' Cristo spoke now, the sound of each word carefully enunciated.

'And in doing so you may well crucify your sister. Better to let the matter rest, laugh it off and kick any suggestions of misbehaviour back in the face of those who swear them true.'

'As you are apt to do?'

'English society still holds to ridiculously strict rules of conduct, though free speech is finding its way into the minds of men who would do better to believe in it.'

'Men like you?' Taris stood. His reported lack of sight was not apparent as he stepped towards the window, though Tay saw the oldest brother watch him carefully.

Care.

The word reverberated inside him. This was what this was all about, after all: care of each other, care of a family name, care in protecting their only sister's reputation from the ignominy of being linked with his.

Protection was something he himself had never had. Not from his parents. Not from his grandmother. And particularly not from his uncle. It had always been him against a world that hadn't taken the time to make sure that a small child was cherished. The man he had become was the result of such negligence, though here in the salon of a family that watched each other's backs the thought was disheartening.

He made his way around a generous sofa. 'I have an errand to attend to, gentlemen, and I find I have the need of some fresh air. If you will excuse me.'

'WHAT DO YOU make of him?'

Asher asked the question a few moments later as Cristo crossed to the cabinet to pull out a bottle of fine French brandy.

'He's hiding something.' Taris accepted a drink from his brother. 'For some reason he is trying to make us believe there was only necessity in our sister's foolish midnight tryst in the carriage with him and that she was never at Alderworth.'

Cristo swore. 'But why would he do that?'

'Even a reprobate must have his limits of depravity,

I suppose. Lucinda's innocence may well be his.' Taris drank deeply of the brandy before continuing. 'He studies the philosophy of the new consciousness, which is interesting, the tenets of free speech being mooted in the Americas. Unusual reading for a man who purports to be interested in nothing more than sexual mayhem and societal anarchy.'

'I don't trust him.' Asher upended his glass.

'Well, we can't hit a man wrapped in bandages.' Cristo smiled.

'Then we wait until they are removed.' There was no humour at all in the voice of Asher Wellingham, Duke of Carisbrook.

LUCINDA WHEELED HERSELF to the breakfast table, her muscles straining against the task and her heart pounding with the effort. It had been almost two weeks since the accident and the feeling that the doctor had sworn she would recover was finally coming back, though she had been left with a weakness that felt exhausting and a strange and haunting melancholy. Now she could walk for short distances without falling over, the shaking she had been plagued by diminishing as she grew steadily in strength. The wheelchair was, however, still her main mode of getting about.

Posy had spent much of the past week at the town house, her horror at all that had happened to Lucy threading every sentence.

'I should never have taken you to Alderworth, Luce. It is all my fault this happened to you and now…now

I don't know how to make it better.' Large tears had fallen down her cheeks before tracing wet runnels on the pink silk of her bodice.

'You did not force me to go, Posy. I remember that much.'

'But while I was safely locked away in our bedroom, you were…'

'Let's not allocate any more blame. What is done is done and at least I am regaining movement and energy.'

It had taken Lucinda a good few days to convince her friend that she held no malice or blame, Posy's numerous tears a wearying and frustrating constant.

Asher was sitting in the dining room, reading *The Times* just as he usually did each morning, and he folded the paper in half and looked closer as something caught his interest.

'It says here that the Earl of Halsey has suffered a broken nose, a black eye and twenty stitches in his cheek. The assault happened in broad daylight four days ago in an altercation outside the livery stables in Davies Mews right here in Mayfair. There were no witnesses.'

His glance strayed to Lucinda's to see how she might react. The whole family had tiptoed around her since the *unfortunate happening* as though she might break into pieces at any unwanted reminder of scandal and she was tired of it. Consequently she did nothing more than smile back at her oldest brother and shrug her shoulders.

'Footpads are becoming increasingly confident, then.' Emerald took up the conversation as she buttered her bread. 'Though perhaps they do us a favour, for isn't he the man who has constantly insisted Lucinda was underdressed at the Alderworth fiasco? Without his voice, all of this could have been so much easier to deal with.'

Lucinda knew Richard Allenby, of course. He had always been well mannered and rather sweet, truth be told, so she had no idea why he should be maligning her now and in such a fashion. Yet a shadow lingered there in the very back of her mind, some nebulous and half-formed thing trying to escape from the darkness. Wiping her mouth with the napkin, she sat back, the food suddenly dry in her mouth and difficult to swallow.

'You look like you have seen a ghost, Lucy.'

'What exactly was it that the Earl of Halsey said of me?'

'He has been spreading the rumour that you may have been intimate with Alderworth at his home. He says he saw you in the corridors on the first floor of the place, searching for the host's bedchamber.'

Her brother's tone had that streak of exasperation she so often heard when speaking of her escapades, though in this case Lucinda could well understand it.

'Intimate?' The shock of such a blatant falsehood was horrifying. 'Why would he tell such a lie? Surely people could not believe him?' Wriggling her foot against the metal bar of the wheelchair, she checked for any further movement. Over the past few days the tingling had gone from her knees to her feet as the numbness receded.

'Unfortunately they are beginning to.' Asher's voice no longer held any measure of care.

'What does Alderworth say?'

'Nothing and that is the great problem. If he denied everything categorically and strode into society the same way he strode into Wellingham House, people might cease to believe Richard Allenby. But instead the man has disappeared to the country, leaving chaos behind him.'

'Alderworth came here? To the town house?' Lucinda frowned. There was something about him that was familiar, some part of him that she remembered from… before. 'What did he want?'

'Put bluntly, he wanted to be rid of any blame as far as your reputation was concerned. He made that point very plain.' Asher put his paper down and watched her closely. 'The man is a charlatan, but he is also clever. The slight whiff of an alliance with us might be profitable to him.'

'Alliance?' Lucinda's mouth felt suddenly dry.

'A ruined reputation requires measures that may be stringent and far from temporary.'

'You mean a betrothal?' Horror had Lucinda's words whispered. Low. She had heard all the stories of the wicked Duke. Everybody had. He was a man who lived by his own rules and threw the caution most others followed to the wind.

As her heartbeat quickened, memory fought against haze and won. Dropping the teacup she was holding, she stood, liquid spilling across the pristine whiteness of an antique damask tablecloth, the brown stain widening through the embossed stitching even as she watched.

The naked form of Taylen Ellesmere came through the fog, unfolding from a rumpled bed, each long and graceful line etched in candlelight, the red wine in a decanter beside him almost gone. She knew the feel of his skin, undeniably, for they had been joined together pressed in lust, his velvet-green eyes close as he had leaned down and kissed her. No simple chaste kiss, either, but one with a smouldering and virtue-taking force.

Shock kept her still, as she looked directly at her oldest brother.

'What is wrong? You look…ill.' Real concern crossed his face.

'I am remembering things and I th-th-think everything Richard Halsey is saying of m-me might indeed be tr-true.'

Her weakened legs folded beneath her just as Asher caught her, the hard arm of the chair slamming into her side.

'You are saying you lay with Alderworth. Unmarried.'

'He was naked in his bedchamber. He touched me everywhere. The door was locked and I could not leave. I tried to, but I could not. He took the key. He was not safe.' A torrent of small truths, each one worse than the last.

'My God.' She had never heard the note in her brother's voice that she did now, not once in all her many escapades and follies. His fractured tone brought tears to her eyes as she felt Emerald's hand slip into her own and squeeze.

'YOU WILL MARRY my sister as soon as I can procure a special licence and then you will disappear from England altogether, you swine.'

Asher Wellingham had already laid a good few punches across Tay's face and Cristo Wellingham was still holding him down. Not the refined manners he had imagined them to have, after all, each blow given with a deliberate and clinical precision. His nose streamed with blood and he could barely see out of his left eye. The two front teeth at the bottom of his mouth were loosened.

'If you kill me…a betrothal might be…difficult.'

Another blow caught him in the kidneys and, despite meaning not to, he winced.

'You will tell Lucinda that it was completely your fault she was at Alderworth in the first place and that your heinous, iniquitous and pernicious sense of social virtue was lost years before you met her. In effect, you will say that she never had the chance of escaping such corruption.'

'C-comprehensive.'

'Very. But as long as you understand us we will allow you to at least take breath into another day whilst we try to mitigate all the wrong you have heaped upon our sister. She is distraught, as you can well imagine, and names you as the most loathsome of all men. A reprobate who took advantage of her when she was drunk.'

'She told you that?'

'And worse. But although she might hate you, she also knows that you are the only man who can restore her shattered name in society when you marry her. In that she is most adamant.'

'A sterling quality in a bride.' Even to his own ears his voice lacked the sting of irony he usually made an art form of.

'Well, you can laugh, Alderworth, but if you believe we will let you anywhere near Lucinda after the ceremony is performed then you have another think coming. You have already done your damage. Now you will pay for it.'

Tay coughed once and then again, his breath difficult to catch. When the younger brother allowed him to drop heavily to the floor he felt the arm that had been hurt in the carriage accident crack against hard parquet, pain radiating up into the shoulder socket.

Ignominiously he began to shake and he swore. It had been a long time since he remembered doing that, his uncle's face screwed up above him in the wrath of some perceived and tiny insult, the summer winds of Alderworth hot against the wounds that lashed his back. Bleeding, everywhere. No mercy in the beating.

Standing uncertainly and holding on to the edge of a chair, he raised himself before them. 'Your sister's memory is faulty. I did not touch her.'

'She says exactly the opposite, and anybody who knows Lucinda knows, too, that straightforward honesty is one of her greatest strengths.' The embossed ducal ring on Carisbrook's finger caught the light as he moved forwards. 'Frankly, given the number of your dubious guests who have not ceased gossiping since the accident about what went on at Alderworth, I find your whining and feeble excuses insulting. A man worth his salt would simply own up to his mistakes and take the punishment he deserves.'

From experience Tay knew when to stop baiting a man who would hit him until life was leached from truth. He nodded an end to the dispute and saw the answering relief on Asher Wellingham's face.

'We will pay you to leave a week after the wedding. A considerable sum that should see you well on your way to your next destination. After that, you will never again set foot anywhere near London or our family.'

'Alderworth is almost bankrupt. Your father's debts were numerous and you will not have enough equity to continue the repayments after the year's end.' Taris had taken up the reins now, from a sofa near the fireplace, his voice steady and quiet. 'You have been trying to trade your way out of the conundrum, but your bills are becoming onerous and a lifestyle of indolence is hardly a profitable one. Accept our offer and you might keep your family inheritance for a few years yet. Decline and you will be in the debtors' prison by Christmas.'

'Will your sister know?'

'Indeed. Lucinda wants it.' Cristo stepped forwards, disdain in his eyes. 'She wants you out of her life for ever.'

Marriage as a bribe to keep the Alderworth estate. Tay thought of its roofline under the Bedfordshire sky, the golden stone against the sun and hundreds of acres of fertile and green land at its feet. His father had forsaken the place, but he could not. Not even if the alternative meant selling his soul.

'Very well.' His voice was hoarse and he felt his honour breaking, but he swiped the feeling away as a quill was inked and a parchment made ready. He was the only Alderworth who could save four hundred years of history and Lucinda Wellingham hated his very guts.

CHAPTER FOUR

LORD TAYLEN ELLESMERE, the sixth Duke of Alderworth, had the appearance of a man who had been in a particularly rough boxing match when Lucinda saw him for the first time at the top of the aisle in the small chapel in London's Mayfair.

He did not turn to look at her, his profile granite-hard, his left wrist encased in a bandage and a large cut running along the whole side of his jaw. The muscles beneath the wound rippled with anger, a barely held wrath that was seen in the straightness of his posture and in the rigidity of his being. His hair was shorter, shaved almost to the skull, a single white, opaque scar snaking from the edge of his right ear to his crown. One eye was blackened.

Even Asher looked slightly taken aback by his appearance, but at this stage of the proceedings there was little anyone could do.

The die was cast after all. She would marry the Duke of Alderworth to redeem her place in society and he would marry her because her brothers had made him do so. She had sinned and this was the result. Love existed nowhere in the equation and the empty pews in the chapel reflected the fact. Her siblings and their wives sat on her side of the church, as well as some close friends, but on his side...there was nobody.

Lucinda speculated as to who might stand up as his witness, the question answered a moment later when Cristo moved across to him. Her youngest brother looked about as unhappy with the whole thing as Asher was, a duty performed out of necessity rather than respect.

Every other Wellingham wedding had been a joyous affair, celebrated with laughter and noise and elation. This one was sombre, quiet and dismal. She wondered how long the Duke of Alderworth would stay in London after the ceremony and just what words she might use to explain away his absence. Asher had said that he would remain in the capital for a week or more, so that appearances could be upheld. After that they would be glad to see the back of him.

Her brother had breathed this through a clenched jaw as if even a day in the company of her soon-to-be husband would be one too many.

Lucinda swallowed away dry fear. This was the worst mistake she had ever made, but the consequences of her own stupidity had brought her to such a pass, her whole family entwined in the deceit. She wanted to throw down the bouquet of white roses interlaced with fragrant gardenias and peel off the ivory gown that had been quickly fashioned by one of London's up-and-coming modistes. The veil helped, however, a layer of lace between her and the world, sheltering confusion.

A week ago she would not have been able to walk or to stand for such long periods, but today the utter alarm of everything allowed her to keep any pain at bay.

Posy Tompkins stood to one side of her, her face drawn. Her friend had been nothing short of horrified about the consequences of their ill-thought-out visit to Alderworth and had been attentive and apologetic ever since. She claimed she had managed to avoid the worst of the excesses by locking herself in her room.

'Are you sure you want to go through with this, Luce?' she whispered. 'We could disappear to Europe together otherwise. I have more than enough money for us both. We could go to Rome or Paris to my relatives.'

'And be for ever outcast?'

'It might be better than…' She stopped, but Lucinda knew exactly what she was about to say.

It might be better than being married to a man who looked for all the world as if he was going to his own funeral. With an effort she lifted her chin. It was not as if she was happy about anything, either, although some quiet part of her buried deep held its breath as green eyes raked across her own, the red streak in one of them bright with fury.

'This is 1831, Luce, not the Middle Ages. If you truly do not wish to do this, you only have to say. No one can drag a reluctant bride to the altar even if the alternative is enormous scandal.'

'I do not think your words are helping, Posy.'

'Then let me call it off. I can say that it was completely my fault I took you to Alderworth in the first place and procured the dress and...'

But the minister had begun to speak in his low, calm voice and Lucinda knew that to simply walk out on her last chance of salvation would be to cut herself off from a family that meant the world to her.

She had brought this upon herself, after all, and she just could not think of another more viable solution. A marriage ceremony. A week of pretence. And then freedom. Lord, she would follow the straight and narrow from now on and, if God in all his wisdom allowed her the strength to get through these next hours, she would promise in return an eternal devotion to His Good Works.

WHEN TAY TOOK a quick look at his bride-to-be he saw that under her veil her hair was plaited in a crown encircled by pale rosebuds. Today she seemed smaller, slighter, less certain. The lies she had spun about them, he supposed, come home to roost in front of the altar, no true basis for any such betrothal. He was glad of the lace that covered her head because he did not wish to see her deceitful eyes until he had to. The gown surprised him, though. He had thought she might balk at making any effort whatsoever, but the dress fitted her perfectly, spilling in a froth of whiteness about her feet. A dainty silver bracelet adorned her left wrist, four small gold stars hanging from it.

A continual whispered dialogue with the bridesmaid began to get on his nerves and he was glad when the minister, dressed in flowing dark clothes, called the place to order.

Everybody looked tense. The bride. The brothers. Even the minister as he held his hand up to the organist and called for quiet.

'Marriage is a state that is not to be entered into lightly, or with false promise. Are you happy to continue, Lady Lucinda?'

Tay bit down on chagrin. Of course she would be. His title was one factor and her ruin was another. He wished the man might skip through to the final troths and then all of this would be over.

But he did not. Rather he waited until the bride before him nodded her head without any enthusiasm whatsoever. 'Then we are here today to join this man and this woman in the state of Holy Matrimony...'

For ever and for ever. It was all Tay could think as he gave his replies, though his parents had never let such pledges inhibit them in their quest for the hedonistic. For the first time in his life he partly understood them and some of his disillusionment lifted.

But it was too late for such understanding now, with his years seemingly destined to run along the same chaotic and uncontrolled pathway as those that he had sworn he would never follow. He was his father's son, after all, and this was a universally ordained celestial punishment for what he had become. The thought calmed him; fate moving in ways which allowed no redemption and if it had not been this particular sticky end that he had met, then undoubtedly it would have been another.

'Will you, Taylen Andrew Templeton Ellesmere, take Lucinda Alice Wellingham as your lawfully wedded wife…?'

The words shook him from his reverie. Her middle name was Alice and it suited her. Soft. Pale. Otherworldly.

'I will.'

Resignation tempered his pledge.

When Lucinda Wellingham gave the troth her tone was shaken, a thin voice in a house of God that held no message of joy within it.

And finally it was over.

Because it was expected he turned to face her and lifted the veil slowly. The church had been a place of refuge for him as a child and he still believed in the sanctity of religion despite everything he had become. The woman who stood there, however, was different from the laughing brave one in his bedchamber in Alderworth. This girl had dark rings beneath her lashes and eczema on her cheeks. Her eyes were flat blue orbs with no sparkle at all and the bump on her head from the accident was still visible. Exhaustion wove paleness into her skin.

As hurt as he was. A shared damage.

He felt his hand move to touch the wound and stopped himself. Theirs was a marriage in name only and the Wellinghams had been insistent that he understood this was for public consumption. A week or two at the most and then they wanted him gone. Her brothers had said that was her wish, too, his bride who, after uttering only lies, would not carry out even the pretence of a union once her ruin was minimised.

A travesty. A perversion. A shameful parody of something that should have been finer. Lord, the notion that survival justified the use of immoral means to achieve the required end was rubbing off on him in a melancholic and peculiar discontent. *'He who neglects what is done for what ought to be done effects his ruin...'* Machiavelli. The memory took him back to the night she had burst uninvited into his room, her colour high and the red dress low across her breasts.

Tay wished Lucinda Wellingham would take his hand again and hold it as she had at Alderworth, her fingers entwined into the worth of him as if she knew things that nobody else had ever discovered. He shook his head hard at such nonsense and she chose that moment to look at him directly, pale blue searingly condemnatory, the lies between them settling into an uncrossable distance.

'It cannot be easy to be the bride of ruin.' His words made her flinch, but he did not take them back. He wished that amongst those gathered there had been one person who might have welcomed his company. But there wasn't. All the wives of the Wellinghams had drawn Lucinda into their bosom, their eyes slicing across his like sharp knives—a rancorous truce, the white flag of surrender raised across his spilled blood and bruising. If he had by chance dropped dead due to some unforeseen and dreadful ailment he thought a party might have ensued, this veil of pretence transformed into a celebration of death.

He had never felt so unwelcome anywhere.

THE SHAKE OF Taylen Ellesmere's head made Lucinda turn away, the tears she felt smarting at the back of her burning eyes threatening to fall. He did not look contrite or penitent or even slightly apologetic. He looked implacable and indifferent, this man who had disgraced her through fine red wine and a callous disregard for innocence, and was now making no effort whatsoever to assuage such poor behaviour.

The Bride of Ruin, indeed. Her husband now. Judas. Shylock. Marcus Brutus.

Lucinda could not even bear the thought that he might reach out and touch her.

She had been destroyed and she could remember none of it. She had been deflowered by a master with only the slightest jolt of memory remaining. Her brothers stood around her, a wall of masculine prickliness, sheltering her from the canker this betrothal had spawned, her sisters-in-law stalwart in the next ring of protection.

Alderworth had not apologised to them. Rather he had laughed in the face of their accusations and sworn free will was a liberty that all were entitled to.

Free will to take an innocent beneath him and to ravish her under the influence of strong wine; free will to take her to his bed and to say nothing to obliterate the raging gossip that swirled around the circles of society.

Lucinda Wellingham, the harlot. Lucinda Wellingham, intrinsically flawed.

Like the spoilt centre of a fruit, she thought, and was glad Posy Tompkins had also pushed in beside her because at least her friend's perception of the nuptials was laced with some sense of excitement.

'You will be free now, Luce. A married woman has so many more liberties.'

'I doubt another invitation will ever land upon my mantel, Posy.'

'Then we shall hold our own soirées, brilliant cultured gatherings that shall be the talk of the town.'

'Like courtesans?' Lucinda could not take the sting of it from her words for, all of a sudden, the whole world seemed meaningless and hollow. Posy had no notion of the signed agreements designating the boundaries of this marriage. She had not told her.

'Taylen Ellesmere is titled and handsome. There will be many a woman who might envy you such a husband. Believe me, be thankful he was not old and grey with no teeth and bad breath.'

Despite everything Lucinda smiled. Trust Posy to see the bright side of it all. Taking her friend's hand, she held her fingers in a tight grip and turned away from the worry of her family. The promises had been given and the deed was done. The only way on from here was upwards and Lucinda swore that when she was finally free of all this she would never allow her life to be mired again in such a shambolic wreck of betrayal.

'THE WEDDING BREAKFAST has been set up, Lucy. Asher asked if you would come now so that we can get this… finished with.' Beatrice spoke softly so that no one would overhear. The Wellinghams could manipulate to avoid disaster, but they wanted no others to understand that they did so. The twenty or so outside guests who had strong ties with the family beamed at her from one corner of the room of Falder House.

They had been invited to make this farce seem… legitimate. With the knowledge of what might happen next her brothers had at least given her back her shattered name. But after this she would only garner pity; the bride who was left summarily by a husband who had never loved her.

Threading through the room, Beatrice, Taris and Asher led the assembly along to the blue salon. If she had wondered before at the control her brothers liked to wield, she understood now the very essence of it. The tables were dressed lavishly, the settings of the finest bone china and sterling silver. French wine had been brought up from the cellar. No shortcuts to encourage gossip. No small errors that might make the invited guests wonder. Nay, beneath the polite banter another reality lingered, stronger and unmistakable, but only if your name was Wellingham.

Taylen Ellesmere was sat next to her, his nearness

making her shake, though when his leaf-green eyes brushed her own she felt…dizzy and disorientated.

Some worry leaked through her anger, a quiet emotion in a room full of tension. Bruising lay beneath his one blackened eye and there was a cut upon his bottom lip that she had not noticed before. Despite it all his beauty shone through, no slight comeliness, either, but a full-on barrage of masculine grace.

Unnerved, she shifted the lengthy veil which had pulled in beneath her, the lace of the Carisbrook's heirloom fragile in the play of sunshine from the window. She felt as though the breath had been knocked out of her lungs by one hefty punch of misgiving, but another truth also lingered.

Her husband was not all evil. There was a goodness in him that no one had discovered as yet.

She knew this as certainly as night followed the day, even though on his left hand beside his marriage band other rings glinted in the light—perhaps reminders of love from other women he had once admired before he had been made to marry her by her brothers? His name was always linked to paramours, after all. Was there one who he might have wished was standing here now in her stead?

Her cheeks itched with the eczema she always got when misgiving consumed her and the idea that her good name might be salvaged by such a course of action suddenly seemed foolish and ill advised. She wished she did not feel so shamefully heated by his presence at her side, the indifference she sought so far away from this undeniable awareness of him.

'The carriage accident hurt us both? I have been told how very lucky I was in not being killed by it, for with only a small movement things could have been so very much worse and I may never have walked again or even spoken and according to Doctor Cameron there might have—'

He stopped her by raising one hand. 'Are you nervous?'

For the first time she could ever remember in her whole entire life, Lucinda blushed. She felt the slow crawl of blood fusing her cheeks and held her hand up to the heat.

'Why would you say that?'

'Because you confided in me once that you talk too much when you worry.'

Her mouth dropped open.

Such a private honesty and one that she had never let another soul be privy to. She seldom shared her secrets, keeping them close to her heart instead, safe from derision or discussion. When and why had she told him such a thing? Perhaps the wine had made her speak? The exasperating fact of her lack of memory was both tiring and worrying.

'Surely you remember. It was just before I kissed you.'

Should she tell him that only a minuscule recollection remained from the time that they had shared in his chamber? *His nakedness. The wine. His mouth upon her breast. Her nipples hardening.*

Now that was new. Sitting up, she tried to remember some more, but couldn't. A new resolution firmed. He had taken her maidenhood without her consent and now would pay for it.

The laws of the land were there to protect the innocent and every Lord in his position had been brought up to acknowledge such a code. Ethics safeguarded chaos. When such tenets were broken, this was the result: a hasty marriage between strangers, flung together by the flimsy strands of expedience.

'I was foolish to come to your house in the first place, your Grace, and more foolish to stay. This is my penance.' She kept her tone distant, formal, just a polite conversation. When she leaned forwards she caught sight of herself in the wide shiny silver of an unused platter. Her cheeks were worse, even in the few short hours since leaving her chamber. She doubted she had ever looked quite so awful and her groom's handsome visage just made everything a hundred times more humiliating. Shallow, she knew, but in all her girlhood fantasies she had not imagined herself appearing so very bedraggled at her own wedding feast.

Lord Fergusson came up behind them, placing one hand on each of their shoulders. 'If you can have a marriage like I had for forty-three years, then you will be well blessed.' His old eyes brimmed with kindness.

Tay Ellesmere simply looked across at her. Answer

this as you will, he seemed to be saying, shards of irritation noticeable.

'Indeed, Lord Fergusson,' she replied, remembering Mary-Rose, his beautiful wife, who had passed away suddenly the previous summer.

'But may I offer you a few words of advice? What you put into a marriage is what you get out from it and agreement is the oil that smoothes the way.'

'Then with all the agreements between us, ours shall run most smoothly,' Alderworth observed.

He had changed the meaning of the word 'agreement', but Lord Fergusson did not understand his reference. Her new husband's hands were in his lap. Fisted. Not quite as indifferent as he made out to be. Another thought struck her. Every knuckle had been grazed as though he had only recently been in a fight. Was that why his eye was black and his jaw cut? Please, God, let it not have been her brothers who had hurt him.

'I knew your uncle, Duke.' This was said tentatively. 'The Earl of Sutton.'

'Unfortunate for you.' Her groom's tone was plain ice and Lord Fergusson left as quickly as he had come, a frown on his face as he scrambled away.

'He is an old man who would do you no harm, your Grace, and he has only just lost his wife. Besides, this is a wedding and people expect—'

He broke in before she had finished. 'What do they expect, Lucinda? All that is between us here is dishonesty and farce. The charade of a marriage and the farce of a happy ever after. And now you want me to lie about an uncle who was not fit to be around children, let alone one who—' He stopped suddenly, his green eyes as dark as she had ever seen them, fathomless pools of torture. The real Taylen Ellesmere who lived beneath all he showed to the world was evident, the pain within him harrowing.

'You speak about yourself as a child? This uncle, the Earl of Sutton, he was your guardian?'

Only horror showed now, though the shutters reflecting emotion closed even as she watched and the implacable ruthless Duke was back.

'Enjoy your day, my dearest wife, because there are not many left to us.'

With that he stood and walked out of the room.

CHAPTER FIVE

GOD, SHE KNEW. Lucinda Alice Ellesmere was guessing his secrets as easily as if he had written them down for her, one after the other of sordid truth.

He should have remained silent, but the old man and his useless dreams had rattled him, made him remember his own hopes as his mother and father had spat and hissed each and every word to the other, unmindful of a small child who heard the endless malice and rancour. He had promised himself he would never marry and yet here he was, chained to a family who would like nothing better than to see him dead and buried.

'If you slope off now you won't get a penny, Alderworth.' Cristo Wellingham came to his side, the room they were in empty. Unexpectedly Lucinda's youngest brother produced a cheroot. 'You have the look of a man who might need one,' he said, offering a light and waiting as Tay took the first few puffs. Smoke curled towards the ceiling, a screen of white and then gone. Tay wished he could have disappeared as easily as it did and, closing his eyes for a second, he leaned back against the wall, enjoying the first rush of its effects.

'I look forward to the day when the guilt of your sister's lies finally brings her to her senses.' The exhaustion in his voice was disconcerting, but the day had taken its toll and he was tired of the pretence.

'When you will likely be squandering what is left of your blood money in some poverty-stricken dive, remembering the ill that you did to a blameless innocent and wondering how you came to such a pass.'

He laughed at that. 'You did not enjoy a few of your wife's charms before marrying her?' A shadow rewarded the query and so he continued. 'I kissed your sister and brought her home. That was all. If she insists otherwise, then I say she lies.'

'With a reputation as disreputable as your own, a lack of belief in anything you say cannot be surprising.'

'Then allow me one boon, Lord Cristo. Allow me the small privilege of some knowledge of how your sister fares once I have gone.'

'Why would you want that? You have made it plain enough that a substantial payment constitutes the sum total of your care.' He stepped back. 'There won't be more from where that came from, no matter what you might say.'

'You will always hold her safe, then?' Tay had not meant to ask the question, but it slipped from him like a living thing, important and urgent, the last promise he might extract before he was gone.

'Safer than you damn well did,' came the reply, but in Cristo Wellingham's dark eyes puzzlement flickered. Using it to his advantage, Taylen pressed on.

'If I wrote, would you give her my letters?'

'Yes.' Ground out, but honest. When Lucinda's brother turned and left he was glad he had been given even that slight hope of contact.

LUCINDA FELT EXHAUSTED by all the smiles and good wishes given with such genuine congeniality that the scandal disappeared into a God-ordained union that restored the balance of chaos in a highly regulated world. A violation covered up. A wrong righted. A happy ending to a less-than-salubrious beginning.

She had been surprised at the way the Duke of Alderworth had stood next to her for the past twenty minutes, his manner with the guests at odds with his self-proclaimed lack of interest in polite society. Perhaps he, too, had finally seen that in a good show of pretence there lay freedom. When his arm touched hers the full length of warmth seared in, the shock of contact electric, her breath held still by an awareness that she had felt with no other before him.

If only she might remember what a night in his bed felt like. The very idea made her frown, because in it she sensed she was missing something important.

'You look concerned.' Alderworth used a gap in the line of well-wishers to address her directly.

'It seems for all your reputation, people here are inclined to give you a second chance. I was wondering why.'

'Perhaps it's because you stand up as my bride, a Wellingham daughter who might deign to lend her name to my sullied one.'

'No. It is more than that. They accord you a certain begrudging respect, which is interesting.'

'Vigilance might be a more apt word!' Unexpectedly he smiled at her, the green in his eyes relaxing into gold, and with the colour of his skin burnished into bronze by the outdoors and his dark hair so shortened, he looked… unmatched. Her brothers were handsome, but the Duke had some spark of incomparable beauty that set him apart from everyone else Lucinda had ever seen.

The vapidity of her thoughts held her mute.

'Frowning does not suit you as much as laughter does,' he remarked.

'Of late there has not been too much to be delighted by.'

'I am sorry for that.'

'Are you?' Even amidst a crowd of family friends she could not leave the question unvoiced.

She saw him glance around to check the nearness of those in his vicinity before he gave a reply.

'I lived with lies all of my childhood, Duchess, and do not wish to encourage them. If you insist on such deception then that is your prerogative, but I will never understand it.'

Both her new title and his unwarranted anger made Lucinda step back, the same scene she had remembered at the breakfast table a week ago replaying over and over in her head.

His nakedness, the red wine, the feel of his warm skin against her own. The door locked and the key hidden. No opportunity to simply leave.

'London is a haven for gossip, Duke, and because of your actions my name has been slandered from one edge of it to the other.'

'A reputation lost for nothing, then.'

Lucinda paled. Did he speak of her virginity in such scathing terms? She was glad her brothers were nowhere nearby to hear such an accusation.

'For nothing?' She could barely voice the question. 'You are a reprobate, your Grace, of the highest order and the fate that flung us together at Alderworth will be regretted by me for the rest of my life. Bitterly.' There was no longer any conciliation in her tone.

He had the temerity to smile. 'Then it is a shame you did not make full use of our evening together and understand the true benefits that uninhibited sensuality can bring. Better to have enjoyed a night in my bed learning all you needed to know about the art of love and regretted it, than repenting the "nothing" you have been crucified for.'

Shocked, she turned on her heels and left him, not caring who saw her flee. He would castigate her for her poor performance in bed when she could recall none of it. Her blood rose to boiling and she hated her pronounced limp.

'Are you feeling well, Lucinda?' Emerald waylaid her before she had reached the door.

'Very.' Even to a beloved sister-in-law she couldn't betray him entirely, a trait she did not understand at all.

'Alderworth will be gone before the end of this week and you will never need to see him again.'

The absurdity of such a statement suddenly hit her, the first glimpse of her life after today. Was she destined then to always be alone, marriage-less and childless? Would she now linger in the corner of society with those hapless spinsters who spoke of unrequited love or of no love at all? Not ruined, but blighted by her lack of adherence to the normal conventions and suffering because of it.

The headache she had been cursed with all day bloomed with a fierce pain, blurring her vision. A migraine. She had had them badly ever since the accident.

Understanding her malady, Emerald took her hand and led her from the room, the familiar flight of stairs to her childhood bedroom welcomed. A refuge. A place to hide.

With care Emerald helped her undress and pulled down her hair till it fell about her waist, the heaviness of it causing her temples to throb harder.

'Marriage has made everything worse, Emmie.' The ring Alderworth had brought with him glinted on her finger and she looked down at it. A single ruby in white gold. Surprisingly tasteful. 'Before it was only my reputation immured in the sludge, now it is my whole life as well.'

'When your head does not ache as much and you realise you can once again participate in all the things you love doing, the world will look rosier.'

'As a widow? As a wife? As a spinster for ever doomed to sit in the corner, waiting for a husband who is gone?'

'You are saying that you wish he would not disappear?' Her sister-in-law's voice was sharp.

'No.' Shaking her head violently, she remembered Taylen Ellesmere's caustic disparagement of that which had been between them. She also remembered the way it had felt when their arms had touched and he had not pulled away.

She shook away the thought with a hard anger. Her husband saw her as a woman to be pitied, a poor excuse of a girl with her puritanical take on life and her inability to embrace his darkness.

They would ruin each other. It was as simple as that. All she wanted was to be between cool and crisp linen sheets, the world dissolved into dreams and ease and far from the reality of being bride to a groom who had not said even one kind word to her across the whole awful charade of their wedding day.

The Bride of Ruin. Indeed, she was exactly that.

'LUCINDA IS IN bed with a headache and won't be joining the family again this evening. To say that she is disappointed in you would be putting it mildly.'

Asher Wellingham stood before Tay, a glass of brandy in a sizeable goblet in his hand. He did not offer the chance of the same to him. Taris Wellingham leant against a window in the far end of the library. As reinforcement, Taylen supposed, the quiet stillness of the middle brother as alarming as it always was.

'You will be allotted a chamber here, Alderworth, to allay any rumour or gossip. Then you will accompany Lucinda to the Parkinsons' ball tomorrow evening. The

Duchess and I will attend as well, to make certain that you play the part of a doting and besmitten groom.'

'Another staged affair, then, though I cannot quite understand what you plan to do about the legal fact of our union in the future. Marriage is usually for ever.'

'Death negates a marriage.' The words were said without any emotion whatsoever as amber eyes met his own.

'You are threatening me?'

'I am the head of a family who is trying to make sense of a senseless act of treachery.'

'Treachery? I kissed your sister once and then bundled her into the carriage to bring her home. An accident prevented us from reaching this town house. Where is the treachery in that?'

'I am more inclined to believe my sister's version of the story above your own.'

'The ravished, ruined version?' Tay could not help his sarcasm and the Duke of Carisbrook's brow furrowed.

'If I hear even the slightest hint of rumours that you say differently, I will make it known you demanded money from us for the sole purpose of your own benefit. Blackmail, if you will, with no thought for your innocent bride.'

'A fabrication that will have me drummed out of London whilst you condemn Lucinda to the life of a nun?'

'Better a nun than the harlot you have already made her.'

'Better than a misguided girl who invents tales to

trap me?' Tay had had enough of carefully tip-toeing around the issue and the gloves were off.

Intent darkened his adversary's eyes. 'You came into our lives by an accident, Alderworth, and you can depart on one just as easily.'

'More threats?'

Turning away from Asher Wellingham, Taylen took in a breath. Let him strike like a coward and see what happened next. He had had it with headaches and warnings just as he had had it with utter lies. This was his wedding night and the only one he might damn well ever get, given these ridiculous edicts, yet here he was trading insults with his…new brother-in-law. Such a thought made him maudlin.

He could not win any concessions here tonight when tension, mistrust and fury coated every word between them. Better to wait until the morrow and have a conversation with his new bride that was long overdue.

'I am returning to my own town house and, short of rendering me unconscious and tying me up to a bed here, you can do nothing to stop me going. I will be back tomorrow after midday in the hope that your sister will be well enough to sit down and talk sense. Make sure that she is here, Carisbrook.'

As the door closed and Alderworth's footsteps receded into the distance, Taris rose. 'There is a note in his voice that concerns me, Ashe.'

'How so?'

'He seems to genuinely believe he is the innocent party.'

'The guilt of the damned is never simple. His is just more complicated than most.'

Taris drained his glass. 'Emerald said that Lucy never wants to see him again.'

'A difficult emotion, given that a marriage ceremony has just been performed and he was promised a week.'

'We might be rid of him if we were to leave London at first light and make for somewhere he could not find us. I think both parties need some time to take stock of what has happened and see a way through this. I doubt he would make a fuss with the threat of the removal of the promised remuneration hanging over his head.'

Possibilities roared between them as the fire carved shadows across the ceiling. A clean break would make certain that Lucinda was safe and it would also calm the troubled waters until they might make something else of the conundrum. The fine strong brandy in each of their glasses after such a harrowing day made their best intentions seem more…persuasive, less high-handed.

Always they had cared for their little sister, rescuing her from this scrape and then that one, smoothing down conjecture and controlling any whispered gossip. Always, until now.

'Have we made a mistake, do you think, insisting on this damn marriage?' Asher's voice was grave, copious liquor and contrasting emotions clouding certainty.

'Too late for second thoughts.' Taris swore even as he said it, a ripe curse that reverberated around the library. 'We did what we could. It is far past time for Lucy to understand the repercussions of her mistakes.'

'Loneliness might be one of them.'

'Aye, it might. But better than being tied to a man she loathes, I'd be thinking, and if we play it right he will be gone and she can get on with a new sort of life. These awkward alliances happen all the time, but with good management they can be manipulated to appear to be nothing like they actually are.'

'Successful?' Sarcasm dripped from the word.

'I was thinking more along the lines of moderately satisfactory to both parties concerned. Lucinda gets her freedom and Alderworth his money. At least it is a way past ruin.'

CHAPTER SIX

HANDS KEPT SHAKING her awake, insistent and unrelenting.

'Come, Lucy, we need to be up and about, for Asher wants us out of London by daybreak.'

'Why?'

Taking a quick look at the clock on her bedside table, Lucinda determined it to be very early in the morning. The birds had not even called yet and Emerald looked in a hurry.

'Alderworth is rescinding his promise to leave. He seems to think you will be accompanying him north to his estate.'

Sitting up, Lucinda pushed the covers back, the bruises on her legs dark against the whiteness of the sheets.

'He wants that of me?'

Her sister-in-law shrugged her shoulders. 'Given his character he probably wishes to haul you off to Alderworth and keep you there.'

'Like a prisoner?' Tremors of fear made her feel ill.

'Of course not. But it might behove us to make certain that he understands exactly what you do want.'

'Nothing. I wish for nothing between us.'

The wedding dress stared at her from its hanger across the wardrobe door, the white, pristine silk more than she could bear. Getting up, she threw the thing into the cupboard, the veil of gauzy lace joining it.

One day when she was ninety and her brother's children's children asked her about her life, she might tell them that the worst moment of all was the one where she had caught sight of herself in the mirror in her bedroom the morning after her nuptials. And when they asked her why, she would say because that was the moment she realised there would never be another chance of happiness for her.

'I will have the housekeeper dispose of the gown, Lucinda, so that you do not need to see the garment again.' Emerald's eyes were a stormy turquoise, but tenderness lay in the hand that came to fall over hers. 'We shall get through this together as a family, for your brothers have ways to right all the wrongs.'

'Divorce is not an easy passage…'

'Annulment, then? That could be an option.'

'I rather think that might have come too late, considering my returning memories and society's talk. I should never have married him at all.'

'Then we just need some time to think about it, some quiet time away from the pressures of London. A solution is always available to any problem and this one will be no different.'

'What if Alderworth comes to find me at Falder and demands my return?'

The silence told her that there was some other thing afoot.

'We are not going to Falder?'

'No. We are making for Beaconsfield and then to a house on the south coast. You can live there with a stipend if you cannot stay close to town.'

'Away from the Duke of Alderworth?'

'He is a dangerous adversary, Lucy. Until we can formulate a plan to keep you safe, it is better to keep you apart. I think such a man would insist on his marital rights.'

The blood simply drained from her face as she contemplated that truth. Would the Dissolute Duke want to take her to his bed? Again? Her imagination ran wild. If she was already pregnant from her ignominious ruin, how would this change things? The very thought of it had her reaching for her thick night-wrap.

'I do not want to see him, Emmie. Asher is right. I wish for some distance between us so that I can indeed think.'

TAY SAT IN his study with the curtains open and a quarter-moon outside in the heavens struggling to find clear sky through banks of high-billowed cloud.

She had left. Lucinda Wellingham had gone with her family from London, running in the early dawn to a place that was not Falder. He had found out this little information from a stable hand he waylaid on the way home from their town house, though the boy had no inkling of their true destination.

His bride had, however, left a note, the words written in his memory like some morbid poem of rebuttal.

I hope that you will allow me a few weeks to recover from the accident and to consider my options.

Please do not come after me. I will not receive you.

If you need to contact me, Cristo will forward any communication and I will answer as I see fit.

The missive was signed formally. *Lady Lucinda Wellingham.* She had not even used his name.

Lifting a glass of brandy to his lips, he upended it, the quiet tonight a pressing and heavy one. The purse of the Wellinghams sat on the desk in front of him, a considerable sum representing a new life, somewhere far from England, perhaps? The Americas beckoned and so did the East Indies. Here he was struggling to keep ahead of the many and mounting debts his father had left him, every pound he made subtracted twice over by the ones he owed. Another few years at this rate and it would all be gone. Alderworth, the extensive land and buildings around it and the London town house, disappeared into the gloom of history.

A new life summoned—a refurbishment of the soul and one with a beguiling promise. The choice was simple. Stay here and fight the power of the Wellinghams for a wife who did not want him, or leave on a new tide and chance his hand at something different. He had never travelled away from the shores of England before, the duties of being the caretaker of Alderworth taking all his attention. If he left half of the Wellingham money here in an account to be drip-fed into the estate just to keep it afloat, perhaps he could build other possibilities?

Flat blue eyes came to mind, the anger in them directed only at him. Lucinda wanted neither his name nor his title and, as tiredness settled, it took too much will to quarrel.

His parents had frittered away their lives together in acrimonious exchanges and he did not wish to do the same. No, far better to welcome change and simply vanish.

His eyes strayed to the band on the third finger of his left hand. To have and to hold from this day forth, his wife had promised as she had placed it there…

Dragging the gold across his knuckles, he threw it into a drawer in the desk. A relationship that had begun in untruth and blossomed under duress was now ended in deceit. He would journey to a far-off corner of the world which laid no claim to the stifling conventions of a society immured in manners.

And then he would be free.

THE JOURNEY SOUTH was hurried and long and as the carriage swayed against a wind from the sea, Lucinda thought that her life from now on might be exactly like this flight into obscurity.

She could not go back and she could not go forwards, the worry of seeing Taylen Ellesmere again precluding any early return to London. Emerald and Asher both looked as tired as she did, the last weeks resting on their faces, worn down by worry. At least the beginning of her menses had come that morning and there was some relief to know she would not be bound to Alderworth by a child. But even that relief was tempered by sadness as she faced the possibility that she might never ever be a mother.

'The air here is so much better than in London, Ashe.' Emerald's observation was falsely cheerful, just words to fill in the heavy silence.

Lucinda nodded and tried to smile, though she doubted that her brother would be fooled by such a forced joviality. With a cursory glance at the sky, Asher brought the subject back to the problem they were all thinking about.

'In a month you can come back to Falder, Lucinda. I will employ guards to make certain Alderworth comes nowhere near you and at least it will be a more familiar setting. I doubt, however, that London will be a destination available to you for a good long while yet. Society has a great need to feed off scandal and this one…' He left the sentence unfinished.

She nodded to please him, but the ache in her breast threatened to explode into an anger she did not recognise. She wished with all her heart that she had not been persuaded to go to a house of such ill repute in the first place, for all that had followed was the result of one injudicious decision.

'Visiting Alderworth was more than foolish,' she

muttered and Asher looked up, the pity in his eyes almost her undoing.

'I have left word to have Alderworth followed so any movements that alarm us will be monitored. Let us hope he has the sense to retire to that estate of his and never again leave it.'

'You think he will stay in England?' As Emerald asked the question something passed between Asher and her—a warning, were Lucinda to name it. A quiet notice of caution with an undercurrent of intent.

Goodness, had her brothers shanghaied her husband already and thrown him on to a ship sailing far from Britain before disgorging him on to some unknown foreign shore? Her mind ran all the possible injuries that Taylen Ellesmere might sustain.

'If you have hurt him…' she began and stopped, dread making her question what it was she was going to say. Ellesmere should mean nothing to her. She should be glad that he would disappear for ever, yet concern lingered.

'He is at liberty to go where he wants. There was no duress in it.'

'You paid him?' Suddenly she understood. 'You bribed him to leave?'

When he nodded, she looked away. Ruined and humiliated. She vowed that there would never be another time when she allowed a man to hurt her.

TAY WATCHED THE coast of England receding into only mist. The sea birds called around him as the canvas of the sails caught the wind, turning the ship east, and an excitement he had not felt before quickened his breath and made him lift his face to the heavens.

Free.

For the first time in his life the debt of Alderworth did not weigh him down with its constant demands and a new horizon beckoned.

A place to make a different mark, a land where no one knew him. The mantle of the past slipped away into the gathering breeze and his fingers curled around the guard rail, holding on to the rusted steel as though his very life depended on it.

'You look as though you could do with a drink.' A tall red-haired man stood next to him, the collar of his coat raised against the weather. 'Where are you headed?'

'Anywhere a fortune is to be made,' Tay answered, a plan formulating as he spoke. He needed money to come back. He needed good hard cash to retrieve his life and make it work in the way he wanted it to. His glance took in the bare third finger on his left hand as the stranger spoke again.

'I am bound for North Georgia. They say that the gold there is easy to retrieve and the veins are rich. Two years I have given myself to find it and my wife, Elizabeth, is already counting down the days.'

'You have experience of mining, then?' A small worm of an idea began to creep up into possibility.

The other nodded. 'With farming as it is I have needed to supplement my income from the family es-

tate by other means. I could do with a partner if you
are interested. A flat fee for the tools we will need and
that will be it, save for lots of hard work and a good dol-
lop of persistence. A sense of humour might help, too.'

The screech of a gull above had them looking up,
the big bird wheeling out of the sky towards them, its
wings outstretched as it landed on a point at the top of
the ship. Hitching a ride or having a rest?

Choices.

They came from the most unexpected places and
from the most unexpected people. Putting out his hand,
he felt the firm grasp of the other.

'Tay Ellesmere.' No title. Nothing to tie him to the
England he was leaving. A different man with another
life.

'Lance Montcrieff. From Ridings Hall in Devon.'

LUCINDA WALKED ALONG the cliffs of Foulness Point and
watched the ocean waves break across the beaches
below, never-ending tides, washing the land clean of
all that it had left there the day before. A constantly
refreshed canvas, the flotsam of life taken away to another headland in a different place, redefined and transformed.

As she was not. Two years of isolated country living
had left her struggling with her identity, Falder and its
environs beautiful, but never changing. Her physical
strength had returned finally, though her memory had
never followed. Oh, granted, she still had headaches
sometimes and when she was tired her vision became

a little blurred, but the bone-wearying fatigue had dissipated and in its place a haunting curiosity had risen.

She wondered where in the world the Duke of Alderworth might now be. Cristo had given her a letter a good year ago and she had opened it with shaking fingers.

His description of a town in the North Georgia mountains in the Americas had been interesting, but had left her hollow. He had written nothing of his feelings or of his intentions or of any new relationships he might have formed. A half-page long, and wholly factual, the message could have been written for anyone.

He had signed it Tay Ellesmere. No title. Just the diminutive of Taylen. *Tay.* She had run the word a thousand times off her tongue ever since reading it and hated herself for doing so.

She wanted him back. She did, out here in the wind and with the sound of the ocean all around her. She wanted to feel his skin against her own in that particular way he had of heightening her senses and making her feel alive.

Dead. She had been dead since he had left, on an early morning ship out of St Katherine's Dock, Asher had said. Sailing for the Americas and a new life without any of the burdensome encumbrances that he had been tied to in England and so unwillingly.

Paid to take ship from London and never return? She had heard that, too, when she had listened in to a conversation between Taris and Asher. All she had picked up in their tones was relief that Alderworth was gone and so she had tried to forget him, banishing all thoughts of a husband from her mind.

And failing.

She hated this limbo she was in, caught between marriage and widowhood, and never a chance of moving on. Sometimes she hated Taylen Ellesmere so much that her skin shook with the loathing.

A voice calling took her thoughts away and she saw Lord Edmund Coleridge, a friend of Cristo's, walking towards her.

'Cris told me that you would be here,' he said as he came close. 'He also said that I was to ask you for a dance tonight at Graveson.'

'Florencia's party?' The house had been awash with busy hands since it had been decided to throw a birthday party for Cristo and Eleanor's oldest daughter.

'Seven is an important number. She has asked her father if she might invite Bram Crowley to help her celebrate.'

'Young love.' Lucinda smiled and shook her head. Brampton's father owned the property bordering Cristo and Asher's holdings and, although the family were not titled, they were by all accounts very rich. Florencia had liked him from the very first moment she had arrived with her mother, and the boy had done much to bring a frightened and retiring child out of her shell.

'I hope you might save a waltz for me, Lady Lucinda.' Edmund took her hand, surprising her. 'I would dearly like to get to know you better.'

'I am married, my lord,' she returned quickly. 'There can be no gain in aiming your sights at me.'

His laughter floated on the wind around them, a happy, free sound that made her relax.

'Your brother told me that you were forthright and now I believe him. I will swap you one waltz for the chance to tool my greys around the Falder course on the morrow.'

'A difficult thing to refuse. Did Cris also tell you of my passion for horses?'

'He did indeed. He said I was to expound on my expertise in archery as well.' His eyes lost their humour as he continued. 'It is just a dance I beseech, Lady Lucinda, and the chance of friendship.'

For the first time in a long while Lucinda allowed a man to hold her fingers for more than a second without pulling away. There was none of the magic there that she had felt with Alderworth, but it was not unpleasant, either. With blond hair blowing in the wind and his dark eyes soulful, Edmund Coleridge had his own sort of appeal. Lord knew she had heard he was popular with all the young ladies of society and she could see how that could be so.

But he did not smell of wood-smoke and lemon and his eyes were not the colour of the wet forests at Falder. Nor were they underlaid with a thrilling lust that made her whole body sing.

LUCINDA WORE A new gown that evening, a red silk that was edged in gold. Such a combination might have been showy, but the dressmaker had played up the under-lights in the silk and matched them exactly with the trim.

'You look beautiful tonight, Lucy.' Emerald was the first to see her as she came downstairs, and indeed as she caught a reflection in the large mirror at Graveson she did look...different.

Sorrow had stalked her for so long since the fiasco in London that Lucinda had almost got used to its sombre presence. Tonight, however, her spirit was lifted. Perhaps it was because of something as uncomplicated as the beautiful gown or the fact that Eleanor's maid had fashioned her hair in a new style. Or perhaps it was just the fact of a family celebration and the excitement of Florencia, Cristo and Eleanor.

Edmund Coleridge was the next one to compliment her and he did so with a raft of words.

'I could compare your hair to moonbeams or sunlight or to the sparkling fall of water over rocks, my lady.'

Despite the flowery rhetoric, Lucinda laughed. 'Please do not, my lord.'

She liked the warmth of his hand and the smooth feel of his skin. His hair tonight was Macassared and it suited him; made him look more dangerous. She shook away the thought. Safety was what she was after. The consequences of following reckless paths had ruined everything, after all, and she had promised herself to walk a discreet and scatheless way in future.

'Your niece has been asking after you. I think she wants to give you something.'

As if on cue Florencia appeared before them, a beautiful gardenia in hand. 'Everyone has to wear one tonight, Aunty Lucy, because they are my very favourite flower.'

Lucinda noticed the bottom of the stalk had been wrapped in brown paper, a pin secured in the folds.

'Is this your handiwork, my love?' she asked as she took the bloom and smelt it.

'Mine and Mama's.' Her dark eyes crossed to Edmund. 'But you are wearing yours upside down.' A wide smile lit up her face as Coleridge knelt and fashioned his flower exactly as she wanted it.

'Is this better?'

'Much. Now I just have to find Uncle Taris. I think he is hiding from me because he thinks flowers are for girls.'

With a whirl she was gone, with her little basket of gifts and a jaunty lilt to her step. Lucinda remembered back to when she had first met Cristo's daughter. The change in her demeanour was heartening and it seemed Coleridge was thinking exactly the same thing.

'Cris is lucky with his family and is happier than I have ever seen him.' The flower had wet the fabric of his coat where water seeped through the paper, but he only wiped it away.

Edmund Coleridge was a kind man, a good man with high principles and moral worthiness. She caught Eleanor watching them with a smile on her face and thought briefly how easy it might have been had she chosen a man like this one. Her family liked him, society lauded his goodness and he observed her as though he was inclined to know her better.

When a waiter passed with a tray of drinks in tall and fluted glasses she picked one up and drank it quickly before returning for a second.

'My brother knows his wine. French, I should imagine, and very smooth.'

The first flutter of warmth stirred in her stomach, the drink relaxing a tension that was ever-present in her life. More usually she stayed away from anything that might not allow her control, after her last débâcle, but tonight she felt able to risk it.

She nodded as Edmund Coleridge took her hand and asked her to dance. A waltz, she realised, as he led her to the floor, the slow languid three-beat music swirling across her senses.

He was thinner than his clothes suggested, but as her fingers came across the superfine of his jacket a sense of masculine strength made her breath come faster. It had been so long since she had touched a man like this.

Taylen.

Swallowing, she made herself stop. Alderworth was not here and would never be so. He had gladly gone to the Americas, paid handsomely by her brothers to abandon any husbandly duty. The ache in her chest made her breathe faster.

'We can sit this out if you would wish to?'

Concerned dark eyes washed across her own.

'No. I would like to dance.'

The music of the orchestra was beautiful and the

smell of the gardenia wafted up from her gown. She had to learn to live again, to laugh and to dance and to touch a man without pulling back. The wine was beginning to weave its magic and at the side of the room she could see Asher and Emerald watching her without worry marking their eyes.

Two years of dislocation. The silk of her chemise felt cool against her skin and Edmund Coleridge's fingers curled with an increasing pressure around her own.

Claimed. Quietly. She did not look up at his face. Too soon. Too quick. She wished the fingers that held her own were covered in golden rings, an old scar visible just beneath the crisp white cuff of shirt.

Taylen.

Sometimes she could smell him, at night when everything was still and when she reached into the deepest place of memory. Lemon, woodsmoke and desire. She bit at her bottom lip and sent the thought scattering, leaf-green laughing eyes and short dark hair dissolving into nothingness.

'Will you come back to London soon?'

Another voice. Higher.

Edmund.

'I am not entirely certain. My brothers think that I should, but…'

'Come with me, then. Let me take you to the Simpson Ball.'

Now his interest was stated and affirmed, the *perhaps* that Lucinda had been enjoying transformed into certainty. The game of courtship had begun, all chase and hunt, and her heart sank.

'I am a married woman, my lord.'

'A married woman without a husband.' The dimples in his cheek made him look younger than he was, an amiable and gracious man who had taken the time and effort to try to humour a woman of little joy. Cristo's friend, and a man that her other brothers approved of, all the parts of him adding up to a decent and honest whole.

She allowed him the small favour of bringing her closer into the dance so that now his breath touched her face.

'I should like to see you laugh, Lucinda.' When his thighs pushed against her own, the pulse in his throat quickened. Coleridge was so much easier to read than Alderworth had ever been, his secrets hidden in an ever-present hardened core of distrust.

Breaking off the dance when the music finished, Edmund led her into the conservatory at the head of the room. Stars twinkled through the glass overhead and myriad leafy plants stood around them in the half-light.

She knew he would kiss her even before he leaned down, she could see it in his eyes and on his face, that desire that marks even the most timid of men. She did not push him away, either, but waited, as his lips touched her own, seeking what it was all lovers sought, the magic and the fantasy.

A light pressure and then a deeper one, his tongue in her mouth, finding and hoping. She felt his need and tried not to stiffen, understanding his prowess, but having no desire for a mutual understanding. Just flesh against flesh, the scrape of his teeth upon her lip, his wetness and the warmth. Ten seconds she counted and then twenty until he broke away, a flush in his cheeks and a hoarseness of breath.

Sadness swamped her as he brought her in against him. Nothing. An empty nothingness. Wiping away the taste of him when he was not looking, the weft of cotton felt hard against her mouth.

'Thank you.' His words. Honourable and kind.

Even as she tried to smile an aching loss formed, the mirthless harbinger of all that she had wasted. Alderworth had ruined her in more ways than he knew. Edmund Coleridge was exactly the sort of beau she should wish to attract and yet...

'Perhaps we should go inside. It is chilly out here.' The shaking she had suddenly been consumed by was timely.

'Of course, my dear. A dress of silk is no match even for a summer evening. I should have realised.'

Manners and courtesy. The smile on her face made the muscles in her cheek ache as she accompanied him into supper.

'EDMUND SEEMS MORE than taken with you, Lucy.' Cristo approached her as she returned from having a word with Beatrice. 'He is a good man who has long wished to know you better.'

'Well, I am sure he is besieged by all the lovely young

women in society. His manners are faultless and he is such congenial and unaffected company.'

Cristo frowned. 'Such vacuous praise is usually an ominous sign...' His dark eyes watched her, the gold in them easily seen in the light from the chandeliers above.

Lucinda rapped him with her fan. 'I am not in the market for a...dalliance.'

He laughed at that, tipping his head up with mirth, the sound booming around them.

'I hope not. It was something more permanent Edmund was angling for, I would imagine.'

Taking one of her hands, he chanced offering advice. 'If you do not choose to move on with your life soon, Lucy, the opportunities may not keep coming.'

'You speak of suitors as if I were a widow, Cris.' Anger tinged her words and she was surprised as he shepherded her from the salon and down the corridor to his library. Once there he poured himself a generous brandy, restoppering the decanter when she turned down the chance of the same.

'Another letter has come.'

The words shocked her. She felt the blood drain from her cheeks and her heartbeat race.

'From Alderworth? When?'

'Last week. The mark on it is from Georgia.'

'Yet you did not think to give it to me sooner?'

'I knew Edmund would come tonight and he had asked me for the chance to court you. I had hoped...'

'Hoped for what? Hoped that the law might have dissolved all that was between me and Alderworth?

Hoped that I might finally find a man that you all approved of? Hoped that the scandal of my disgrace may have been watered down by the pure goodness of your friend? That sort of hope?' Her voice had risen as she shook away his excuse. 'Where is it?'

Digging into a drawer at the back of his desk, Cristo laid an envelope down on the table. The writing was large and bold and not that of her husband, for the hand was completely different from the one correspondence she had received. Her excitement faded.

Lady Lucinda Ellesmere.

Graveson.

Essex.

Lucinda held her fingers laced together so they would not snatch at the paper. Was Taylen dead? Was this a missive to tell her of an accident or an illness or of the wearying of soul and a final resting place?

Had he married again, had children to a new lover, found gold, lost a hand, suffered a horrible and gruelling death in the throes of dysentery or smallpox or the influenza?

Finally she moved forwards and picked it up. 'Have you told Ashe of this?'

He shook his head.

'Then please do not.'

'You need to be careful, Lucy. Alderworth is a reprobate and a liar. He uses women for his own means and does not look back over his shoulder at whom he has hurt. Coleridge, on the other hand, is trustworthy.'

The sound of the orchestra winding up an air and the deep voice of Asher took them from the moment.

'The speeches.' Lucinda was glad for the interruption.

'We need to return to the ballroom.'

Folding the note, she stuffed it into a small compartment on one side of her reticule. Cristo made no comment as he gestured her to go before him and doused the lamp on his desk.

As soon as she was able to escape the party without raising any eyebrows Lucinda did so, climbing the steps to the room she had been allotted at Graveson with a mixture of hope and trepidation.

She could feel the presence of the envelope in her bag almost as a physical thing, prickling inwards.

Gaining her bedroom, she asked her maid to unhook the buttons at the back of her gown and, feigning tiredness, dismissed her. Locking the door behind the departing woman, Lucinda sighed with relief as she leaned back against heavy oak, free at last to see just what the letter from Georgia contained.

With agitation she slit open the top of the paper, carefully and precisely so as to do no damage to anything within.

A newspaper clipping confronted her, the folds of print displayed in such a way as to show a headline.

'Ellesmere strikes gold in fine style'.

The hazy distorted ink spoke of Tay Ellesmere celebrating with a great number of women in some sleazy saloon, the text citing details of a raucous party lasting well into the early hours of the morning, the guests invited unsuitable and rowdy.

As infamous as his soirées at Alderworth? Unchanged. Unabashed. She was in England pining for something that he had not spared a thought for, while he partied with women who were probably inclined to give away any and every favour he would want.

Swallowing, Lucinda let herself slide down the door frame where she sat pooled in red silk, her first finger tracing the exploits of a husband who on each turn of events seemed destined to disappoint her.

Another smaller piece of paper suddenly caught her eye and she lifted it up.

Lucinda
I presume that this is your runaway husband. Perhaps, given the goodly amount of his newly found claim, you should be seeking him out again.

I have sent this letter to Graveson in the hope that your brother might pass it on as I have no notion of your new address.
Yours
Anthony Browne

Screwing up the paper, Lucinda crossed the room to the fire, hurling the letter into the flames. The paper caught at one edge and blackened, embers glowing red before turning to a dull and dusty ash.

Anthony Browne, the brother of a school friend. She had always detested him.

Her glance returned to the newspaper cutting. If she had any sense she would consign this to the fire, too. But she didn't. She hated the tears that fell down her cheeks and the gulps of grief that she tried to quieten.

He would never stop hurting her, Taylen Ellesmere with his wild and ill-considered chaos. Another episode in a far-off land, his name slandered and his intentions dubious.

This was the man she had married, unstable, volatile and lawless.

Wiping the moisture away as a tear slid unbidden down the newsprint, she cradled the missive in her palm before bringing it to her heart.

'Where are you?' she whispered into the night.

CHAPTER SEVEN

London—1834

The gold coins were heavy in Tay's hand as he hoisted them up on to the desk. They clinked against the dark mahogany, solid and weighty, the letters of the Federal Mint at Atlanta imbued in red ink on the fabric of the bag.

'Here's the return of your bribe, Carisbrook, with more than interest in full. Now I want my wife back.'

Asher Wellingham stood as the words echoed around his library. 'You accepted our sum to disappear for ever.'

'Your expectation, Carisbrook, not mine. My Duchess and I shall leave for my country estate first thing in the morning and you can do nothing to stop us.'

'Over my dead body, you bastard.' Without warning the Duke was at Tay's throat before he had time to react, the chair beside the desk overturned and the strength of his fingers cutting off breath.

But Taylen was a good ten years younger than Lucinda's oldest brother and had more in muscle. His time in Georgia had also given him plenty of battle practice.

With a quick twist he rolled away, fists up and waiting as the other angled in.

'I don't want to hurt you, Carisbrook. All I want is what is mine.'

'My sister isn't yours.'

'In God's eyes and anyone else that counts, Lucinda is my wife.' He had not meant to get into an argument, but the history between them was murky and here, in this same room he had been pummelled over once before, he found it difficult to temper back wrath.

'We should have killed you when we had the chance.'

Tay laughed and then moved quickly as a punch almost connected. He couldn't afford for his dinner dress to be bloodied as his next pressing destination was a ball. Waiting for his chance, he moved in, fingers reaching for the arteries of his adversary's throat.

It was over in two minutes, the point of pressure allowing an easy end. The fights in Dahlonega in Lumpkin County had been rough and a lucrative stake in gold at Ward's Creek in the North Georgia mountains always had to be defended. He almost felt sorry for the Duke of Carisbrook laid out on the floor but, when he checked, his breathing was deep and regular and tomorrow he'd barely feel any effects. Save embarrassment, probably, but he'd given Tay a good measure of the same treatment almost three years ago so Tay could not be remorseful.

Straightening his jacket, he caught sight of the clock at the end of the room. Ten-thirty. His wife was spending the evening at the Croxleys' ball in Culross Street and it wasn't far. He smiled. Almost too easy.

Letting himself out of the library, he closed the door behind him. Then he took his hat and cloak from the waiting servant and thanked him with a coin before walking into the night.

HE WAS BACK.

She knew he was from the frantic whispers swirling around the ballroom, his name on the edge of every one of them.

'The Duke of Alderworth is here, returned from the Americas and twenty times richer than his father ever was.'

Lucinda felt all the eyes upon her as she stood near a pillar in the Croxleys' ballroom, Posy Tompkins to one side gripping her hand. Three years of dreading this very moment and it had finally arrived. The breath congealed in her throat and her heart beat so fast she was certain she would keel over.

No. She would not faint or fall or run. None of this was her fault, after all, and she would not allow Taylen Ellesmere to make her feel that it was.

'He is coming this way, Luce.' Posy barely managed to get the words out. 'And he is looking straight at us.'

'Then we shall give him exactly what he does not expect,' she replied, plastering a practised smile upon her face. Almost simple to do, she thought in surprise, the warmth of greeting a foil to the inquisitive faces turned her way.

'Your Grace.' Lucinda tried to make her tone convivial, a meeting of acquaintances, a trifling and inconsequential thing—a figure from the past to whom she had given no consideration since last seeing him.

'Duchess.' His voice had deepened in the years between their forced marriage and this unexpected return. 'I did not think to find you here in town.'

He was still beautiful. His hair was much longer than when she had seen him last and it made him look even more menacing.

Intimidating.

It was the only word she could come up with to describe him as he stood before her, dressed in black from head to foot, save for the white cravat at his neck fastened loosely in the style of a man without much care for fashion.

'Do you still enjoy the art of untruthfulness?'

The effrontery of such a question almost undid her and she answered with one of her own. 'Do you still enjoy despoiling innocents on a whim and all in the name of free will?'

A fiery glint in his eyes was seen fleetingly in a face hewn from cold stone.

Urbane and distant. Anger made her fists ball at her side, though she unclenched her fingers as soon as she realised what she was doing. She was pleased Posy had had the sense to retreat so that their conversation remained private.

'I had heard that you were back in England, your Grace.'

'Your brothers gave you the news, no doubt,' he returned, taking her hand in his own and pulling her towards the dance floor. 'But come, let's confuse the wagging tongues and stand up together. It will give us some space to talk.'

Short of creating a scene, Lucinda allowed herself to be led into a waltz, his arm encircling her back and drawing her towards him.

'The gossips have placed you on the Eastern seaboard coast of the Americas for many years, your Grace, taking part in all the temptations the cities there have to offer, no doubt.'

He laughed, a deep rumble of amusement; a man embedded in scandal and savouring it. Her ire rose unbidden. She had seen the evidence of his immorality, after all, in the headlined cutting Anthony Browne had sent her.

'Your brother Asher said much the same to me when I saw him this evening.'

'You have been to the Wellingham town house already? Why?'

'Paying my dues,' he replied obliquely, 'and stating my intentions.' He stopped for a moment as though gathering the gist of what he might next tell her. 'Not every one of them, though. I saved the best proposal of all for your ears only.'

A streak of cold dread snaked downwards. 'You want a divorce, no doubt?'

At that he laughed, the sound engulfing her.

'Not a divorce, my lady wife, but an heir, and as you

are the only woman who can legitimately give me one the duty is all yours.'

She almost tripped at his words and he held her closer, waiting until balance was regained. Their eyes locked together, no humour at all in the green depths of Taylen Ellesmere, the sixth Duke of Alderworth.

He was deadly serious.

Shock gave her the courage of reply. 'Then you have a problem indeed, your Grace, because I am the last woman in the world who would ever willingly grace your bed again. Surely you understand why.' Disappointment and anger vibrated in her retort as strains of Strauss soared around them, the chandeliers throwing a soft pallor across colourful dresses resplendent in the room. The privilege of the *ton* so easily on show.

Scandal had its own face, too!

It came in the way his fingers held her to the dance even as she tried to pull away, and in the quiet caress of his skin over hers.

Memory shattered sense and the salon dimmed into nothingness; the feel of his hands upon her nakedness, the smell of brandy and deceit and a wedding quick and harrowing in that small chapel.

Even the minister had not met her eye as he said the words, 'To have and to hold from this day forward...'

Taylen Ellesmere had stayed less than a few hours.

Her husband. A different and harder man from the one who had left her and now back for a legitimate heir. She wanted to slap him across his cheek in the middle of the ballroom and he knew it. It took all of her will not to.

'If there wasn't a male left in Christendom save for you, I still would not—'

He broke over her anger.

'I will gift you the sole use of the Alderworth London town house on the birth of our first son and pay you a stipend that will keep you independently wealthy in fine style.'

Blackmail and bribery now. She shook her head against such a promise, but did not speak.

'One heir and then the freedom to do whatever you want for the rest of your life. A safe haven. The power of independence and autonomy. One heir whom you shall have the right as a mother to raise until he is ten. Eton should see to the rest.'

'And if the child is a girl?'

'Then I will dissolve all contracts and allow you what I offer regardless. I would not tie you to such a bargain for ever should you in good faith produce only a female Ellesmere.'

She frowned, barely believing the words she was hearing. 'There are other women here who would jump at your offer, your Grace, if you obtained a divorce and remarried.'

'I know.'

'Then why?'

'Salvation.' He gave no other explanation as he smiled at her, the deep dimple in his right cheek caught in the light. So very beautiful.

Lucinda felt the muscles inside her clench.

Freedom for the use of her body? He had had his fill

once and she was no longer young. The very memory of it all took her breath away.

'I will not rape you if that is what you are thinking.'

'A mutual consent may never happen, your Grace.' She put as much disdain into the words as she could manage.

'I stake all my gold on the fact that it will.' His voice was overlaid with a certainty that was worrying.

Could she do it? Play the whore to a husband she could not trust and sell her body for a freedom she had never had? The girl she had been almost three years ago now would never have considered such a monstrous proposition, but the woman she had become did.

'I want it in writing. I want a hundred pounds for every time I lie with you and a hundred more for every month it takes to become pregnant. No one must know of this bargain of ours, however, and in public you will only sing my praises. Do you understand? I shall not be the subject of any scorn whatsoever, for if my brothers ever found out exactly what you have proposed...' She could not continue.

'They would offer more threats.' He said this not as a question but as a truth. 'However, I would like to add one more condition of my own. For the conception of an heir I would require the whole night in my bed, at a time of your choosing. No rushed affair. I wish to lie in the moonlight and know your body as well as you know it yourself. Hedonistic and unhurried.'

She turned her face away so that he would not see what she imagined might be there—horror vying with avidity. The muscles deep inside throbbed in a promise that was like the echo of memory. She would not show him the hurt or the anger or the plain recognition of the choking shame she had lived with since he had gone.

She would tell him none of it until she could take the papers for the town house and fashion a separate existence.

Salvation, he had said. Perhaps it would be hers as well, this unexpected departure from being beholden to her brothers' generosity and benevolence. The gossip that had never died down as she thought it would, but had followed her with every step that she took.

The forgotten wife. The abandoned bride. The willful Wellingham sister whose reckless antics had finally caught up with her.

'My carriage will collect you the day after tomorrow from Wellingham House and bring you up to my seat. It would be an early departure so you would need to make sure that you are ready when it arrives.'

She shook her head, sense returning in the indifferent way he gave her instruction, like a Lord might order his valet to set out his clothes. 'My brothers will stop me.'

'Then it is up to you to persuade them otherwise. But know that we are married in the face of God for ever. I have given you my terms of agreement and I would never consent to a divorce.'

When the music stopped he escorted her back to her place near the pillar and into the company of Posy.

'I shall expect you to be ready by nine o'clock on

Thursday with any luggage you require. I will join you
later on the Northern Road.'

Without further word, he left.

HE HAD DONE IT. He had struck the bargain that he
needed with less difficulty than he might have imagined. The line of the Ellesmeres of Alderworth would
be saved.

Tay breathed in hard even as he walked through the
crowd, wondering why it was he felt so damned uncertain. His wife still wore the ring he had given her,
he noticed. The rest of her fingers were bare. The scar
on the back of her hand was faded now, but under the
light from the chandeliers he had still been able to see
it. The carriage accident had left marks inside and out.
Shaking his head, he cursed.

She was a hundred times more beautiful than she had
once been. He remembered her eyes to be darker, but
they were the blue of the early springtime sky, bright
with promise. Her curves had matured as well, and her
skin was still silky smooth and pale. He brought the
edges of his jacket further around his body, angry at the
reaction she so carelessly extorted from him.

Looking back from the doorway, he tried to find
her in the crowd and there she was, taller than most of
the other women present and graceful. Her bones were
small, the thinness in her arms giving the impression of
a dancer. The dark-blue gown she wore with a froth of
lace at the neckline emphasised the colour in her eyes.

'Hell.' He swore and as if on cue Jonathon Wigmore, the Earl of St Ives, joined him.

'Is it the swarm of admirers around your wife you do not like, Alderworth? You might need to get used to that, for since her return to London last year every man with any sense has courted her. Lord Edmund Coleridge, of all the swains, has been the most constant fixture. She allows him more of her time than any other. We all thought you were gone, you see.'

'So you were amongst her ranks of admirers, too?'

'Indeed I was, though with little success, I might add. Her brothers are ruthless in the protection of their sister.'

For the first time since arriving back in England Tay smiled and meant it. He had something to thank Asher, Taris and Cristo Wellingham for, after all.

'There was always something damn fine about Lucinda Wellingham. I could never understand why you left when you did.'

'I was twenty-five and foolish.'

'And now?'

'Now I am older and wiser.'

The first notes of the next dance made it hard to hear and Tay watched as his wife was handed into a quadrille by Coleridge, the look on his face suggesting that he was escorting a rare and valued treasure. He looked away as her hand rested upon his shoulder and she allowed him a closeness that was improper.

Deceit came in a beautiful package with every appearance of veracity. He recalled his entrapment by the

Wellinghams with an anger that was as raw as it had been all those years before.

Turning, he left the house and hailed a hansom carriage for he had not bothered with his own. Habit, he supposed, and the habitual saving of pennies even though he could now afford any number of carriages that he wished. Sitting back on the seat, he closed his eyes, the quiet noise of the hooves of the horses echoing in the street.

His wife was beautiful. But it was something else that he saw in her pale-blue eyes. Sorrow lingered there now, the sort of sorrow that had been the hallmark of his childhood: fear overlaid with caution. It did not suit her, this new wariness, this vigilant and all-encompassing apprehension.

Breathing out hard, he cursed the Wellingham brothers their heavy-handedness, but at least, according to Jonathon Wigmore, they had kept Lucinda safe. Tay knew if he was to have any chance of successfully taking his wife to his own estate he would need to get one of them, even begrudgingly, upon his side.

Taris was the one he would target. The middle brother would not grab him in a headlock and try to pummel the daylights out of him with his failing sight and he was tired of defending himself physically every time he came into their company.

A group of women standing on a street corner beckoned to him through the window, the sort of women who had been two a penny in the gold-mining towns of Georgia. Good women some of them, with hard-luck stories almost the same as his own. There was not much to separate success from ill fortune and he had never been a man to judge another's way of dealing with the varied hands that life dealt.

He had always felt alone. Right from the first moment of perceiving that his parents saw him as a nuisance rather than a blessing and had sent him off to anyone who would have him, little care taken in making certain of the reliability and soundness of their protection. He would never bring his own children up the way his parents had him. He would love them and cherish and honour them.

He laughed to himself, although there was no humour in the sound. The heirs he hoped for were poised precariously between his wife's hatred and her brothers' aversion.

He suddenly and sincerely wished that everything could just have been easy.

LUCINDA HAD SEEN Taylen Ellesmere walk for the door in the company of Jonathon Wigmore some five minutes ago.

All she wished to do was to leave, to run from the farce and close the door against gossip. But to do so would be adding to it and so she stayed, her conversation amenable and her smile bright. Only Posy watched her with any idea of the truth and she made a point not to look in the direction of her best friend at all.

Tonight she was the woman she had fostered so diligently to appear to be since she had arrived here a year before. Poised. Mannered. In such armour she was left alone, the figure of pity waiting plaintively for a husband who she thought would never return diminished into the new persona.

And now he had returned, taller and more imposing, striding into her life as if he had not left it and demanding the production of an heir. As she bit down on her disbelief, the reality of all she had agreed to seemed far more terrible without him here in front of her, yet in the recesses of places she had long since neglected a sense of excitement moved.

She would lie with him for all the long hours of the night. Had he not said so himself? A half-formed smile lifted her lips, and when Edmund Coleridge came to claim a dance she curtsied prettily and allowed him her hand.

LATER AS LUCINDA lay in bed she replayed the conversation she had had with Taylen Ellesmere over and over in her mind.

He had promised her the freedom of deciding the time that they would lie together and he had also promised that she would enjoy it.

Such arrogance was something she would normally find most unappealing, but with Taylen Ellesmere there was a certain truth that saved him from sounding smug. Besides, when he had danced with her at the Croxleys' ball the touch of his skin against her own had made her feel…excited. Excited for the first time in years, the vibrating possibility of it all leaving her breathless.

He did not wish for a quick tumble, either, but had stipulated the promise of a whole night. It was not some momentary and sordid tryst that he was proposing, but the vow of a lengthy coupling that was...unimaginable. She was beyond the first flush of youth and had never known the things that he spoke of. A sad statement of fact, but true. Pushing back the sheets, she took off her nightgown and wandered across to the mirror on the far wall of her room.

She was not a siren with her small breasts and thinness, but everything looked to be in place, did it not? Turning to one side, she tried to make her stomach extend outwards by arching her back so that an impression of fullness was gained. What would it feel like to hold a child inside her? His child? One hand fell to the curve and she smiled and straightened, her hair falling away from her body in a long and pale curtain. Taylen was probably used to experienced, curvaceous women, women who knew what to do to make a man feel...more than she could. How would she compare to them? The smile on her face was lost.

A knock on the door had her scrambling for her nightdress and dressing gown.

Emerald walked in as she called out for her to enter and her sister-in-law did not look pleased. The conversation they had had when she had come home, she supposed, and the discussion about her intentions of joining Taylen Ellesmere.

'You do not need to leave with him, Lucy. I would

bet my life on the fact that Alderworth is bluffing and if you call it he will be forced to back down completely.

'Ellesmere is not a man you can play with, Lucinda. He reminds me of the sailors on the *Mariposa:* harsh, raw men with blood on their hands and childhoods that have crushed any kindness from them. He is worse than your brothers.'

'He is not a pirate, Emerald. He is a Duke.'

'The difference only of a title. If he wants something, he will get it. I hope that thing is not you, for if he hurts one hair on your body I will—'

Lucinda interrupted her. 'I am married, Emerald, and I want to know what that feels like. I want a child and I want a home that is mine.'

'This one is yours.'

'No. It is Asher's, a ducal residence that is passed down across the generations to the next inheritor of the title. I do not wish to still be here when I am thirty and that is not far away.'

Unexpectedly Emerald began to laugh. 'Asher is hardly sleeping for the worry of what will happen and here you are actually wanting what it is he thinks you do not. Do you love Alderworth?'

'I barely know him.'

'But you are happy to take the chance of doing so?'

'Yes.'

Silence reverberated around the chamber for one long moment and then two. 'I wish to give you something.' Emerald reached into the bodice of her nightdress and slipped a necklace from around her throat. 'I have no more use for this, Lucy, but I swear that it is a formidable talisman.' She placed the green jade carving in Lucinda's outstretched hand. 'For happiness,' she explained. 'An old woman in Jamaica gifted it to me and I rarely take it off. But I want you to have it now because in wearing it I will feel that you are safe.'

Lucinda's fingers closed around the treasure still warm from Emerald's skin. 'A well-paid-for heir' did not quite seem in the spirit of the happiness the jade was imbued with, but she said nothing.

'And one more thing, Lucy. Men are simple, remember that, and you will know exactly what to do to please them.'

In the light of the candles with her hair down and her turquoise eyes bright with promise, Emerald had the look of an enchantress from one of the story books of Lucinda's childhood.

'Simple?'

'Happy with small pleasures. Sex. Food. And love if it is honest.'

Which mine is not. She almost said it, but didn't, choosing instead to slip the necklace over her head and position it above the warmth of her heart.

TAYLEN MET TARIS WELLINGHAM at the pub of the Three Jolly Butchers in Warwick Lane and was glad when Lucinda's brother dismissed his servant to another, distant table on his arrival. He had sent the note to Taris after breakfast, hardly daring that he might heed it.

'Thank you for coming. I know it is short notice.'

Wellingham laughed. 'The idea of meeting you in a crowded pub allayed my concerns that the engagement would become physical, Alderworth. Words, however, can have the same effect of wrapping their meaning around your throat and squeezing.'

'Free speech in the broadest sense of the term?' Tay could not help but feel a certain respect for the man's intellect as he replied.

'Exactly. What is it you need?'

'I have asked your sister to come with me to Alderworth Manor tomorrow, and she has agreed.'

'You have asked her already?'

'Last night at the Croxleys' ball. She has agreed.'

'Then there must have been a strong reward to entice her to such a promise. She is not apt to sing your praises about anything.'

Disconcerting opaque eyes watched him with all the focus of one who could see to the heart of the matter clearly.

'Lucinda hates you. How plain do you need to hear it in order to go away, Alderworth, or are you one of those obtuse men who fancy they see hope where there is none and would batter their heads against a brick wall for the rest of their days rather than facing a truth they do not wish to hear?'

'Going away is no longer an option for me.' Tay kept his voice low. 'Lucinda is my wife according to the letter of the law and under the authority of the Church, and I would never agree to a divorce. Besides, I have enough money to care for her now and the desire to do so.'

'Desire?' Unexpectedly Wellingham leant forwards and one hand shot out to entrap his in a grasp that was unyielding. A surprising accuracy, too, given his lack of sight. 'Desire to bed our sister again and then leave her? Desire to beget an heir upon her and then be on your way into the shady corners of the world when nothing turns out quite as easy as you expected it to? That kind of desire?'

Had his wife already spoken to her brothers about their bargain? Surely not. His hand ached with the force of strong fingers wrapped into flesh, but he did not pull away. Let the bastard see how little anyone could ever hurt him again. Aye, Taris Wellingham could break every damn bone in his hand and he would allow himself no reaction.

And then Lucinda's brother let go, simply sitting back against the fine leather chair and lifting his glass to drink as if nothing had happened.

'My *desire* to protect your sister is none of your business, Lord Wellingham.' Taylen did not make any effort to accord the words politeness, scrawling them instead with the seedy innuendo her brother had read into their meaning.

The show of force from the older man was a smokescreen. He could do nothing legally to stop them leaving and he knew it. Threading his hands in his lap to prevent himself from retaliation, Tay waited. This meeting was not going anything like he had hoped that it would.

'With a name slathered and immured in depravity, it might be hard to protect anyone or anything, Alderworth. Your history of wildness and debauchery does not make for good reading and a hundred men and women of the *ton* would swear you are the Devil incarnate. No.' He shook his head. 'If we are looking into the etymology of words, I doubt *protection* in your book has the same meaning as it does in mine.'

The stubborn anger in Lucinda's brother's voice was more than evident—a man who was at the end of his tether and showing it. Taking in a breath, Tay took a different tack. 'Does Carisbrook know you have met me here this morning?'

'He does. His instructions were to stick a knife through the place where your heart should be.'

'Explicit.'

'Very.'

Tay detected the beginnings of a smile. 'Then perhaps we could forge a bargain that might suit us all.'

'Indeed?' The tone was not encouraging, but he needed to get at least one of the Wellinghams on his side and he had long admired Taris.

'I propose that my wife continues to reside in your family's town house for the next few weeks on the condition that I can escort her to various public functions of her choosing. That will allow you to see that I am not as black as you might paint me and give her time to see that I am not the bastard she thinks I am.'

'Asher has control of Lucinda's assets and all of her money.'

'Good.'

'And you will get none of it.'

His words were bland, no true reflection at all of the topic under discussion.

'All I want is a chance.'

'I can promise nothing without talking to my sister. I will, however, be advising her to run as fast and far away from you as she can and to refuse to partake in further dialogue or to accept other correspondence. If it is simply a case of enough money to be rid of you, then we have the means...'

'It isn't.'

'I thought not.'

He raised one arm and his man came immediately to his side. 'If Lucinda feels she would be interested in finding out more about the sort of man she has married, then I will not stop her and neither will my brothers. But it will be her decision, Alderworth, not yours.'

When Tay nodded and held out his hand, Taris Wellingham failed to respond. Laying his fingers upon the pristine white cloth covering the table, he stood as the other did and watched him leave, a tall dark-haired man who made his way with his servant beside him across the salon of a busy public bar, his lack of sight completely hidden to all those observing him.

CHAPTER EIGHT

'You do not have to go to this ball with Alderworth, Lucy. We can fight any allegation he might make through the courts and completely ruin his name.'

Taris took her hand and tears pooled behind Lucinda's eyes at both the familiarity and the safety.

'The Church recognises the sanctity of holy marriage and Taylen Ellesmere made it clear that he would never agree to a divorce.'

'Then let us talk to him again…'

'No.' She was most adamant about that. There was nothing more to be said. The Duke of Alderworth had offered her a proposition and freedom looked admirable after years of being shackled to a missing husband. All her friends, save Posy, were married and bearing children whilst she had wilted, growing old upon a shelf of her own making, withering into someone she had never thought to become.

She could bear it no longer, this middle land of no choice at all, and, standing here in her best dress of light-blue shot silk, she knew that she wanted more.

'I need the chance to understand the only husband I am ever likely to have.'

She did not tell Taris that she had never been the slightest bit attracted to any other suitor in all her years of being out in society or that there was something about Taylen Ellesmere that made her heart run faster. She did not say that his green eyes had a promise in them she had found shocking because of her own capacity for response or that when he had spoken of the things he might like to do with her body at the Croxleys' ball she had finally felt…aroused.

Beatrice, from her place on the other side of the room, joined in the conversation.

'You are sure that this is what you wish, Lucinda? Alderworth seems both dangerous and alarming, a man who might be hard to tame.'

'He is my legal husband, Bea.'

'Your husband of only a few hours.' Her sister-in-law's voice was tight, though beneath it lurked a tone that was surprising. If Lucinda could have named it, she might have chanced humour.

Taris interceded. 'If there is ever any danger and you feel…'

'I am going to a ball a half a mile from home, Taris, with hundreds of people I know all around me. How could that possibly be dangerous?'

'Alderworth will not come here to get you?'

She shook her head. 'He said he would wait for me at the Chesterfields' in Audley Street because he does not wish for another contretemps. Every time one of you meet him someone has been hurt so I can well understand his point.'

'Then I will ask you to give him this.' He pulled a letter from his pocket sealed in an envelope. Looking over at Beatrice, Lucinda knew the pair must have fashioned the missive last night when she had returned with the news of her imminent departure, a plan that had been changed that very morning to include at least two weeks in London.

'What is in it?'

'A warning. If Alderworth does anything to hurt you, anything at all, Asher, Cris and I will hunt him down to the very edges of the earth.' He swiped one hand through his hair, pushing back the darkness and looking as angry as she had ever seen him.

Goodness, if her brothers had any inkling of the agreement she had consented to regarding the conception of an heir, she doubted that they would have sent only a note.

THE CHESTERFIELD TOWN house was one of the prettiest in Mayfair and one of the grandest, too, the sweeping drive of white pebbles leading to an imposing portico. Two men in livery stood at attention at each side of the wide flight of steps, Taylen Ellesmere between them, the darkness of his attire in complete contrast to the bright scarlet jackets they sported. He came forwards as he saw her and opened the door of her carriage, gesturing the Chesterfield servants away and shepherding her down a side path lit with lanterns, where they were hidden by trees.

Tonight he was dressed in charcoal, his long-tailed

coat and breeches of the best-quality superfine. His cravat was loosely tied, no artifice in it, the snowy white of the fabric showing up the darkness of his skin and hair. A tall man and graceful with it. Where he touched her arm she felt the heat of contact. The ring she had given him all those years ago lay on his wedding finger and the small spark of recognition made her feel warmer. She was sure he had not been wearing it yesterday.

'I did not think you would come.' Lucinda could smell strong drink on his breath as he turned and stopped.

'I have a message for you.' In his company tonight she felt…uncertain and she hated the fact that she did. But in a crowded ballroom she knew she could simply slip away if she needed to. The thought calmed her as he turned the envelope over and looked closely at the writing. Breaking the seal, he opened the letter, reading it quickly before handing it back to her. 'This concerns you.'

Alderworth. One wrong move with our sister and you will pay for it.

The message was unsigned, but the parchment had the Wellingham insignia emblazoned at the top, an eagle argent on sable.

'You are fortunate in your protection.' His voice was an echo of some lost thing, surprising her.

'My brothers have been the most wonderful support in the world but… I am tired of being for ever thankful.'

Sacrilege to even utter such a sentiment, but she did, the words running into the silence between them like sharp daggers. Taking a breath, she looked around her at the other carriages coming up the drive. She was glad for the privacy the trees here afforded them.

'And the proposition I gave you yesterday?'

'You said you would not rush me, your Grace.' This time she looked directly at him, catching his eyes with her own in challenge.

'So formal?'

'We are strangers, you and I, who have been tied by the binding agreement of a marriage that is to neither of our liking. I barely know anything of you.'

'Which might be a good thing,' he returned, his words overlaid with just a tinge of regret. It was enough for Lucinda to press her conditions further.

'I couldn't tolerate the sort of parties you have made famous. An endless list of drunken guests parading through the places I reside within would be abhorrent to me and until...'

She could not finish because he leant forwards to take her hand, stroking the palm with his thumb so that small *frissons* of desire ran in ever-increasing strength up her arm.

'Until you are ripe with child?'

The shocking reality of the words made her pull back. That she could even have thought to control a man like Taylen Ellesmere, whose very world was so far from her own, was naïve.

'You may well laugh at our situation, your Grace, but I know that you accepted a large sum of money from my brother to disappear for ever. It is hard to trust a groom who only thinks to profit substantially from his bride.'

He looked away, a muscle in the side of his neck rippling with the tension only the guilty could feel. Asher had told her last night of the enormity of the sum Tay Ellesmere had taken and for a moment she had thought to rescind every agreement between them completely. But she had not. *Why* was a notion she found difficult to fathom, the thought of being tied to a man who had gained much fiscally from her misery more than demeaning. Lucinda waited for him to explain, to find some honour in his actions and clarify his reasons, but he stayed silent.

She felt the breaking of hope almost as a pain.

He was greedy and he was reckless. He was also dangerous, distant and intimidating. But there lay beneath the image he showed to the world other shadows, too, quieter and more beguiling. Tragedy was one such veil. She had seen it once when he had spoken of his uncle.

Secrets and silence stretched between them, the sound of the world around distant, though her heartbeat drummed at a frantic rhythm in her ears.

HE COULD NOT bring himself to say he had paid her brother back each and every single penny twofold, penance for the only time in his life where his integrity had been held to ransom. Not now. That would come later, far away from accusation and dishonour and the reality of an enticement he had succumbed to in desperation.

Breathing out hard, he tried to take a stock of things.

His estranged wife looked a little like his mother used to, beautiful and prickly and angling for a fight, wanting high emotion to wreck what little peace he had left.

God. Patricia Ellesmere had used every single second of her life to make it harder for those near her and as her son it had often been him. Tay did not want acrimony and argument. He did not want greed and wrongdoing to punctuate everything that he was now, leaching out contentment and serenity.

Had he made a huge mistake by coming back after all, searching for an elusive something he could not quite forget? Almost three years of separation had hardened Lucinda. He could see it in her eyes. She was a different woman now, less innocent, more worldly.

'If it is of any use, I would apologise for the way I left. Excuses can only go a certain way in the alleviation of great pain so I won't bore you with them.'

'I have not heard even one explanation as yet, your Grace.' Her blue eyes were reflected in the silk of her dress, almost a match in colour.

'The dukedom was bankrupt.'

Surprise crept across her face. 'Surely my brother did not promise to rescue the Alderworth estate in its entirety?'

'No. He gave me the chance to do that myself. I hit a rich seam of gold in a river at the foot of the North Georgia mountains and had the luck to sell my claim for a tidy sum. After that I invested in the only services on a gold field that truly raise capital, the transportation facilities. The fortunes in mining are random, you see, but the large profits in the adjoining industries are not.'

'So you have arrived home rich?'

'I have.'

'And because of it you feel the need of an heir.'

He nodded.

'An unbroken line?'

'Precisely.'

'The saying that one person's luck is another's misfortune comes to mind.' Her mouth was a single tight line of fury.

She spoke as the forgotten wife who was suddenly recalled for duty a thousand days after he had left her. Such a thought was sobering, the contract for an heir stretching between them.

'If there is someone else who has gained your affections whilst I have been away, then I would—'

She did not let him finish. 'There isn't.'

Tay could not even begin to understand the relief he felt at her answer.

'After...us... I was largely left alone by others. Ruin has its own particular brand of isolation that is not easy to shake off. Besides, your reputation for debauchery and sexual experience meant all were wary.'

'When did you return to London?'

'Last year. My brothers insisted on it and their influence paved my way. It was all going well until...'

'I came back.'

She nodded and looked aside.

'Why, then, did you agree to come with me?'

He thought for a moment that she might not answer, as her eyes flinted in anger, but then she did, her voice shaking. 'Because anything is better than the stigma of abandonment.'

'I should not have let your brothers threaten me. I should have stayed and taken you to my home.'

'And forfeited your gold?' Her tone was neither soft nor conciliatory. It was hard and biting. 'No, your Grace, your promised largesse will go a long way in allowing me the freedom of a future I want.'

Tay shifted his stance and looked at her closely. She made him feel like the low-life he had not been, her lies cornering him into defending himself before her brothers, the licentious duke who had ruined a favoured sister.

Only he hadn't.

He had bundled up a woman who, with little persuasion, would have been easy to bed, but instead he had ordered a carriage and driven her home.

He had been paying for it ever since, by God, because the Wellinghams bore a grudge with great persistence, even one based on deceit.

He had sent his own correspondence, too, of course, a few careful letters explaining his daily routines and the harsh beauty of the countryside around Dahlonega. His wife had never written back. Not once. Tay wondered if Cristo Wellingham had stayed true to his promise and delivered the notes.

He could ask her, he supposed, pull the truth out of lies, but he had no more stomach for it and an idea hatched in the lonely fields of American dreams made little sense here.

The brothers' latest missive sizzled in his hand full of threat, the careful illusions of their wedding day dissolved here into only disappointment.

For them both.

'When we go to Alderworth Manor you will be given your own suite of rooms. I shall not presume on you for anything save for the fulfilment of our bargain.'

He turned away as she nodded and felt his body respond in anticipation of all that was implied.

I SHALL NOT presume on you for anything save for the fulfillment of our bargain.

A duty that had turned into obligation, the giving of her body for a sum of money and the promise of future freedom. A chore and a task that sounded onerous tonight. Lucinda couldn't decide just where she had lost all sense of herself: at Alderworth Manor three years ago or here, hurtling towards her marital requirements, only a womb for rent.

She could find no common ground with a husband who was a stranger, forged in hatred and anger by a family that gave no credence to close bonds or honest discourse.

'If I come, I would need at least a few weeks to settle in.' She blurted the words out, each one running on top of the other in a stream of quickness. 'I could not just be...'

She found it hard to finish.

'Pounced upon?'

Humour laced the query and she was glad for it, but still she pressed on.

'I would also require some sort of kindness, your Grace.'

This time he did laugh. 'How many men have you slept with, Lady Lucinda?' He did not use her married name and she did not answer. The corded arteries in his throat were raised in the dim light.

'I realise, of course, that you are used to faster women, women who would think nothing of sharing around their charms and making certain every man got their portion, but I am not of that ilk, your Grace, and if you think that I might change...'

'I do not wish for that at all.'

'Oh.' All of the wind went from her sails and she stood there, exposed and waiting. 'I need at least a few weeks,' she repeated, the quiver in her demand easily heard. Should she have bargained for more time? A month. A year?

'Very well.' His voice was hoarse, a promise co-erced only under duress. When he turned and offered her his arm, she could do nothing other than take it as he walked her back to the portico. Joining other couples who made their way up the wide staircase, the light from the lamps showed up his face as a handsome and distant mask.

Lucinda had not understood just exactly what it meant to be at the side of a man who was the most vil-ified and envied Duke in all of London. When their names were called as they stood waiting to go in, she heard the distinct murmur of surprise and a momentary lull in conversation of the three hundred or so guests present.

'The Duke and Duchess of Alderworth.'

'Notoriety has its own set of drawbacks and this is one of them.' His voice was soft and steady, not a care in the world showing as he smiled at those who might crucify him. 'Let us just hope that your unblemished pedigree shelters you from some of it.'

'With an attitude like that it is a wonder you still receive invitations to anything at all, your Grace,' she replied.

'No one wants to be the first to leave the lofty ducal title off their guest list and especially now they know all the coffers are full.'

'How full?'

The tone in his voice changed somewhat as he replied. 'Full enough to call in the chits of men with fewer morals than I have.' As she pulled back he made an effort to lighten such darkness. 'Full enough so that you could order as many gowns as you desire and I would barely notice, Duchess.'

'Tempting.'

His hand closed tighter in a movement that claimed her as his wife and Lucinda was pleased not one of her brothers was present as they walked down into the crowd. Edmund Coleridge was at the front of the group and smiled at her fondly, but she did not encourage him to come forwards because a small part of her worried that Alderworth would slice any tenderness to pieces should he know of it.

The Beauchamps, Lord Daniel and his French wife Lady Camille, were the first to receive them.

'I had heard you were back, Tay. How long are you here for?'

His brown eyes were kind and Camille Beauchamp seemed just as welcoming. Perhaps this evening would not be as difficult as Lucinda had thought it, her husband's reputation melding with her own to produce some sort of a halfway point of acceptability.

'Only a few weeks.'

'Then you might come to see us before then.' Camille joined the conversation for the first time, her lilting French accent beautiful. 'My husband made a point of telling me that you speak French well, your Grace. I should enjoy a conversation in my native language.'

More couples drifted over towards them, amongst the group an old school friend of Lucinda's. Annabelle Browne was as effusive as ever.

'Why, I just absolutely cannot imagine what it must have been like for your husband to have spent three years in the Americas, Lucy. My brother, Anthony, was in Washington for only a small amount of time and he was most forthcoming about the primitive state of the place.'

'I suspect that Alderworth managed,' she returned.

'The gold fields were dens of iniquity, I am told. It was a shame you could not have been there with him, to guide him through the pitfalls.'

'Oh, I am certain my husband was able to navigate them by himself, Annabelle.' The cutting she had received from Annabelle's brother came to mind and in an effort to change the topic she looked around at the others present. But Annabelle Browne was as persistent as she was dull-witted.

'Tony says the Duke was lucky in his windfall and that he left Georgia under a cloud.'

'A cloud of what?'

'Suspicion. His partner in the mining venture, Montcrieff, was killed and there was some discussion as to who would have benefitted most from such a tragedy. It seems Alderworth did.' She smiled sweetly, setting Lucinda's teeth on an edge.

'I am certain had there been anything untoward, the constabulary would have moved in.'

'But they did, you see, that is my very point. Tony said that your Duke was supposed to come before the courts in Atlanta, but—'

She stopped, aware of Alderworth's glance upon her.

'I was freed, Miss Browne, as an innocent man. The law has its uses after all, even though most of the time it is an ass.' His smile was languid, the creases in his cheeks deep against his tan and in a room full of men who had spent the good part of the day getting ready for this evening's entertainment he looked untamed— a ranging wolf amongst dainty chickens. The vibrant green of his eyes added to his menace.

Annabelle turned red and for a moment Lucinda viewed the world as Taylen might have, the innuendo and aspersion on his character a constant presence. She made herself smile as she faced her husband.

'It is most trying when people insist on passing on false rumours, do you not think, Duke?'

'Indeed,' he returned, and they both watched as the woman gave her goodbyes and dragged the man she was with away.

'I do not need you to defend me,' he said as Annabelle Browne moved out of hearing and the anger in his voice was sharp.

'Do you not, your Grace? I should have thought the very opposite.' She stood her ground as he loomed above her.

'Doubts begin to creep in if one crows one's innocence too loudly, I find.' He was back to his most infuriating best.

'It is more than doubts that hold those in this room enthralled in the saga of the Alderworth family. Were I to name it I might chance…fear.'

A small flicker of doubt came into his face. 'Do you fear me then, too?'

'No.' Surprisingly she did not. The answer tripped from her tongue in truth as their glances met and held, a living flame of heat that curled around sense and wisdom. She should fear him because every single thing she heard about him compromised all she had known before and just as they were finding a footing together some other new and terrible story pushed all accord aside leaving only this…attraction.

It would never be enough, she knew, tragedy and disaster trumping proper judgement and good sense. But she could not help it.

Intrinsically flawed.

And she was.

LUCINDA WAS LOOKING at him as though he might stab the next person who came to talk to them. The aspersions just aired, he supposed, as the face of Lance Montcrieff rose up in memory, an accident with their rudimentary stamp mill in Ward's Creek slicing through his thigh just below the groin.

It had taken less than ten minutes for him to bleed out, despite Tay's efforts to staunch the flow, and Tay had held his hand through every long and harrowing one of them, willing his friend to live even as breath dulled and stopped. Gold took no account of the integrity of its victims, for if it had it would have been him lying there with cold blue on his lips and death in his skin, thousands of miles from home.

Another loss. Another brush with the law. Another woman without a husband, another child fatherless.

Swallowing, he pulled himself back into the ball-room on Audley Street with its chandeliers and wide curtained alcoves, marbled pillars and liveried servants.

A gentle England that had not been his for a long, long time. He had forgotten its beauty and peace, he thought, as his wife swayed unconsciously to the beat of music, deliberately not looking his way.

'Would you dance with me again?'

He expected her to refuse, but she did not. Instead

he found her fingers within his outstretched hand and then they were on the floor amongst the other couples, the music of a waltz beginning.

He had always liked the way she fitted into him, her head just under the curve of his chin, liked how she allowed him to lead her, an easy flowing dancer with a light and clever step.

He did not usually dance at these social occasions, but spent the hours in the card rooms drinking away the night.

'How did the man in America die? The one Annabelle spoke of, I mean?' Her query was soft and he could think of no other of his acquaintance who might have asked this question so directly of him.

'His name was Lance. Lance Montcrieff. We set up a stamp mill outside Dahlonega to crush the ore from the tunnels and release the gold. When the sapling holding the structure broke and it all came down on him, he never stood a chance. We were ten hours from the nearest township, you understand, and a lot of that was over rough terrain.'

'Why did they blame you?'

'Gold has the propensity to make fools of every man and a rich claim incites questions. I was the one who would profit most from his death, after all, and there was no one else about to vouch that my story was true.'

Her breath hitched against the skin at his throat. Another truth she did not want probably. Another way she would be disappointed in him.

'Trouble never seems very far away from your door, your Grace. Do you ever wonder why?'

Shaking his head, he was amazed when she let him pull her closer, their bodies now touching almost like lovers. The firm daintiness of her breasts rubbed against his chest and he pushed his groin against her own in a quiet statement of intent.

Slender fingers tightened on his hands. Their bodies talked now in the smallest of caresses, almost accidental, never hurried—a slight pressure here, a small stroke there, too new for words, too fragile for any true acknowledgement. Taylen had never been in a room before and felt so removed from everybody in it. Save her. Save his wife with her straightforward questions and her unexpected allegiance.

'What is Edmund Coleridge to you?'

'A friend who has helped me to laugh again.'

'That is all. Just the laughter?' He did not care for the hesitation in her words or the sudden stiffness in her body.

'Why all these questions, your Grace?' She smiled as she asked, a smile that made her look so beautiful, with her deep-set dimples and pale spun-gold hair, that he had to glance away.

'My father may have had no problem with being cuckolded, Duchess, but I most certainly do.' He did not like the unease he could so plainly hear in his words.

'Three years of absence makes your insistence on celibacy rather hard to take, your Grace. Perhaps I should inform you that a woman, contrary to belief, has as many needs as a man.'

'Needs I wish to fill, sweetheart, and tonight if you would let me.'

He felt shock run down through all the parts of her body in a hot and hard wash, and was glad for it. If he had been anywhere else save in a crowded ballroom, he could have used such a reaction to persuade her to take a chance on him. Such an easy seduction. He had done it so many times before, after all, and not one woman had ever held complaint.

Yet as he gritted his teeth those faceless paramours dissolved into the ether just as they had done for a while now, lost to him and formless, lovers with the word skewered into only faithless lust. The broken promises of his childhood bound into the present.

When the music stopped they came apart and he was glad for the distance as he went to find a drink.

Lucinda felt giddy. A ridiculous word, she knew, but it explained her lack of certainty entirely. Taylen Ellesmere threw her into a place that was without compass, directionless and wanton.

Wanton? Another word she smiled at. Tonight her vocabulary regarding misdirected emotions was growing and she did not wish for it to stop. Already she looked for him across the room, tall and dark amongst a sea of others.

She was like a moth to his light, fluttering unheeded, waiting to be burnt. Her brothers had warned her, her sisters-in-law had told her stories about him and none of the tales had been kind. Yet still some invisible bond drew her to him, the wedding ring circling her finger a part of it, but nowhere near the total. Her nails dug into the soft flesh of her palms as she pondered her intentions.

What did she want of him? She could not even begin to name it.

Posy Tompkins came to her side and took her hand. Lucinda liked the warm familiarity of the action.

'You look beautiful tonight, Luce, and I think that fact has something to do with the return of your mysterious husband. Edmund has already been whining to me about your lack of attention.'

'You never liked him, Posy. I am not certain why.'

'He is a boy compared to the Duke of Alderworth, a boy who in the end would disappoint you.'

'And you think that the Duke would not?'

'I think he has been misjudged by society. I think he is strong like your brothers and honourable in his way. I think, if you gave him a chance, he might surprise you.'

'You were always the romantic, Posy.'

'To find the happiness you haven't had ever since your wedding, Luce, you might need to allow Alderworth some ground for compromise, for a bending is better than a breaking. If it were me, I would grab him with both hands and never let him go.'

'Fine words from a woman who has sworn off relationships for ever.'

Posy's more normal optimism was sliced by a sadness Lucinda had sometimes seen in her friend before. 'He reminds me of a man I knew a long time ago, in Italy.'

Their conversation was interrupted by the arrival of the Elliott twins, their voices louder than they needed to be.

'Lucinda, it is so wonderful that your husband is finally back. You must be thrilled that he has returned after all this time?'

Elizabeth Elliott was as effusive as her sister, Louise. 'Everybody is talking about him, of course, and it seems he has arrived back in England a lot richer than when he left it. Perhaps you might both come to our ball on Saturday night—for Edmund Coleridge had already said that he will be there.'

The questionable undercurrents of the *ton* at play, Lucinda thought, and was glad when Posy took charge.

'I had heard a rumour that you are to be married, Lady Elizabeth. Is it true?'

A scream of delight and then much was made of a ring on the third finger of her left hand. Lucinda scanned the room for any sign of her husband and was disappointed when she could not see him at all. Had he simply left or was he in the card room, drinking himself into oblivion and losing a fortune? The excitement she had felt before was suddenly changed into cold hard worry and she did not like the feeling at all.

Ten minutes later she made her way to a large terrace overlooking the garden and was about to walk out on to the edge of it when a scuffle and shouting at the far end caught her attention. Richard Allenby, the Earl of Halsey, was pummelling someone on the ground, a number of others around the prone body adding their particular attentions. Turning away in order to find somebody to help, she saw the profile of the person they were hurting suddenly in the light.

'Taylen.' Shouting, she moved forwards, catching the group unawares, each one of them looking towards her with a varying degree of disbelief on their faces. Then she was amongst them, sheltering her husband with her body and daring them to go through her person to get to him.

Blood was on his nose and his chin, a long cut across the back of his head and a metal bar lying down beside him. He looked groggy and dazed, his collar crooked and his jacket torn.

'You have no business here.' Allenby's voice. She turned to face him with pure wrath.

'No business, Lord Halsey?' Her hand came out to push him back. 'Will you hit me next, then? Do you creep up on defenceless women as well as men?' She stooped as she spoke; her fingers found the bar and she raised it above her head. 'If anyone comes closer, I will use it on them and I will scream the place down as I do it, you understand. And then when people come running I will tell them exactly what I saw; a bunch of cowardly thugs beating up a badly injured, half-conscious man in their midst and enjoying it.'

Silence reigned except for the breath of her husband,

taken noisily through blood and mucus, then they were gone, all of them, the door to the ballroom shutting, leaving them alone.

She leant down to him, his blood staining her blue silk as she tried to mop up his face with her hem. Her hands shook with the shock of it all and she made an effort to still them.

She knew the moment he came back into full consciousness because he stiffened and tried to stand, coming up to his haunches in a way that suggested great pain and swaying with the movement.

'The bastards hit me from behind.' His fingers worked around into his hair, finding a gash as he looked at the bar. 'They used that, I suppose. Halsey always was a coward.'

Lucinda thought that his pupils looked larger than they should be, green shrunk into darkness. He blinked a lot, too, as though his vision was impaired and he was trying to find the way to correct it.

'There are stairs at the other end of the terrace. If we went through the garden, we could get to the road to find your carriage.'

'You would come with me?'

'Of course I would. You need help.'

'If people see us, they will talk.'

When she laughed it felt free and real and good, a surprising discovery with the trauma of all that was happening around her. 'They talk now, your Grace, and there is too much blood to go back into the ballroom. If they see you like this, everything will be worse.'

Nodding, he came up into a standing position, though his hands used the balustrade to steady himself, to find his balance. 'I have ruined your gown.' His top lip was thickening even as he spoke.

'A small consideration given all of the others.'

The music had begun again, calling those present to the dancing, and Lucinda was pleased for it. With so much happening inside it would be far less likely for a guest to take the air on the terrace. Placing her arm across his, she led him down the steps, the small pathways amongst the plants lined with white chip stone which made it easy to traverse in the moonlight. Before a moment or so had passed they were out at the gate and Lucinda hailed the Alderworth conveyance, which languished further down the road, the driver throwing a cheroot to the ground and stomping it underfoot before climbing up into the driving box.

Another moment and they were inside with the door closed behind them and, for the first time since finding her husband at the feet of his assailants, Lucinda took in an easy breath. They would not be discovered like this, battered and bloodied after such a scandalous attack. They were safe.

Reaching into her reticule, she found a handkerchief. 'Here, let me help you.'

His hand came out as he shook away the offer, anger evident in his refusal.

'Why would Halsey waylay you in the way he did?'

Taylen Ellesmere raised his head slightly and had the temerity to smile.

'Because, once upon a time, I did just the same to him.'

CHAPTER NINE

'YOU CREPT UP on him like a coward and knocked him out?'

He shook his head and then clutched at the side of it.

'With a whole group of others to help you do your dirty work?'

'Of course not.'

'You used an iron bar on his scalp and hit him with it from behind, allowing him no chance to defend himself, and when he was down you kicked at his face?'

He seemed to suddenly lose patience with her questions, leaning forwards to take her hand into his.

'Thank you, Lucinda.'

'You are welcome, Taylen.'

His blood had made his palm sticky and he was careful to wipe her fingers with the tail of his shirt when he let go. Such a simple action and so much imbued within it. She looked away so that he would not see the emotion on her face. Outside the London streets were as busy as usual, nothing changed. Inside her world had shifted, though, the touch of his fingers against her own different now, more familiar. His smell. His warmth.

The breadth of his thighs as they pressed against the velour on the seat.

'My parents always believed in the concept of treating everyone as an enemy. Tonight I forgot.' The words were said concisely, as if he would place a point on each one of them.

'Advice like that makes me wonder whether such people have the right to offspring. Surely no child deserves to be brought up under such a cruel misconception.'

The sound of his laughter filled the small space, allowing accord to push through shock and anger. 'Are you usually so forthright, Duchess?'

'Indeed I am, Duke. My family would tell you that it is one of my greatest faults.'

His head shook as the Wellingham town house came into view, the action shadowed on the wall of the carriage behind him by the light from the portico. His hair had worked free from its leather strap and lay around his shoulders, darker than the darkness.

'But I would not. Free speech has always been a particular preference of mine. I think it a residue of being raised by parents who never said what they actually thought.'

'Because they were trying to protect you?'

He laughed again and was about to say something more when a movement on the stairs before them caught his attention. 'It seems we have a welcoming party.'

Lucinda's heart sank. With the blood from his nose

still smeared across his face, a rapidly darkening eye and a thickened lip, Taylen Ellesmere looked exactly like the reprobate her brothers had good reason to think that he was.

'I won't come in. I doubt my body could take another beating.' The dispassionate and cynical Duke was back, no warmth in his eyes at all as the footman opened the door and the light spilled upon them.

'A further rowdy night of fighting, Alderworth?' Asher's question was layered with disgust.

'Someone has to subdue the scum of London. It may as well be me.'

'No, it isn't as you think it—' Lucinda began as she stepped down from the coach, but her husband cut her off.

'I will see you tomorrow, Duchess. Thank you for the most interesting of evenings.'

A rap with his cane on the roof had the horses moving, the perfectly matched pair of greys gathering speed as they disappeared down the road.

'His blood has ruined your gown.' Asher ground the words out as they walked back inside.

'Halsey did it. Halsey and a group of his cowardly friends. They caught him alone on the terrace at the ball in a planned attack. He had no chance against them.'

A look crossed her brother's face, dark and unexplainable, and a terrible idea suddenly occurred to Lucinda.

'You did not pay anyone to do that to him, did you, Ashe?'

'Halsey is a weak-willed and arrogant sycophant. If I wanted the job done, I would do it properly myself.'

'Well, don't.' She stood to her tallest height in her stained and crumpled gown, the shock of the evening on her face and an anger boiling beneath everything that was dubious. 'Hurt Alderworth, I mean. I am tired of being the forgotten wife and I want at least the chance to…' She stopped, not quite able to voice what it was she did want.

'The chance to what?' His dark eyes were filled with an urgent question.

'To…know something of the man I have married.'

With that she swept past, making for the staircase and the privacy of her room.

TAY HELD A hand close against his chest. He was sure a few of his ribs were broken and knew they would hurt like the devil in the morning. Breathing shallowly, he leaned forwards, finding in the movement a slight relief. The wedding ring he had retrieved that morning from the bottom drawer of his library desk felt solid on his finger.

Lucinda had seen him helpless at the feet of a pack of cowards who had crept up on him as he was lighting a cheroot, the evening with his wife making him less vigilant than he normally was. Usually the *ton* avoided any contretemps or whiff of scandal, but Lucinda had come forwards with her integrity and her honour, ad-

monishing grown men with words that he could not
have bettered.

Like a fierce and urgent angel. Lord, he was the
sinner married to a saint and with his past it would be
her paying for such loyalty again and again and again.
The shock in her eyes, her trembling fingers, her ruined gown and disappointment scrawled in deep lines
across her brow. He had seen her stiffen when her oldest brother had come out to meet them. Another mor-
tification. He smiled at the word and then regretted it
as the skin on his top lip stung.

Without Lucinda here everything hurt, badly, a cold
emptiness closing in about him. He would not meet
her tomorrow or the day after that, for he needed time
to nurse his wounds and to try to find some idea as to
where to go to next.

He could not keep putting his wife into danger or
see her compromised by his own lack of regard for the
law and there were more of the ilk of Halsey out there
than he would have liked to admit.

Remembering Lucinda's words in the carriage as
she had tried to explain to him why he was nothing
like Richard Allenby, he smiled. No one had ever been
on his side before, not like that and in the face of such
damning evidence. The feeling was…warming.

Shaking his head hard, he told himself to put such
nonsense aside. Twenty-eight years had taught him a
few home truths and one of them was to depend upon
nobody.

Treat everyone as an enemy.

His mother and father's son after all, the words scrawled into his flesh like a tattoo. Ineradicable and permanent.

LUCINDA DID NOT see Taylen Ellesmere the next day or the day after. No note of explanation came.

Her brothers had ceased to talk of Alderworth whatsoever, hoping perhaps that by ignoring him he might go away, but she haunted the wide front-window bays like a wraith, glancing out each time a noise caught her attention or the sound of hooves echoed on the street, her breath catching with every newcomer turning into the square, eyes picking out their livery with interest. He might be laying low, but the bargain for an heir that they had struck between them still simmered underneath everything, calling through the silence.

'You seem jumpy.' Eleanor sat on the small sofa in the blue room working on a tapestry.

Smiling half-heartedly, Lucinda picked up her own needlework, but the stitches blurred before her, the counting of each one difficult today.

'I did not sleep well last night or the one before that.' Goodness, that was an understatement. She had lain awake almost till the dawn, worrying.

'I could make you one of my tonics if you like. It is bound to help you relax.'

As Lucinda shook her head to decline the offer, the needle pierced her finger, drawing blood, yet instead of wiping it away she watched as the red of the wound spread into white cotton. Other blood came to mind.

The injuries Taylen Ellesmere had sustained were substantial and damaging and she wondered how he fared now. Who would tend to him and make certain he was not becoming worse? His breathing had been laboured, after all, and she was sure his nose had been broken.

Standing again, she walked to the window, unconcerned as to what Eleanor might make of her distractedness. Outside drizzle coated the world in grey, a few leaves falling on the gardens with their ragged yellow edges brittle. Like her. She felt the tension in all of the corners of her body, scraping away contentment, panic close to the skin. Tears pooled at the back of her eyes. One step forwards and then two steps back. She was tired of the uncertainty and the confusion.

'Is the contretemps at the Chesterfield ball worrying you?' Eleanor came to stand beside Lucinda, the palm of her hand making contact.

A nod brought the hand fully around Lucinda's shoulders.

'Cristo thinks Alderworth may have been the one to deal with Halsey three years ago, which would explain the attack upon him in Mayfair after the carriage accident. He said that he may have misjudged him.'

'Alderworth would not thank him for the compliment were he to hear of it, Eleanor.'

'Because he is prickly and distant and completely unmindful of a reputation that is hardly salutary? Or because he likes to hide behind an image that is not entirely the truth?' The tone in her words was a worried one. 'His grandmother used to hit him, you know.

Hard. She thought such training would make a man of her grandchild because her own daughter had become such a biting disappointment with her many lovers and her drinking.'

Bile rose in Lucinda's throat as she turned to her sister-in-law. 'Who told you that?'

'Rosemary Jones, my maid's older sister. She works at Falder now, but as a young girl she was employed by Lady Shields at her home in Essex.'

'Many children are punished, Eleanor.'

'Not in the way he was. According to Rosemary, he spent months away from the family in a hospital in Rouen after one particular incident. Then his uncle took him away.'

'An uncle? Which uncle?'

'Hugo Shields, Lord Sutton, I think was the name mentioned. His mother's brother. Rosemary did not see any of the family again because she was asked to leave. The old lady had some inkling of her disapproval, I suppose, and did not wish to be reminded of an unsavoury period in her life.'

Goodness. The whole horror of everything began to mount inside Lucinda. Between a heavy-handed grandmother and a brutal uncle, the small Taylen Ellesmere never had a chance, just as he did not now with the building censure of a society that barely knew him.

'I think I will take the carriage out, Eleanor. I need to see my milliner about a hat.'

'I will tell your brothers that you have a few errands to do, Lucy. I know there are a pile of library books well overdue from Hookham's Lending Library if you would not mind dropping them off for me.'

'Certainly.' She smiled as Eleanor did. Both knew that the Ellesmere town house was only a few hundred yards from the mentioned establishment, a distance easy to walk.

THE DOOR OF Alderworth House opened almost instantly after her maid rang the bell, a tall man ushering them into a room which was light and airy, the windows looking out on to a garden filled with greenery. A mismatched set of a sofa and two chairs were arranged before the fireplace and there were faded areas on the walls where pictures had been removed and never replaced. Lucinda wondered why the Duke had not had the place refurbished after his windfall in the Americas.

'I'll tell his Grace you are here, your Grace.' Ellesmere's butler's face flushed at the recognition of her name and he seemed to hesitate for a moment as if he could not quite decide what to do. 'It might take a few moments,' he managed finally. 'A maid will bring tea and cakes into you while you wait.'

'Thank you.'

Claire, her maid, stood by the door, her face a careful blank canvas. She was probably balancing the luxury of the Carisbrook houses against the frugality here, a topic that would be faithfully reported back to the downstairs staff at the Wellingham town house to mull over and discuss. Lucinda wished she might have asked her to wait with the carriage, but to do so would have invited questions.

She heard a cat howling outside somewhere close. Further afield the faint trip-trop of a carriage wending its way was audible above the ticking of an ancient ornate clock in the corner, its glass face shattered on one side and the time running a good half an hour slow.

The piece had already boomed out twice before the door opened again and Tay Ellesmere stood there, formally dressed and his gait stiff. His hair was wet, giving the impression he had just bathed, and it was pulled back into a tight tail falling to his shoulders. One eye was ringed in black whilst the white of the other had changed into a violent red, deeper marks of the same colour snaking into his hair at the temple. He smelled of soap and of lemon, a combination that was appealing, but all she could think of were Rosemary the scullery-maid's words: a small battered child lost behind hard green eyes.

'I am sorry. I did not realise we had arranged a meeting.'

'We had not, your Grace. It is just the last time I saw you it looked as though your injuries were worse than you let on and I thought to check to see if you were… well?'

'I am. Entirely.' The puffy edge of his right eye had made it close at one end. Lucinda wondered if it blurred his vision because he squinted as he watched her, the tick in his swollen eyelid clearly visible.

'I see.'

She wished with all her heart that they might have a moment in private. He seemed to understand her reticence as his glance took in the servants. 'Bingham, would you take the Duchess's maid to the kitchen and find her something to drink.'

'Very well, your Grace.' It took only a moment for the room to be cleared and the door to be shut behind them.

'A walk in the park would be out of the question, I suppose?' She kept her tone light as she broke the awkward silence.

'Unless you want me to scare small children.' His smile went nowhere near his eyes. 'Why are you here?' Tiredness draped the query.

'I have waited for you for the past two days and when you did not come I wondered if you had the medical help that you needed...'

'I do.'

He did not even look at her now.

'What was the reason for your attack on Halsey all those years ago?'

That brought his attention back. 'Allenby broke one of the most important rules of my house.'

'Which was?'

'What goes on at Alderworth stays there.'

Disappointment welled. So it wasn't solely because he had been trying to protect her, after all.

'It seems to me enforcing such a rule would require much effort?' The sharpness in her voice was not becoming, but she could no longer hide it. 'Why seek more battles when you had enough of your own to fight?'

'Usually I am more handy with my fists than you saw me to be at the Chesterfields', and making certain scandal does not follow each of my guests home has not been unduly onerous before.'

Today Taylen Ellesmere was exactly the Duke his title proclaimed him to be, the solemn answers at odds with his damaged face and eyes. He stood strangely, too, straight-backed and erect, the pose making her wonder what other injuries he had sustained under the ministration of Halsey and his cronies.

'But scandal follows you regardless, your Grace. Your own reputation has been the talk of the town for years.'

He moved towards her and reached out his hand, one finger tracing its way down her cheek.

'Every opinion should be allowed to be given freely, I believe, but it is wise to remember that what is said is not always the truth.'

The warmth and the strength of him flooded into her being, a touchstone in the scattered uncertainty of her life, drawing her home.

Hold me closer, she longed to say, as if their history together melded only into the bright promise of this moment, but his hand fell back instead.

'If you don't wish to be in my company for a while, I would quite understand. I cannot promise that there will not be another contretemps, you see, and if you were to be hurt because of it…'

He stopped.

'I am no weak-willed girl, your Grace. Were I to be pitted against your own skills with a bow and arrow I may well win the competition.' She held her palms face up. 'I have the calluses to prove it.'

For the first time that day true humour crept into his face. 'My Diana.' The words were whispered and then regretted. She could see the wariness in his eyes.

'Do you have any other family at all, your Grace?'

His brow creased at the subject change.

'Why do you ask?'

'You seem so alone sometimes. I only wondered if there were others you might rely on.'

He shook his head and crossed to pour himself a drink, lifting a brandy decanter to offer her one as well. Declining, she waited until he began to speak.

'I have an aunt, but I lost any contact with her years ago.'

'A fading line, then?'

His smile was wicked. 'Which brings us back to our agreement.'

The heir. With a thick cloak on, servants just outside the door and her maid presumably returning at any moment Lucinda also smiled. 'A broken nose and cracked ribs have probably put paid to any designs you might have on me at the moment.'

His laughter filled the room, deep and resonant. 'Injuries such as these have not stopped me before.'

'I read of you once. A story in a newspaper when you had first struck gold.'

'Where did you get it from?'

'An old school friend's brother sent it to me. The author of the piece made certain that the readers understood that the women you were partying with were…"' She could not quite find the word.

'Fallen?' He provided it for her. 'The difference between the *ton* and those who ply their bodies for money on the street corners of hopelessness is smaller than you might imagine. Believe me, I know it to be true.'

Was he speaking of his childhood? she wondered and braved a question. 'How did your uncle hurt you?'

'Badly.'

A truth, without an embroidered qualifying word attached? Lucinda could barely believe his honesty.

'He should have been shot.'

'He was.'

'Oh.'

The words were on her tongue to ask by whom, but the gleam in his green eyes stopped the question. She wanted amiability and agreement to be between them, even if only for this meeting.

'Would you ride with me tomorrow, your Grace? In the park. I usually go early before the crowds arrive.'

'Yes.'

She could hear the voices of her maid and one of the Ellesmere servants in the hallway coming closer. 'Shall we say nine o'clock?'

He reached over and rang the bell, the same man she had seen before hurrying back in. Claire also rejoined them, standing behind the sofa, a heavy frown upon her brow.

'Thank you for taking the time to see that I was regaining in strength, Duchess, and please do give my regards to your family.'

'I will, your Grace.'

So formal. So many undertones. She hoped with all her heart that her maid would say nothing of the visit to Asher's valet before she had had the chance to tell her brother.

'I WENT TO see Taylen Ellesmere today,' Lucinda announced at dinner just as the main course was being served. On the journey home she had decided that honesty would be the best ploy with her family and bringing things out into the open was far better than having them simmer and boil over in the shadows.

'How is his face?' Emerald asked, her smile belying any more sinister purpose.

'I do not know if his nose is broken, though the boots of Halsey's minions did a good job of trying to do so. Both his eyes are blackened and there is a sizeable cut to the back of his head. Perhaps other injuries linger beneath his clothes. He certainly moved as if they did.'

'Trouble follows him like a stray dog after the meat man.' Her brother's voice was wary.

'I remember a time when it seemed to follow me with as much tenacity.' Emerald looked directly at Asher and the spark that ignited between them had Lucinda glancing away. Passion in a marriage bed was something she had never experienced, the burn of it rolling across ordinariness and lifting everything up. Every one of her siblings had that sort of feeling with their partner and she was suddenly tired of her own lack of hope for the same.

'I have asked the Duke to accompany me on my morning ride in the park tomorrow.'

'And he has agreed?' There was no warmth in her brother's query whatsoever. 'You may regret allowing a man who seems to find a fight at every opportunity, un-provoked or not, back into your life, Lucy.' Fury raised the tone of his voice.

'He is my legal husband.'

'A matter that was supposed to be resolved three years ago by a large sum of money. We hoped never to see him again and we would not have, save for a lucky strike in a Godforsaken goldfield miles from England which allowed him to crawl back.'

Lucinda stood, breath coming almost as fast as her heart was beating. 'Perhaps that is divine intervention, then. Gold for gold and the recommencing of an or-dained union promised before a minister of the Church. Surely when you hatched this plan of matrimony a small part of you thought that it might just…stick?'

Asher stood now, too, and Lucinda was glad that the table lay between them, a solid wide slab of oak that divided the room down its length.

'God damn it, you are my sister and I was only trying to protect you.' For the first time in memory her oldest brother sounded…defeated, the strain of the last week showing on his face in deep lines of regret.

'And you do that well, but I do not wish to live with you for ever. I need to find my own life, too.'

'I will gift you Amberley Manor in Kent, then. That estate is more than ample for your needs. You can stay there with a stipend if you cannot stay here.'

'But I will still be beholden to your generosity, don't you see, and with no recourse to marriage again it will always be that way. For ever. Until I am old and childless and alone.'

'So you would agree instead to give the benefit of doubt to a Duke who displays neither morality nor virtue? A man you hate?'

'Eleanor seems to think he is more virtuous than any of us might realise, Asher.' Emerald came around the table to stand by Lucinda, her turquoise eyes deep pools of worry. 'She says that the servants at his London town house have a great deal of regard for him.'

'You imagine that is enough?'

'Cristo said Alderworth dealt with Halsey when he was spreading rumours of Lucinda's…dalliance. He seems to believe Halsey waylaid him to pay him back. If that is the case, we ought to be thanking him, not maligning him.' She stopped for a moment before carrying on. 'It is also rumoured that Alderworth still supports the wife and children of his mining partner, killed in an accident in America. Only an honourable person would do that.'

Unexpectedly her brother began to laugh. 'Lord,

Emmie, if we want to find out about anyone it would be wise to ask you first.'

'All I am saying is that he may be a good man whom you have not given a chance to.'

'A good man who locked my sister in a room against her will and had her way with her. That sort of a good man?'

'Well, if Lucy finds that she cannot bear him, then she can take you up on your offer of Amberley. It is not medieval England after all. Alderworth cannot keep her anywhere against her will.'

The thought that he might do just that showed on Asher's face as a dark uncertainty, but the heart of his argument had been taken to pieces and Lucinda knew that Asher would allow her the freedom she asked for. However, when she exchanged a smile of gratitude with her sister-in-law, she saw in the turquoise eyes a quick burst of puzzlement and pity before she turned for the door.

CHAPTER TEN

As LUCINDA BRUSHED away a curl that had escaped her bonnet in the wind, a movement to one side of the park caught her eye.

Taylen Ellesmere watched her from a distance and she waited as he threaded his way towards her on a large dark stallion.

'You ride well,' he said as he reached her. Today his bruising looked less and he moved with more ease, though his right eye was still brutally red.

'You have been watching me?'

'I had heard you had a good seat.' His left hand shifted on the reins and the rings on his fingers caught in the sun, underlining the differences between them. Such adornment seemed an over-embellishment and foreign, though she was pleased to see that the ring she had given him as a wedding vow still lay amongst the others. He hailed from a world that was so far removed from her own that Lucinda wondered if she might ever truly know him.

When he saw where she looked he stilled, the vigilance that seldom left his eyes easily seen.

'I ride here most days when I am in town, your Grace. It is a freeing thing.'

'I have also heard it said that you tool a barouche like a champion.'

She laughed. 'Taris taught me.'

'You are fortunate, then, in the care your family gives you.'

She wished her brothers had heard the compliment he gave them, for perhaps then they might not have been quite so averse to any communication. The breeze caught at a line of oaks to one side of the path, sending a scattering of green leaves into the air.

'I think the early morning shows Hyde Park at its best,' she chanced when he did not deign to speak.

'Indeed. My grandfather loved it here, too. It was the closest he ever got to a peaceful and solitary life given my grandmother's disposition, for he spent all of his hours wandering the parks and gardens when he was in town.'

'He sounds kind.'

'He was.'

'How old were you when he died?'

'Six and a half.' So precisely known, Lucinda thought.

'I met Lady Shields a few times. She seemed difficult.'

'And now she lies beside my grandfather in consecrated ground for all of eternity.'

'Matrimony being the most onerous of bonds to break away from?' The sting in her voice did not become her, but his last words made her wonder if that was what he might think of their union, too.

He was quiet for a moment. 'There are things about marriage that one could find…addictive.'

She thought he meant sex and stiffened, but when he kept on talking she knew that that was not what he was alluding to at all.

'A person to watch your back and be on your side no matter what happens is one of them. I do not think I thanked you enough for doing just that the other night at the Chesterfields' Ball. No one ever has before.'

Again she saw behind the mask, a quick glimpse of a man she could love. A lot.

'I was glad to help.' So precise and stilted. She wished he would dismount and reach out to thank her with his body, but he did not, his attention caught by others riding behind them.

SHIFTING IN HIS SEAT, his horse shied to one side and he gentled him. A few other souls had now ventured out on the same pathways, tipping their hats as they passed and looking back with more than interest on their faces. Tay knew the gossip mills had been grinding ever since his return to England and that the betting in the clubs were riding fifty to one he would have his estranged wife beneath him before the week's end.

He might have enjoyed the irony of it all, but such a gamble cut too close to the quick and fifty to one still seemed like damn long odds. He hoped that the

Wellingham brothers had no knowledge of the punters' flutterings.

The stakes were rising and he could not get Lucinda to himself until at least after the promised two weeks.

Breathing deeply, he bid his horse on and was glad when his wife followed his lead, the path wider now and more conducive to a canter. There was nothing like a ride to free a soul of tension and the heavy muscles beneath him were soothing and easeful.

Lucinda rode like the youngest sister of three brothers who had all left the mark of their tutorship upon her, fluid and daring, and he allowed her by him so that he might watch. She did not flaunt her gift, but every movement and command had the sort of controlled gentleness that even great horsemen struggled to achieve as she galloped in front of him. Her laughter rang in the air as she pulled in her mount, waiting as he drew up beside her.

'I don't know of another female who can ride with the expertise of a jockey.'

'You disapprove?'

'Far from it, my lady wife. I hail it. At Alderworth you will find fine tracks to ride along, though the stables have been largely depleted.'

'But you will replace them with new stock?'

He shook his head. 'To get the production from the land up and running again is my first priority.'

'You do not sound as dissolute as they say, then.'

'It is my experience that no one is ever as good or as bad as society might paint them.'

A slight flush crawled into her cheeks. 'Expectations are certainly bonds that tie you down. The Wellingham name held me captive for years in that I could never truly be myself.'

'And now?'

'When everybody disapproves so firmly of my actions, it gives a freedom to do just as I want.'

There it was again, that sadness. The accident, a hasty marriage and his three years away had all had their part in drawing a melancholy hue over her pale-blue eyes. Ever since they had met they had hurt each other, Tay thought, his demands for an heir adding to the burden. He was suddenly tired of it.

'Lucinda. Luce.' A sound from a distance had them both turning. A young woman hailed them from her mare, her groom left far behind.

'My friend, Posy Tompkins. You will remember her from the wedding.'

'She was the one who brought you to Alderworth in the first place?'

When she nodded Tay thought he had a lot to thank Miss Tompkins for. He watched as she came closer.

LUCINDA WISHED THAT they had ridden further into the greenery where they might have been more alone to talk. Already she could see the intrigue on her friend's face.

'I have been following you,' Posy said as she joined them, 'and I still think you should not take such risks on a horse, Lucy. How many times have your brothers admonished you not to gallop so fast?'

'Oh, I lost count months ago.'

'The doctor told you another bump on the head could be dangerous…'

'He did?' Taylen Ellesmere sounded nothing like he had a few moments prior. Nay, now he sounded exactly the same as Cristo, Asher and Taris.

Posy nodded. 'He said that she was to lead a careful and circumspect life and that he had seen many a patient becoming gravely ill if they did not heed his advice.'

The green in her husband's eyes displayed no humour now whatsoever.

'Something about blood vessels bursting, I think he said. The walls of the brain are thinner where they have been damaged. Because of that it is easier for them to erupt again.' Listing the medical information using her fingers, she bent down each one after every fact stated.

Posy did not look at her, but at Alderworth, an expression that Lucinda recognised on her face. The same look she had seen in their earlier days when together they would stage outlandish tragedies for the family to watch, the curtains in the downstairs salon of Falder fashioned into a theatre. She was baiting Alderworth for some reason and Lucinda could do nothing at all to stop it.

'Posy is exaggerating and I hardly think that will happen, your Grace—' she began, but Taylen interrupted her.

'Are you a physician now, too?' The tone in his voice was furious.

'No.'

'Then you should heed a warning from a man who is obviously qualified to give it.'

'And never race along the gullies and cliffs at Falder? Never clear another fence in my life?'

'If that is what it takes to be safe from any danger, then yes.'

Posy's laughter brought an end to the bickering. 'Asher has used the same arguments as you do so many times, your Grace, but to no avail.' Posy raised her eyebrows as Lucinda frowned at her and smiled congenially at Alderworth.

Amazing, Lucinda thought. Posy had never approved of any of her suitors. Not one. It was the creases in Taylen Ellesmere's cheeks, she supposed, and the way the light played upon his eyes—a man who was no one's lackey. The only white he wore was in his cravat and it showed up the tan of his skin. She could suddenly imagine him far from London in the back country wilds of Georgia, traipsing across swollen rivers and steep craggy mountains. Any information she had ever read on goldfields described them as hard and dangerous places, spawning hard and dangerous men.

'My brothers have this idea that I need to be looked after all the time. I find it easier to simply get on with my life in the way that I wish to and allow them to do the same.'

'In other words, you do not tell them of the danger
you are placing yourself in.'

'Exactly, and I would appreciate your discretion in
the matter, too, your Grace.'

'Then I hope you will at least have the sense to walk
your horse home.' He tipped his hat. 'Miss Tompkins,
it was my pleasure.'

Then he was gone, cutting across the park on a path
Lucinda seldom used, body rising and falling with each
movement of his horse in an effortless display of skill.

'Alderworth rides well, Luce.'

Anger seeped into her reply. 'Why would that be
important to me, Posy? If it was left to everyone else,
I should be in my drawing room at home, pursuing the
gentle arts of needlework or playing music.'

*Or lying in bed on my back, trying to produce an
Ellesmere heir.*

She bit down on chagrin.

'WHAT THE HELL are you doing here, Alderworth?'

'White's is my club too, Wellingham, and I want a
chat with you.'

Cristo Wellingham did not assent, but neither did he
get up and leave. Rather he sat with his drink in hand
and waited until Tay had taken the chair opposite.

'Your sister is recklessly galloping in Hyde Park
when, according to a Miss Posy Tompkins, her doctor
has expressly discouraged such behaviour.'

The other took a large swallow of his brandy before
putting it down. 'And now you want to stop her?'

'I do.'

'Well, good luck with that. Asher's response was to take her horses away for a month, but she only hired other more dangerous ones. Taris endeavoured to send a man with her every time she used the stables, but she gave him the slip more times than not. I took her to Graveson where she rode along the beaches until she got bored with them. A number of approaches, you see, and none of them worked well or for long because she is as stubborn as a mule and twice as difficult.'

'A true Wellingham, then?'

Cristo tipped back his head and laughed. 'If you were not such a bastard, Alderworth, I might even like you. What is in it for you, anyway, this sudden and touching concern for my sister?'

'I do not wish to be a widower.'

Again Cristo laughed. 'You have not as yet been a husband and, if my family has its way, you never will be.'

Ignoring the criticism, Tay went straight to the heart of the matter. 'What else interests her?'

Cristo leant forwards, a frown on his face. 'She enjoys archery. No danger and a quiet walk to the target. She is also inclined to drawing. But be warned that if you play false with her emotions this time, Alderworth, there won't be any second chances.'

'Word has it that you got one with your wife.'

'Word has it you were in gaol in the Americas for taking the life of another.'

'Gold makes bad men greedy and rumour is always overstated.'

'As greedy as you were when you hived off with the Wellingham booty after despoiling our sister?' The quiet of Cristo Wellingham's words belied the fury inside each one.

'You know as well as I that I have paid every pound of it back and Lucinda was an innocent when I left her, no matter what she remembers.'

'Edmund Coleridge may have changed that, of course.'

Tay's fist came down on the table. 'If I hear even the slightest of whispers from him saying anything of the sort, then he will be a dead man.'

'I will tell him when I see him next. He is a personal friend of mine.'

'You do just that.'

Swallowing the last of his brandy, Taylen stood, the peers of the realm of England watching him over their tipples. The Alderworth ducal title sat squarely on him, but he had never felt that he belonged here, the stuffy manners and pretensions of these men so far from his own road in life.

He wanted to get back to Alderworth and he wanted to take his wife with him. The face of Edmund Coleridge rose into his consciousness and he stalked from the room.

COLERIDGE WAS KISSING Lucinda's hand when Tay met her next at an afternoon soirée at the house of Daniel and Camille Beauchamp.

His wife had not frequented the pathways of Hyde Park that morning to take her exercise. He had been waiting, after all, but as the minutes had turned to hours he knew she would not come.

He was therefore both relieved to find her here and furious to see who she was with, for the man was virtually making love to her with his lips and she was allowing it. Her compliancy had him grating his teeth together. Hard.

'Duchess.'

She frowned and he was pleased to see worry in her eyes. 'Duke.'

Coleridge made no attempt at all to distance himself from her side and Taylen looked at him pointedly as his wife began to speak.

'Cristo said you might want to talk to me.' The statement left Tay speechless. 'He said you had a proposition you would like me to know. Something about spending my days in the parlour with my embroidery or being coddled in the garden painting flowers?'

'Your youngest brother has a sense of humour.'

'You went to see him after our meeting in the park? You went to tell him about my galloping when I so expressly asked you not to?'

Coleridge was taking in every word between them with interest and Tay had had enough. 'Would you excuse us?' Without waiting for a reply he shepherded his wife to an end of the room sheltered from the notice of others by a narrow alcove.

'I did not expect you to be so…underhanded,' Lucinda said as they stopped, her eyes shimmering with anger. Taylen changed tack altogether.

'I told your brother I did not fancy living alone for the rest of my life if anything were to happen to you. Did he tell you that as well?'

She shook her head.

'Edmund Coleridge wants you in his bed.'

'A fact that makes him little different from you then, your Grace.'

He ignored her criticism completely. 'Yet knowing that, you still allow him to court you openly?'

'He is a friend. I allow him friendship.'

'Your brother thinks he would like to be very much more.'

'It sounds like you had a long discussion about me. Pity I was not there to set wrongs to right, but then my siblings have always been more than quick to make judgements about the suitability of my various beaux.'

'Various?'

'Indeed. You didn't expect me to be pining for the company of a husband who did not think to remember that he had a wife for three long years until the necessity for a legitimate heir brought him back?'

The four small stars on her bracelet sparked gold as her hands underlined her words.

'The newspaper cutting you spoke of, the one in the paper from Georgia. It was not as it was reported. Since marrying you I have always respected my vows and I have not…cheated.' He finished each word with a sharp honesty. The muscles in his jaw rippled with the effort.

Damn, Taylen thought, what the hell had made him confess that to his estranged wife here in a crowded room in the middle of a public soirée?

He was known for his waywardness and his belief in free speech and action, flamboyant and untempered by the conventions attached to society life. He had lived his whole life in the pursuit of the hedonistic and the liberal, escaping the dreadfulness of his childhood with fine wine and finer women.

Until he had married!

Then something had happened that he could not explain. His libido, long since more than active, had simply dried up and he found it difficult to touch a woman without thinking of his parents' licentiousness. Six lovers had trooped through his younger life on his mother's side and many, many more than that on his father's. And they had left their mark.

He remembered the chaos as if it were yesterday and had vowed every moment of his early years never to repeat it if and when he finally married.

His hands tightened at his sides, fisting into hardness. It was why he had returned to England, after all, to understand just exactly what it was that simmered between him and this woman he had been forced into a union with.

Lucinda, the only wife he was ever likely to have and to hold. If it had not all been so deadly serious he would have laughed at his conundrum. A sinner caught by a saint and made impotent to boot by the memory of his parents' unfaithfulness.

Nothing made sense any more and had not done so for a long time. He wanted his certainty back and his conviction and one small part of him understood that only with Lucinda at his side might he be able to regain it.

It was the reason he had pressed her so hard with his need for an heir—a way to bring her to him on his own terms. A way to bed her.

LUCINDA COULD NOT believe what she had just heard. The Dissolute Duke of Alderworth was telling her he had been faithful to her memory? All those years. All those temptations. Three thousand miles from home and a stranger in a land that was as harsh as it was different and yet he had never cheated? A Duke who was known for his dalliances and excesses? She was astonished.

'Why are you telling me this?'

'Because I want to know that any child we do have is actually mine.'

The anger in his voice contradicted everything he was confessing. One moment she understood him and the next...

'I was brought up with a father who never believed that I was his, you see, and treated me accordingly. Seeing what such distrust does to a man, I should not like to repeat it.' No softness lay in his brittle green eyes, the bruising around them adding to his menace. 'It is not necessary that you like me when you provide me with an heir, Duchess, but I do need to be certain that you have not allowed another the same delights.'

My goodness, she could barely breathe with her anger and confusion, the joy of the disclosure eradicated completely by a reading of her character that was hardly salubrious.

He imagined *her* wanton? The pulse in her throat was beating like a drum as she stood speechless. At that moment she hated him with a passion and she could not keep the emotion from showing on her face.

'I shall be leaving London for Alderworth on the morrow. I will send the carriage back for you when I have word that you wish to join me.'

He was disappearing again, the tenuous truce that she had felt between them across the last week dissolving. Even in the face of her fury she could not just watch him go.

'What time will you leave?' Her voice sounded broken and hoarse.

'In the morning. There is no point in staying here longer.'

'Then I will come, too.'

For the first time a spark of life entered his eyes. 'Very well. My carriage will be at the Wellingham town house at ten o'clock. Be ready.'

He did not speak again before he turned and walked away, Edmund Coleridge joining her the moment he was gone.

'You look pale. If Ellesmere has threatened you—?'

'No.' She did not let him finish. As a friend of Cristo's she realised he might know more of the relationship she had with Alderworth than others did. 'I think I am just tired.'

Taking a breath, she tried to regain her lost composure, all the while her eyes scouting to check if Taylen Ellesmere was still anywhere in the vicinity.

'I am retiring to Bath next week with my family, Lucy. If you should wish to join us, you would be more than welcome. My mother would enjoy having you to stay, I am sure.'

Edmund's eyes were warm with promise, but Lucinda knew she could no longer lead him on with hopes that would never come to pass.

'I am sorry. I shall be rejoining my husband at Alderworth tomorrow. It has just been decided.'

'I see.' He stepped back. 'Does Cristo know what you intend?'

'Not yet, but he will.'

'He won't be pleased.'

Ignoring his condemnation, she carried on. 'I wish you well in your Bath sojourn. I imagine it is lovely there at this time of the year.'

Platitudes, she knew, but her husband's unexpected confession had taken her from one place to another.

Taylen Ellesmere had never cheated on her, but had held their marriage vows safe and close. She felt the smile blossom on her face as she gave Coleridge her goodbyes and went to find Camille Beauchamp to thank her for the soirée.

CHAPTER ELEVEN

'I WOULD FEEL far happier about all of this if you would take a few of the Wellingham servants with you.'

Lucinda shook her head at Taris's words. She did not want those in the employ of her brothers to see the truth of the relationship she had with Taylen Ellesmere, for undoubtedly such a detail would leak back to Falder. She was pleased when the conversation was interrupted.

'The Alderworth conveyance is here, my lord.'

'Very well. See that Lady Lucinda's luggage is stowed on board.'

Taris turned to her as the butler left. 'Asher and Emerald have decided not to see you off and Eleanor and Cristo were called back to Graveson yesterday afternoon. Perhaps it is best that it is just us.'

When her middle brother stood she went into his embrace, his arms warm around her, the solid strength and honesty of him so very familiar. Part of her wanted to hold on and stay here, under the shelter of home and family, but another part needed something different and that was the voice she was heeding.

Disengaging her arms, she moved away, trying to keep her emotions in check.

'I shall send word as soon as I am there to let you know that I am safe.'

'It is not the journey worrying me, Lucy, but the man who you will live with at destination's end.'

The amber in his eyes was clouded and she could see worry there. It broke her heart to sense her brother's concern. Just another betrayal she had heaped upon the family. Beatrice, however, was smiling.

'Go with hope, Lucinda, and find the way of your life.' She pressed a small package into her hand. 'I have wrapped up a book for you I have recently enjoyed.'

And then Lucinda was outside, the façade of the town house behind her in the wind. Looking up at the third-floor window, she fancied she saw Asher, but the shadow was gone before she had time to be certain.

One step, two steps and then three, her feet like leaden weights dragging towards the carriage. Taylen Ellesmere sat inside and gave Taris a cursory greeting which was given back with an equal lack of warmth. When the door was closed between them, her brother's open palm splayed out upon the window.

I love you. She mouthed the words, but knew that he would not see them. Biting down on the soft flesh inside her bottom lip, she sat back as the horses gathered their rhythm.

'I am not taking you away for ever, Lucinda. You may return any time you wish to visit your family. The carriage shall be at your disposal whenever you have need of it.'

She nodded because she did not trust herself to speak and he swore beneath his breath.

'My own family was not close so it is something of a novelty to see such affection in others,' he offered finally as she kept her silence. 'In fact, I would say loathing was the nearest term to describe any family dynamics that I recall.'

'That must have been difficult for you.'

'Well, it was always easier when distance parted us.' He smiled through the gloom of the day, a laconic devil-may-take-it smile that negated all that she had ever heard of his upbringing. 'I would be farmed out to others, with no thought given to my schooling. My life truly began when I eventually got to Eton.'

A new and interesting turn. 'How old were you?'

'Twelve. My parents had died the year before, but I was an independent child for my age so their deaths barely affected me.'

'Callous.'

'I prefer to call it practical.'

A dead end of insults slung across lies.

'One of the maids at Falder used to work for your grandmother at about the same time you did not return from France.'

He stiffened and Lucinda felt a creeping coldness. A muscle along the bottom of his jaw ground out movement when she chanced a peek at him.

'Rosemary Jones made some mention of your uncle.'

This time he sat forwards, his hands together so that his fingers were entwined in the position Lucinda remembered placing her own in one of the favoured games of childhood.

Here is the church and here is the steeple...

Ditties that he would not have played as he was fighting for his life in a hospital bed in Rouen.

'She said that you were often hurt.' This was blurted out before she lost her courage altogether.

'All children need to stand corrected in the name of good behaviour.'

His eyes flinted, the anger in them causing her to simply fold. She could have said more, could have told him everything that the maid had confided, but it was too soon and the facts were too raw.

'Of course they do, your Grace.' She sounded like a thousand other wives in London who only wanted a life that was peaceful and easy, the truth tearing what contentment was left into pieces.

Outside the road ran along fields of green and the sky was blue, a cold blue, the colour belying the temperature. It was chilly inside the carriage, too, and she was pleased for the woollen blanket that was over her lap.

She wondered where the accident in the carriage had occurred when they had come this way all those years ago. She had been told the name of the place, of course, but with no little memory left of the time, she could be certain of nothing. Still she felt a familiarity, a knowledge of having passed this way before and she was glad that the journey would be only a few hours in length.

Taylen Ellesmere had ceased to make any effort at conversation at all, his glance drawn by the views outside, his face a blank mask of indifference. If he remembered the accident, he did not show it.

Over the past week she thought she might have been getting closer to him, but this morning they sat opposite each other like strangers hurtling towards a new life together and one it seemed that neither of them wanted. When her fingers closed around the jade talisman of happiness that Emerald had bequeathed her, she frowned.

She wished she might ask him to explain more of his surprising confession from yesterday and that this time instead of anger there could be dialogue. But his expression stopped her from such an action and so she turned to look out at the countryside.

ALDERWORTH WAS A substantial mansion built of stone and wood, the wings around a large central edifice a matching image of each other. The parkland it sat in was extensive, rows of old trees stretching as far as the eye could see. A lake of some proportion lay at the bottom of a rise, the old stone walls radiating out from the driveway alluding to another, more ancient dwelling.

Lucinda had come last time under the cover of darkness. She knew because Posy had filled in many of the details of the visit that she had forgotten. She hoped that the servants would not remember her and that enough time had passed for the incident to be consigned to history and to never be recalled.

'When my parents were alive they used to line the servants up around the front driveway every time a

guest came to stay in a sort of skewed sense of importance. I have never been so formal.'

'It looks…' She could not quite voice what she meant
to say.

'Less than well cared for?' His eyes took in the lines
of the house. 'Much of the money at the moment is
going into increasing the production of the agricultural
yields.'

'Cristo has been doing the same at Graveson.'

'Then perhaps we have more in common than I
thought.'

'So there are no more parties here?'

He turned towards her and Lucinda felt breathless.
'The shallow follies of youth have much to be account-
able for. I spend money on far more important things
now.'

Like the production of an heir?

She almost said it. Almost blurted it out, so that it
was there in the open instead of seething underneath
each and every word, a contract penned in pragmatism
and shame. Instead she smiled, in a tight and vapid way,
the movement taking the humour from his eyes.

'You will have your own set of rooms and a maid
to see to your needs. The house has suffered across
the years from inattention but I am aiming to see it restored.'

'You love Alderworth, then?'

'History is to be valued,' he answered in a measured
way. 'If too much of it is left to waste, there will be no
lessons to be learnt by those who come after us.'

The topic of the heir again, winding into conversation and strangling any hope of accord. Best to remember that she was not here as the cherished new wife of a Duke who would love her, but as the sole hope of ensuring that a questionable family name might march into yet another decade of unbroken lineage.

When the carriage stopped and Lucinda was helped out by a servant who welcomed her, she was achingly aware that Taylen Ellesmere neither took her arm nor gave her the courtesy of any introduction as they walked inside.

Not quite the wife he wanted, but at least the country air made her feel stronger and more in control.

Everything here was in need of attention: the flaky stone, the gardens, the few servants in their old and faded uniforms. Ellesmere had not lied when he had proclaimed the finances of Alderworth had suffered.

But beneath the lack of care, peeling paint and rotten woodwork was a beauty that lay in the very bones of the place, the house's roofline raised to the sky in a proud exclamation of old wealth.

The quality of the timber was undeniable, the ornate cornices alluding to a time where such frippery was the vogue. She vaguely remembered parts of it from the last time she had been here and did her best to recollect more, but to no avail. Darkly fashioned paintings of ancestors stared down from the walls in every room, sombre harsh people whose eyes seemed to follow this new generation with a disapproval that was tangible.

Two large portraits of his parents had pride of place

above the fire surround in the main salon and Lucinda saw the small holes a dart might fashion in both of them before she had looked away, not wishing to pry further. A green *chaise-longue* with carved mahogany feet took up the space in a bay window, the sun lightening the fabric in all the places that it had touched, leaving the seams dark.

Taylen Ellesmere had disappeared almost immediately, leaving her in the hands of a middle-aged housekeeper, Mrs Berwick, who had hurried her up to the first floor and finally to her bedchamber, a room nearly at the very end of a long corridor. She had pointed out a pile of bath cloths and two decanters with brandy and whisky, equally filled on a table by the bedside.

An evening tipple? The single glass provided looked spotlessly clean.

'There is a light meal set out for your lunch in the small dining room, your Grace, and dinner will be served at six. When you require a maid to help you dress you only have to ring the bell and she will come.'

The bed was tiny, a child's cot that gladdened her heart, for there was no possible way her large husband could share it with her.

After the accompanying luggage was lifted into place she thanked the two men with a smile. Around the edge of the room stood many tallboys and wardrobes, the array of old furniture giving the impression that many of the unwanted accoutrements of the Ellesmere lineage had been dumped here, a last resting place before being disposed of or burnt.

When the woman didn't leave, Lucinda knew there was something important that she wished to impart to her. 'The master has brought new life to Alderworth, your Grace. The house may not be as magnificent as it once was, but the farm cottages have been refurbished and the people here appreciate his endeavours. He is a good man despite all that might be said of him in London.'

The woman hurried out after she had delivered her words, a swish of skirt and then gone.

A good master who was appreciated here? Lucinda turned the words on her tongue, liking the endorsement.

Nerves had taken away hunger, so she walked to the window to gaze down upon the gardens, the formal lines of hedges lost in the march of time. No one had tended to anything, it seemed, the wild and rambling roses climbing in a tangled heap of runners with the occasional misshaped flower blooming amidst green. The hand of good fortune had disappeared a long time ago from the estate of Alderworth, leaving disorder in its place. Her mind dwelled on the fact that her husband was a Duke who would make sure others were well housed before he turned his attention to his own living quarters and she smiled.

A movement caught her eye in the very far corner of her view. Ellesmere was hurrying towards the stable courtyard a little way off, his demeanour brisk. He had dispensed with his jacket and his hat and the white linen of his shirt stretched across the muscles of his back, his dark hair trailing across it. Another came out to meet him, a small round man waving his arms madly as if in some important explanation. The Duke in contrast stood perfectly still, a quiet centre in the midst of all that moved about him.

Taylen Ellesmere did that often, she thought, as though testing the air, like a deer might in the high hills of some undisturbed place just to make certain of safety.

Then a horse came forth, a stallion of a height Lucinda had not seen before, the lines of Arabia in its form. She saw her husband run his hands across its flanks, quiet and gentle, before he mounted, easily managing the skittish response of the animal. The Duke of Alderworth looked as though he had been born there, the flow of man and beast joined in a languid and perfect balance as he turned towards the hills beyond the gardens and disappeared.

Then there was nothing, only trees and leaves and the scudding clouds across the afternoon sky wending towards a dark forest in the distance.

She wished she could open the doors that led out on to a balcony to see if she might catch more of a glimpse of them, but they were nailed shut—another oddity in a house full of neglect. Lifting her hand, she wrote her initials on the inside of the window. With a flourish she surrounded her name with the shape of a heart and then rubbed the whole thing out, her fingers made dirty by the dust on the glass.

Falder, her family home, had the lines of love running through it, generations of Wellinghams enjoying the promise. Each day a legion of staff cleaned it from top to toe until it was polished and gleaming, the small decay of everyday living repaired before any damage had the chance to spread further.

The sun broke out quite suddenly, enhancing the green in the fields behind. Here in the rolling hills of Bedfordshire and far from the expectations of London there was a certain peace and freedom she had not felt in years. It lay, she supposed, in the march of time drawn across a fading splendour. Once Alderworth would have boasted grandeur and sumptuousness, but there was a mellow truth about its present-day meagreness that was beguiling.

Finding her satchel, she drew forth her drawing equipment and laid a parchment on the desk, liking the feel of charcoal, the dusty ease of a long-time friend calming in the face of the unknown. She drew, from memory, the house and its lines and Taylen Ellesmere on the horse, his hair against the wind, his forehead strong.

She stopped after sketching his eyes and rested because the quickness in them was disconcerting, knowing, a question framed in them that held all her own fears naked in the afternoon light. She wanted to rub them out, wanted to scrawl across such eyes with a hard strong stroke, but she couldn't. Couldn't countenance destruction of such raw and angry beauty. His lips followed, full and generous, lips that had offered her the promise of liberty for the price of a child. Yet he had qualified such an unexpected option with salvation and loyalty and she believed he had meant it.

Placing one finger across the drawing, she felt an easing of spirit, a lessening of tightness. A slight question of flesh? Revealing. Unforeseen.

'Taylen.' She whispered the name into the quiet and even as she watched his lips seemed to turn. Upwards. The black of charcoal moving in a way it never had before. Living. Breathing. Laughing. She did not dare to impart more form to his figure as she buried the sheet of paper in her sketchbook.

A flash of some hidden thing ripped through Lucinda, beating at truth. The headaches she had had after the accident had largely gone, yet here they threatened to return in the same intensity as they had whilst convalescing.

A room came through the fog, a room at the end of a long corridor and a man sitting in bed and reading.

Spectacles. She had the vague idea it was Alderworth. She squinted her eyes to try to remember the title of the book in his hands because she thought it was important in some way. But no more memory surfaced.

Rising, she picked up her cloth bag from the place she had left it in one corner and extracted the wrapped present that Beatrice had bequeathed her in the moments before her departure from London. A novel confronted her as she ripped off the bright blue paper and a note was threaded with ribbon around the cover.

Lucy,
The dependence of women on marriage to secure social standing and economic security can be un-

derpinned with something far more wonderful. I
have a suspicion that you will find what I allude
to with Taylen Ellesmere. Anne Elliot certainly
did in this story.
All my love,
Bea

Jane Austen's *Persuasion*. She had not read this book
and was glad for the chance to do so here, though Beatrice's note seemed more than odd. She knew her brothers hated her husband with a passion and had thought
her sister-in-law might have felt the same.

Something wonderful? Such hollow hope was layered with a reality far from any such truth, the unfamiliar environment here increasing her homesickness.

When tears welled up behind her eyes she did not
try to stop them as they ran down her cheeks and on to
the small book across her lap, blurring the inked note
in Beatrice's handwriting.

TAYLEN WADED NAKED into the lake behind the house and
waited as the icy water numbed his feet and his legs, the
shadow of Valkyrie reflected in the silver before him,
low in the water. He had named this dash of raised-up
land as a boy and had used the island as a fortress many
times, a stronghold against a coercive uncle and a place
to assuage the remnants of betrayal.

'Betrayal.' He whispered the word to himself and
watched how the warm air fogged. He had never had
a chance against his mother's brother with his corrupt

tastes and easy smile. The fact that he was a child whose parents saw responsibility only as a nuisance and had gladly given up any claim on a son who was alternatively badly behaved or withdrawn aided such tendencies.

Innocence was such an easily taken commodity and Taylen knew that his had gone a long time ago.

Like the small hut he had built on the rise, left to the birds and the ghosts and the wind. Only echoes in the inlets and silence in the few remaining trees, the black outline of wood sharp against the dusk where it had fallen at an angle against the sky. No longer a shelter.

Picking up a handful of sand, he let it filter through his fingers—Alderworth soil, the mark of a thousand years of ancestry imprinted in the earth. His land now, to have and to hold as certainly as a wife brought from London under the dubious flag of obligation.

He shook his head hard, the strands of wetness falling into his line of vision before he wiped them away. The air here strengthened him and gave him resolve. Lucinda would be sitting in the room beside his and wondering what exactly might happen next. He hated the fact that she would be frightened, but there was no other way of resolving this impasse, and he knew without a single doubt that had he left her in London her brothers would have made certain any access was limited.

Lord, but was it any better here? The whole place teetered under a strange spell of melancholy, the staff left reduced to a bare handful of overworked servants.

He had left it too long to return, he supposed, but the memories here had always repelled him, the child without rights struggling inside the man he had become, dissolute and uncaring. Swallowing, he fisted his hands hard against his thighs and lifted his face to the rain that had begun to fall in a mist.

Back. Again. This time with a spouse who distrusted him and the threat of retribution from the Wellinghams should he ever hurt her.

A flash of lightning above the hills to the east reflected in the lake. A sign, perhaps. A portent of battle.

THAT EVENING LUCINDA came down the wide staircase with a feeling of disbelief, her heart tight and her stomach filled with butterflies. The dress she wore was her newest, light-yellow silk shot through with gold, the *décolletage* on the prim side of fashionable heightened by a line of frothy Brussels lace, her arms covered by a shawl against the cold. Her hair was pinned to her head in a tall and elegant chignon, with a few curls left to frame her face, that had taken a maid a good hour to complete. On her feet were slippers of fine calf leather, the lacings drawn in tight.

The Alderworth servant accompanying her stepped back as they came into the front salon. In the ensuing silence a bead of sweat traced its way between her breasts to fall across the skin above her ribs.

Taylen Ellesmere was already there, dressed entirely in black, the collar at his neck open. A gentleman at home and at leisure or a man expecting a woman to entertain him?

'Duchess.' His teeth were white and even and perfect.

Part of her wanted to run, wanted to lift the embroidered fall of silk and make for the safety of her room, negating any contract between them.

I do not think he would stop me if I went! The thought came from nowhere but it was there in his eyes, soft velvet with a sort of pity.

She did not wish for that. Raising her chin, she walked through the opened door and tried not to flinch as it shut behind her.

His eyes took in her gown and her hair, his expression tightening. 'I have something to show you,' he said as the silence lengthened. 'It is this way.'

He did not take her hand or shepherd her forwards. He did not touch her at all, but walked in front through the long corridors of the place to a room filled with books. Two glasses sat on a desk with a bottle of white wine chilled in a bucket of ice.

Intentions, she supposed, a heady amount of alcohol to loosen the restraints of almost thirty-six months of distance.

'Please, take a seat.'

She chose a chair with enough room for one person. Unexpectedly, though, he pulled a stool over to where she was and sat in front of her. A shaft of light bathed him, turning his hair to shining raven black. Like the cut sides of coal. He was the most handsome man she had ever met. She could not dispute that fact.

'I was not intimate with you three years ago no matter what you might say, Lucinda. I put you in the carriage before anything could happen between us and tried to take you home. If it had not been for the accident, I would probably have succeeded.'

Lucinda felt her insides curl. Taylen Ellesmere had always used words well to suit his intentions.

'You were in bed. I remember you…touching me?'

'You ran into my room to escape from the Earl of Halsey. I kissed you once. That was all.'

'No.' She shook her head. 'You lie.' Her eyes flicked to the line of her breast though she could not bring herself to voice all that she remembered.

His fingers at her nipples, the feel of him hard against her skin in places no one had ever touched before. The full naked size of him as he stood before her. Shocking. Thrilling. Forbidden.

Reaching over to the wine, he poured her a glass, fine crystal, and the stem vibrated under the pressure of her fingers as she took it. As easy to break as her innocence had been?

'Perhaps a drink might refresh your tangled memory,' he toasted, shattering the bubble of *détente* completely. A sharp bud of shock took her breath as hard eyes gleamed, the warmth of his glance searing through silk.

HER FACE WAS PALE, the smile she had forced upon it tightly stretched.

A small droplet of wine lay on her top lip. Once he

might have leant over and licked it away, but he had never been a man to take a woman against her will and the wariness on Lucinda's face was easy to read. Drawing back, he opened the folder on the table beside him. There was a file fat with the transfer-of-ownership documents tucked inside the front cover. He pushed the papers across to her.

'I have signed the town house over to you already. The terms allow you sole use of the place until you die. Then it shall revert to our heir…or heirs if sins of the flesh are as enjoyable as I think you will find them to be.'

Worry brought lines to her forehead and the tip-tilt of her nose against the light made him look away. He remembered running his finger down the gentle slope and on to the plump rose of her lips. Once she had watched him as if he were the only man in existence. Once she had taken his breath away with a single stolen kiss. Now suspicion and wariness were the only expressions that he could read and the disappointment was disquieting.

'I have a pouch, too. A hundred pounds for the first time you lie with me and a hundred more for every time after that.' The heavy thud of the leather purse sounded on the file, like the promise of Antonio's flesh from the pen of Shakespeare. A pound for a pound. Payment for an heir.

Her teeth worried her bottom lip and shadowed eyes perused the bounty, but she did not reach out, leaving the largesse exactly where it was. Then she lifted her glass and had a generous gulp of wine before chancing a second and a third. Tay wanted to warn her of the strength of the draught, but in the circumstances he refrained. A relaxed Lucinda would be so much easier to handle than an angry one.

'So you are saying that when I become pregnant the bargain will be fulfilled?'

The catch in her voice nearly broke his will and for a moment he thought to nullify everything and walk away. 'A doctor will need to verify your condition, of course.'

'Like a brood mare,' she returned. Against the candlelight her pale hair shone and her eyes were back to flinty, fighting blue. During all his travels amongst the most beautiful women in the world he had never seen another like her.

He did not want her subdued. He wanted her like this. In bed she would be magnificent.

The thought had the flesh in his trousers swelling and he cursed, feeling like a boy again with no control over any of it. If he had any sense at all he would reach out now and strip her naked, demanding the rights all husbands received at the marriage altar and be done with any bargains. It was a God-given privilege, after all, and he had paid for her in blood and in gold.

He knew she saw the thought, too, for her hands tightened.

'I would never hurt you.' It was suddenly important that at least she knew that.

'Then let me go.'

'I can't.' Two words that stripped the life out of everything and his heart beat faster than ever it had during the bleak and lonely watches in the Americas when death could be forthcoming in one moment of inattention and often was. With care he reached out to gather a long curl of pale flaxen, turning it in his palm as the light caught wheat and gold and silver. 'I can only hope for release from the demons that have hounded us for three long years. Will you be brave enough to trust me?'

'Do I have any other alternative?'

He shook his head and the pulse at her throat slowed marginally—small signs of surrender.

To take the charade further he allowed her glance to escape from his own, falling out of contact. Eyes can take much from the soul, he thought, as she jammed her hands into the yellow silk of her skirt. He hoped dinner would be served soon. Eating would ease the tension that words were failing to do. How often had he plied an adversary with food and wine before picking the flesh of secrets clean away from the bone?

The thought that he did not wish to hurt Lucinda in any way at all left him struck dumb with shock.

Her innocence again and her goodness. He had had this same trouble in his bedchamber three years ago with the heady sighs of sexual release reverberating all around them—wholesomeness like some sharp-edged sword smiting evil with a conscience he had never felt so keenly before.

SHE WAS VERY WARM. A fire burnt low in the grate, sending out a glow of red, and she was too hot even in her light clothing. She loosened her shawl. The scent of herbs wafted in the air around her. Lavender. She would never again smell the bloom without thinking of this moment, the documents and money spilled across the table before her, sordid rewards of lust.

'Marriage has left us both in a difficult position,' he continued, 'a no-man's land, if you like, precluding any other relationships we might wish to pursue. But if we use the situation wisely, we may at least enjoy it.'

The shock of his words made her draw in her breath. She was twenty-seven years old and, apart from one night three years ago, her sexuality had lain dormant and curdled.

Until now! Until a husband straight out of the pages of some improper and implausible fairy tale had walked back into her life and demanded this.

The Duke of Alderworth was not soft or quiet or gentle. He was hard and strong and distant, his eyes devouring her and the lavender blurring her senses. When she shook her head he laughed and broke away.

'May the Lord above help us then if you think we might spin this out for all of a week, Duchess.'

Such brutal masculine honesty reminded Lucinda of her brothers and a further ache of homesickness claimed her. 'The trouble is that I do not know you at all, your Grace.' She had agreed to come to this place, agreed to the things he had said. She could not pull back now. But she did need time to adjust.

'I thought you had made it plain to everybody that

you did. Intimately. Your three brothers at least will swear to it.'

'Much of what happened before the accident is lost to me,' she continued as if he had not spoken, 'though I know in my heart that you enjoyed far more than the mere kiss you acknowledge.'

He stood very still, watching her. 'More?'

'You wore no clothes.'

'I had retired for the night and you surprised me. There is no crime in that.'

'There were red marks upon my breasts.'

Laughter reverberated around the room, his face made years younger by mirth. She had not seen him like this before, humour sparkling and a dimple in one cheek.

'Fine breasts they were, too.'

Now he *was* lying, for she knew she had none of the form of those women of society whose charms were followed by the eyes of men.

'You think it cannot be so?' He walked across to her and traced his fingers down the line of her bodice, his touch running softly over the skin above the lace.

'You are a beautiful woman, Lucinda, and the pleasures of the flesh have their own reward.' The sensuality in his tone was beguiling and his touch made her draw in her breath. But she was neither gullible nor stupid.

'Lust is a base and shallow emotion, your Grace. It could never be enough to sustain a marriage.'

'You would want more?' He said this in such a way that Lucinda knew the thought of love had not occurred to him at all. Probably he found the softer emotions laughable—sensations that were as foreign to his world as easy and gratuitous sex would be to hers. The gap between them was a widening abyss.

'Hell and damnation,' he said, pushing back the hair on his forehead. Another opaque scar lay under the hairline and the anger on his face was unhidden.

LOVE.

She was speaking of that. He knew that she was and cold dread seeped through him.

Love only hurt. Enjoyment was better, of the mind or of the body it mattered not which. Enjoyment allowed the ease of parting when it was time to say goodbye and move on to the next place or person. Enjoyment was not the trap that love was.

Lord, he was paying his wife enough for such enjoyment and he was even biding his time to enable her to get used to the idea. He did not know of one single person who sustained their marriage in the way that Lucinda seemed to think was normal, the congeniality of two souls for ever linked.

This was the stuff of fairy tales and operas and the books that flooded out of the Minerva Press. He had read one once, just out of interest, and laughed at such an implausible nonsense.

His uncle had whispered the word in his ear, too, as he had hurt him. 'This is because I love you, Taylen. Only that.' The last time Tay had kicked the bastard hard in the balls as he had lunged for him and run to the door. The key hadn't turned, though, stuck in the lock as his fingers fumbled to release it and Hugo had caught him easily, holding his shaking body close and telling him he loved him over and over.

That was love. That was his memory of love, bound by blood and hurt to all the adults in his life, until one day they had simply washed their hands of him and sent him off to boarding school.

His deliverance. The few canings there were nothing compared to his regular and systematic abuse at Alderworth, and in the summers when all the other boys save him returned home the masters had allowed him the free run of the place. To read. To walk. To fish.

Lucinda was watching him closely and it was disconcerting with his past rushing in between them.

'Our bargain consists of a hundred pounds each time you lie with me, the end coming when you conceive an heir.'

He knew such words would cut the talk of love to ribbons, but the sweat had begun creeping up his body. He needed to get away before she understood more about him than he wanted anyone to know and there was no kind way to say it.

He gathered the heavy leather pouch and the papers he had meant to have her sign. 'I find I am not hungry, Duchess. My servants will see to your evening meal.' With that he left her.

CHAPTER TWELVE

A SOUND WOKE HER, a groan muffled by something, but close. Lucinda sat up in bed and listened, the moon coming in through a gap in the curtains. It was nighttime and late. She had spent a short time in the dining room and then retired upstairs as soon as she was able. She had seen no further sign at all of the Duke of Alderworth.

Another cry had her up on her feet and she walked to the door, placing her ear against the wood and listening. No footsteps hurried along the passageway, no hint of someone else hearing and helping. An owl called from the trees that marched in a line up a hill near the mansion, plaintive and lonely. Otherwise there was only silence.

Her feet were becoming cold on the parquet floor and she was about to get back into bed when a further sound came. This time she recognised the voice. Her hands opened the door and she was through it in a second, slipping through the unlocked door of the adjoining chamber. For a second dizziness made her clutch at the oak, this room familiar somehow and dangerous.

A candle burnt on a low bedside table and her husband was caught in a tangle of sheets, his hard body brown against the white, not asleep and not awake, but somewhere in a halfway place that was haunting.

'Wake up.' She shook him, the opened shirt he had on drenched in sweat, but his hand pushed her away. Not gently, either, but Lucinda had been raised in a house full of brothers and she pushed back.

'Wake up.' Louder now and more insistent. The bottle in front of him was drained and the smell of strong drink lingered around the room.

On the floor lay a book in Italian, the corners on one page turned down. A pile of other tomes in English, Italian and French sat in a nearby pile: Voltaire, Rousseau, Dante, Thomas Aquinas, Adam Smith and Machiavelli's *Il Principe*. Another flash of him reading this same book came to mind, the room draped in shadow save for a single candle. Before. She strained to recall other things, but could not.

'Taylen. Taylen. Wake up.' He came to in an instant, one moment boneless and the next ramrod stiff, the distant and vigilant Duke back in place.

The redness in his eyes was marked, the green of his iris darker against the colour. 'I shouted out?'

'Loudly. No one else came.'

Looking away, he reached for a fob watch positioned near the candle and checked the time. When his shirt dropped down a little as he stretched, Lucinda gasped. A whole row of scars slashed into the smoothness across the top of his back and she could barely believe the damage.

However, if he saw her looking he gave no sign of it, shrugging his shirt on further, fingers on the collar pinching both points of it inwards. His hands shook so much Lucinda thought that he would not be able to hold it closed.

All his rings had been stripped off, save their wedding ring and she wondered what that might mean. Sweat glistened on his face and his hair was plastered to his forehead, a worrying unsteadiness visible as he pushed himself up.

'Are you drunk?'

He laughed at that and shook his head. 'If only it was that simple…'

'Nightmares, then? When I was a child I had—' He stopped her with an impatient flick of his hand.

'I will ask Mrs Berwick to place you in another room in the morning. That way you will not be disturbed again.'

'This happens every night?'

'No.' He was so quick in his answer that Lucinda knew he lied.

'Exercise helped me. My mother insisted I rode each day for hours and after that I slept so much better at night.'

She could tell he was listening and so she carried on. 'I was a wilful child, you see, and always in trouble. My mother thought it would have been best had I been a boy, but I wasn't.'

A slight upturn of his lips had her carrying on.

'My brothers would be assigned each in turn to watch

over me. Ashe and Taris were far older than I was and they took the duty seriously. Cristo was more my age and seemed to get in worse scrapes than even I was capable of. Alice was not a woman to be too bothered with children, you see. Her garden was her great love.'

'And your father? Where was he when all of this was going on?'

'Overseeing the running of the estate. Ensuring the lineage of the Wellinghams remained financially viable. He died of a heart condition when I was young. I would probably have been a disappointment to him had he lived.'

'Were I a father I would hold no impossible expectations of my children.'

A father! There it was again, that same old hint of why they were both here. She could see he also was reminded of the fact because his eyes turned smoky and he pushed himself up out of the bed.

He had fallen asleep in his clothes and his boots, the rumpled linen of his shirt sticking to his skin where the sweat had gathered. The nightmares had carved deep lines of desolation across his face. Almost as deep as those on his back. Could they be the marks of a careful and judicious beating administered to a child with as much hatred as was possible?

She held her breath with the enormity of it all, watching as he poured himself a generous glass of a drink that did not look alcoholic and finished the lot. Her nightgown felt insubstantial and she wished she had stopped to put on the matching negligee. Outside the moon was low and the night was dark, a mounting wind throwing the branch of a tree against the glass in his window.

'Tomorrow I shall take you riding…sedately.' For a moment she could not quite understand what it was he spoke of. Then she did.

'My mother will be smiling down from Heaven.'

'Or warning you away from me as all your brothers have done and hoping like hell that you heed her.'

'You keep on telling me that you are not safe.'

Walking to the window, he pulled back the curtain of heavy burgundy velvet.

'Come and look, Lucy.' It was the first time he had called her the name that her family did and she went across to him. He did not touch her, but positioned himself behind, his breath warm against her neck.

'As far as the eye can see it is Ellesmere land. From the hills against the sky here to the place where the moon shines on the lake there and behind the house a thousand acres yet again rising through the valleys. This is the safety that my father squandered and my mother cared not a jot for. This was the reason I took the money from your brother to disappear after our wedding. It was never meant as a slight to you.'

'A precious bequest?'

She felt him nod.

'If it were Falder I would have done exactly the same.'

'Thank you.' His hand came down upon her shoulder, the pressure gentle at first and then building as it slid across silk and shadow to rest on the sensitive skin at her neck. She wanted to lean in and keep him there, all the pent-up loneliness bursting forth into a simple need.

He was dangerous and difficult and menacing. He was also the only lawfully wedded husband she was ever likely to have. When he turned her slowly, the greenness in his eyes was darkened by half-light and gentle honesty, a man woken up by his past and trying to come to terms with his present.

His confession of faithfulness in the Beauchamps' salon made her braver and she brought her arms up around him. She could feel the welts of the old scars, the cotton in his shirt hiding nothing. Drawing one finger along the length of a twisted ridge, she suddenly had an image of the past. She had wanted him then as she did now.

'I remember pieces. I remember this.'

His only answer was his mouth upon hers and then she forgot everything as his tongue slanted inwards. Pure masculinity found her essence through touch and taste and she knew in the first second of his onslaught exactly what it was all those society women who watched him through their hooded glances had known.

He was both tempered steel and quicksilver, the opposites melding wonderment and delight and he wanted from her what men like him had wanted from a woman through the centuries since the very beginning of time. The quiet kiss she had thought to offer was overtaken by a storm of sensation.

There was no sense in it left, no moderation, no limit on the depth of her feeling, no careful prudence. All

there was were heartbeats and warmth. Unable to understand what was happening, she simply closed her
eyes and let him take, the magic finally in her grasp.

HER BOSOM HEAVED as he moved closer, drawing his
thumb along the edge of her throat and across the bones
of her chest. When he sucked at his forefinger and ran
it fast over one nipple, she arched back, her nightgown
leaving nothing hidden, and the languid glassy abandonment of passion showed in her eyes before she closed
them. His woman. Paid for and bought. Legally bound
until the very end of time. No confines on anything.
He could use her exactly as he willed.

He wanted to rip away the rest of her clothes and
have her there now upon the floor, emptying himself
into her time and time again until there was nothing left
of three years of desperation and urgency.

The more worrying thought that a woman like this
could in some way inveigle herself into a corner of his
heart confused him. He felt as if he could tell her things
he never wanted another to know and break covenants
that he had always kept.

Carefully he pushed her back, his thumb running
across the soft line of one cheek and then the swelling
of her lip. Bewilderment lay in her eyes, demanding
explanation, but the nightmares always left him exhausted—too exhausted to deal with the complex lab-
yrinth that was a relationship.

'Why is it like this between us?' Her question,
dredged from the depths of need.

'I do not know, sweetheart, but now is not the hour to find out. It is time you were back in your bed.'

She looked away, pulling the silk of her gown back into place at her neck, a prim and proper covering of what had been there only a moment before. Her hair had escaped the loose plait she had worn when she had entered the room and fell in waves across her shoulders, the paleness caught between candle and moonlight and the length emphasising her slim height as it fell to the curve of her waist.

His fingers tightened against his thighs and he wished she would leave, shutting the door behind temptation because if she stayed much longer he did not trust himself enough not to reach out and remove any choice.

'Goodnight.' Her voice was strained and low and a few seconds later she was gone.

LUCINDA SAT ON her bed, trying to catch her breath, her heart pounding in her chest.

She wanted him. She did. She wanted him to show her what it was that had boiled between them when he had kissed her. Her fingers traced down the line of her bodice, cupping one breast through the layers of fabric, feeling the same things that he had. The thought had her standing because she had never been a woman who was overtly sensual, the men in London society leaving her with no true desire other than a residual and slight interest in what happened between the sexes. Nothing more.

Until now.

Different. Alive. Aching everywhere. For him. The

skin around her nipples tightened as she imagined his mouth upon them, the place between her legs throbbing in anticipation. The jade Emerald had bequeathed her lay between her breasts. For happiness, her sister-in-law had promised. She wondered what this emotion she felt now was. Certainly there was an excitement that was foreign and wonderful.

Could one be married in lust and not in love?

Would that be enough?

Or might the agreements between them eventually ignite the sort of marriage her brothers had, the for-ever-and-ever sort that lasted through thick and thin?

Her husband did not seem to think so and yet he had kissed her in a way that made no sense of the distance he offered. His heart had raced as fast as hers, she had felt it where their skin had touched, the heat in his eyes belying the aloofness he brokered.

When he had stood behind her at the window, offer-ing an explanation why he took money from her brother, she could almost imagine him standing there as a loving husband who cared for her feelings and who wanted her to understand that it was not insult but truth he sought.

She wiped away the tears in her eyes with the back of her hand, a quick angry movement because such a maudlin wallowing was useless.

She had been lonely for years, lost in her own com-pany amidst a family who all had partners. The shared glances, the careful smiles, the way a hand was given in complicit understanding. These were the things she had never discovered, never desired until now.

The moonlight drew mottled, patterned trails across her skin, paleness overlaid by shadow. The artist in her enjoyed the line and the beauty of the design, but the woman only saw the desolation of solitude.

How would she be able to go through with this bargain of conceiving an heir if every part of her wanted so much more than he would give?

CHAPTER THIRTEEN

LUCINDA SPENT THE morning on her own. There had been no sign of her husband at all, no movements from his room. She knew this because she had been listening most carefully, getting up to place her head against the door at any sign of noise.

Mrs Berwick bustled in just before twelve.

'The master was asking after you, your Grace.'

'The Duke is up already?'

'Indeed. Riding across the top valley would be my guess, on that black horse of his that goes like the wind.'

Lucinda crossed to the wardrobe to find her bonnet and coat. Within a moment she was on the front portico, Mrs Berwick pointing out the formal gardens and the small pathway to the Ellesmere stables.

Finally she was alone, the wind on her face and the sun appearing from time to time between ominous banks of high, dark cloud.

A dog joined her on her walk a little way into the tumbled-down garden, his coat mangy and his head hanging. She could not even make a guess as to its pedigree, for the animal had the head of a Labrador, the body of a much thinner hound and the hairiest and longest of legs. Usually she was frightened of dogs, as she had been bitten badly once at Falder and had not been much in their company since, but this animal with its trusting brown eyes, its odd shape and a tail that curled twice before tucking under its back legs was so comical it was comforting. All day she had been alone, so when the animal's wet muzzle came into the curl of her fingers she laughed.

'Who are you?' Her voice brought it to a stop.

'His name is Dog.' Taylen Ellesmere was suddenly behind her, his riding clothes splattered with mud and no sign on his face at all to indicate he had any memory of last night. Perhaps he had felt nothing. Perhaps for him the kiss had been like one of the many others he had bequeathed to countless beautiful women across his lifetime.

'Is he yours?' Lucinda hoped that the rush of heat on her cheeks did not show.

'My carriage almost ran him over on the London riverfront and so I had him brought up here.'

'When?'

'The first day I arrived back in England, a month and a half ago now. It seemed a sign,' he added, an unexpected lopsided smile having a strange effect on the area around her heart.

'A sign of what?'

'A sign indicating that I was meant to stay. An anchor, if you like.'

'Mrs Berwick told me you had concentrated your

efforts on bringing the farm cottages up to a habitable standard.'

'The estate needs work, though there are some who do not like what I am trying to accomplish.'

'Change always polarises people. Asher says that often.'

He smiled, and nodded. 'In a year I could have Alderworth profitable again...' He stopped, a sense of wariness in the words. 'But you probably have no interest in such things?'

His query trembled into the space between them.

'On the contrary. If this is to be my home, I could help you.'

'Our home.'

And just like that she was back again into breathlessness, enchantment shimmering in the air between them.

'Do you have your riding clothes?'

'Of course.'

'Then come with me and I will show you Alderworth from the hills.'

'Now?'

Nodding, he called the dog back to his side, its mangy spine rising into his hand where he patted it.

'Give me ten minutes,' she answered before breaking into a brisk walk.

TAYLEN STOOD AND watched her leave, desire seeping into a cold dread.

Hugo Shields seemed to reach out from the grave and deny him any thoughts of hope, years after he had died with a bullet through his heart. His uncle had gone into his afterlife muttering the threats he'd made such an art form of whilst living, insults softening into pleas and then whimpers as the life blood had run from him. Tay had allowed him no forgiveness, simply watching with distaste and relief as he took his last and final breath. The Italian nobleman, who had shot Hugo as a card cheat, had taken ship back to the Continent that very night and a youthful Taylen had never spoken of the incident to anyone.

Secrets and lies. It was who he was, what he had become, and no amount of longing could change it. It was why the nightmares never left him, but spun into the release of sleep like a spider gathering corpses. He could not hide the darkness inside him from Lucinda and if he tried to…

He shook his head. He would have to be honest, for he owed her at least that.

The dog's whining made him tense.

WITH HER RIDING habit in place Lucinda rejoined Taylen at the front of the stables.

The large black horse she had seen at a distance from the window of her room was twice as impressive close up. She stayed a good ten feet away from him as she looked over the lines of his body.

'He is beautiful. What do you call him?'

'Hades. My father brought his grandsire out from France after winning a lucrative hand of faro.'

Taylen Ellesmere never seemed cowed by scandal;

rather he threw any caution in the face of the wind and challenged comment. Attack was better than any defence. He used the maxim like an expert.

'Your family is unusual.'

'There isn't much of it left.'

'The very opposite of mine, then. Sometimes I used to think there were too many Wellinghams, but now…'

She trailed off, but he finished the sentence for her. 'Now when you see the alternative it makes you realise how lucky you are?'

'I think that is true. They are not so bad, you know, my brothers. It is only that they are trying to protect me.'

'From further ruin?' He smiled unexpectedly, the green in his eyes paler today than she had ever seen it. The Dissolute Duke who watched over his estate out of a duty he could have refused, but didn't.

Sometimes her husband was so very like her brothers. Confusion made her ramble.

'It is good to be away from town and Alderworth is a beautiful place despite the disrepair or perhaps because of it, I think, although I can imagine my mother's displeasure at the state of your garden.'

'I would be more than happy if you wish to oversee any repair, Lucinda.'

She laughed. 'Gardening being such a quiet and docile hobby…'

'At least it might stop you from galloping *ventre à terre.*'

She knew he would kiss her before he leaned over. She could see it in the way his face softened, humour changing to some other thing less discernible. As the wind lifted her riding skirt and blew the falling leaves into eddies around their feet, she simply closed her eyes and felt his warmth against hers and his solidness, his fingers on the skin of her arm, stroking down to catch her to him, no questions left. Just them with a beautiful horse standing behind, the yellow sandstone of the stables pitted with age and the peace of the early afternoon settling in.

This kiss was different from the one they had shared the night before. This kiss came with all the knowledge of what they both wanted—nay, what they needed from each other.

They came together with a hard edge of disbelief, thrown into a storm of movement, his hand around the back of her head, his body pressed against her own. This time she did not limit what she gave in return, her teeth biting down and tasting the power of abandon. She was not careful or circumspect or quiet. She was all woman released from the fetters of years of manners and demeanour that denoted a Wellingham daughter, the expectations of society a distant and unpleasant memory.

She could no longer care. Her fingers wound through his hair as his tongue came inside her mouth, rough and urgent, no quiet asking in it as he held his hands on each side of her face.

This was what she wanted, the taking and taking, moulded into desire, the loss of self in a thrall that held no end. A moment or an hour? It was his choice. She would have lain down upon the grass beneath the roses if he had asked her, opening to him, accepting the roaring release of a womanhood for ever tied to agreements and conditions and plain cold reason. Respecting the fact that he was a man caught in the complexities of family and trying to make the best of it, she could deny him nothing.

Nothing. Her mouth widened as he came within, tilting her, his breath hoarse and raw, his thumb on the nape of her neck as she arched back and simply enjoyed.

HE COULD NOT remember ever revelling in the company of another as much as he did his wife. He had never had a confidante before, a person who might guard his back against the world despite everything that was said of him. The wonder of it was humbling.

Lucinda kissed like the most skilled of all courtesans, allowing him things most ladies didn't, gentle softness dispensed with under a building and aching need. When her teeth came down on his lip he smiled, the pain of it inciting urgency as he took her breath into his own, swallowing her air and exchanging it for his. He bound her mouth in a tight seal of authority, pressing down so that she had to trust him. She did not fight, though her eyes flew open, watching, glazed into submission, waiting while he fed her breath.

He had never felt such a compelling insistence for any woman, not in all the years of his life enjoying the fruits of a reputation he had earned at the hands of parents who taught him not to care for anything or anyone. So very easy to take and to leave.

But with Lucinda there was a betrothal that was impossible to break before man and before God, the edicts written in the law of the land and handed down through many centuries of union.

Unions that produced the next generations, heirs who could hold the great estates in the palms of their hands and care for their longevity as no outsider would ever be able to.

His heirs. Their heirs. The children of Alderworth who would follow in his footsteps. An agreement bound by time and gold.

Breaking away from her, he ran his hands through his hair and swore. This was not how it was supposed to be, this desperate need to be inside her, a sense of for ever in his thoughts that was as scary as it was impossible.

No one had ever stayed at his side through thick and thin, through richer and poorer, through the vagaries of trouble and the inadequacy of laws. No one at all, save Lance Montcrieff, who had died trying to show him such friendship was possible even as the last piece of life had bled from him, warm on the dusty turnings of earth and in a land that was far from home.

His breath felt shaky and he turned from his wife's sky-blue gaze, not wanting her to see things he had shown to no one before. Give a little of yourself and be punished for it. Trust another and that emotion would be thrown back as corruption and abuse. Or loss.

After his grandmother's betrayal he had allowed his uncle to see his vulnerability when he had come to collect him from the hospital in Rouen. Then another sort of deception had begun, one worse than his grandmother's heavy hand, one wrapped in soft bare flesh and whispered words. It was then he had understood that love equalled pain and shame. When he had finally rid himself of his uncle's depravities he had found a different enjoyment of the flesh. One that required neither trust nor honesty. One that allowed him the freedom to move on from a woman before there was ever the chance of more than a way to pass the hours of his life, superficial, numerous and unimportant.

'I know there is a lot I need to learn about the art of kissing…?'

He stiffened as he faced her, hating the worry so evident in her voice.

'But I no longer wish to wait to make an heir. I want to know where a kiss like that one might lead to next, Taylen. I am twenty-seven years old and I do not wish for another single day to pass before I know.'

Raw and honest with her chest heaving, Lucinda reminded him of everything that was good in the world.

'Now?' He did not recognise his own voice.

She nodded, a small hint of nerves, but still she stood before him, unflinching.

Tay could not believe she might mean it and yet in the aftermath of their kiss his body had hardened and risen. He took the chance of waiting no longer by simply holding out his hand.

Her fingers laced about his own, intertwined.

'Come, then.'

Calling to his man to unsaddle Hades, he strode back through the gardens along the white shell paths, ten steps and then twenty, always assuming that she would pull away. She did not.

He walked through the main salon at the bottom of the house, the servants watching them, a strange juxtaposition of the normal and the absurd.

A bargain.

A payment.

An heir.

He had never felt as he did at that moment, leading his wife towards his bedchamber and knowing what would happen once they got there.

Mrs Berwick asked him a question and he answered, the warmth of Lucinda's fingers burning need into his soul. He saw his wife's eyes were lowered lest the truth of what lay inside was seen. Speaking in words that were empty, his mind replayed other words, stronger words, words that would change both of their lives for ever. He felt as if they were tied by a quivering single thread, its quicksilver need running through all the parts of him. Forcing him on.

Up the stairs they climbed, Lucinda's breath strained. Not from exertion, but from anticipation. He almost smiled then, although humour was far from what he felt.

Then through the door they went, the heavy oak of it shutting behind them and the locks turning. The noise elicited a small involuntary flinch from Lucinda, but she did not speak. Pocketing the key, he moved away, dropping the contact, needing the space. For the first time in a life filled with indulgence and dissoluteness he did not know where to begin.

His wife did it for him, undoing her jacket buttons one by one, her small hands mesmerising. The shirt beneath was of the finest linen, inset with lace, her flesh peeking through where the pattern of the stitches changed. He stepped forwards.

'Let me?'

She nodded, stood still as he drew her hair into his hands and released the mass of gold and wheat from restraint, running his fingers through the curls so that they were freed from the heavy chignon. He wanted to see her tresses against her pale skin, enveloping the curve of her breasts and hips. He wanted to lay her down upon his bed and mould the shape of her to his so that she would never forget him, marked and branded.

The racing beat of her heart belied the bravado she was showing him as he undid the small mother-of-pearl buttons that held the last of her bodice together.

He had done this before, in this very room three years ago, unlaced Lucinda and understood the beauty beneath the cloth, but this time was different. This time she was his wife, promised to him, bound in law and troth and honour.

Marriage. His parents had never venerated the spirit of such a union, but to him… He stopped.

Not empty words after all. The wedding ring he wore glinted in the light, catching gold.

'Only for an heir…?' She phrased this in a question,

running her tongue around the dryness of her lips as her head tilted back.

Asking for more.

He pulled the cloth away and her breasts fell out into his gaze, then his hands lay across them, the fullness firm and pale.

Lust ruled now, heating blood, shallowing breath, raising skin. His mouth came around one rose-hued peak and he sucked, hard, the burn of want and need, the ache of completion, the trembling primeval blaze. She groaned and he kneaded the other nipple, the thread between them snaking into hardness, snaring desire.

'Now.'

Her voice, and no longer a question. Raising his head, he simply picked her up, her bodice trailing downwards and the skirt she wore pulled up across his arms, the dainty beauty of her ankles and shins on show.

She did not fight him, but lay still as he placed her on his bed. No resistance. His hands came beneath her skirt, into the silk of her petticoats, under the thin nothingness of her drawers. Until only skin remained, thick and swollen and soft feminine skin, wet with her wanting.

'It may hurt, my love.' He had to warn her as he unbuttoned his trousers. She did not look at his nakedness, for her eyes were closed now, the quiet blush of need on her cheeks, the trembling, too, of something unknown. He wished he could find the words that she wanted him to give her, but the truth was more important.

'I need you, Lucinda. I need all of you.'

At that she opened her eyes, acquiescence and knowledge now in the blue as one arm reached out to caress the planes of his stomach before falling lower. An elemental virgin-siren, the release of her breath heard in the quietness, a thin line of beaded sweat on the top of her lips.

Kicking off his boots and trousers, he lifted her skirt and opened her legs, the searing flesh of his manhood stilling as his fingers parted heat—balanced, waiting, poised on that moment of change that comes to every new bride.

Slipping inwards, driving hard, breaking flesh as she arched up to him, slick in the coupling. Her hands tried to push him away, her nails digging into his back, the terror of it written into one single keening cry. And then stillness as he waited, engorged, filling her, tightening, the deep pain of loving changing into a different consciousness.

Her breath came quick now, the dead weight of him pinning her down, unmoving.

'Wait, sweetheart.' It was all he could say. *Wait until we become accustomed to each other. Wait until your body answers. Wait until the waves of response begin.*

And then they did. A slight quiver of flesh, an easing, a softening, the first call of her body as she moved and allowed him a different access. Slowly. Out and in again. Deeper. Faster. Wider. Harder. Again. And again. He prayed that the pain was lessening and changing into some life-filled thrall that was indescribable and heightened. He knew that he had her when her hands came around his back and she held him to her as if she might never let him go.

SHE COULD NEITHER breathe nor think. Every part of her was centred in the place between her legs where he was in her, joined by flesh, the hurt leaving now, not as ragged, and another pain building. A different pain. One that held her stiff and breathless, reaching for what was promised.

One that made her shake and groan and stretch as his movements quickened, needing the beauty of it, feeling the togetherness of what brought a man and a woman into a single person, nothing between them save the knowledge of each other. His breath against her throat, the movements faster now, reaching up and racing against hope and heat and desperate need.

And then a release, a melting ache of absolution quivering through the stiffness, widening and deepening, rolling across her stomach inside everything. She shouted out, her voice heard far away, the beaching waves unlike anything she had ever felt or known.

Lost in sensation. Adrift. Satisfied. Crying. Her tears hot on her cheeks and brushed away softly by a husband who had astonished her.

She heard the thundering of her heart inside her head, a languid lethargy in her limbs, the weight of Taylen and the heat of him drawing energy away.

Still joined. She could feel him twitch, the thick engorgement inside. Sweat ran through all the places between them.

'Thank you.' His words, caught between deep breaths.

Smiling, she closed her eyes, unable to say more,

tears drying tight against her cheeks. She wanted to stay here just like this in the silence, wrapped inside each other's skin, the sun slanting across the room in a yellow curtain of light.

Heaven.

'I always wondered why my brothers were so…happy being married. Does everyone feel this?' She had to know, had to understand.

'No. My parents hated each other with a passion.'

'So they sent you away?' She watched him, his body bare in the light, the edges of the marks on his back creeping round on to his ribs. One finger traced a scar in wordless question.

'On occasion. And when I was here they ignored me,' he said, watching the ceiling, and Lucinda knew from the tone in his voice that the things he was thinking had been stored inside him for a long, long time.

'Lady Shields's maid said that you were in hospital in France?'

'In Rouen. My grandmother hurt me when we were on holiday there. I had asked one of her friends if I could live with them, you see, and she found out and was furious. But it was only after my uncle came to pick me up a good month later that I understood the true meaning of…brutality.'

He whispered the word, softly, anger leaving him stiff and motionless. 'My mother's brother decided I needed lessons in…obeying him and took such tutorship to heart.' He looked at her then full in the eyes, the torment of memory bright and fierce.

'I was twelve years old and my parents had both died the previous summer. Twelve is no age to fight back, you see…and I couldn't. He…he…'

Shaking her head, she placed her fingers on his lips as if to stop what he might say next. 'I love you, Taylen. I love you because the things you have been through have made you who you now are. Strong. Certain. I think I must have always loved you, even then, when we first met, even without the memory of it.'

A single tear traced its way down the side of her face and he kissed it away before covering her lips and taking all that she said inside of him. Again.

TAY WATCHED HER as she fell asleep, lost safe in the arms of dreaming. Her lashes were long and curled, the tips dipped in lightness and even in slumber her dimples were still apparent. Three years of waiting for her and he had ruined it with his stupid truthfulness.

He slipped away from her body and sat on the bed, the blood of sacrifice easily seen on the top of his thighs.

How could she love him after the things he had told her? How could she find it in herself to do that? Maybe now it was possible in the first flush of passion, but tomorrow when the truth settled? What might happen then?

Every confessed word had been wrong and heavy and he swallowed twice, guilt rising with anger as he fumbled with the drawer to one side of his bed and extracted a hundred pounds.

Hers for the bargain.

He placed the notes carefully upon the counterpane and did not look back again as he stood to collect his garments and leave the room.

IN THE MORNING he rode to the home of Lance Montcrieff's wife a good five miles from Alderworth. He had installed Lance's widow in one of his smaller estates since his friend's death when she had been ousted from her home by the heir and had visited her a number of times since returning to England a month and a half ago. He knew that Elizabeth Montcrieff wanted more from him than he could give and part of the reason he needed to see her this morning was to put an end to the hopes of any type of relationship between them.

Lance had loved his wife, well and truly, and Tay knew that his friend would have wanted his family to be settled and secure. Without any other relatives to help her, he felt she was his responsibility.

The butler took him straight through into the library and he was greeted almost immediately by Elizabeth.

'I did not know you were coming this morning, Duke.' The velvet in her voice was smooth. On her lips was the lightest of colour. The heavy perfume she favoured filled the air between them.

'There is a chance of leasing a town house in London, Elizabeth. It is central and there is a school just around the corner suitable for the girls. I think you would be happy there with the chance of more society and a wider group of people to talk to.'

She watched him intently. 'I hear that your wife has

arrived at Alderworth. It is the only topic of conversation one hears at the moment around here.'

Her brown eyes were resigned, her smile calm. She was not a woman given to histrionics and she was sensible enough to understand he did not wish for tears.

'I am sorry if I have given you any cause to think there could have been something more between us…'

'You have not, Duke. You have been most circumspect and generous.'

'It was Lance's final wish as he died. He made me promise to look after you, but life has changed and my wife is…' He stopped. What was Lucinda to him? A mother for his child? Or much, much more?

Her hand came down across his own. 'I understand. You have helped me with a home and a living, Duke, and for that I shall be for ever grateful. You have done your duty ten times over.' Unshed tears banked in her eyes. 'I could not have wished for a more thoughtful man in the face of my own loss and loneliness. I hope her Grace knows what a treasure she has in you.'

He smiled at her words. 'My lawyer says that you have not touched the money I deposited into your account.'

'I have not needed to. Everything has been provided for me here. But now…' She hesitated. 'Now I think I will repair to London and see what that town has to offer us. You have been more than generous and I will always be grateful.'

'Nay. It was Lance's share.'

She shook her head. 'I know the real money did not

come in until after his death when you diversified into other areas. I am certain that you know that, too.'

Elizabeth Montcrieff had never looked so beautiful to him, a woman of honour and integrity. He hoped that she would find what it was she needed from London and that somewhere in the future he might bring Lucinda to meet her.

'There is one more thing,' he said as he turned to leave. Reaching into his pocket, he extracted the ring Lance had worn in Georgia and handed it to her. 'This should be yours.'

He laid the gold in her palm. *LM.* The initials of his first real friend. But now he had another. The thought came from nowhere, but the truth of it was undeniable.

Lucinda.

Suddenly exhaustion overtook everything. He wanted to be away from this house and out in the open again, feeling the wide space of freedom over his head and the chance of redemption in his heart. He couldn't go home, not just yet. He needed the hope of Lucinda's words for a while longer, unspoilt by the consideration that must blossom when she had time to think about all that he had told her.

Saying goodbye to Elizabeth, he rode for the village to buy a drink.

CHAPTER FOURTEEN

'HIS GRACE HAS been called away to one of his other properties, your Grace.'

Mrs Berwick gave her the information as Lucinda came down to the dining room for breakfast.

'Did he say when he would return?' Lucinda kept her voice even and controlled, though her hand shook as she helped herself to bacon and eggs.

'No. He did not. Sometimes it is a few days before he is back, but this time…?' The housekeeper left the question unanswered.

'I see.'

And she did.

Taylen Ellesmere had run from Alderworth as fast as he had been able to even with her ill-given exclamation of love. It was the blood. Her blood. Her virgin blood of pure deceit. He had been trapped into a marriage, beaten by her brothers and forced into years in a far-off land with no hope of return and all because of lies. She knew that now, the proof of it on the bed sheets and in the soreness between her legs. He had never touched her there.

It was her husband who had held her neck still after

the accident and made certain that the damage was not worse. She remembered that, too, the paleness of his face above her as he had strained to keep her immobile, the cold rain streaming down upon him and shattered glass in all of the broken and damaged lines of his skin.

Every single thing he had told her family had been true about the lack of relationship between them and she had sacrificed him because of it.

Only an heir. She understood the words now as she had not before. An heir from the only wife he was ever likely to have and all because of her lies. The notes on her bed when she awakened came to mind, spread out beside her. It looked a lot when counted in falsehoods.

But other thoughts also surfaced. The secrets that he had shared with her last night were not easy or small truths, the gift of confidence surprising and humbling. He had laid his soul at her feet even as anger had marked his eyes, brittle, shameful fury stained in green and he had not turned away when she said that she loved him.

One hand strayed to her stomach. *Please let his seed take. Please, please let a child grow.*

She prayed for that with all her heart.

She wanted him back. She wanted to tell him that her lie had been sorely mistaken and that she was sorry. She wanted to hold him against the hurt of his youth, in her arms away from the loss of an innocence that should have been safeguarded.

But he would not come and the only companion left to her was the unkempt dog who followed her back to her room.

'I am not certain if you are allowed in here,' she said in the lowest of voices, for she had already seen the animal being shooed out a number of times today. Kneeling, she offered her hand to him and he sidled over, his tail fixed as it always was between his legs.

'Are you hurting?' The query had her placing her fingers upon the matted hoary coat and wondering what other care the animal had missed out on. Perhaps he was more like his master than she had originally thought, tossed out from home and beaten.

She reached for one of her brushes and began to try to untangle the knots. Surprisingly a coat that was both lighter and longer began to emerge, the dog looking more and more presentable with each stroke.

'Like a swan,' she said to him and laughed as he lay down, his body comforting against her own. 'If you were mine, I should call you Swan.'

The sudden and unexpected sounds of feet moving along the corridor outside made her stiffen as the door-handle turned. Her husband appeared, dressed in his riding cape with a hat in hand.

His eyes went to the dog, a frown lingering as he called to the animal. It stood instantly and walked across to stand beside him, the bony ridge of its back prominent.

'He followed me in here.' It was all that Lucinda could say, banal and hackneyed, she knew, but her tongue was tied and she could not decide how to greet him, a stranger who had been a lover and was now back in the guise of a man who looked…unknown.

Confusion and ire surfaced and as he came closer she scrambled upright. A strong perfume was evident on his clothes.

'Thank you for last night, Lucinda.'

Another flush of red crawled up into her face. If he would not castigate her over her mistake, then surely it behoved her to mention it.

'My memory was faulty after the accident in the carriage. I believed that you had…enjoyed more than I wanted to offer.'

'And now?'

'Now in the light of yesterday I can see that I was mistaken in my accusations.' She made herself hold his glance. 'It cannot have been easy to have had your reputation so unkindly maligned and for that I apologise.'

He smiled, his skin creasing at the corner of his eyes, an outdoor man, a man who did not bother too much with the fripperies of fashion. 'My reputation was maligned a long time before you added to it. What do you remember?'

'Running into your room. You were reading and naked. I remember that clearly. Machiavelli in Italian? I thought you had kissed me?'

'I did.'

'I also think you might have touched me.' She raised a hand and placed it across her breast. 'Here.'

'That, too.' His right hand joined hers, cold from the morning outside. She shivered and his other fingers drew a line down her cheek. 'I touched you like this,' he offered, 'and like this,' he added, cupping the flesh under her bosom. Even through the material of her gown her blood began to pump.

'And I wanted you to?'

He nodded.

'You must have hated me then, after my brothers told you I had said that you ruined me?'

Only for an heir. Only for an heir.

'I do not hate you.'

'But the payment you left on the bed. Is that only what this is?'

He stopped her questions simply by holding her against him, tightly bound, his jacket sprinkled with rain and wet.

'Last night…the things I told you…' He stopped, holding her close with the dog around their feet. She could not see his eyes or his face, but she could hear the beat of his heart against her ear.

When he did not speak she began to. 'Everyone has their secrets, Taylen. I ran away with a man when I was seventeen. Emerald, my brother's wife, stopped me before I boarded a ship and married him. It would have been a huge scandal if anyone else had known.'

'But they did not?'

'My brothers hushed it up and nothing else was ever said. I saw him again about five years later and thanked the Lord that I had been caught.'

'That bad?'

'He became a dandy, a man who enjoyed puce waistcoats and powdered hair. I doubt he thought of anything else at all. Then when I was twenty-two I fancied myself in love with another swain who turned out to be married already and just wanted a…dalliance. He was Italian, you see, and had not mentioned his family circumstances.'

'How did you find out?'

'My brothers never liked him and they sent a runner to Rome. I cried for a week until I understood that it was my fault really that any of these things had happened. After that, until I met you, I was quite circumspect. And when you left after our wedding I was virtually a recluse.'

'I wrote to you three times from Georgia, but you never replied. Did Cristo not give you my letters?'

'He did, Duke, but all you talked about in them were the environs where you now found yourself and a duty message was not what I wanted at all. So I decided that it was in my best interests never to think of you again.'

'You did not think I would come back to you?'

Lucinda breathed out. Every day she had hoped it. Every day she had held her breath and wondered would it be this day that Taylen Ellesmere might come home. To her.

The knock at her door had them both turning, however, as the butler appeared in the doorway.

'Mrs Moncrieff is here, your Grace, and it seems that one of her daughters has gone missing. I have placed her in the blue salon.'

'Thank you. I will come down.' Anxiety covered Taylen's words as he accompanied his servant from the room. Not knowing whether to follow or to stay,

Lucinda hesitated and her husband was gone from her sight even as she tarried.

Montcrieff. Was that not the name of Taylen's partner in the gold mine in Georgia? Shutting the door behind her, she made her way down the stairs after them.

In the blue salon she found a beautiful woman weeping in her husband's arms, her head against his breast.

'Emily has not returned from the Partridges and I sent a servant for her but there was no sign at all. When you came to me, Duke, I think she overheard that we might be leaving Tillings and going to London and she has made friends here and did not wish to go.'

She burst into noisy sobs and Lucinda could only stand and watch the spectacle like an outsider. The same perfume that had hung heavily on her husband's clothes was in this room as well.

She could see both the lines of guilt on his forehead and the familiar way the woman curled into his strength. Elizabeth Montcrieff wore his ring, too, she noticed, on the third finger of her left hand, the gold engraving glittering in the light.

Betrayal? Every part of her body wanted to deny what she was seeing, but she could not. Turning back to her room, she raced up the stairs as if a ghost was on her tail.

'I do not hate you.' He had said those very words not ten minutes before, but he did not love her, either. Not enough. For all his fine words, perhaps he was a cheat. A man with as many mistresses as he had years still to live; so many, in fact, that here was one straying into

their very home, a demi-wife with his ring on her finger to prove the commitment.

She was glad for the key Taylen Ellesmere had given her and, locking her door against any intrusion, she tried to think of just exactly what she would do next.

ELIZABETH HELD HIM as she might once have held her husband and as Tay tried to disengage her grip he saw a quick flash of a dark dress.

Had Lucinda come down the stairs behind him? Had she seen Elizabeth entwined about him and sobbing? Lord, if she had, she might imagine other things, too.

With a real effort he moved away from Lance's widow and poured her a brandy.

'Drink this. It will help.'

Thankfully she did swallow the draught without question and the tormented and hysterical crying stopped.

'If I have lost her, too…'

'You won't have. Emily will have gone to one of her friends' place to hide or to wait and see what you do as a result of it.'

Hope flared in dark eyes. 'You think she might have?'

'I do.'

The sobbing began again, quieter though now. 'She has been difficult since her father's death and I have not been as strong as I have needed to be.'

'Then take a lesson and begin in London, Elizabeth. The school there is a good one and the girls will have all the care and direction they require. A new start is exactly what you all need.'

'Could you come back to Tillings with me now and talk to her, when we have found her? She listens to you just as she used to listen to her father.'

Tay's heart sank. He knew that it would be dark before he could return home to Alderworth. He was also worried about Lucinda, but with a carriage waiting outside and an anxious mother inside he had no time to go upstairs and explain everything to her.

Tomorrow he would take his wife out riding and show her the estate. Perhaps if she was willing he could also take her back to his bedchamber and find the same magic that they had discovered last night.

It was already morning. Lucinda had fallen asleep fully dressed under the cover of a thick blanket that lay at the bottom of her small bed after waiting nearly half the night to see whether Taylen would return.

But he had not come home. He had gone with the beautiful dark-haired woman and as the hours had tumbled one across the other she knew that he would not be back. She felt sick with the implications of what that might mean.

Had he left again, this time with the full intent never to return? My God, her brothers had been right. Exactly right. She should have heeded their word and refused to accompany him to his estate. Once a snake, always a snake. Yet he hadn't been that at all. He had been hon-

est and honourable. It had been her memory at fault and
he was the one who had suffered.

A knock on the door had her sitting up, running the
back of her hand quickly against her eyes and trying to
place a smile where anguish had just been.

'May I come in? I have your breakfast tray.'

Scrambling up, Lucinda unlocked the door and a
maid came bustling in with freshly baked rolls and a
pot of tea.

'Mrs Berwick said I was to tell you that the master
will be a-riding home this morning from the direction
of the local village, your Grace. She said that the groom
could find you a mount should you wish to venture out
and meet him.'

The idea appealed. A ride might blow away the cob-
webs Lucinda felt building and give her freedom to
think. The added bonus was that meeting him out in
the open would allow them to talk in private.

If she got one of the stable hands to show her the way
she would not get lost and the weather outside looked
finer than it had in weeks. When the dog came through
the door she decided to take him, too, reasoning that
the exercise would be good for the hound.

THE HORSES STANDING in the stables were by and large
older hacks, though one smaller filly caught her attention.

'What of that one?' she asked the stable boy. 'The
roan mare at the end?'

'Her name is Venus. She's a mite skittish in temperament, though, for she came with his Grace's black as a pair and when Hades is gone she's apt to fret.'

The perfect ride, then. If she had any chance of meeting up with the returning Duke, the odds had just got better.

'Who usually takes her out?'

Silence told her that nobody did.

'I can saddle up a more docile horse if you would rather, your Grace.'

'No. This one will be fine.' Lucinda liked the lines of Venus and she felt desperate for a good long stretch. None of the other horses here looked as if they would give her any more than a slow canter.

With anticipation she mounted and was surprised by the docile way the horse allowed her a seat. The day was blue and it had been a while since she had sat on the back of a horse in the countryside and raced across the land, feeling the wind in her hair and liberty in her veins.

After all that had happened she needed to simply feel. The wonderment in such an unexpected loving still left every fibre in her body alive with promise and had her heart racing.

She had lain there when she had awoken and felt... different. A woman who understood exactly what it was that others spoke of in the hushed tones on the far side of rooms. Yet now with Taylen's absence everything had returned to only bewilderment.

Veering left at the main gate as the stable boy had directed, she allowed Venus her head, racing across the line of fence and bush with the sun on her shoulders. The silence of the place was absolute, the birdsong long since diminished and the day shaping up into a glorious one. The dog loped at her side in an easy gait.

At the top of the incline the lands of Alderworth spread out around her as a tableau and Lucinda wished she had brought her drawing things to capture such a view. Her eyes searched out the paths coming in from all directions, but there was nothing. Perhaps Tay had stayed on longer, lying entwined in the arms of the beautiful widow, and regretting the confidence he had allowed in his marriage bed.

A brace of loud shots had her turning as a group of men burst from the trees a good five hundred yards away.

Hunters. Lucinda felt the quiver of her horse's fright even before she bolted, whipping the reins from her hands and tearing off in the opposite direction from where they had appeared.

She could only hang on, her fingers entwined in the hair of the mane and her feet solid in the stirrups. A hundred yards and then two, the hilly terrain giving way to a long valley and trees. The branches whipped her face as she tried to stop, shouting at her horse to slow as hooves beat faster against the muddy ground. Then she was off, flying through the air with the rush of landscape beside her and down on to the slope of a gully. She might well have stopped if there had not been a disused well at the bottom, the slopes rolling into the mouth of it and over into darkness.

A good six feet down she clung to the roots of a tree and tried to force her body into the space between earth and wood. Already she felt sick, disorientated, dizzy. Pain brought her back to the moment and the last thing she remembered was the dog looking down before turning away from the gap in the sky, the sound of his panicked barking disappearing on the wind.

ONE OF THE lads came out to meet him as Taylen cantered in to the stables. He had left the village as early as he could and made excellent time back to Alderworth. Looking at his timepiece, he saw it to be twenty minutes short of twelve. Emily had been reunited with her mother after a number of hours of searching and was suitably apologetic, though with a night behind him in the local inn Tay was glad to leave and head for home.

A sort of panic had gnawed at him for hours, the idea that something was not quite right pervading all his thoughts.

'Will you be joining her Grace out riding, your Grace?' The young stable hand's face was tinged with worry.

'The Duchess has taken out one of the horses?'

'Venus, your Grace.' A full frown now lingered on his forehead.

'You let her take Venus?'

'I offered her the choice, but she was most insistent. The stray dog went with her, your Grace, and I had the impression she hoped to meet you on the way.'

Tay scanned the hills behind Alderworth and the pathways to the front.

'What time did she leave?'

'Two hours ago, your Grace.'

'Saddle Exeter for me then, and see to Hades. I will be back in fifteen minutes ready to leave.' Dismounting, he took his leather satchel and hurried inside.

Mrs Berwick was in the kitchen when he found her and up to her elbows in flour.

Tay tried to temper his worry so as not to disturb his housekeeper, but he could hear it in his voice nevertheless as he asked his question.

'Did the Duchess tell you where she was going riding today, Mrs Berwick?'

'Towards the village,' the other answered quickly. 'I gave her the directions for the pathway you would take home and she rode out to meet you.'

A whining at the door stopped him and the dog came in, panting from its exertion. Relief budded for the stable hand had said Lucinda had left with this animal, so perhaps she had already returned. The arrival of the same lad a second later put paid to such a hope.

'Her Grace is still not back, your Grace. The dog came a few minutes ago and I thought she would follow. But nothing…'

Mrs Berwick was now wiping her hands off, a look of alarm spreading across her face. 'The weather is changing, your Grace. I think it will rain soon.'

'What was my wife wearing?'

'Her riding jacket and skirt. They looked both serviceable and warm.'

Almost three hours since anyone had seen Lucinda after she had left. Kneeling down, Tay lifted the front paws of the dog and saw the telltale red dirt of the hills to the east on his feet. He had not crossed a river then or the silt would have been washed away. The choices narrowed.

Venus was not an easy mount and the terrain became hillier past the track into the village. Other more sinister thoughts followed. Had Lucinda fallen and knocked her head? He distractedly swiped away his hair. The Wellingham physician had been most explicit about the consequences of such a mishap.

HALF AN HOUR later Tay rode across the land to the east calling Lucinda's name. Six Alderworth servants fanned out on horses all around him doing the same and at every pathway that dissected the main trail he sent a man off to see if she might have branched off. Forty minutes and then fifty went past, with not a stirring of anything untoward.

His hands gripped the leather reins as the thought of not finding her consumed him. He seldom panicked, yet here he was allowing ideas to come that took him to the edge of it.

If she had hit her head somehow... The warnings that Posy Tompkins had spoken of in the park had been specific. Even a little knock might do it...

His wife's soft honesty, her smell, the way she smiled

at him and stood by him. The colour of her hair falling across his body, pale against the dark, a perfect match. He could not have just found her to lose her again. The dog ran next to him, easily stretching to the pace of his horse, as one by one the miles were swallowed up.

SHE WAS SHIVERING and even that small movement dislodged dirt from the spaces between the timber, hurling them down the steep sides of the hole where they fell into water.

Fifteen feet, she reasoned.

Two hours at least since she had been here, the sky above darkened with rain. Her head ached with the fall.

'Please, God, don't let it end like this,' she prayed and then found herself shouting Taylen's name, as loud as she could manage again and again into the silence.

A spider startled her as it jumped on to her riding jacket. She had always hated insects, but as this one with its tiny spiky legs tiptoed up her sleeve, she felt strangely aligned with it, both of them down a hole in the cold and far from safety. She watched as it crossed to a leaf further away towards the light.

'Go well,' she whispered and watched as it spun a web and swung up to another twig and then another. If only she might do the same, she thought, but her hand could not reach the branch above and the lip of the well on the other side was just too far away with skirts to hinder her.

Her throat was scratchy from shouting and her only hope of rescue lay in Dog. *Please let him have gone back to Alderworth,* she prayed. *Please let him bring help.* Her husband would come, she knew he would, and surely at the house the alarm must have already been raised.

But what if he did not come by dark? The thought crept into panic, stuck down here amongst what was left of the old tree roots. What would crawl out when the sun set and the moon rose and the cold of the night became apparent?

Again she shook away such thoughts. She was a Wellingham and she was strong. A little dark and cold could not hurt her and spiders did not bite.

She would sing, that is what she would do. She would sing and sing until they came, with her rusty voice and her lack of tune and her spirits would be raised. Sound would echo from the hollow stone and if Taylen was somewhere nearby he must surely hear it.

A SEA SHANTY he remembered on the ship back from the Americas rang out around the small glade that Tay had followed Dog down to and he tilted his head to ascertain the exact direction.

Oh Blow the man down bullies, blow the man down,
Way, hey, blow the man down…

Lucinda. She was alive. He did not question the pure ache of relief as he dismounted and ran to an old disused well on the side of a hill.

Not wishing to scare her by suddenly appearing, he chanted the next line of the words back to her loudly.

A pretty young damsel I chanced for to meet...

The only sound then was that of sobbing, heartbroken wailing that had him lying across the edge of the opening.

When he looked down fear caught in his throat.

His wife was positioned precariously and the only thing allowing her any purchase was an old rotten tree that had fallen over, creating a makeshift ledge.

Nothing looked stable or safe.

'I think the bough beneath me will break if you come down here,' she said, her voice strained and hoarse as she tried to contain her crying. Even as she said it more dirt dribbled down the wall to be lost in the darkness of the bottom. A splash told Tay that water lay below. 'There are spiders here, too. At first I did not mind them, but now...' She stopped, giving the impression she had made herself do so.

'Stay very still, then. Don't move at all.' He glanced around for something to tie a rope to and found it in the trunk of another tree.

'No. If you fall...'

'Then we both go,' he replied, and across the rain and the dirt and in the space of eight feet their eyes caught, saying things to each other that they had not been brave enough to voice as yet.

'Is she your mistress?' Her quiet words were lost in worry.

'Who?'

'The woman I saw you with in the downstairs parlour?'

'Elizabeth Montcrieff. She was Lance's wife, my partner in the gold mine in Georgia. I have been helping her financially.'

'But the ring you were wearing was on her wedding finger?'

'Because it once belonged to her husband and I gave it back to her. That was all.' Her chin wobbled and he saw her swallow, but another falling piece of the ledge brought them back to the present danger. 'Don't move while I get the rope and push yourself to the very back so that I can come down to you.' The dog ran in circles around the top of the well, barking wildly.

A moment later he had the lifeline fastened and started to climb down the side of the drop. When he reached Lucinda he simply laid his arms about her and held her close. She was cold, her teeth were chattering and her hair was plastered to her head with the rain. It felt so good to hold her and cast away all the nightmare thoughts he had had on the ride here.

'It will be all right, sweetheart. Here, grab the rope and I will push you up.'

He took both her hands and guided them about the thick plait of jute. 'Don't look down. As I push you need to pull as hard as you can and try to scramble up on the rope. When you get to the top, find the tufts of grass and heave yourself over. Do you understand?'

She nodded.

'Are you ready?'

She nodded again.

Making a stirrup with his hands, he got her to place her boot upon it before bringing it up as far as he could go. 'Can you see the edge?'

He felt her flurry of movement though he could not look up, his face jammed against the earth and his breathing heavy. Then the weight was gone, her boots disappearing as she levered herself across the mouth of the hole, a few errant stones coming down upon him and stinging his back.

She was safe. Lucinda was safe. He thanked the Lord for her deliverance just as the ledge crumbled away completely and he disappeared into the blackness of space.

CHAPTER FIFTEEN

TAYLEN WAS GONE. The rumble of earth had taken him to the bottom, the tree he was jammed in against disappeared with him, leaving only emptiness where a second before he had stood.

There was no reality to it, no recognition of the horror of it all, only an aching searing loss that had Lucinda lying down on the grass and screaming out his name.

She could just make him out at the bottom of the hole, partly buried beneath a pile of rocks and dirt, his head turned downwards. Thankfully the width of the old tree had missed landing on him and lay at an angle to one side. Grabbing the rope, she measured the full length of it and determined it finished a few yards from the bottom. Could she get down there or would she dislodge more of the crumbling walls and damage him further? The rain solved the question completely as she saw the water running in a steady stream. He would drown if she waited too long.

Removing her stockings and boots, she tied hooped knots all the way along the stem of the rope in the way her brothers had shown her how to do so many times in her youth. Coiling the rest of the line, she then threw it over the edge, watching as it swung heavily against the side of the well. Would it hold? The tree Taylen had fastened it around had not moved at all and the anchor looked well fashioned. Fear made her sweat, the close cloying air in the hole would be even worse at the bottom and she could not see how she might be able to climb out carrying him. She would be stuck there again until help came.

Swallowing away panic, she took a deep breath before making two good tight fists and levering herself over the side, the knots and their hoops allowing both her fingers and toes a good grip as she descended.

It was easier than she thought and within a few moments she was at the bottom of her lifeline. It was a few feet short and, letting it slip from her hands, she dropped the rest of the way to land on her feet to one side of Taylen, the mud slithering between her toes and the water icy cold.

He was still alive when she touched him, still breathing as she sat to take his head carefully upon her lap, away from the water.

'Please, please be safe,' she whispered, the echo of it hollow in the depth of the earth. Blood dribbled down his face from a cut on his brow and there was a large swelling at the crown of his head. Reaching for the hem of her riding skirt, she wiped at his cheeks, the red and brown of blood and mud strangely mixed, and his skin pale beneath their hues.

Her brothers had bought her a gift of inestimable value, a man she could respect and admire and adore—

a man who had risked his life to save hers and who now lay unconscious as payment for his valour.

Already the sun had fallen, daylight leached from dusk, the long shadow of night upon them. Holding him closer, she tried to impart some of her warmth into his cold, her fingers tracing the shape of him in the darkness.

He was hers and she would protect him. At Alderworth now the alarm would surely have been raised and help would be coming.

THE SOUNDS OF others came quietly at first and then more loudly, the length of rope trailing above twitching and raised. She could see nothing now, the black complete.

Then there were more voices, men's voices. She recognised some of the tones of the Alderworth servants as another line dropped down beside her. A thicker rope this time and longer.

When a figure came from out of the gloom she could only watch, scared to move in case she hurt Taylen further.

A tinder flared and then there was light, a face outlined by the flame. He pulled three times on the rope and another one dropped, a man she did not recognise at all on the end of it. In his hands was a long roll of heavy calico, the ends tied to folded poles of wood.

'Briggs, your Grace. The dog led us here. Has he woken at all?'

She shook her head in answer.

'The doctor has been summoned and will be at the house by the time we are back with him.'

Laying the fabric of the stretcher to one side, they pulled the contraption into a narrow bed. The mud and water had soaked through the canvas even before they lifted Taylen slowly on to it. The pain must have leaked into his unconscious mind for he groaned, the ache in his voice making Lucinda grimace.

'Be careful,' she pleaded as the stretcher was hoisted, one foot up from the ground and then two, both men steadying an end each as they all rose, the eerie shadows of the torches showing up broken patches of the sheer earthen walls.

She was the only one left down here now, and she got to her feet unsteadily after such a long time sitting, the stretcher disappearing over the top of the lip in a calm and easy way.

Safety. Lucinda could almost taste the relief of it. The dog was barking and more lights above took away the gloom. She could make out the flares against the black sky as another figure descended. Briggs again and holding the rope she had fashioned into foot and finger holds out to her.

'I will come up beside you, your Grace. Just hold on and they will pull you up.'

A moment later jostling hands helped her over the top and she was once again standing in open air, the huge blackness of sky above her, a few stars twinkling through the gaps in the clouds.

Taylen lay motionless, his cheeks pale and the dark

runnels of dried blood powdered on his temple. He barely seemed alive, though when Lucinda laid her hand against his he tried to turn and say something. His green eyes were lost in the swollen bruising.

'You are safe now,' she said. 'There will be no more pain, I promise.' As if he understood his eyes closed of their own accord and he breathed out, heavily.

The blankets covering him were thick and warm and Lucinda felt someone place another one across her shoulders. When a cart was drawn into place a few yards away she watched as more blankets were laid down on the floor as a cushion to transport her husband back to Alderworth.

Swan the dog crawled in beside him.

'THE DUKE WILL need complete rest and quiet,' the doctor proclaimed as he regarded Taylen a few hours later. 'He has had a nasty knock to his head and concussion has resulted. From my experience with similar cases it may be a week or so until he comes to his senses, for Briggs told me it was at least twelve feet to the bottom of the well.'

The Ellesmere physician stood to one side of the bed as he stated his findings, a passionless man with little in the way of a comforting bedside manner.

'But he will recover?' Lucinda asked the question with trepidation, for Taylen was looking worse and worse as the hours marched on.

'The brain has its own peculiar timings and reasons to stay inactive; some people come back to consciousness very quickly, others languish on the netherworld for weeks or months or even years. Some stay there for ever. It is God's will. Talk to him. Tell him all the news of the house. There is a new school of thought gaining traction that says those in a deep coma are none the less aware of things about them if they have a constant source of translation from a loved one.'

A loved one? Did she qualify as that or would any interaction between them make him even worse?

'If you need me in what is left of the night, send a messenger. Otherwise I will return tomorrow afternoon to see how my patient is progressing.'

Then he was gone, Taylen lying still and Mrs Berwick fussing about with the sheets at his side.

'Are you certain you do not wish me to stay, your Grace?'

Lucinda shook her head, not trusting herself to speak and when the woman finally took her leave she sat on a chair beside her husband and reached for his hand. The nail on his right thumb had been pulled off and there were cuts across the fingers. 'If I could heal you, my darling, I would,' she murmured, tucking the blanket in further and dousing the candles so that only one still blazed, protected by a glass cover as a precaution against fire.

SHE WATCHED HIM as the sun appeared above the hills that she held no name for, the horizon aglow with pink and yellow. She watched the rise and fall of his breath, too, and the pulse in his throat where the stubble of a twelve-hour growth darkened his skin.

His chest was bare and she could just make out the tail end of the scars by his neck where the marks had curved around from his back and licked at the sensitive folds of his throat.

Hurt by life and by his family, and then censured by society and tossed out of England all because of her lies. And all the time he had stood up to her brothers with the knowledge of what he had not done. Halsey, too. The broken ribs and the ruined face. Nobody had ever believed in him and loved him as they should have.

Nobody until now. Her grip tightened.

'I love you, Taylen. I love you so much that it hurts.' She hated the tears that were gathering in her eyes. 'If you die I don't know what I will do because there is nobody else who understands me, who makes me feel… perfect.'

Not flawed, not foolish, not merely pretty, but beautiful and strong and completely herself. Finally after all these years she knew what she had been missing, a friend, a lover, a man who might sacrifice his life to save her own.

Anger came next and she shook his hand before holding it to her lips. 'Don't you dare leave me, Taylen, because if you do I will kill you, I swear that I will…'

'Water?' The voice came croaky and deep as dark-green eyes found hers, dazed with the strong painkillers. She could not quite believe that he was conscious. 'You can hear me?'

He nodded. 'You were...threatening me.'

'And loving you.' She had to say it, had to make him understand.

'That, too.' The creases around his eyes deepened.

'For ever. I will love you for ever.' She did not try to stop the tears now as they fell in runnels down her cheeks.

Tipping his head, she offered him a drink of boiled water from a jug, careful to give only small sips in the way that the doctor had directed.

Pain scrawled deep lines into his face and he grimaced as he tried to move.

'You have a bad bump to the head and your ankle is sprained. The doctor says you are to stay very still. He will be pleased to know you have woken.'

'How...long?'

'Just a few hours. It is five o'clock in the morning and they brought you to Alderworth last night after eleven.'

Reaching for her hand, he held on.

'Don't go.'

Before she could even answer he had fallen back to sleep.

EVERYTHING HURT. HIS HEAD and his eyes and his neck. He had a tight bandage wound around the top of his forehead and a flickering light had been left beside him.

Lucinda—his last moments of seeing her safe, climbing up the rope from the well at the bottom of the Thompson's Ranges. She had spoken to him some time later in the cold and the mud and then again somewhere else.

Here. His bedroom. A small hand entwined in his own. Warmth and hope and safety, her breathing even and deep beside him and the moon waning towards the dawn. Home. With his wife. Closing his eyes again, he fell asleep.

ASHER WELLINGHAM WAS there when he next woke up, stretched out on a chair, his long legs before him. Lucinda had gone. He felt around for her with the hand that she had held and found the bed empty.

It was almost noon because the sun was high and the shadows at the window folded down on to one another. The blue openness of sky through the drawn curtains hurt his eyes with its brightness.

'You saved Lucy and put your own life at risk. I want to thank you for that. If you had not come when you did...' He stopped, regrouping emotion before beginning again.

Seeing him awake, Asher spoke, as if his message was urgent. 'Lucinda has told us that she was mistaken about her allegations of intimacy with you at Alderworth three years ago. We had you thrown out of England on a lie, Alderworth, and you would have good reason to hate us.'

All these words at once, Tay thought, tumbling into the air around him. Where was his wife? He wanted her back.

'Lucinda?'

'She has slept beside you for the past three nights since the accident. We all thought it was time she looked after herself and took a break, though I should imagine she will be back before the clock strikes the next part of the hour. It seems she cannot stay away.'

Exhaustion hammered at Tay like a mallet and he let his eyes close.

THE NEXT TIME he awoke it was night and Lucinda was there, watching him.

'Welcome back.' Her smile was shy and her hair was loose, dancing in pale waves across her shoulders and down her back.

'Beautiful.' And she was, in every single way that he might imagine.

'Thank you for saving me, Taylen.' Her fingers traced the lines of a scratch across the back of his hand as though measuring the hurt. 'If you had not come...'

He stopped her. 'But I did.'

Tonight the world was sharper, less hazy. He could even lift his head from the pillow and it did not ache.

'How many days?'

'Four.'

He brought up his free hand to feel the bandage.

Memories. After Rouen. A small child without a hope in hell of protecting himself.

Lucinda knew everything hidden and still loved him?

A bunch of wildflowers sat in a vase opposite the bed, and for the first time ever the bile did not rise up in Tay's throat as he thought of his uncle. It was over, finished, and there was all of the future to look forward to. The peace of it made him smile as he spoke. 'You look happy.'

'I am. With you here next to me and a whole night of just us. Ashe also sat with you each time that I did not. Taris came, too, and Cristo. They all hope you can forgive them.'

This time he laughed. 'Forgive them for forcing you upon me? Forgive them for making my life…whole?'

Catching her hand, he brought it to his lips and noticed an injury on the top of her knuckles from the fall. Further up on her wrist an older scar from the carriage accident lingered. He wanted to wrap her in his arms and keep her close.

When she lay down beside him to sleep he knew that he would never be lonely again.

THEY WERE ALL in the Alderworth dining room at the end of dinner, celebrating the first time that Taylen had been able to come downstairs unaided.

A week since he had fallen down the well. Lucinda thought it seemed like a lifetime ago.

Everyone was present, her brothers and their wives and Posy.

Cristo made certain that a comfortable chair was angled in the best way for Tay to sit in and Asher got him a drink. It was strange to see her brothers fussing over a man they had hated not so very long ago.

When Taris raised his glass he gave a toast. 'Here is to you, Taylen, and a warm welcome to our family. The beginning may not have been exactly comfortable, but we have many years now to make up for it.'

Tay smiled and took Lucinda's hand. 'Without your… help—' he gave the word the inflection of a question and everybody laughed '—I may not have found my wife.' He raised his own glass now and looked directly at her. 'To you, Lucinda, and to family.'

His green eyes brimmed with a happiness that softened the lines in his face. To Lucinda he looked the most beautiful man in the world, her man, and a husband who made her feel strong and real.

Intrinsically flawed? No, she felt far, far from that.

'To life and to laughter,' she toasted in return and looked around the table at the smiling faces as she held up her glass.

Happiness was a feeling that was almost physical. Emerald's jade talisman was warm in her palm and she knew for certain that she would ask Emerald if she could give it to Posy, who sat next to her with a look on her face that she thought might have been her own a few months back.

An observer of life, but wanting so much more.

'Has your memory returned fully yet, Lucy?' Beatrice asked the question.

'It hasn't. But there are new memories now which have replaced those old ones.'

'Then let us drink to that.' Cristo stood and poured fresh brandy into all the glasses. 'But be warned, Duke, once a Wellingham, always a Wellingham. Eight of us now and that is not counting any of the children.'

Lucinda's eyes met her husband's. Children. How she hoped that the time would come when she held the heir of Ellesmere safely in her arms.

CHAPTER SIXTEEN

London—three months later.

TAY HAD ALWAYS hated these big society events for all of
the falseness and the inherent censure within them. As
the Duke of Alderworth he had been invited because
of his title, but the *ton* had tiptoed around him, feared
him, he supposed, and worried about what he might do
or say next, every new and over-exaggerated myth that
had built up around him adding to their trepidation.

An outsider. A Duke asked because it was harder
to leave him out, such a slight a reminder of how far
the Alderworth star had indeed fallen. Oh, granted,
there were those amongst the *ton* who would gravitate
to him, but they were often men he felt no true com-
munion with or else young bucks satisfying their first
urges to kick the traces and to irritate their more-than-
disapproving families.

But tonight with the lights of the chandeliers full
upon him and a dozen of the Wellinghams around him
it was different. Every eye in the place might be turned
towards their party, but the usual alarm that prickled
inside him on entering such a salon was missing.

Safety. Belonging. The feel of his wife's hand tucked through the crook of his arm and her oldest brother beside him.

'A smile might persuade those who are here to criticise you to do otherwise, Tay.'

'You think it that easy?' Months of getting to know Asher Wellingham had brought them together as friends.

'The *ton* revolves around a large measure of deceit. Surely you have learned at least that?'

Such an answer did make it easy to smile, to simply laugh at all the implied deceit and make use of it. Taylen saw Taris smile, too, his wife, Beatrice-Maude, beside him in the company of Cristo, Emerald and Eleanor. Asher's friend, Jack Henshaw, also lingered amongst them, Posy Tompkins on his arm and dressed in the most absurdly expensive gown, the diamonds on the cloth glittering in the light. The plain jade pendant she had around her throat seemed very out of place in the ensemble and Tay remembered seeing the piece around Lucinda's neck and wondered.

Altogether they made up a high-ranking and prominent group and although the power of money and title was behind them, it was something much more than that again that made Tay's heart swell with pride.

Respect was something he was not used to, but it came tonight in waves from those who watched them, the consequence, he supposed, of the years of good works and care of others the Wellinghams had been involved in. And he belonged, not in the game room amongst the card sharps and the drunken care-for-nothings, but here in the bosom of the protective custody of the Carisbrooks. One of them. For ever.

His hand tightened on his wife's. 'Can I reserve every single dance, sweetheart?'

'I have already pencilled you in, Tay.'

In a light gold dress Lucinda looked unmatchable, her hair wound into curls and the *décolletage* on her dress showing off the creamy skin of her breasts.

'Should your bodice be quite so revealing?'

She simply laughed. 'This from a man who insists I come naked to bed every night?'

'There it is only us, but here…' He looked around. A good percentage of the men in the room had their eyes fastened upon his wife and he knew exactly why. It was the joy that seemed to well up in Lucinda like a fountain, spilling around her as laughter and honesty and delight. And there was something else that only he was privy to, a wild and wonderful secret that had not yet been told to anyone, save him.

They would have a child in less than six months, and there had been no payment except for love involved in its conception.

His whole being filled with a feeling that almost frightened him with its intensity and yet when he looked at Taris and Ashe and Cristo he saw the same desperation in their eyes, too. Men made whole by their women and astonished by the fact over and over again.

'How many hours until we can be back in our bedchamber?' he whispered and saw the flush of pleasure stain her cheeks. God, he loved her puritanical bent because it was so much fun dismantling it every single night.

'Five waltzes at least, Duke,' she replied, knowing how he enjoyed holding her close to feel the slight swell of her stomach between them. Three months along. The newest Ellesmere. Another Wellingham. A cousin for all the numerous children who ran and laughed in the great estates of Falder and Beaconsfield and Graveson. Another belonging. More protection. A tight circle of safe-keeping.

Like an onion, he thought, and Lucinda was his very centre.

A soulmate. He had never expected one, never believed that after all he had been through he might find such paradise.

Tripping as he walked, he clutched at the stick he needed to use now, a reminder not of his infirmity, but of their survival.

Asher's arm came out and steadied him. 'If you get tired, we can go home.'

Tay knew Asher hated these large gatherings and smiled at the hope in his voice. 'I have promised your sister that I will dance with her.'

'You feel up to it?'

'My balance is getting better with each passing week. Doctor Cameron said that soon there will be only a little of the vertigo left.'

'A lucky escape. It could have been so much worse.'

'Lucinda could have fallen instead of me.' Taylen had

relived this horror during so many nights that the dread of it was like a familiar stranger walking with him.

'No, I meant for you, Tay. You could have died.' Amber eyes looked grave.

'But instead I found everything I was looking for.' He gestured to Lucinda and to the Wellingham family all about him.

'And as Cris said, once we claim someone we keep them for ever.' Taris added this from behind, and laughter accompanied the group as they walked on to the overcrowded dance floor.

A FEW HOURS later Lucinda and Tay lay in bed with moonbeams across their bodies and the winds off Hyde Park making the trees sway as shadows on their walls. Swan the dog lay in his own bed of fur by the window, tucked into sleep. He accompanied them everywhere now, his fearful demeanour changed to one of contentment.

'I love you,' Lucinda said softly to her husband, her fingers moving across the skin of his chest and feeling his heartbeat strong and even.

'And I love you back,' he replied, the smile in his voice bringing her in further. It was colder tonight and he always felt so very warm. 'When I found you at the Croxleys' ball and offered you money for a legitimate Ellesmere heir, I did not realise that it was my heart I was giving away instead.' He stilled her hand. 'You have it all, Lucinda, every piece of my love and if anything was to happen to you…'

'It won't.' She turned over and lay across him, his face within the veil of her hair and his worry vanished to be replaced by a look that simply took her breath away.

'That first time when you came to my room at Alderworth I thought…' He stopped and swallowed. 'I thought that you might be the one to save me and I was right, sweetheart.'

'We saved each other, Taylen, and this child shall be the beginning of a whole new dynasty of Ellesmeres.'

Turning her beneath him, his lips came down across her own, all the magic that she had felt from the very first second of meeting him beginning over again.

* * * * *

We hope you enjoyed reading

FOUR IN HAND

by #1 *New York Times* bestselling author

STEPHANIE LAURENS and

THE DISSOLUTE DUKE

by SOPHIA JAMES

Both were originally Harlequin® Historical stories!

You dream of wicked rakes, gorgeous Highlanders, muscled Viking warriors and rugged Wild West cowboys from another era. **Harlequin Historical** has them all! Emotionally intense stories set across many time periods.

www.Harlequin.com

NYTHRS0816

Joanna fell into his comforting embrace and the temptation in his kiss. Her heart pounded with the risk and the thrill of his body against hers. She rested her hands on his chest and his strong pulse beneath her fingertips reminded her she was young and alive and all her dreams might still come true. A shiver coursed through her as he traced her lips with his tongue, his breath one with hers as he held her close. He tasted like the drink of strong port she'd sneaked once at a soirée for the school patrons, rich, sharp and forbidden. She savored him as she had the liquor, each illicit taste making her crave more.

She slid her hands up over the sturdy curve of his chest, past the white cravat and collar surrounding his neck. With small circles she traced the smoothness of the skin before raising her fingers to slide them into his hair. In the circle of his arms was a belonging she'd never experienced before. Despite her being hidden away and ignored, he'd seen her for who she was and he wanted her. It almost made every risk she was taking with him worth it.

A faint darkness crept in beneath her bliss, like a mist along the ground at dusk. He had little to lose with this liaison while she might sacrifice everything for a fleeting bit of happiness. She clung to it like she did his biceps, his muscles hard beneath her grip, trying to forget reality, duty and consequences. Beyond the strength of his kiss, the tightness of his fingers against her back, nothing else had changed, not his situation or hers.

She withdrew her fingers from his hair and broke from his lips, but not his embrace. He eased his arms from around her waist, but left his hands to linger on the narrowness of it. Every argument against their being together nearly died on her tongue as she held his fierce gaze. The dreams of being with him that she'd entertained in the middle of the night felt more real than anything she'd experienced at Huntford Place. Her heart urged her to embrace whatever was happening between them and perhaps gain everything she'd ever desired.

Don't miss
THE CINDERELLA GOVERNESS by Georgie Lee,
available September 2016 wherever
Harlequin® Historical books and ebooks are sold.

www.Harlequin.com

HARLEQUIN®

HISTORICAL

Where love is timeless

Save $1.00

on the purchase of
ANY
Harlequin® Historical book.

Available wherever books are sold, including most bookstores, supermarkets, drugstores and discount stores.

Save $1.00

on the purchase of any Harlequin Historical book.

Coupon valid until October 31, 2016. Redeemable at participating outlets in the U.S. and Canada only. Not redeemable at Barnes and Noble stores. Limit one coupon per customer.

52614196

5 65373 00076 2 (8100)0 12209

NYTCOUP0816

THE WORLD IS BETTER WITH

Romance

Harlequin has everything from contemporary, passionate and heartwarming to suspenseful and inspirational stories.

Whatever your mood, we have romance when you need it, wherever you are!

HARLEQUIN®

A *Romance* FOR EVERY MOOD™

www.Harlequin.com

#RomanceWhenYouNeedIt